# ECHOES OF NIGHT

BOOK
ONE

DAUGHTERS OF THE SHATTERED MOON

# CAITLYN MCFARLAND

OLIVERHEBERBOOKS

*For Kristin, Lindsay, and Jordan. Favorites.*

*Echoes of Night* is intended for mature audiences.
It contains graphic violence, explicit sex, depictions of abuse, and other adult content.

# Daughters of the Shattered Moon Timeline

AD – *Anno Domini*
WW – Woken World

The Waking – June 1996 AD
January 1, 1 WW – January 1, 1997 AD

Wars of Power – approx. 2–55 WW
Alaric Bane founds Conqueror's Moon Pack – circa 59 WW
Height of Conqueror's Moon – approx. 68–85 WW

Founding of Shattered Moon pack – June 99 WW

## One

*December 100 WW*
*Shattered Moon pack lands, Missouri Ozarks*

### KILLIAN

The winter air is thick with the stink of blood and sour sweat. The cold bites my chest, my back. My hands and everything below my knees went numb long ago. Dizziness turns my stomach as I crawl through wet, crusted snow.

The snow. There's something wrong with it.

"Grace?" I barely recognize my voice. My throat feels shredded, like I spent the night screaming.

Screaming.

"Grace?" I stumble onto unsteady feet and call my mate's name again. I'm in a clearing. The Ozark woods are all secretive hills and winter-bare trees so tightly packed that they obscure anything past a hundred or so feet, even without leaves. The sky above the clearing is a perfect overturned bowl. Stars scatter the western half, but in the east, it's turning gold.

Dawn. Is it dawn? The last thing I remember is night. Vandran told me Grace was seen leaving the pack house in the company of Jackson Beaumont, and I went to find her—

*Killian, stop! Please!* Grace's voice.

*Alpha, you need to calm down.* That memory is Jackson, the heir of the Redcedar Hollow Pack.

And then Grace again, her voice rising in fear. *Killian, what is happening—?*

Screaming. Snarling. Giving in, because I had no other choice.

The snow is red. That's what's wrong with it.

I see Grace then. Not in memory but in the growing light of dawn. Her broken body is only feet away. Her chest is torn open. Blood and viscera ooze everywhere. Her bright aqua eyes are clouded and empty as the sky. A breeze stirs the chestnut hair that frames her lifeless face.

"Grace!" I stagger to her and fall to my knees. She's as cold as the snow. I pick her up and pull her close. She'll come back. She has to come back. This isn't real.

*Help me!* Her voice rings in my memory, but she remains so terribly still. *Why is this happening to me?*

Next to her is the body of Jackson Beaumont. The Redcedar Hollow heir is about twenty-two, the same age as me. Blond. Athletic. Good-looking. Or at least he was before something opened up his torso and ...

I turn to one side and am sick in the snow. Screaming and screaming so loud in my head, I don't hear the footsteps approaching.

"Killian!" A new voice. "Grace! Why the hell have you been outside all—?"

I look up to see Asher framed between the trees. Tall and rangy with chestnut hair that flops over his eyes, just like Grace. The Beta of our new, rapidly growing pack. My best friend.

Her brother.

Asher takes in the blood. The bodies. His wolf flashes bright blue in his eyes, the same color as Grace's were before the yellow.

"Asher ..." I can't find my voice. I don't know how to explain what happened or why my mate and the heir of the neighboring pack are lying dead together on the ground. I don't know what happened. Except ...

I do. The memory is there, surrounded by tatters of yellow mist and sprays of blood.

This is my fault. I did this.

My stomach churns, and I'm sick again. I swipe bile from my mouth with the back of my hand and taste iron.

My hands are covered in blood.

Asher grips the hilt of the sword at his hip until his knuckles turn white. "You killed them. You killed Grace because she was out here with *him*."

Sharp pain in my chest. She was out here with Jackson, and I killed her.

"Yes." The memory is graphic. Vivid. I know exactly how it felt to open her from navel to sternum. How much resistance her flesh offered. I can picture the steam as her insides spilled out into the cold.

Asher draws the sword his family named Argathach and spins it around his hand, fluid as water. Light glints from the rippling Damascus steel blade and gleams along its silver edge.

Then he attacks.

The Quinns are an ancient werewolf bloodline. That sword is hundreds of years old. It survived the Quiet, when magic slept, and was still in Quinn hands a century ago, when magic flooded the world again.

I'm a stronger Alpha than Asher, but the Quinns are steelborn. He and Grace have trained with blades since they were toddlers. Asher is fast, precise, and agile. When he shifts, the sword melds with him and becomes his claws, and he's immune to silver.

He could kill me.

I want him to fucking kill me.

He makes a solid start, tearing open my back, my chest, slashing at my face. Only instinct makes me flinch back so that he slices the middle of my left eyebrow and splits my lip instead of taking out my eye.

But when I don't fight back, he stops.

"Fight! Do to me what you did to them!"

I just sit there on my knees.

"Bastard!" He kicks snow into my face. "I thought you loved her!"

"I did—I do."

He's told the pack. I can feel them stirring through the pack tie, all one thousand of them seething like a kicked anthill. Sofia, my Gamma, keeps trying to speak in my mind, but I close myself off.

Asher flips the sword around his hand, then rams it into the meat of my chest just beneath the right side of my collarbone. An animal sound escapes my throat. The silver on the edge of the steel blade burns as it tears through me, then yanks free. Agony radiates down through my torso and up my neck.

"Why?" Asher screams. He looks at his sister's body. Tears streak his face.

Something terrible moves in the dark abyss of my mind. A whisper. A madness.

... *breakthemkillthembleedthemeatthem* ...

Terror of that whisper grips me. Terror of what it means. I've dreaded and waited for this moment my whole life—for my father's violence to surface in me.

I know what she did.

I know what I did.

Jackson's pack is going to demand vengeance.

"Why?!" Asher screams again, lifting his sword to shoulder height and leveling it at me.

Dizzy with the loss of blood and grief, I leap to my feet and roar, "I don't know!"

Alpha energy explodes out from me like a bomb. Asher braces, but it pushes him back, leaving muddy skid marks in the mud and snow.

I fall to my knees again and look up at Asher. "Kill me."

His face is a rictus of grief. He holds Argathach angled toward the ground, crimson blood dripping from the tip to join the thousands of droplets spattered all over the snow and churned mud of the clearing.

He's hesitating. He's not going to do it.

"Kill me!" I throw all of my power into the command. I am his Alpha. He has to obey me. "It's my fault. She was my mate." My voice breaks.

The veins in Asher's neck and arms bulge as he fights the compulsion. Every other wolf in my pack would crumble beneath my power, but Asher is too strong. He follows me because he chooses to. He doesn't have a head for running a pack. He never has. Even back in our petty crime days, I'd plan, he'd execute. When we were enforcers working under the warlord of the Fall Line Protectorate, it was the same.

Finally, he snarls, "I'm not going to kill you."

"What?"

Chest heaving, eyes wild, Asher presses the tip of his sword to my throat. "Swear on her blood you'll never take a mate again."

"Just end me!"

"*Swear it!*"

"I swear." I sound broken.

I am broken.

Asher does something far crueler than killing me.

He lets me live.

He leans in close. "Break that promise, and I will come back. I will kill whoever you take as a mate in front of you, and then I will kill you. That is, if the Beaumonts don't rip your worthless guts out first."

A little way from Grace is a brown leather belt. It was hers, and it must have broken when she shifted. On it are the two sheathed quillon daggers she called Sgàth and Sgàil, siblings to Asher's Argathach.

Asher takes the belt, daggers and all, then disappears into the trees.

When he severs his side of the bond to the Shattered Moon Pack—to me—it's like having a blade driven through my chest all over again.

THIS AREA USED to be a state called Missouri. This region, which begins roughly in the middle of the old state borders and spreads south into what was Arkansas, is still called the Ozarks. It's an eroded highland plateau older than even the Appalachian Mountains, a place full of caves and hollows. Full of eldritch beasts and restless dead.

At the end of the twentieth century—a hundred and six years ago, now—magic returned in an event called the Waking. It restored magic to about half the human population, reopened the doors to the fae Realms, awoke eldritch monsters, and reminded the lands and waters they were alive.

For fifty years after that, the Wars of Power raged. When they ended, the world was shattered. Unrecognizable.

Then, a warrior and commander on the same level as Alexander the Great or Genghis Khan rose and swept across the eastern half of North America. He styled himself a king. He was a werewolf named Alaric Bane, and he commanded a horde of wolves one hundred thousand strong.

My father.

When I was born, being Bane's son didn't make me special. He was so obsessed with legacy that he fathered over a hundred children. Then he went insane, hunted them all down, and killed them.

Except me. Before he could find me, the seemingly unkillable Alpha was murdered. Not by another warrior or any great weapon, but—if the rumors are true—by a small handful of the mothers of his slaughtered children.

The pack scattered. Bane's kingdom, which stretched from the

Great Plains to the Atlantic coast, was ripped apart. Trade stopped. Rule of law ended. Lives were lost. That was fifteen years ago.

Two years ago, I was brought out of hiding with a few friends—including Asher and Grace—and sent by the warlord of the Fall Line Protectorate to bring peace and trade back to the Ozarks by reuniting part of my father's old pack.

No Alpha since he died has had the power to command a hundred thousand. Most can only command hundreds. A few can command thousands. A handful, ten thousands. Only Bane could command more.

Until me.

At first, bringing peace to this area got off to a good start. We united several of the smaller packs, made allies, and took a solid chunk of territory, including my father's castle-like pack house on a southern branch of the winding Lake of the Ozarks.

The pack house sits close to the eastern edge of my territory—only twenty miles from my border with Redcedar Hollow, but I thought I could make peace with them.

Now their heir is dead. Jackson's parents, the Alpha Lord and Lady Beaumont of Redcedar Hollow, won't let that go unpunished.

I've spent my life afraid to snap the way my father did. Asher and Grace and others close to me said it couldn't happen, but I knew. I *knew.*

Grace is dead, and it's my fault.

Vandran was right. I never should have asked her to be my mate.

One night crawls by after I kill her. A second, a third. Every sundown, whispers start. Yellow fog rises. The monster that takes me over wants to go to the pack house, take the castle room by room, and tear apart everyone inside. Every member of my pack. Every person I love.

I won't.

If I stay far enough from the pack house at night, I can stop the monster from going there. But I can't stop myself from becoming the monster.

On a miserable, cold day one week after Grace's death, I watch her funeral from the branches of an oak tree that lets me see over the Shattered Moon compound wall. The pack house rises in the distance beyond the graveyard, a castle on a cliff we've only half-rebuilt.

Sofia, Fate Reader Diya, and the new Beta, an older man named

Deacon Jones, officiate. The whole pack turns out to say goodbye to their Alpha Lady despite frigid sleet that spits from a gray sky.

When they all leave, I slink through the graveyard gate and kneel beside the newly turned earth. Sleet spatters my bare torso. I don't care. I can't remember where I was last night. I can't remember what I hunted. I smell like sick sweat. My mouth tastes like animal blood. It's been a week, but the feverish nights won't stop. I can't rest.

I don't deserve to rest.

I lean my forehead against her blue-speckled pink marble headstone, not caring how the mud seeps into the knees of my shredded pants or the cold of the stone into my forehead and palms.

I want to be ice. I want to be stone. I want to be in the ground with her.

"I know what she did."

A low growl rumbles from my chest as I turn to face my mother.

Claudia Darrow stands at the foot of Grace's grave, all in black, her shawl fluttering in the wind, red stain on her lips. Even from here, I can smell the wine on her.

"Whatever you think you saw, you didn't," I snarl. "You were drunk."

A smirk curves one corner of her mouth. "No. I wasn't. I followed you to the woods that night, my poor, sweet Killian. I saw what happened to you, and then I saw Grace—"

I rise and loom over her. I don't ask why she followed me that night. Blackmail is Claudia's bread and butter. The woman gave birth to me, but left solely in her hands, I never would've survived my teen years. "If you say a word to Eva, I will kill you."

My mother backs up. Fear flashes in her eyes, but then the courage from the wine kicks in, and she straightens. "You know I have particular lifestyle standards, Killian. Make sure they're met, and I'll make sure Eva Quinn never discovers the details of her daughter's final moments. Let's see. To start, I'd like to be moved up to the top floor with the other senior pack members. Eva's apartments are there, and you're not even her son."

There are footfalls in the snow, and I look beyond the mother of my birth to see the one of my heart. I bare my teeth at Claudia. "I'll make sure it's done. Just leave."

My mother's smile is fierce. "Of course. Anything for you, dear."

She turns to go and passes Eva, who I thought had returned to the castle but is now coming toward me. My stomach tightens as they cross paths. I wait for Claudia to make a cutting remark.

To my surprise, she puts a hand on Eva's shoulder, murmurs something, then walks on.

Eva Quinn turns her attention to me. Her gray waves are held in place high on her head with a crescent moon clip. Her bright blue eyes pierce me with their grief. Dread fills the pit of my stomach.

"Killian." Eva holds out her hand, and I want to run away.

For a week, I've been too much of a coward to face Grace and Asher's mother. Because of me, she has no daughter. Her elder son is gone. Her mate died long ago, back in the rogue Free Cities before I formed Shattered Moon. Eva and her adopted youngest son, Maddox, are all that's left of their family here.

Now that I've brought war to our pack, they're in danger too.

Nothing can make up for what I've ripped from her.

I must look feral, unwashed, covered in forest detritus and mud. Maybe blood too, from whatever I've been killing in the forest. I don't know.

She gets close enough to block the sleet with her umbrella. I bow my head, and words spill from me. "I'm sorry. I'm sorry. I'm sorry. I should have known I would snap—it's in my blood. I should've known no one near me could be safe. It's my fault. I never should've asked her to be my mate."

Eva grabs my chin with one strong hand, forcing me to look into her eyes. They overflow with tears. "Killian, my sweet boy, whatever this is, it wasn't you. Word just came. Eli Whitlock, the warden of Rowan Ridge who serves as Vandran's first arcanist, hasn't stopped researching what this might be since he returned to Fall Line. It's not madness—it's a curse. It sounds like you have an enemy who made a deal with an eldritch. Come inside. Come home. You need food and warmth. We'll figure this out."

"A curse?" Curses are outside the scope of wolf magic. Only witches can perform curses. Or—if someone has enough hate and is willing to make a sacrifice—the eldritch. "Who would curse me? Why?"

"I don't know, baby. I don't know." She strokes my hair. Then she lifts my hand and places something in it. A heart-shaped golden locket.

I don't open it. I already know what's inside. A picture of Eva and, on the opposite side, a recent picture of Asher grinning with his arm thrown around Maddox's shoulders. Maddox is fifteen and gangly, with black hair and a contagious grin that could almost convince me he was born a Quinn. Engraved on the back, the locket says, *For Grace, Love Killian.*

"She would want you to have it," Eva says.

I close my fingers around the small metal heart, rise, and pull away.

A curse.

Who would curse me?

Silly question. It's obvious. Someone—probably someone I've never even met—is afraid I'll become a marauding Alpha king at the head of a werewolf army tens of thousands strong. Just like my father.

I can't blame them.

It might be that I could summon the eldritch on my own, but that would be more destructive than doing nothing. They'd demand some kind of great sacrifice—my life, the life of the person I love most. And their deals always turn out to be poison.

"I'm glad to hear the warden is searching," I say. "Tell me when he discovers more."

"Killian—"

"I'm going back to the forest. I'll patrol the borders. I'll keep the pack safe from the retaliation that's coming because of my actions. Until this ends, that's where I'll be. It's too dangerous for anyone to be near me."

If I could leave the pack, I would, but an Alpha can't stop being Alpha. Any wolf in the pack can leave me if they disengage from the pack tie, but I can't leave them. The only way for me to get out of my responsibilities is to die. I can be challenged and killed by another Alpha blood wolf, who then becomes the nexus of the pack as long as they're strong enough to hold as many wolves as I can. Or I can die from another cause, and the pack goes to my heir. If there is no heir, it goes to the Beta.

I really should cut my side of the connection to Asher, but I can't bring myself to do it.

"Be reasonable," Eva pleads. "Please. Come in. Get warm. Eat. Rest. You look exhausted."

"No." My voice sounds like it's been dragged from the depths of hell. "Until it ends, I have to keep everyone safe, and that means keeping them far away from me."

# *Two*

December 105 WW
*Redcedar Hollow pack lands, Missouri Ozarks*
*New Moon*

## SELENE

Howls echo off the hills, discordant in the night. They're so close.
"Run, Finn!"

My brother is only seven. His little legs work as he sprints through the grasping winter-dry undergrowth in the dead darkness of the new moon night, his breath coming in giant gasps.

My heart pounds against my ribs like it's trying to splinter them into shrapnel as I push him along in front of me. We're so close to the edge of Redcedar Hollow territory. So close, I can taste freedom. If it were just me, I could've been away a long time ago, but like hell will I ever leave Finn behind.

For hours, we've run along the border where the lands of our pack, Redcedar Hollow, touch the lands of the monster Alpha of Shattered Moon. I dare to unshutter our lanterns only once in a while, trusting my faint wolf instincts to keep us inside our territory and out of his.

Now we're far enough north that we're almost out of the forested hills and to where the land flattens into plains. Where the Alphas Prime of the Great Lakes Steel Alliance offer refuge to all who need it.

Even wolves like me, who don't have enough magic to shift.

My pack doesn't consider me a wolf at all. The only one who did has been dead for five long years.

"I'm trying!" Finn's voice is a wheezy sob. His fear breaks my heart, but the frigid air streaming past my face steals my tears before they can fall.

I scoop Finn up and swing him onto my back. A burst of pain erupts from the old injury between my collarbone and left shoulder, but I hold on. I'm not as strong as other wolves, but my legs are longer than my brother's.

He scrambles to arrange himself, and for a moment, his fingers catch in the servant collar locked around my neck. It's made of finely woven steel wire and threaded through with silver. Wolfless like me are virtually immune to silver's poisonous effects, and my pack loves to use the collars as a constant reminder of the magic we don't have. I cough as the pull chokes me a little, then Finn adjusts his grip.

I pelt through the woods with my brother on my back, my arms up to ward off low, whipping branches.

More howls, closer. Twigs snap and leaves crunch as pony-sized wolves scramble closer. Closer. A terrible, familiar hopelessness almost brings me to my knees. This isn't the first time my sister Bianca has run me down. Usually, though, she does it for her own amusement. This is the first time since I was thirteen I've tried running for my life.

Now the howling is so loud it might as well be in my ear.

*No,* I want to sob. But I won't let Finn see my despair.

We're still a mile from the northern edge of our territory. Even if we make it, there's a chance my pack will cross to grab us and hope the Steel Alliance never finds out.

But there's one line they will not cross. One line that has been absolutely forbidden to step a toe over ever since the Alphas signed the treaty a few weeks ago. A border that's only a hundred yards away.

Do I die at my own pack's hands, or do I risk entering the territory of the monster Alpha of Shattered Moon?

I veer toward Shattered Moon, running down a hill, then down into a fold where two hills meet. Then, when I have no other choice, up another slope, lifting my feet high and praying I don't hit roots or mole tunnels. It's so dark, and my night vision isn't as good as theirs. As a child, Finn doesn't even have a wolf yet—we gain our ability to shift at puberty—but his senses are still better than mine.

He thrusts a finger over my shoulder. "A tree! Move right!"

I jump right. His night vision is a good sign he has a wolf, and I'm grateful. I don't want him to end up like me. Wolfless are less than nothing in pack society. Lower than low. Forced to serve "true" wolves in whatever way they see fit from the time we fail to manifest a wolf until the end of our short, brutal lives.

Not that having a wolf will save Finn when my mother wants him dead so very badly.

Branches snap. A growl reverberates in the dark. Then it's there, around us—the oppressive terror of the hunt.

The first Redcedar Hollow wolf erupts out of the forest behind me, snarling and snapping at my heels. I sob and force an extra burst of speed. Shattered Moon territory is so close. So, so, so close.

More wolves lunge out of the darkness. I'm less than fifty feet away from the border, and I'm not going to make it. I'm not going to make it.

I'm not going to make it, but Finn can.

"Finn," I gasp, "Run straight for two hundred steps, then turn northeast. Run until the trees disappear. There's an old highway. Follow it. Find a person. Tell them you claim refuge."

A normal child might be confused, but Finn has lived through too much. His arms tighten around my neck. "No! Selene, no! You're supposed to come with me!"

I reach up to where his hands are laced over my neck and squeeze his fingers. My throat is thick with grief, but there is no time for tears. "I'm always with you, Rocket."

A pure white wolf emerges from the darkness in front of me. As if she's been waiting. She probably has.

I yelp and swerve to one side. Bianca snaps, her teeth closing on air as I dodge around her. Then I'm past. One step, two, three ...

Her teeth close mercilessly around my ankle.

I scream as she jerks her head back, tripping me. Finn goes flying over my head and rolls. Pain bursts through the old injury in my shoulder.

"Run!" My voice is ragged.

I'm not sure he'll do it, but Finn pops up and obeys. Even as Bianca drags me back. Even as the rest of the wolves of Redcedar Hollow close around me, my brother crosses the line to freedom.

Now he just has to survive the night.

I'm not a praying person. Since the Waking, religion has become a tangle of gods and fates and who knows what else. But I pray anyway, sending a plea to the universe or whoever is listening.

*Don't let the monster find him. Let him live.*

Bianca snarls and bites down hard on my ankle. I arch my back but throw my arm over my mouth to stifle my scream.

I won't let them lure Finn back now.

There's a smoky scent and a ripple in the air, and the wolf at my feet becomes a lithe hybrid female.

A hundred years ago, when magic reawakened in the world, about half of humanity discovered that they had some aspect of magic running through their veins. Werewolves, vampires, sirens, elemental mages, witches, nature-touched—too many to name.

Within each aspect are further divisions. Most werewolves are just werewolves. They can shift from human into giant wolf. But the strongest werewolves have Alpha blood, which means that they have the right kind of magic to become the nexus for a pack tie.

That power often, but not always, runs in families, and where normal werewolves have only two forms, Alpha blood wolves have a third—the hybrid form.

In her hybrid form, Bianca stands six and a half feet tall, with snow-white fur and green eyes that luminesce in the darkness. She snaps at the others, and they draw back. Then she falls forward so her clawed hands thud into the ground on either side of my head and leans down so her wet canine nose is a breath away from nuzzling mine.

"That was stupid, Selene," my sister purrs. "Daddy won't like that you sent his bastard to be killed by the Beast of Shattered Moon just like Jackson was, and Momma won't like that you spoiled her fun."

She bites at the air. I turn my face away from her snapping teeth. "He'll be out of the territory before Killian Darrow ever knows he's there. And he's a child. Children are protected by Conclave law."

There's a chuckle from the handful of wolves powerful enough to have an Alpha hybrid form. As hybrids, they can speak. Those in regular wolf form can't except in their minds through the pack tie that connects them all.

Now that I'm not running, I recognize the wolves around me, half-glimpsed in the darkness, nightmares that have been with me since childhood. Aside from my sister, Bianca, there's one of Redcedar Hollow's multiple Betas, Harper Lloyd. Daniel, the disgusting middle-aged man I'm always hiding the wolfless girls from. Zachariah, the hard-eyed

Gamma who's supposed to keep the peace between pack members but always turns the other way when the abused is wolfless.

The others here remain as full wolves, which means they're mid- to low-ranking pack members, but I'm sure I know them too.

Leaves rustle as footsteps approach. The wolves around me glance over their shoulders, and I feel *their* power wash over me.

The Alpha Pair of Redcedar Hollow.

My parents.

They arrive in their human forms, carrying a camping lantern and dressed in fitted combat clothing in our pack's forest green and gray. My father, Frank Beaumont, is a tough, rangy old man who looks more like a farmer than a powerful Alpha Lord. His salt-and-pepper hair is kept short, and his face is weathered, tanned, and deeply etched with lines. While he looks at least a decade older than his actual age—somewhere in his fifties—my mother looks ten years younger. Bianca is basically her clone, but where Bianca is tall and muscular, Delilah Beaumont is a delicate little thing.

Bianca huffs a laugh and stands languidly, gripping the front of my too-thin coat to pull me upright. Pain lances through my ankle, and I favor my good leg.

My father looks at me with the same dead-eyed stare he gives all the servants. "Where is my son?"

It's hard to see in the lantern's glow, but my mother's mouth tenses at the mention of Finn. He's my father's, but he's not hers. No, her precious boy died five years ago.

That's why she's so dead set on killing Finn. She can't stand the idea of him replacing Jackson's memory.

Bianca gives a tinkling little laugh. "Didn't you hear over the pack tie, Daddy? Selene practically threw him across the monster's border and told him to run. Finn is as good as dead."

Courage drains from me as the blood drains from my father's face. He strides to me and—*Crack!*

The slap snaps my head to one side. The fact that my skin is half-frozen makes the pain so much worse. He moves as if to grab me, shaking with rage, but stops himself.

"If I didn't have a use for you, I would tear your flesh from your bones," he snarls.

A tremor runs through me. Once before—only once—I tried to run away, a few months after discovering I was wolfless and being forced into a life of abuse and servitude. It was my father who found me. My father who beat me, at thirteen years old, to within an inch of my life.

My mother and Bianca just looked on, Mom with dead eyes, Bianca with a secret little smile.

I know Bianca is the one who told him I ran.

"Well, how tragic," Delilah says. "But we can't cross tonight, Frank. It will ruin everything."

I resist the urge to roll my eyes. My mother thinks I've done her job for her. She's spent the last seven years hating Finn. She would've spent that time hating his mother too if she hadn't had Hayley turned out and run down by the pack for sport when Finn was three.

Hayley was wolfless. She was my friend. I've done everything I can to keep her son alive since.

I swallow and repeat, "Children are protected by Conclave law."

My father lashes out again. *Crack!* This time, he let his claws grow a little. This time, I bleed from three ragged, shallow lines down my face. My whole body is laced with scars like these. Shallow cuts that heal pale, hard to see on my moon-white skin but present nonetheless.

"As if that creature gives a shit about the law," Bianca snipes. "If he did, Jackson would still be alive."

I should bite my tongue, but I already can't escape what's coming.

"He gave a shit enough to sign a treaty that says he has to marry *you*," I shoot back with venom.

The war between Redcedar Hollow and Shattered Moon has raged for half a decade, ever since the killer Alpha, Killian Darrow, murdered my older brother, Jackson, in cold blood.

My parents were justified in seeking revenge on Darrow, but that's never been enough for them. They want to crush his pack and everyone he loves. They thought having an insane man for an Alpha meant Shattered Moon—which is half our pack's size—must be easy pickings.

It took them five years and nearly a hundred pack soldiers dead at Killian Darrow's hands to figure out they were wrong. It might have taken even longer if not for pressure from the Conclave. After a century of upheaval, this part of the world is desperate for peace.

Despite his insanity and propensity for tearing out the entrails of his mates, Killian Darrow is apparently in favor of peace too. He came to the treaty talks. Negotiated. Signed. I wasn't there, but Bianca and her friends wouldn't shut up about how he wasn't what they'd expected.

I have no idea what that means. I've never known much about

Alaric Bane's mad son except that he emerged out of nowhere seven years ago to reclaim the heart of his father's old territory, haunts his own land day and night, and kills our soldiers in droves.

Bianca shifts down into her human form, completely nude, her fingers still gripping the front of my coat. As a human, she's a tall Amazonian blonde with apple-green eyes, a flawlessly carved face, and a perfect, fit body. As malnourished as I am, it's easy for her to wrench me off my feet and shake me like a rag doll. "But I'm not marrying the monster Alpha of Shattered Moon, am I, Selene?"

She grins, and even in human form, her canines are long and sharp. "All we promised him was 'the daughter of the Alphas of Redcedar Hollow.' It's not my fault he assumed that meant me instead of useless, powerless, wolfless you."

Tears burn behind my eyes. My parents have always been distant, always favored her. But Bianca and I were sisters once. Real, true sisters so close in age that some assumed we were twins even though we look nothing alike. She's twenty-five, and at almost exactly eleven months younger, I'm twenty-four.

But whatever love was between us died the second it became clear I was wolfless. My parents made me a servant, yes. They mistreated me.

Bianca, though? Everything in her world has to be perfect, and suddenly, I wasn't. In some circles, an Alpha family producing a wolfless child is the greatest shame possible. As soon as other pack children teased her for having a wolfless sister, all Bianca's love for me evaporated and she became my cruelest tormentor.

Jackson used to stop her. He was the only Alpha blood who's ever been remotely kind to me. But Jackson is dead thanks to Killian Darrow, and I've been without protection for a long time.

Bianca tilts her head, smiling wickedly. "That's why you left, isn't it? Your little network of servant spies overheard what we have planned, and they told you."

In opposition to Bianca's purr, my mother's voice is clipped and brisk. "Is that true, Selene? Did one of our own disloyal servants eavesdrop on the Alphas?" She tuts. "We protect our wolfless. Feed them. Keep them housed. This is going to require severe correction."

"No!" It takes everything I have not to fall at my mother's feet in a pleading heap. I can't let them punish the other wolfless for my actions. The others don't have the dubious defense that sharing Beaumont blood provides me with. If my parents think they were betrayed by their own servants, more than one will die. "It was me. I overheard. I eaves-dropped!"

"When?" Bianca asks. She's got a shit-eating grin on her face. Life, death, and politics are a game to her, and she loves to play. It's a game my parents taught her. A game all Alphas indulge in. And the ones who don't, like Jackson? They die.

I hate them all.

I falter, but my mother shrugs. "If Selene is such a glutton for punishment, she can take the blame."

An odd, out-of-proportion rage flashes across Bianca's face. "If the wolfless are conspiring, Mother, we need to keep them in line."

"It was me!" I repeat, words spilling from me like water from a faucet. "I heard the whole thing. Killian Darrow is expecting to meet in the canyon between our pack lands in three days. He's expecting to take the beautiful, powerful Alpha blood Bianca back to Shattered Moon, where they'll mark each other as mates and finally end the pack war. Then the Conclave can stop dealing with us and have its uninterrupted trade routes to the south back. But instead of Bianca, I'm the one who will be given to Darrow."

Not in a public wedding ceremony, like Darrow is expecting and like Bianca would have gotten. No, I'm going to be sacrificed in the dark, dragged over the border into his territory at night. "He'll find me, assume I'm a random wolf from Redcedar Hollow violating the treaty, then murder me."

Which would be within his rights if I were a random wolf. "You'll claim he knew he was getting me all along. That you gave him your beloved daughter and he killed her in cold blood. The Conclave will send a combined military force that will fall on Shattered Moon and rip it to shreds. Whatever is left will belong to Redcedar Hollow."

I'm left breathing hard, like I ran another fifteen miles with Finn on my back instead of revealing my parents' plans. Even Greta—the older wolfless woman who overheard all this and warned me—hadn't actually heard this much. But I've spent my life watching, listening. I always have to be five steps ahead to survive.

She heard they wanted to give me to Darrow in Bianca's place. I put together the rest. My parents can't defeat the Shattered Moon Alpha, they can't kill him, so they're going to trick him into bringing about his own pack's doom. They won't lose one second of sleep over the fact that it will have caused my death as long as it allows them to avenge Jackson and take what they covet.

My father snorts, almost sounding impressed. "Must've been you that overheard it for you to know so much." He stamps his feet and looks at the sky, then peers off into the darkness toward the border with Shattered Moon.

For an insane moment, I wonder whether he might actually cross the border to chase down Finn. He has never let my mother kill him and became even more protective of him after Jackson died. But I don't think it's out of love. I think he likes to use Finn as a thorn in my mother's side when they aren't getting along.

*Make it, Rocket.* Finn got the nickname because he was obsessed with stories about how pre-Waking humans used to go to the moon. I snuck so many books from the pack library to read to him at night. I even taught him to read from a book about the solar system.

Then my father shakes his head, and I sag with relief.

He's not going after Finn. If Finn makes it, he can be free.

In the instant of reprieve I have, I close my eyes. I ground my feet in the earth, the air brushing past my skin. When Finn was little, he used to hide from me sometimes. Once, it was getting dark and I couldn't find him. I shouted for him for half an hour. I thought he might have been dead.

Out of desperation, I followed my instincts and felt for him.

I may not be a strong wolf, but I am a wolf, and my brother is mine. As long as he's not too far, I might be able to sense him.

The sensation of rushing through the forest fills my head. Cold wind blows through my body. I breathe in and ... there. He's sprinting through Shattered Moon territory, speeding away from me toward the northeast. Relief washes through me.

He's going to make it.

"Well," my father says at last, "we're not going to let the plan go to shit now. It's cold. Bring her home and lock her up, Bianca. She's got a wedding in two weeks."

I expected a beating. I swallow but don't let relief show. My parents have mellowed over the years, their violence becoming more intentional, less frequent.

Bianca, however, looks scandalized. "That's it? You're not going to punish her?"

My father's gaze goes unfocused, distant. He's speaking to someone through the pack tie, already mentally checked out of this moment. "Eh. She'll be dead soon enough."

The words are so cold, they hit harder than any physical blow could.

My parents don't even look back when they leave.

I stand there, sweat freezing to me, teeth chattering. Bianca still has a hold of me. She waits for our parents and most of the other wolves to leave until it's just her and her cronies. Then she smiles.

My sister has a lovely smile. It makes the venom behind it so much more poisonous. "Our parents are getting soft, Selene. But don't worry. I'm not."

Relief evaporates. Dread returns. I can't let it show either. She likes the fear. It's what she's after. Nausea roils in my belly at the knowledge of what's coming.

I've scraped by for years, doing my best to protect Finn and the other wolfless and, as an afterthought, myself. My parents, my sister, even visiting Alphas—nothing can stop them from doing whatever they want. Alphas are evil. Every last one of them. Power makes them evil.

I bare my teeth, then spit in her face. "Fuck you, Bianca."

She throws me on the ground, and I yelp with pain as my ribs crack against a rock. She strides away, barely visible in the dark, naked hips swaying.

She waves her hand at the half dozen wolves that crouch all around and drops her voice back into a purr. "She made us chase her for miles in the cold. And she killed Daddy's bastard boy ..."

I turn on my side and curl into a ball, my hands over my head, and swallow a whimper.

*Finn is free. He's going to make it. He's going to live. Finn is free. Finn is free.*

"... make her regret it."

The blows begin to fall.

# Three

≈

*January 106 WW*
*Shattered Moon pack lands, Missouri Ozarks*
*Full Moon*

## SELENE

I will die with dignity.

It's my first thought when I wake. I open my eyes as breath plumes from my lips, silvering as it's caught in the light of the full winter moon. A thin, sheer whiteness blurs the night and makes my lips feel warm and damp when I exhale. Fabric. A veil?

I tilt my head forward. The sheer white ripples and shimmers as I move, catching the moon in thousands of rhinestones that glitter along its edges. It is a veil. I also wear an elaborate white satin dress, stark against the blackness.

Memories rise in a drowning tide. Running. Finn's escape. The beating that came after. The treaty with the Beast of Shattered Moon.

Oh, that's right. I'm a *bride*.

The taunt of the dress seems at cross purposes with making Darrow believe I'm a random wolf. I assume—as I suspect my parents do—that he'll kill me before noticing my clothes. And if my corpse is dressed like a bride, it will be that much easier to convince the Conclave that Darrow knew who I was when he murdered me.

I take in my surroundings beyond the veil. Here, in the secretive cave- and cliff-riddled forests in the central highlands of the once-United States, it snows only a few times a year. We haven't had any heavy snows yet, but it's still cold enough to freeze. The skeletal umbrella of twisting bare branches overhead provides me with no shelter. Also, I'm dangling, suspended by my wrists from the reaching, horizontal limb of an ancient oak. It's incredible how much light the full moon casts in contrast to the grave-dark night when Finn and I tried to flee.

My heart aches at the thought of my little brother, and tears gather in my eyes.

There's been no word of him. I'll never know whether he made it, whether he's safe right now, whether the Steel Alliance is finding him a new home.

I have to believe he did. That I didn't send Killian Darrow another son of Redcedar Hollow to devour.

For two weeks, I've been kept drugged and quiet. After the fury and rush of my escape attempt, I've had nothing but time. That feeling of slow calm lingers, even though tonight is my final night.

My icy feet barely touch the leaf litter. My shoulders burn. My hands are numb. Between the lack of blood flow and the cold, I'm afraid to know what state they're in. A trickle of blood stains the dress on my left shoulder. The scar there is just a puckered pink slash, but sometimes it tears open and bleeds. Even with the infinitesimal amount of werewolf magic that trickles in my veins, its metallic scent is blade sharp, a harsh contrast to the cold-earth smell of the forest.

From miles away, across hills and bluffs that bare cracked layers of limestone like broken bones jutting from the soil, an eerie, multitoned howl drifts on the shivering air.

It isn't a wolf. It's something wilder, more ancient. Howlers are a type of lesser eldritch—the monsters that came back to haunt the world when the Waking brought back magic. With their bearlike strength, impossible speed, and mind-altering venom, they are particularly well-suited to hunting werewolves. But their howls carry for miles, and these sound distant. I'll be dead long before they can find me.

"Ngh." The agonized little noise bubbles up as I let my head fall back. Another long stream of steaming breath escapes my lips with the sound.

Soon, the mad Alpha son of Alaric Bane will find me and put me out of my misery. Because he will kill me; there's no doubt about it. I'm a slap in the face. A hard slap in the face. An underfed stand-in in a bridal gown and a servant's collar. Best of all, wolfless. Honestly, I can't think of a way Redcedar Hollow could've insulted him more.

Pack magic works like a feedback loop—Alpha to pack and back again. The stronger the Alpha, the larger the pack. The larger the pack, the stronger the Alpha. But when there are two mate-bonded Alphas, the whole thing amplifies exponentially. Wolves in a pack like that are faster, stronger, more closely tied. Everyone in the pack benefits.

Wolfless can't mate bond. Even if he did want to keep me, I'm useless to him.

Alphas have no mercy for the useless. Maybe I could scrub his toilets, but I'm sure Shattered Moon has plenty of servants of their own.

My collar burns icily against my skin. I had hoped to die with it off. Maybe Killian Darrow will do me a favor and make that happen. Or maybe he'll just rip out my guts. That's what he did to his mate. Rumors say that she died trying to protect Jackson. Maybe soon I'll be able to thank her for it.

Awareness prickles at my vestigial wolf senses.

I am not alone.

Something huge moves through winter-brittle twigs and the carpet of rotting leaves. *Shuffle, snap. Shuffle, crack.*

Bit by bit, the strangling power of an Alpha aura creeps over me.

Killian Darrow has arrived. He lurks beyond the gnarled reach of the oak, where a scattering of redcedars casts pools of shadow that hide him from the moon.

He's watching me. I feel his gaze like crawling flies. My vision blurs as moonlight catches, crystalline, in the tears collecting in my eyes.

I'm about to die, and I never got to live.

I'm leaving them behind. Finn, Jenny, Greta, Sam, and a dozen others.

The Alpha doesn't move. He's taking his time with me, drinking in my suffering.

Is this how he stalked Jackson?

The thought sparks blue fire within me, illuminating the glacial rage that I keep buried so deep, I forget it's there. Rage I've pushed down and kept frozen for over a decade, knowing I'm too weak to fight back against the powerful who rule every part of my life.

Why bother hiding it now? There's no one here the Alpha can

threaten to keep me under control. No one but me and the monster enjoying my suffering.

If I can't die with dignity, let me die with rage.

"Killian Darrow!" Tears spill hot from my eyes and burn down my frozen cheeks. "I know you're there. Come out and get it over with!"

A deep, velvety growl winds out from the darkness, twining around my body, my lungs, my throat. Two pale sickly yellow orbs flicker to life, glowing out of a redcedar shadow not twenty feet away. His eyes sit higher than I expected—at least seven feet off the ground. His power swells, the invisible insistence of his magic pressing, suffocating, crushing.

"I said, get it over with! I've heard you have a taste for my family's blood!"

A cold wind knifes through the trees. His Alpha aura presses down on me like a horse stepping on my chest. I can't take my eyes off his sickly irises.

Then death steps into the moonlight.

My stomach drops. Confusion and fear dull the edge of my anger.

As an Alpha, Killian Darrow would have a hybrid form, and that's ... almost how he appears. Near seven and a half feet tall, shoulders twice as broad as a man's, a lupine face, and shaggy silvery black fur. Moonlight flashes off inches-long canine teeth that glisten with saliva.

But there's something wrong with him. His fur is patchy. His muscles bulge like they might burst from his skin, but he's also emaciated. Skeletal and elongated with razor claws eight inches long. Those yellow eyes are flat and soulless. Whatever looks out from them is not a wolf. It's mindless, ancient, alien, and cruel.

He's not a figurative monster; he's a literal one. Like one of the eldritch.

Is he ... possessed? Did he let it in on purpose? Is that why he's so strong?

My people have fought this monster, but so few have survived. Those who have ... I never believed them when they told stories.

I should have.

He approaches slowly, giving me time to taste the bile rising in my throat, to fight my bladder's urge to release. His scent washes over me, and it's just as cold and alien as his eyes.

He gets so close, I have to tilt my head back to meet his gaze. I do, refusing to show my gut-churning fear. "Get. It. Over with."

A rumble reverberates from him. A languid, cruel wolf's chuff of a laugh. His eyes trace over my body, from my bound hands to my face to my breasts and down. He lifts a too-big hand. I try to jerk away, but it only sends agony through my shoulders, which are growing insistently more pained every second.

Slowly, deliberately, he places the tip of a needle claw at my elbow and drags it down the underside of my arm, splitting my skin. I cry out as the cut opens and I bleed.

The monster Alpha inhales, like he can breathe in my pain, and makes a demonic sound of satisfaction.

His cruelty reminds me of Bianca. In the spirit of her memory, I draw my head back and spit in his face.

He flinches, then lurches forward with a roar, fetid breath streaming over me. He snatches the ropes where they're tied around my wrists and presses the tip of another razor claw to the base of my throat. He lifts it and lowers it to my belly, just below the center of my ribs.

The meaning is clear. He's going to do what he did to my arm, drag it down, split my skin, open my body, spill my organs onto the dry oak leaves. Just like they say he did to his mate. Just like he did to Jackson.

The claws draw back, then slash. I cry out, but only fabric tears as he cuts the thick straps of the dress, then down the center of the bodice. Beneath, I'm wearing a corset and a silk slip. The dress falls to my hips and catches. The monster chuckles.

I was wrong. There will be no dignity in my death. Only the cruel glee of an Alpha who doesn't care about anyone weaker than him. Only the powerless rage that's failed to ever make a difference. Only pain.

I can't take it. Something in me breaks.

I change my mind. I won't go gently into death, and I especially won't do it for the sake of my power-hungry family.

I jerk against the ropes, trying to kick him, but the skirts of the wedding dress tangle around my legs. His hand on the rope slips, and he grips my arms just beneath. His skin touches mine. His palms are as scratchy as the pads on wolves' feet.

"Killian Darrow," I snarl, "you will *not* murder me!"

Suddenly, there's a blazing silver light. I don't know where it's coming from, but it illuminates the monster's terrible face in stark black and white.

His eyes are wide, with me reflected in them.

The light is in my skin. It's coming *from* me.

The creature in his eyes, the ancient thing ... it looks shocked.

It looks afraid.

Then the light pulses outward, engulfing him. He makes an inhuman sound, and his hands tighten on my wrists until my bones grind together. I cry out, arching on toes that already barely support my hanging weight.

He shakes his head, blinks. Then it's like he ... softens, though that isn't the right word for it at all. His body becomes less exaggerated, his clawed hands proportional, his whole shape less like the embodiment of hollow hunger and more like a normal—if massive—Alpha wolf in hybrid form. His eyes are no longer yellow but a warm topaz brown. Not alien. Human, and confused.

A keening howl tears from his throat. He crumples to the ground, going to his knees before me. As soon as he releases my arms, the silver light in my skin wanes. His howl turns into a snarl. The yellow returns to his eyes.

"Stop!" I command. On instinct, I lift my frigid bare foot. He's wearing the fitted black combat pants Alpha bloods favor, but they're old and torn. A patch of fur shows through a hole ripped right across his quad, and that's where I put my foot, digging beneath the fabric to ensure contact, seeking skin. His body is hard, like he's carved from heated stone.

He wraps a claw around my ankle, and I feel his coarse palm again. The silver reappears in my skin, and the edges slough from him.

This time, the transformation doesn't stop at his hybrid form. Fur melts into pale flesh. His body shrinks from lupine humanoid to well-built human man. His sandpapery wolfish finger pads become a heated, callused palm pressed against my ankle.

Finally, the elongated canine muzzle flattens into the most striking face I've ever seen. A carved jaw covered with black stubble, parted full lips, a nose that looks as if it's been broken at least once, sharp cheek-bones, and dark brows under a tousle of thick, almost-curly black hair. A long scar slashes his cheek, his lips, and one of his eyebrows. His breathing is labored and his eyes dart like he doesn't know where he is.

I don't know how I would have pictured Killian Darrow as a man. But the one who kneels before me is definitely not it.

His gaze locks with mine, unfocused and wild. Slowly, his breathing eases. His expression changes, brows coming together in dazed confusion.

"You ..." His voice is rough with disuse, deep and dark. It slides across my ears like imperfect silk.

I search for words, but I can't find my voice.

Why is he looking at me like I can save his entire world?

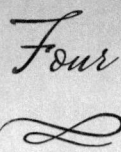

*Four*

## KILLIAN

The hunger goes quiet, and I come back to myself on my knees on cold earth, staring up at a veiled woman like I'm a supplicant and she's a saint.

The moon shines directly overhead, illuminating her pale arms and glittering along the edges of her veil. Her visible skin shimmers subtly with silver, like it's lit by shifting stars from within. The light is a balm. It's sanity. Her foot is on my thigh. Pale, delicate, but so cold that even in the moonlight, I can see her toes are red. I place my hand on top of it. For a second, I believe the old gods are real or that this woman is the Fate of the Moon, who the Weave Readers claim created werewolves and chooses fated mates.

Then I see the rope binding her wrists. The way the bodice of her white dress has been slit and drapes over a full skirt hanging from her thin hips. Above the skirt, she wears a corset over a slip that does nothing to hide her half-starved feminine form. Just beneath the hem of the veil, her chest heaves, and ragged breath mists up from where her mouth must be.

Waking from the curse is never easy. My mind is sticky, groggy, achy, shrouded in yellow mist. As it finally clears, I realize this is no goddess, no fate. Just a woman.

I can't see her face, but something pulls me to her.

Then I realize: a woman. Alone. With me.

I jerk away. Grace's locket hits the back of my hand, the leather cord that binds it to my wrist loose now that I'm in my human form. "You can't be here."

My voice sounds like it crawled out of a cave. Pain lances the back of my skull. The beast rears up and digs its claws into my mind, cold and ancient and hungry. So fucking hungry, and it smells the blood that's dripping slowly from her arm.

Memory rises. It did that. *I* did that.

*BREAKTHEMKILLTHEMBLEEDTHEMEATTHEM!*

The yellow fog comes for me again, but it doesn't take me as fast as it usually does. It shies away from her light.

Despite knowing I should be up and running, putting as much distance between us as possible, I lunge for the sanity of her skin. She squeaks in fear and tries to pull back as I wrap my hands around her ankle. The monster snarls and claws at my mind but retreats. From her. From this ... bride?

The fog around my mind clears again as I breathe her in.

It's her. Touching her skin quiets the curse.

Behind the blood, she smells like Redcedar Hollow. My knee-jerk reaction is to pull back again. To shift. To rend and tear. This is a trap. It has to be a trap. Frank and Delilah Beaumont found a way to momentarily strip me of the monster so I'm easier to kill.

I bare my teeth and scan the area, waiting for the attack. I smell more Redcedar Hollow wolves around the tree but only traces of them, hours old.

And then there's her. Her scent is ... strange. Elusive and enticing but hollowed out, like most of it is missing. Even that elusive half scent, like a fresh, clean spring surrounded by wildflowers, makes my chest ache for things I haven't allowed myself to think about for five long years.

"Are you going to kill me or not?" The words sound like they're being forced through gritted teeth. She wiggles her foot, but I only tighten my grip. There's no way I'm letting her dislodge me.

"You're Redcedar Hollow, so I most likely will." Guttural gruffness clings to my words still. The forest is so quiet and the veiled woman so ethereal, I'm not sure this is real. "Who are you, and what are you doing in my territory?"

"You're asking?" There's bitter amusement in her voice. "And they were so sure you'd just tear me apart."

I growl and rise. I can't break contact with her skin. Every time I do, there's the pain in the back of my head. The yellow fog reaches for me again.

My palm is wet with her blood. It drips down my fingers and leaves dark smears as I draw my hand up her calf, then trail my fingers beneath her skirt, dragging its heavy weight up to her thigh before I can reach up and grasp her bare, bleeding forearm with my other hand.

I'm unsteady on my feet, but that's nothing new. The curse makes it so I run rampant all night. Being an Alpha means I keep running all day. The only time I rest is on the single night of the month the curse leaves me alone—the night of the new moon.

The woman makes a muffled sound as I lean on her too hard, her blood leaking over my hand as I struggle to right myself, trying not to squeeze too hard. Her arm is barely more than bone and skin.

When I'm steady, I pull away the veil. It comes easily, sliding with barely a breath of sound to pool, shimmering, in the leaf litter.

I am arrested by what's beneath.

Her skin is bone-white, her hair silver and roughly cropped at the length of her delicate, too-sharp jaw. Her nose is narrow and upturned, her eyes too big on her hollow face. Stranger, their irises are frost-white ringed with black. I've never seen eyes like that before. She looks like a ghost. The restless dead aren't uncommon in these hills, and they sometimes wander from their hollows.

I can't decide whether she's beautiful. She's underfed, bordering on brittle. I prefer my women healthy, whatever their size.

But those eyes. I fall into them, caught in a moment that stretches for an eternity. Seared inside and out and *seen*.

Only after three too-long heartbeats do I shake out of my trance and realize her skin, which is like ice on the surface, hasn't actually lost its living warmth. That, plus her scent and the fact that I can see her breath misting in the air between us, mingling with mine, convinces me she's alive.

Her elusive scent is wolf, but it lacks the smoky undertones of a wolf who's been through their first shift. At her clearly adult age, that can mean only wolfless.

And there's also the less subtle hint of the collar around her neck.

I shake the rope and snarl, "Do your Alphas think I'm stupid? What is this? Where are they?"

Her head bobbles, and she cries out in pain that has me snatching back my hand before I remember I can't let go and grab her again.

She bares her straight white teeth in a pup's imitation of a snarl. "Do you see this wedding dress? Have you noticed I'm not Bianca? This is my Alphas telling you to go fuck yourself, Killian Darrow. They're not here."

"Is that what the message is?" I wrap a hand around her slender throat, stroking the chill silk of her skin with a thumb. I have no patience for this. I don't know what scheme the Beaumonts have concocted, but I will end it.

I expect her to whimper, beg, or scream.

Instead, she glares at me. Her body trembles, and tears bead at the corners of her eyes. She's so afraid. But more than afraid, she is enraged.

She lifts her chin, giving me easier access to her neck. "Go ahead. Strangle me. But you're playing right into their hands."

I stand there, muscles straining, pushing back against instinct, against the easy violence that has saturated my life for too long.

This isn't what I always would've done. I used to be patient. Tactical. I used to have compassion.

"Well?" She says it like she's irritated I'm not killing her fast enough.

I drop my hand and laugh without humor. "Well. I'd hate to give the Beaumonts anything they want. Tell me who you are."

Her spine straightens as much as someone hanging by the wrists can straighten her spine. She inhales sharply through her teeth at the movement. "Isn't it obvious? I'm your intended."

My lip curls. "We've established that you are not Bianca Beaumont."

I've seen the Beaumont daughter at the treaty negotiations more than once. She looks like her dead brother and a warrior version of her mother. I've heard she's an incredible fighter and a powerful Alpha, but I never could get past the way she looks like him. Or the way she smiled at me. Like she was looking forward to killing me in my sleep.

The joke's on her. I barely sleep at all, and over the years I've discovered I'm nearly impossible to kill. But if she can manage, she is entirely welcome to do it.

The woman in front of me is trembling, her teeth chattering. She tries to hide it, like being cold is a weakness despite the fact that it's

January and she's barefoot in the woods in nothing but a thin satin dress and a corset that doesn't fit.

For a third time, my eyes rove the surrounding forest. I listen for movement. Scent for other wolves. I even lean back and look up at the ropes, then kick at the leaves around my feet to see whether there's a net or snare.

Nothing. They really just left her here.

"Have you figured it out yet?" she asks. Her thin face has grown taut with pain, and she keeps shifting restlessly, trying to ease the strain on her shoulder. "Do you see the trap?"

"Enlighten me."

She grins, but it's more like a baring of teeth. "My name is Selene Beaumont, and you're *supposed* to murder me."

Again, I nearly step back. Again, I barely remember in time to keep my hand clamped firmly around her arm.

My mind goes back to the section of the treaty that talks about Bianca. It never listed her by name; it only referred to her as "the daughter of the Alphas of Redcedar Hollow." Sofia thought it was odd, but Deacon didn't. I listened to my Beta and brushed my Gamma off. Besides, by the time we noticed it, the sun was setting behind the stone walls of the canyon. My time before the curse would take me was limited, and I was sick of going back and forth. I just signed.

"A second daughter?" I snarl. It's rare for Alpha blood families that strong to produce wolfless offspring, but it's not unheard of.

They left her here for me to find. No one outside of my pack council knows about the curse. From what I've gathered, the wider world assumes that I inherited my father's violent insanity, which is the same thing I assumed in the first week after Grace's death.

For five years, I've dispatched every Redcedar Hollow wolf that crosses into my territory. That's what they expected me to do tonight. She's right. They expect me to kill her.

Rage builds deep within me. "They're trying to trick me into breaking the treaty. They want the Conclave to help them take over Shattered Moon."

Selene raises a brow and nods, like a teacher surprised by a slow student getting an answer right.

I growl. Damn them. I want peace. I thought they were ready for it too.

Apparently the war isn't over.

I am so tired of killing.

"You don't look like a Beaumont," I snarl. "You don't smell like them."

"My family and I have different lifestyles," she says dryly. "Unfortunately, the scent of soap and vinegar will never quite rival the perfume my mother had imported for Bianca from Paris."

"Paris?" I let out a low whistle. "They must have a better relationship with some smuggler than I do."

"No, they're just idiotically rich."

I know that. Just like I know exactly which smuggler they hire to get goods from across the Atlantic, and which one they hire to get things from the ocean ports up the rivers. Travel over open water is no easy thing since the Waking, when the seas and larger lakes filled with monsters. Only ships with a siren sea-singer can travel any distance safely.

If I know that much about the Beaumonts, is it possible they've discovered my secret, as well?

"What about the curse?" I demand before I can stop myself. Because there is no other explanation. The Beaumonts know, and they found some way to dampen the curse's power, which means this girl might know who is behind it.

I shake her again, harder. "How are you controlling it? Tell me!"

"What curse?" she gasps.

She sounds hurt, exhausted, and like she genuinely has no idea what I'm talking about.

"Don't pretend," I snarl.

"I'm not." Her protest is weaker than before. She's stopped shivering, and there's a blue hue to her lips and skin that's more than just the moonlight.

I might not believe her, except that it's clear the Beaumonts sent her here to die. If they knew about the curse and her power to dampen it, they would be here. There has never been a better time to kill me.

Selene's head lolls and her eyes flutter closed.

I've let this go on for too long. I won't get any answers if she's dead.

With a snarl, I reach up and slice the ropes suspending her from the tree.

*Five*

## SELENE

The ropes holding me up break. My body falls against his. He slides a knee between my thighs and wraps his arm around me. My arms fall from their too-stretched position, and my bound wrists go around his neck.

My shoulders scream. I let out a helpless cry at the agony and curl forward, bracing my forehead against the shoulder of Jackson's murderer. I don't want this monster to know how weak I am, but I can't see, can't think. I can only whimper, "Ow, ow, ow."

The Alpha's arms tighten around me—does he think I'm going to run? The movement presses our bodies together, spreading his warmth, surrounding me with his scent. Not the inhuman wildness of the monster I caught before but cedar and rain on a clear night when the forest is just waking after a long winter.

With all the panting from the pain, the scent goes to my head, and I feel drugged all over again. The wedding dress slips down my hips. Darrow drags it up, settling it where it goes as best he can and holding it there. Then he reaches behind his head to where my bound hands rest, touches the rope, and swears.

I wiggle, trying to get away. I should detest his touch. I'm horrified to find it's the opposite. Not that it matters. Every time he releases me, the yellow returns to his eyes and it looks like he begins to turn into the monster. Somehow, touching my skin keeps it from happening. But that's crazy, isn't it?

Isn't Killian Darrow simply insane and violent?

What did he mean when he asked about a curse?

He ignores my weak escape attempts. Slowly, he eases my hands over his head and brings my wrists to his mouth. His warm breath mists over my skin, a sharp contrast to the frozen air, and goosebumps break out on the back of my neck.

"Let me go!"

"Be still."

He bites down on the rope, slicing through it. Blood flows through my wrists into my palms and purplish fingers with abrupt, agonizing pins and needles. I grit my teeth but can't help releasing a small sound of pain.

Relief tugs at me as I see he didn't bite through the tattered, clumsily knotted sky-blue-and-lavender friendship bracelet around my right wrist. Finn made it for me, and it's the last bit of him I have.

Looking at my hands brings my attention back to the light moving softly beneath my skin. If I concentrate, I can feel a warm hum in my chest. But that could be my imagination. I'm so numb, my brain could believe it feels anything.

"You are too fucking cold," Killian grumbles. "And you're still bleeding."

"You did that," I say absently. I *am* too cold. Much too cold. Or maybe the slice in my arm is pumping out too much blood. I can't fathom why he cares, though. He murdered Jackson like it was nothing, and I'm just wolfless.

"I have to take care of this."

I watch in horror as he leans forward, places his tongue on the cut, and draws it up the sensitive skin of my arm.

"Oh ..." A warm wave pulses through my body. Liquid heat flows through my face, my chest, then lower. Despite the cold, the night, the killer who holds me, the sound that escapes my throat is pure, sensual enjoyment.

Then my mind unfreezes a little, and embarrassment tingles in my numb cheeks. Alphas have healing enzymes in their saliva. He's not licking me out of some twisted sexual blood lust. He's healing me.

I try to get out of his arms again. This is Killian Darrow, son of

Alaric Bane, the monster of Shattered Moon. Jackson's killer. I should be repulsed and terrified.

Instead, my entire being is taken up with the sheer physicality of this man, like there's something deeper between us. More.

His gaze slides to my lips. He brushes the pad of his thumb against the bottom one. Whatever this strange, unearned connection is, he feels it too. "Selene."

Hearing him say my name makes me want to drop my head back, expose my neck, feel his mouth on the skin there too. So when he lowers his face until his lips are a hair's breadth from mine, I don't move.

When I don't move, he kisses me.

The iron tang of my blood is on his lips. Maybe I should be revolted. I'm not. Welcome heat sears through me. Pleasure floods my brain. It's so intense, I can't think. Can't breathe. Can't do anything but cling to him and feel.

His tongue touches the seam of my lips, and I open for him. He deepens the kiss. A moan rumbles through his chest. I shift restlessly, as if it would be possible for me to get closer to him than I already am.

His response is to dig his fingers possessively into my hip and the small of my back and nip at my bottom lip, a flash of almost pain that sends a thrill all the way through me.

But my desperation to have this murderer's hands all over me finally breaks through the pleasure and terrifies me. I struggle again. I'm afraid he won't let me go. My entire life has been dictated by the will and pleasure of more powerful wolves. They wouldn't release me.

But Killian Darrow does.

"What the hell was that?" I demand. We're both breathing raggedly. I already want to kiss him again.

He scowls. "Years of isolation, probably."

This is too much, too fast.

I lean my head away, not sure what to feel and reaching for anger because if I'm not angry, I'm going to be lost and undone, and I refuse to make myself that vulnerable to him.

When leaning doesn't create enough distance, I shove at him despite his implacable grip. "Go ahead, then. Do what Alphas do and take what you want. I'm only wolfless."

He drops me onto the leaves and takes a full step back. His eyes flash that inhuman yellow, and the musty scent of eldritch magic permeates the air.

He's turning back into the monster.

We move at the same time, me springing up and him grabbing me but holding me at arms' length. The ground is ice. The air is freezing. I didn't realize how warm he was keeping me until just now.

Oh, god. Maybe he really is cursed. But why does he seem to be able to fight it off when he's touching me?

"Take what I want?" The words are a growl that slides into a tortured laugh. "All I want is to rest. I want to know how you are doing this. I want to know what your family knows. I want—"

Then he stops, his eyes caught on mine, like he's forgotten what he was saying.

I don't know what's in his gaze, but I need him to stop looking at me like I'm some kind of answer when I didn't even realize there was a question.

Instead of letting my knees turn to slush, I lift my chin in challenge.

I refuse to look at his lips or sink into his warmth.

Without warning, he swings me up into his arms like the mockery of a bride my parents made me. I smack his chest. I don't expect it to have an effect, and it doesn't. "What are you doing?"

"Taking you where it's warm. There are things I need to know."

I open my mouth to protest, but words bottle up in my throat. What am I going to demand? That he take me home? That he set me loose?

I have no home, and if he lets me go, that thing inside him will resurface.

He starts to jog through the woods. He's barefoot and half-naked, but of course, I'm the one wracked with shivers now that he's warming me up. Once again, I'm not in control, so I fall back to what I know: being practical. "You're carrying me? Like this? How far?"

He glares down at me, topaz eyes flashing. Or maybe they're amber, and I'm an insect caught inside. Every time he looks at me, electricity zings through me.

"Do you think you could hold on if I were a wolf?"

"I could try."

"You'll fall, and then the beast will come back, and you will die."

I bare my teeth. "Or we can go like this and both lose all our toes to frostbite."

"I'm not cold."

"Shift into your hybrid form. You can carry me and be sure to keep one of your hands touching my skin."

He doesn't even look at me. Dismissive, arrogant. Of course; he's an Alpha. Full wolves can regulate their temperature to an extent, but we're near the outside edge of his territory. If he's taking me to his pack house, it will be in the center. We must have miles and miles to go.

"Just *my* toes, then," I say coldly. "Because my body is expendable."

"Tell me, Selene, what do they say about me in Redcedar Hollow? How many of your pack soldiers have I killed?"

I swallow as his power rises around me, but I've had a lot of practice sidestepping the auras of demanding Alphas. I let my gaze bore steadily back into his. "One hundred and three, counting my brother."

Is that a flinch, or did he just shift his weight to avoid the mossy boulder jutting out of the ground?

I'll never know.

"I don't know whether shifting into my hybrid form will activate the curse again. If it does, my kill count for your pack will become one hundred and four. Do you want your toes or your life?"

"What is this curse?"

He regards me, then runs his tongue over his teeth. I can see he's making some kind of decision. "You saw the monster I was."

"Yes." I repress a shudder at the memory.

"Five years ago, I started becoming that thing at night. I have almost no control over it. It hunts and kills anyone it comes across. You should already be dead. But touching you ... " He shakes his head. "I feel ... sane."

This time, the chill I feel at his words goes so deep, I can't repress the shudder. If this is true, he's done a good job keeping the knowledge of this curse a secret, at least from Redcedar Hollow. "Why?"

He regards me again, and I can see in his expression he thinks I'm playing dumb, but he doesn't press. "That's the first question. The second is the one I asked before. Do you want your toes or your life?"

"Both."

He makes a frustrated noise. A second later, he dumps me on the ground. My feet sink into the inches-thick carpet of leaves and I stumble, but he still has me by the hand. He holds my cold palm to the heated skin of his bare chest and says, "Good luck."

My hand rests there for two thudding beats of his heart. Then he shifts. His form blurs, darkens, grows. In moments, my fingers are buried in the silver-tipped black fur on the chest of a massive hybrid wolf. He lowers his big head toward me, nostrils flaring. I hold my breath as I watch his eyes for signs of that sickly yellow.

They stay that pretty, shifting topaz brown.

"See?" I whisper, throat dry.

He rumbles. I feel it through my palm, a sound that might be a noncommittal "Hm."

## KILLIAN

I make my way steadily homeward, even though I should take her to my shelter tonight and let her go in the morning.

It's the least I owe her, this enemy. This insane wolfless woman from Redcedar Hollow. I should let her be on her way northeast, where the Steel Alliance takes in strays and rogues. If she's really a victim the way she claims, it's the safest thing for her.

But she stops the curse. I keep expecting the effect to wear off, but it hasn't.

It took a year after Grace's death for Eva and Sofia to talk me back into the pack house during the day. Since then, I've spent all my lucid time tearing the world apart trying to find a cure or even just a way to lessen the curse's impact on me. I've enlisted doctors, witches, mages, nature-touched. I've even had a seraph researcher out to examine me. Nothing worked.

But now, here I am, in my own territory, holding the answer in my arms. Jackson Beaumont's secret sister.

There's something about Selene. The bitter way she laughs. The resignation when she thought she was going to die. The way she bears pain. Her obvious stubbornness.

I don't think she's a spy—she would be dead right now if not for her strange magic bringing me back to myself. Yes, there's a chance the Beaumonts discovered the curse. A chance they found a magic that allows her to do this. But the odds of both of those things being true feel slim.

Besides, if they had known they could catch me this off guard, they would have lain in wait to kill me as soon as she touched me.

I don't trust her, but I don't want to kill her.

I am so tired of killing.

I am so tired.

Redcedar Hollow sent Selene to insult me. Goad me. Get me to sign my own death warrant and destroy my pack. But they have no idea they've just sent me exactly what I've been looking for—a way to keep the treaty and my promise to Grace and Asher not to take a mate. It was the one thing I wasn't able to figure out a way around with Bianca.

But wolfless can't mate bond.

I can go through with the wedding, and then Selene Beaumont can live her life, and I can live mine. Shattered Moon can have peace. If I'm lucky, the arcanist, Whitlock, can study Selene's magic or her blood, figure out what it is that shelters me from the curse, and break it.

I could be completely free.

"Why are you making that face?" Selene demands hours later, as I turn down the barely detectable remains of an old road. We're little more than a mile from the pack house now, having passed most of the trip in silence.

I glance down at her, unaware that I made a face at all. Then her eyes start to swallow me again, and I look away.

"Shattered Moon and Redcedar Hollow have a treaty, Ms. Beaumont. You aren't the daughter I expected, but you are the one I claim. You belong to me."

## Six

### *SELENE*

He *claims* me? I belong to him, do I?

We'll see how long that lasts once he realizes how much power he's giving up by not taking an Alpha mate. Or once his pack finds out.

No one in this world remains voluntarily weak.

"If you're going to keep me," I spit the words, "I deserve to know what's wrong with you. You might be a tyrant's son, but what I saw in the woods isn't just some evil wolf. Tell me more about the curse. Do you think my family cast it on you to get revenge for Jackson?"

There's no way they did. My parents are cruel, but they're not crazy enough to mess with the eldritch. And while I suppose it could've come from a witch or the fae, what I sensed from him felt like old magic.

Killian doesn't answer for a long time as we walk along the crumbling remains of a country road. There's not much left of it, but you can still tell the smaller roads by the remnants of cracked pavement underfoot and the gap it causes between trees. Some roads are still maintained, but this deep in the forest, most are overgrown except the highways.

Finally, he says, "No. It didn't come from your parents."

I wonder how he knows.

Becoming that thing clearly puts Killian Darrow out of his right mind. If he became that monster when he discovered his mate and Jackson, he wasn't in control when he killed them.

He still murdered my brother, but can the Shattered Moon Alpha be held entirely responsible?

I open my mouth to ask, but as we come around a curve, I run face-first into a wall of déjà vu.

We're on the crest of a high hill. A break in the trees offers a sudden, breathtaking view of the distant lake winding through the forest like a silver snake. The lake was man-made by damming a river system long before the Waking. Even now, likely thanks to naiads who live in the lake and river, the dams hold strong.

In my mind's eye, I see this view during a summer sunset, the trees full and green. Another blink, and I see it again in winter, but the night isn't clear like tonight. The moon isn't quite full, and the lake is shrouded in mist.

But I've never been to Shattered Moon. I've never seen this lake—only farther east, beyond the dam, where it reverts into the Osage River.

If I feel something dreamlike, it must be because of the onset of hypothermia. Or the proximity of Killian's hard body and the fact that no matter how much I breathe him in, I can't stop noticing how good he smells.

I have to shake this magnetic pull. This man killed Jackson. He claimed me like a kid claiming the last piece of candy with zero concern for my agency.

I should be used to being treated as subhuman by now. But, though breaking beneath the unrelenting pressure of my pack's abuse would've been easier, I've never been able to let go of the idea that I am, in fact, a person.

I curl tighter in his arms, with my knees to my chest and my hands balled in fists beneath my chin. Moving carefully, I touch my lips with one finger. Heat slithers through me at the memory of his mouth, the way his hands gripped me, his body against mine.

That should've felt like being used. Unfortunately, I kissed him back in a way that was very, very mutual.

Claiming me for the sake of the treaty means Killian is planning to marry me. Will he want more?

The question turns my brain and body into a weird soup of conflicting thoughts, emotions, and physical reactions that I do not have the wherewithal to examine. Not only disgust and fear but also attraction and a deep reluctance to be physically parted from him that is completely at odds with common sense.

I need to get warm. I need to sleep. Then this pull will be gone, and I'll be able to think straight.

The shuffle of leaves beneath Killian's clawed feet changes to the coarse crunch of gravel, marking a more-used part of the road. But it isn't until the trees clear and we walk into moonlight unfiltered by branches that I look up, and my lips part for the second time tonight at an incredible view and the vivid feeling of knowing it.

But of course I do. I've seen pictures in books I snuck from the library a thousand times.

A walled castle rises before us, perched at the highest point of the land. A cliff drops away to the left. All around, the secretive hills roll away in dark ripples. A clear spring winds around the cliff's base before feeding into the silvery lake.

The pack compound takes up acres and acres, surrounded by that high stone wall. I see only one entrance—a massive gate made up of heavy wooden double doors reinforced with crisscrossing bands of steel.

The books I read did nothing to prepare me for the reality of this place or the castle in particular. How tall. How sprawling. How beautiful.

It's framed by the night sky, limned white by the moon. The base building is a mansion made of stone, broad and square with dozens upon dozens of windows, some lit by an internal glow but most dark. However, it looks as if it's been added onto over the years. Built taller, added onto. The top two floors seem to have walls that are all window.

The Redcedar Hollow "pack house" is several long, low buildings built halfway into the hills, with some of the interiors melding into the caves that are everywhere in this area.

I always felt swallowed by that place. In comparison, Shattered Moon feels soaring, even with the wall. It's easy to picture this place as the impenetrable fortress of Alaric Bane. Easy to see why my father is obsessed with it.

Before founding Redcedar Hollow, my father was one of Alaric Bane's top generals. When I was younger, his stories about the self-declared Alpha King fascinated me. My father liked to make himself the hero in those stories, but as I got older and snuck more books from the library, I got a clearer picture of the truth.

Frank Beaumont broke off from Conqueror's Moon only when the mad king started killing indiscriminately, wiping out his own children, raving about immortality and the eldritch. My father is lucky he left when he did because not long after, an explosion rocked the Conqueror's Moon pack house, killing Bane and the few loyalists he had left.

For thirteen years after that, the half-ruined Conqueror's Moon castle passed from petty Alpha to squabbling, petty Alpha. They drenched the land in blood, and my parents, secure in our territory at Redcedar Hollow many miles to the southeast, were content to let them.

Then, seven years ago, Killian Darrow and about a hundred wolves came out of the Free Cities—the grandiose name for the shanty towns full of rogue wolves that popped up in the Catskills after the Waking—and claimed the ruined castle the way he'd just claimed me. By walking up to it and declaring it was his.

Since the son of Alaric Bane returned to his father's territory, the Conclave have been holding their breath, waiting for him to take up his father's legacy and expand, conquer, control. In those first two years, their suspicions seemed well founded. Killian very quickly added all of the bickering little packs in the area to his number, swelling it to a thousand-plus wolves.

Then Jackson died, and Redcedar Hollow declared war, and it seemed like all of Darrow's dreams of legacy had ended.

If a major waterway and an intact highway—trade routes the Conclave wants safe and open—didn't run through both of our lands, I doubt the war would've stopped until one pack or the other was conquered.

Honestly, if one of us had managed to conquer or kill the other fast enough, I think the Conclave wouldn't have cared about our war. But enduring five years of trade disruptions is apparently where they draw the line.

From what I've overheard as a servant, invisible in my parents' house, the Conclave have Killian hosting their triannual gathering—also called the Conclave, not confusing at all—at Shattered Moon this year. They say it's an honor, but anyone with a brain knows they want to check up on Redcedar Hollow and Shattered Moon. Especially as some of the events will take place at the old park in the canyon that serves as the neutral zone between packs. The same place Killian and my parents signed their treaty a few weeks ago under watchful Conclave eyes.

As we approach the gate, a figure materializes out of the darkness.

It's another wolf in hybrid form. Killian's fur is dark and silver-tipped; this wolf is as silver as a slice of the moon. As tall as Killian but leaner, younger. His teeth are bared, and a growl emanates from him.

I am captured by the newcomer's eyes. He has luminescent black-ringed irises that are a rich bright gold that melds into a deep purple at the bottom.

Gold, amber, green, brown, and blue eyes are common among wolves. But purple? That means he has witch blood in his veins. The air around him crackles with strange energy—an Alpha aura but more. Prickling, electric, and aggressive, charging the air like lightning about to strike.

The cold wind drifts in our direction, and I catch his scent—spices, warm summer earth, and the smoky campfire undertones most wolves share. That scent is … familiar, even though I know I've never met this wolf before. Goosebumps race across my skin.

In response to the newcomer's challenge, Killian's Alpha aura surges, crashing over the younger wolf's like an ocean tide snuffing out a birthday candle. "Stand down, Maddox. It's me."

The other wolf's stance doesn't change, but he stops growling. Warily, he says, "Alpha? It's not the new moon. You're not supposed to be here."

Killian glances down at me, and I bite back on the desire to ask who Maddox is. Has he ever been a rogue? I've met a few. Has he ever been to Redcedar Hollow? How do I know that scent?

Killian's look draws Maddox's attention to me, and suddenly, I'm fixed in his gold-violet gaze. We stare at each other, and I wonder whether he feels the same weird familiarity I do.

"I … found something," Killian says. "An answer. Maybe."

"Who is that?" Maddox's question is sharp.

My stomach tightens in fear. A Redcedar Hollow wolf would be on the ground by now, bleeding from half a dozen wounds and showing their throat, begging for forgiveness, if they spoke to my parents or Bianca with that level of disrespect.

But Killian doesn't move to strike, doesn't growl or demand obeisance. He doesn't even seem perturbed.

"Selene Beaumont," he says evenly. "The other daughter of the Alphas of Redcedar Hollow. They sent her to be my mate."

"Mate?" Maddox growls again. He pins me with a second glare, then blinks, seems to shake himself, and focuses on Killian again. "You said you'd find a way out of it. You swore to him. To me. To Grace. You said you would honor my sister's memory!"

That electric chaos crackles again. There's something off about this young wolf. Something feral and barely contained.

Because I'm pressed against Killian's chest, I hear his heart beat faster. His breath catch. He tenses, then seems to force himself to relax.

"Selene is wolfless," Killian says quietly. "She can't mate bond."

"Do you think that will stop him from coming?" The feral energy grows stronger. I press closer to Killian, which, logically, is a very strange thing to do. But he feels safe, and Maddox doesn't.

"Enough. Stand aside."

The words carry a snap of Alpha power. Maddox flinches like a misbehaving child whose hand has been slapped, and again, I see how young he is. Maybe twenty. Not that I'm much older at twenty-four, but most days, I feel ancient.

"I'm sorry, Alpha. I ... I don't—" He steps aside and lowers his head.

"It's fine. Tell Gamma Sofia I'm here." The command in Killian's voice is natural, easy. "Have Callie tell your mother as well. I'll tell Zev."

"And Beta Deacon?"

Killian hesitates for a fraction of a second. "No."

"What about *your* mother?" Now, when Maddox sneaks a look up at Killian, there's a mischievous turn to his wolfish mouth.

Killian laughs once, sharply. "Absolutely not."

Maddox bows his head again. "As you command, Alpha. They'll be waiting for you."

We pass him. As we do, Maddox murmurs, "He'll find out. He won't be satisfied with 'she's wolfless.'"

Killian hesitates, says, "We'll see," then keeps walking.

An interesting exchange. I tuck the details away.

There's some movement behind the stone wall, and the heavy wooden doors of the gate part to let us enter. A pair of guards in human form eye us. They seem even warier than Maddox.

"Alpha." They bow. Killian nods to them. One says, "It's been a long time since we've seen you on a full moon."

Killian gives the man a long look. He immediately drops his gaze. Then we're moving up the gravel drive and into the pack compound.

"What is it about the full moon?" I whisper.

He doesn't look at me, and his answer is equally low. "I am what you saw in the forest every night except at the new moon."

"Don't they know about the curse? They're your pack."

"Only the pack council. So if you want to live, keep it to yourself."

Buildings are scattered around inside the walls. Some are stone like the castle. Some are made of logs. In fact, there appear to be a few dozen small log cabins tucked away over by one corner of the compound beneath a tall structure I realize is a water tower. Smoke curls lazily from most of the cabins' chimneys. Killian follows my gaze.

"Private family homes. Not everyone wants to live in the castle. Not everyone would fit."

"At Redcedar Hollow, most pack members live in barracks, though mated pairs have small dormitories to themselves."

Killian grunts. "Your parents treat their pack like a military."

"All wolf packs are militaries. Alpha bloods are officers. Normal wolves are soldiers. Wolfless are the labor, worth less than nothing when all wolves value is strength."

Killian carries me up a set of wide, shallow stairs to a huge set of double doors in the same style as the gate that leads into the castle. He pushes them open, carries me across the threshold into a dark, echoing space, then sets me on my feet. The moon drifting in through the door and a few tall windows is the only light. The floor is smooth and hard. Compared to the ground outside, it's blessedly warm.

I'm just below average height for a woman, but the Alpha of Shattered Moon towers over me. He places my palm against his chest, trapping it there with one of his big clawed hands, then blurs and shifts into his human form. He still towers. His human face is even more striking than I remembered. His chest is hard and smooth beneath my hand. My throat goes dry.

"Is that what you think? That strength is all that matters?" he asks.

It takes me a second to find my voice. "It's all Redcedar Hollow values, and they're not the only ones. My father learned everything he knows from yours."

Killian lifts one hand to my neck, his other palm resting heavily on my shoulder. His nail lengthens into a claw that he slides beneath the collar I wear. I am electrically aware of his height, his strength, and the fact that I can do nothing to escape.

He pulls. Wires pop as they're sliced. The weight of the collar falls from my neck. It makes a low, musical, metallic sound as it hits the floor.

Shock steals my voice. I touch my throat. There's a lightness there that's so much more than the loss of the collar's physical weight.

"The wolfless aren't nothing here." He picks up the broken collar, examines it, then crushes it in his fist. Silver sizzles against his skin, but he doesn't flinch. "Not as long as I am Alpha."

My lips part. I can't seem to catch my breath as he casually tosses the tangled, broken mass into a nearby trash can. His hand slides from my shoulder down my arm, and he interlaces his fingers with mine. His palm is warm and rough. His hand is so big, it engulfs mine.

I stare at that trash can while he turns and moves away, only following when he tugs me after him.

I can't stop running my fingers back and forth across my throat as he leads me through the darkened entry hall and up a wide flight of stairs. Sconce-like light fixtures every ten feet or so cast just enough of a dim, warm glow for me to see where I'm walking.

The dreamlike familiarity I can't shake only deepens as I get the impression of patterned marble floors, pale walls, and high, heavy-beamed ceilings. Most of the pack house is shrouded in shadow, but I swear I can picture what it looks like in the light.

As we go, there are sounds of movement in rooms or echoing down corridors, but we don't meet anyone. Eventually, I lose track of the halls and staircases until we must be all the way at the top.

There are more lights on here. Columns lead to arches in the ceiling, interspersed every fifteen or so paces with wide windows that look out onto forested hills illuminated by the setting moon. A golden glow emanates from more sconces and lanterns suspended between each arch. The floor is gleaming, complexly patterned marble tile in shades from chocolate brown to pale cream.

"This is beautiful." My voice is hushed. Now that I'm warm, I'm starting to realize how tired I am. My steps falter, and the Alpha notices.

"We're almost there." He gestures to the end of the hall, where I can just make out a single closed door.

It's blocked by the largest wolf I've ever seen.

"Zev," Killian greets him.

The huge wolf dips his head. Then Killian's eyes flash and go distant in a way that means he's speaking to someone through the pack tie. From the intent way the huge wolf, Zev, is staring at us, I assume it's him. Killian blinks, then scowls.

"What is it?" I ask.

"My Beta found out I'm here. He's waiting for us."

# Seven

## KILLIAN

**M**y hand tightens on Selene's. I nod to Zev. The curse stirs beneath the surface of my mind but as if it's contained behind a membrane or a wall of heavy cloth. I can see the surface ripple as it paws and presses, testing its boundaries, but it doesn't escape. Through the pack tie, I say, *"Thanks for the warning, Zev."*

The head of my personal guard nods his massive canine head, then stands aside. *"I'm here if you need me, Alpha."*

If he's curious about Selene, he shows no sign.

I lead her inside, and we step into the sweeping two-story living room of my apartment. Floor-to-ceiling windows take up most of the walls. An open staircase leads up to the second floor. Beyond the living room is a dining area. A kitchen in the corner connects both.

The lights are on, the place blazing. Even though the color scheme is mostly soothing, stormy grays with some purple-blue scattered around, it's harsh after the dark of the forest and the dimness of the pack house. I'd be annoyed at the waste, but last year, we finally moved to arcane generators instead of gas. Not that paying for the gas was a problem, but sometimes sourcing it was.

I blink, growling at the temporary blindness, and put my arm between Selene and the rest of the space. She releases my hand and presses her palms against my back. My skin is electrified where she touches me, and I have to force myself to pull my focus from her, from imagining those hands on more of my skin. From the way that kiss still burns on my lips. The attraction is confusing, nonsensical, and distracting.

"I thought this was your apartment," she mutters in that dry tone I realize she uses to cover concern.

I don't answer because I don't know why I moved in front of her. I don't like that I did it without thinking.

My eyes adjust in time to see Deacon Jones rise from where he was sitting ramrod straight on my couch, like he expected to be called to attention at any time. He's older, compact, and muscular, with cropped white hair and the precise movement of a seasoned soldier.

"Alpha. Interesting to see you tonight." He doesn't bother to smile.

He's within his rights as Beta to call me out if he believes I'm endangering the pack, but I don't have the energy to debate with him tonight.

"I wouldn't be here if it put the pack in danger," I say, offering nothing else.

Overall, Jones is a good Beta. He doesn't do much to hide how he's feeling, which can make him either easier or harder to work with, depending on the circumstances.

Sometimes, though, he oversteps. Sometimes, even when the sun is up, dealing with the Beta who replaced Asher makes the beast prowl.

I have a feeling tonight is going to be one of those times. Which is confirmed when he says, "Hm. We need to talk. Outside."

Jones isn't the only one in my apartment. My Gamma, Sofia Perez-Costa, is also here, along with her mate Parker and Eva Quinn.

While Deacon is in charge of defense, Sofia oversees the logistical needs of the pack. Usually, she's polished to a high sheen, but her deep red shirt and wide cream-colored pants are rumpled, and her dark hair, which is pulled back into its usual slick bun, isn't quite as slick as usual.

She stands a little away from Jones with her arms folded across her chest, annoyance written across her face. "The Alpha didn't call you here, Beta Jones."

"Which is a problem," Jones snaps. "Pack safety is my purview, and he has offered no explanation for his presence."

Parker stands behind Sofia. She's Zev's second-in-command, tall and lithe with fair skin and red hair that's undercut and pulled into a neat topknot. She doesn't know it yet, but she and Selene are about to spend a lot of time together.

Parker raises a brow at the Beta and shifts so she's in front of Sofia instead of behind. "No need for hostilities, Beta. We were all dragged away from bed, and some of us don't sleep alone and were not actually sleeping."

Sofia smirks, and I suddenly understand why she isn't quite so polished.

Eva huffs a quiet laugh. She stands near Sofia as well, dressed for sleep, her gray curls loose, her shoulders wrapped in a shawl the same bright blue as her eyes.

*"I'm coming inside,"* Zev says as he slips in the still-open door behind Selene, then closes it softly with a push from his back paw.

Eva's attention flicks over my shoulder and lands on my captain, who, when he's human, is a hulking man in his late forties with cropped blond hair and more scars than me. Eva's cheeks turn rosy, and she looks away.

"Alpha," Jones prods. "I don't know how you're in your right mind, but unless you've suddenly broken the curse, you *are* a danger to the pack."

"He's got a point," Eva says gently. "How are you here?"

I shift a little to one side, revealing Selene. "Redcedar Hollow left me a gift in the woods."

Selene peers out at him from behind me, and all of their eyes go to her.

As bright as the room is, I doubt any of them can see the subtle play of light beneath her skin. I'm not sure why, but I prefer it that way.

"A gift?" Jones demands. "Who is she, and what does she have to do with your presence?"

His tone grates. Now that I'm here, it hits me, how tired I am. Tired to my bones. Exhausted with the weight of years. I just want to get Selene into the hands of someone safe so I can retreat, think through what all of this is, what it means, and decide what I'm going to do. "I'm still figuring that out, Beta. You and I can discuss it tomorrow."

His expression flattens. "Will we also discuss why you invited Gamma Perez-Costa and Preceptor Quinn here tonight and not me?"

Eva snorts. "Don't be dramatic, Deacon."

His gaze cuts to her. "Dramatic, Preceptor? Am I the only one here who hasn't lost my mind? And it's Beta." He snarls the last word.

Zev growls. My lip curls. "Look at me, *Beta.*"

The air in the room thickens with tension. Slowly, Deacon turns to me.

I release a fraction of the constant hold I keep on my Alpha aura and let my power rise. Deacon has submitted to me as his Alpha, and that means I hold his mind in mine, like a rabbit in my jaws. Rarely do I remind my wolves what that means, but now I twitch that power, let him feel it.

The Beta goes pale and drops his head. I think I see him sneer, but I know that's the exhaustion getting to me. Jones loves rules and hierarchies. He pushes, but it's always for the good of the pack.

I fight for the patience I used to have and grasp onto a bare, thin thread.

"Sofia is my oldest friend. Eva is my family. They're here for personal reasons. I explain this to you as a courtesy, Beta, because I respect you. But if you come into my home uninvited again or if you address the Preceptor in that tone again, there will be consequences."

"Apologies, Alpha," he mutters.

"Get out."

Deacon goes, sneaking one last look at Selene as he does. She presses against my back, and I swear a wave of heat moves through me.

I'm hallucinating. Maybe losing my mind. Dawn and my blessed few hours of sleep can't come fast enough.

Once he's gone, I pull Selene around in front of me. There aren't many options for places to maintain contact with her skin without draping my arm over her, so I slide my hand against the back of her neck, my fingers dipping beneath the thick strap of the slip.

Selene glances back at me. Goosebumps race across her flesh, her eyes close momentarily, and I swear her breath catches. I tamp down a similar reaction in myself, as well as the urge to slide my fingers up into her pale silvery hair to see whether it feels like silk. To gently grip it, tilt back her head, and see whether she gasps again when I claim her mouth.

"Killian?"

Selene and I both startle at Sofia's voice. Selene turns forward and clutches the wedding dress to her chest with both hands.

My throat is dry, and I have to clear it before I speak. "This is Selene Beaumont. Frank and Delilah's other daughter. We weren't aware of her because she has no wolf."

Sofia's mouth drops open, then she thrusts her finger toward me. "I told you they were up to some bullshit!"

Parker lifts a brow. "She told you."

"Yeah," I say with a sigh as I rub the bridge of my nose with my free hand. "You were right."

Eva tuts and leans forward, examining Selene's ragged clothing. "Is that a wedding dress?"

"My sister's idea," Selene replies. From the tilt of her head, I gather she's looking at the floor instead of the small gathered crowd. "She's ... creative."

"Those bastards," Eva mutters.

"Let's get her in the shower and get her something clean." Sofia is already bustling forward, reaching for Selene. "And you. God, Killian, look at the state of you. How are you here? What happened?"

On instinct, I jerk Selene back against me so that her back, half-bared by the cut of the dress and corset, presses against my chest.

Sensation explodes like fireworks across my skin.

Oh, fuck. What is happening to me? Yes, it's been a long time since I touched a woman I don't think of as family, but that doesn't come close to explaining this. Selene has gone tense; I feel how ragged her breath is. But after a second, she's the one who pulls away, just a little, and puts a sliver of space between us, which makes the wolf inside me snarl.

I try to hide my reaction, but it's beyond too late. Sofia exchanges glances with Parker, then Eva.

"Talk to us, sweetheart." Eva's brow is furrowed. I know why. I'm acting like Selene is actually my mate. Something they'll already know is impossible from her scent, which is a dead giveaway she's wolfless.

I force myself to relax. To pull back, widening the space between Selene and me, only keeping contact with my hand resting on the back of her neck. Then I explain what happened in the woods. Selene remains silent in front of me, her eyes downcast. The longer it goes on, the less I like or trust the show of submission.

"So the curse is, what, dormant as long as you two touch?" Parker asks when I finish.

"So far."

"And you just declared that you claim her?" Eva says. There's a delicate warning in her tone that makes the teen boy I used to be flinch.

"What else could I have done?" I snap.

I drop my gaze as Eva's sharpens. I wish I could speak to her through the pack tie, but Eva can't speak or hear that way.

Next to me, Selene inhales sharply. She's finally lifted her head, and she's staring at Eva. "You're wolfless."

Eva gives her a sideways smile. "Always have been."

"But—but the Beta said ..." Selene looks bewildered, then like she wants to say more. Instead, she closes her mouth and steps back toward me, pressing into me again. I exhale slowly and force my body not to react. It almost works.

Eva moves forward and lifts her hands just below Selene's cheeks. "May I?"

Selene nods stiffly. Eva takes her face in both hands and studies her, turning her back and forth. A look of deep sadness crosses her face. "Oh, my love. Redcedar Hollow is so cruel."

Selene doesn't fight her touch. In fact, she pins her dress in place with her elbow and grabs Eva's hand, clinging to it like she's found a lifeline in a storm.

"He called you 'Preceptor,'" she says desperately. "The Beta did, and Kil—the Alpha. Preceptors are Pack Council. They're senior wolves. You're wolfless."

A wave of protective rage courses through me. It's so strong the curse stirs in the darkness of my mind and presses against that thin shield Selene provides. Fear lances the anger, and I fight for equilibrium.

"Oh, sweetheart," Eva whispers. "You've had a long day. Let's get you two cleaned up as best we can so you can sleep. I promise, you and I will talk about so many things tomorrow. And I think there's someone else here you might like to speak to."

She looks at me, eyes questioning, and I nod. Selene, however, seems distracted by her own thoughts.

"Do I have to sleep next to him? So he doesn't change?"

Selene has apparently decided that Eva is the authority here, which is true in a way.

Sofia moves closer but cautiously, like Selene is a frightened animal. Or maybe because of my reaction a moment ago. She leans close, examining Selene's skin. I see the moment she notices the light. "Oh," she whispers. "That's beautiful."

She tilts her head, examining Selene's face. I see the thoughts whirring behind her deep brown eyes. "If she's dampening the curse, could be bloodline magic."

In addition to Alpha blood, certain wolf families carry deeper powers. Like the Quinns' steelborn abilities, Parker's heightened speed

53

and agility, Zev's rocklike strength, or Maddox's berserker abilities—which is what most wolves are convinced my curse is. Berserker abilities plus the bloodlust and insanity of Alaric Bane. An illusion I've kept up only because I never let them see me when the curse is active.

"Do the Beaumonts have bloodline magic like that?" I ask.

Selene shakes her head. "Enhanced speed and strength on my father's side and a long line of powerful Alphas on my mother's but nothing rare."

"I'll do some research into their genealogy," Sofia says.

Parker scoffs. "In what spare time, Gamma?"

"Hush."

"I'd appreciate it," I say, braving Parker's displeasure. "Delegate if you need to, though, Fia. Don't overwork yourself."

I don't tell them about my other plans yet—to invite Warlord Vandran to Shattered Moon so Whitlock can take a look at her. Or at least get some blood samples Whitlock can test in the lab at his mountain stronghold of Arx Lumen, which was a college campus before the Waking. His and the warlord's access to obscure knowledge is greater than mine. But I want to broach the subject with Selene first.

Sofia snorts. "Don't overwork myself? Rich, coming from you. You both look dead on your feet."

"What time is it?" I ask, praying for it to be close to dawn.

Sofia checks her watch. It's a pre-Waking antique with a gold face and a worn reddish leather band. She spends a ridiculous amount to source the batteries. "It's 3:36 a.m."

Shit. It's the dead of winter. The sun won't rise for almost four hours, which means that's how long I have to stay in contact with Selene's skin.

Deacon was right. I wasn't thinking, bringing her here. Trapping them all with me. A mistake I wouldn't have made if not for how damn tired I am. "Selene needs to see Dr. Bennett, then sleep. Fia, can you find her some clothes?"

"I already have someone bringing them up," she says, just as a knock sounds at the door.

"I'll get them," Zev says.

Something inside me untwists. I'm so used to being alone, coming to the pack house only for the day-to-day work of the Alpha, that I forgot what it's like to be able to rely on my friends.

"You need sleep too, Killian." Eva's tone is sharp.

"Selene doesn't want me in her bed."

Selene moves, stepping away, grasping my hand instead of pressing against me. She leaves a hollow feeling in her wake, even though she's still right there. "Don't speak for me."

I sigh. "Do you want me in your bed, Selene?"

It's the first chance I've had to study her face in the light. There is beauty there, beneath years of harsh living. She's not as pale as she looked under the moon either. Especially not now, as red is blooming like roses on her cheeks. "No."

It's awkward, arguing with a stranger while holding their hand. "All right, so—"

"But I'm not an idiot, Alpha Darrow; I'm not cruel, and I'm not going to be precious about something that has to be done. You have to stay in physical contact with me so you don't murder everyone here? Fine, we stay in contact. You've been up all night? Fine, you need to sleep. We'll bind our hands together, get into bed ... and ... sleep."

At first, her little speech is crisp, clipped. At the end, I get caught in those uncanny eyes, and her words slow. I realize I've pulled her closer again, that I'm leaning down. The others are watching. I'm too tired to care.

"And ... sleep?"

Selene's throat works as she swallows.

"You think that's a good idea?"

Her jaw sets. "It's the only idea."

"I killed your brother, Selene. For all we know, this effect you have on me could end at any moment and I could kill you."

"Killian!" Eva gasps softly.

I don't know why I said it except that I need someone to put space between us and I can't find the willpower to do it. Selene has the will, though, if I push in the right place—I can sense it. She'll tell me to leave, and I need her to tell me to leave, because I want her in bed with me far too much.

My plan backfires. If anything, Selene's pale eyes only get icier. "Do you think there has been a single night since I became wolfless that my life has not been threatened by the whims of an Alpha?"

The words are a cold slap. I lean back. "I can sit by the bed. I'll sleep when the sun rises."

Selene leans forward like I've challenged her. "That. Is. Ridiculous."

"Fine," I snap.

"Fine." She shakes back her short, pale hair and lifts her chin. Her stubbornness would be adorable if she didn't look like the ghost of a bride who starved to death on her wedding day.

"Where is this bed?" she asks tartly. "I'm exhausted."

~

## SELENE

If anyone here has bloodline magic, I think it's Killian Darrow, and I think his power is driving me crazy. Or, potentially, tricking me into making the dumbest choices I've ever made.

He insists on waking up the pack doctor to come and see me. Josiah Bennett is a bald, broad man with a bushy dark beard and deep brown skin. But it's his soothing smile and the quiet way he deals with me that makes me realize how far over the edge I am. Only when I start to feel safe, thanks to the doctor's calming presence and Eva's kindness, do I realize how afraid I've been. Not just tonight—for weeks. For years.

I want to burst into tears, but my brother's murderer—as he has so gleefully reminded me he is—is sitting here holding my hand. He's turned away, but I will not break in his presence.

After Dr. Bennett declares that I won't lose any of my fingers or toes, Killian and I have to figure out how to get cleaned up, change into clothes that aren't bloody and shredded, and do other necessary things while still holding each other's hands. We settle for one of us standing inside the private toilet-only part of his fancy bathroom while the other stands outside with the door mostly closed. Eva and Sofia help me. Zev helps Killian.

And then we're out of ways to delay. Killian and I stand there, holding hands and facing down the bed. I'm wearing the softest, warmest clothes I've put on my body in over a decade. I keep pulling the sleeve between my fingers and rubbing the fabric. Every time I do and realize again how warm and soft it is, I have to fight the urge to cry.

Why am I here? Why do I have this when the other wolfless don't?

Wherever Finn is, does he have pajamas like this?

Maybe someone here will help me find him. Hope is a sudden, sharp knife in my chest.

Eva goes on her toes and kisses Killian on the cheek. "Sleep, love. For once, actually rest."

I frown at that. Everyone keeps referencing how little he rests, and I admit, once we were in his brightly lit rooms, I was shocked to see how pale he is and how deep the hollows under his eyes are.

Killian closes his eyes. "Mom, please."

"Claudia will pitch a fit if she hears you call me that again."

Killian grunts. "You're my mother-in-law."

Oh, my god. Not only is Eva wolfless, she's the mother of his dead mate. She's still here? She still has a relationship with him, despite what he did?

Why?

At the same time, I can't help but hear the wistfulness in Killian's tone. This is the second time someone has brought up his mother, who, if this farce goes forward, will be my mother-in-law.

From the way they're talking about her, I don't look forward to meeting her.

"Parker and I will be here," Zev says. In his human form, he is hulking. When I say "hulking," I mean it. He looks like one of those old pre-Waking cartoons where the men are drawn like wide triangles with barrel chests, giant shoulders, and biceps like basketballs.

"Leave the door open," Killian says as they step into the hall.

Sofia is the last one to leave. She binds my hand to Killian's with some stretchy tan bandages, then pats my arm. "I know you don't know us and you don't believe this yet, but you're safe here."

I give her a tight smile, and then she, too, is gone.

For a long time, we remain there, hands bound together, staring at the bed. I sway on my feet. Killian tugs on my hand. "I can sit in the chair."

"No." There's the insanity again. I think I'm just desperate to prove I have some control in this situation. In any situation, ever.

Before he can protest again, I climb onto the bed and sink into the comforter.

It's heaven. At Redcedar Hollow, my bed is a thin cot with a couple of blankets, and my room is a closet-sized servant dorm I share with Finn. I doubt even half of Killian's bed could fit inside.

I scoot on my knees to the far side of the bed and awkwardly pull down the covers, which I'm kneeling on top of. Killian follows me, but he's smart enough to pull the comforter back before he climbs in.

Alone in bed with the monster who has terrorized my pack for half a decade. My hand bound to the hand that killed Jackson.

But why did Killian kill Jackson? Because this man ... he doesn't seem like a murderer.

There's more awkwardness as we get settled. We have to lie on our sides facing each other, but Killian puts pillows between us, so it isn't as terrible as it could be.

I try to sleep, but for a long time, I can't. I'm too aware of his hand in mine. Too aware of his big body sinking the mattress, pulling me toward him. Too aware of the scent and the heat of him—and the fact that another person is touching me.

It's not like I've never been touched. Back home, there was Sam. He's a good man. He works hard. He did a lot to help me protect the other wolfless. But when Hayley died and I moved Finn into my room, there was no time. How long ago was that? I count back.

Four years. No wonder Killian has this effect on me. He's the unfortunate combination of everything I am attracted to. His build, which is big but not too big. The fact that his face is head-turning but not so perfect that he lacks character, those expressive dark brows, those scars, and those damn beautiful topaz eyes. Everything down to the way he moves captures me, and that's not even getting into his scent ...

I force the thoughts away. I have to remember who he is. An Alpha, Jackson's murderer, and, apparently, cursed.

I also need to remember who I am. What was it Bianca said?

*Useless. Powerless. Wolfless.*

I'll never be anything to him.

Killian's breathing went deep and even a long time ago. The rhythm of it, the warmth of his hand, and remembering my own, small place in the world finally ease me into sleep.

# Eight

## SELENE

*There are things you must know...*

The voice trails me up from the depths like mist around my feet, an echoing wail that belongs in dreams I can't remember. Or maybe I would if I weren't distracted by the coolness of the mattress next to me. Someone is missing. There's emptiness where I never felt empty before.

I crack my eyes. I'm in a massive, soft bed in a room that looks like the inside of a storm cloud. Beyond the windows that take up an entire wall, the horizon is golden with the sun's first light. The scent of rain and cedar surrounds me. I feel so safe that when sleep rises to claim me again, I roll over and let it.

～

I'M DREAMING AGAIN, because I hear Finn. "How long is she going to sleep?"

There's light beyond my eyelids, but I can't remember the last time I slept so well, and I'm so warm. I can't quite break away from sleep, but I need to. I have to make sure coffee is made and that Jenny is up and has started breakfast.

"A little longer, apparently," says an older female voice. "Be patient. She went to bed very late."

The sound doesn't bounce right, as if the room is full of soft things. The mattress on my left shifts, like a small body just sat on the edge of the bed. I want to reach out and hold this dream of my brother, but everything is so heavy and warm. I breathe in. It doesn't smell like cleaning supplies and the nearby kitchen. It smells like fresh-cut pine and vanilla candles ... like cedar and rain.

Memory floods me. Wearing a wedding dress, suspended from a tree. Killian Darrow claiming me as his mate. The castle that I feel like I know. Eva, a wolfless and somehow also a Preceptor—not just part of the pack, not just on the pack council, but an Elder entrusted with the education and future of the children. Eva saying, *I think there's someone else here you might like to speak to.*

Is it possible ...?

I'm afraid to open my eyes, but I do. "Finn?"

He's there. A small boy with a wild riot of sandy brown curls and huge chocolate eyes sitting on the edge of the bed.

I sit up and reach for him.

"Selene!" Finn's face crumples. He launches at me, and I catch him just as he bursts into tears. I wrap my arms around his skinny body, bury my face in his hair, and inhale the child scent of sugar and dirt. My arms and shoulders are still aching from last night, and the old wound in my left shoulder sends out a little spear of pain as he throws himself into me, but I don't care.

"Selene! Selene! Selene!" Finn squeezes me so tight. "They said you would wake up, but I thought you might never, and I missed you so much, and I thought Alpha was going to hurt you because it's not the right moon ..."

He goes on, sobs wracking his small frame. Tears leak hot from my eyes as I rub his back, whispering comforting words. "I'm here, Rocket. It's okay. I'm here."

Alive, alive, alive and here. It's impossible. He moves to hold my hand. He's still wearing the friendship bracelet he made for himself. His is red, yellow, and orange. The knots are a little better than those on the bracelet he made me because he insisted on making mine first.

Eva sits in a chair beside my bed. Last night, she was in pajamas and a shawl with her hair loose. Today, she's got the same blue shawl, but she's wearing a creamy blouse and eclectic jewelry, with her thick hair piled on top of her head and held in place with a wooden pin carved in the shape of what looks like a sword.

Her smile is soft. "We thought you might know Finn. He's been waiting all day for you."

I squeeze my brother close. "How?"

"Killian found him in the woods. It was the new moon. He's ... more himself on the new moon."

So the fates, the gods, or the universe heard my prayer. I almost start to cry again.

I bury my face in Finn's shoulder. "You were supposed to run to the Steel Alliance."

"I tried! But Alpha Darrow found me. He said it was too far to run in the dark and that I could stay here. The next morning, he said it was too far because my stomach was empty. Then he said I should stay and train with the other pack kids until I get a little stronger. Look how strong I am now!"

Finn pulls up his sleeve and flexes his muscles. My jaw trembles from holding back more tears because he does look different. Healthier. I spent so many years hiding every scrap of food I could to make sure Finn got enough, but he started growing so fast last year it never was.

Shattered Moon has been feeding him.

I look up at Eva, but I can barely see her through tears. "Thank you."

She nods and leans forward to brush a tear from my cheek. I resist the urge to grab her hand again. Finding another wolfless here feels like home, even if she hasn't lived the same life as me. Even if she's never worn a collar.

My eyes go wide, and my fingers fly to my throat as I remember Killian slicing through mine. I push Finn back just enough to see that his collar—one he never should have worn so young—is also gone.

"Wh-where is the Alpha?" He killed one brother only to save another. I don't understand, but I have to thank him for Finn.

As soon as I think of Killian, his absence nags at me. Like I just discovered a missing tooth and now can't stop prodding the spot with my tongue. Mentally, I jerk back from the feeling. It's good that he's not hovering. I don't want him here. I don't crave the hand that held mine through the night or the deep breathing that finally lulled me to sleep.

My voice heavy with tears, I say, "I'm not sure what's happening. I'm not even sure this is real."

"It is real! I told them all about you," Finn says, bouncing in place. "That's how they knew I know you!"

Finn sits back, dries his own tears, and pats my face. "Selene, don't cry. There are so many kids here, and I can play with all of them!"

His words are another punch to the chest. Because of Delilah, Finn was never allowed to play with the other pack children at Redcedar Hollow.

His smile abruptly fades. "I know I should miss home, but I don't want to go back. We don't have to, do we?"

"No," answers a voice like rough silk.

The hair on my arms and the back of my neck stands on end as an Alpha aura washes over me. Killian Darrow is standing in the doorway with Zev behind him.

My eyes go to the Alpha, dragged by that magnetic pull I'm starting to worry has nothing to do with my extreme mental state last night. His thick dark hair is pushed back from his face. The dark circles under his eyes are less prominent. He wears black pants and a black sweater with the sleeves pushed up to his elbows. He gives me a wan smile, and suddenly, I can't breathe.

"That's her," someone whispers.

"Oh! She's in the Alpha's room. He must like her."

Three children peer around Zev's legs—two girls and a boy. Heat crawls into my cheeks at a cluster of kids finding me in the Alpha's bed.

"Wow! She just turned really pink. Do you think she likes him too?"

Thankfully, Eva takes pity on me and gestures at the children. "You three. Did you come here with a purpose?"

"Yes! It's school time. You know that, Elder Eva," says a little girl. She waves at Finn. "It's school time!" Then she waves at Killian. "Hi, Alpha!"

Killian waves back at the girl.

Wolves at Redcedar Hollow whisper that Shattered Moon lives in fear of Killian the way Conqueror's Moon did his father, but that was obviously a lie because these children are not afraid.

Finn jumps off the bed. "I have school!" He kisses my cheek and hugs me tight. "I'll see you after, okay?"

"After ...?" I reach, but Finn is gone with the other kids in a cloud of giggles.

"I can have him come back if you'd like," Eva says.

I shake my head and sniff, wiping away tears. "No. He's happy. Thank you for taking care of him."

"We didn't realize you were the sister he was asking for until we saw your bracelet," Eva says. "Finn's work is ... recognizable."

I laugh and hold up the wrist with the clumsily knotted bracelet I never take off. "Yeah, it is."

Killian approaches and sets down a tray covered with a cloth on the bedside table. "He didn't tell us he was Frank Beaumont's son."

Cold fear pools in my stomach. "Please, you can't send him back."

"Am I holding my enemy's heir?"

"No," I snap. "So don't get any ideas about using him as a hostage. He's the son of my father and a wolfless woman Delilah had killed a long time ago. She'll never let him become Alpha."

It's true. I won't let it be anything else. But in the back of my mind, I know if Finn manifests a wolf and he's strong enough, Delilah will acknowledge him. They'll pit him against Bianca, who is older and more ruthless than my sweet little brother can ever hope to be.

Killian grunts as if this has answered multiple questions. "If your father decides he wants him back ..."

"My father thinks he's dead," I say. "I'd like to keep it that way."

Killian's expression remains neutral. "He's an Alpha's son, but the boy was half-starved when I found him. Why?"

"The Alpha Lady is resentful of the reminder of her mate's infidelity."

Killian studies my face, then my body. The way his eyes move over me is clinical, not sexy. "You fed him from your own share of food."

It's not a question. I hug myself, like that can cover up what the years have done. "All of the adult wolfless gave some, and there were a few pack members who'd help from time to time."

"But you were the one who made sure he ate every meal, every day."

"You say it so confidently, it must be true," I retort.

Killian lifts the towel from the tray. Steam wafts off a bowl full of chunks of chicken, carrots, and potatoes floating in rich broth beaded with fat. Next to the bowl are three thick slices of warm, buttered bread.

The Alpha brought me food.

What is happening?

"Eat," Eva chides.

"I ..." I'm overwhelmed again. My stomach knots despite my mouth watering. It doesn't help that they're all staring at me.

63

Like he knows it, Killian rises suddenly. "I forgot something to drink. Zev, come with me."

"You're going to get me a drink?" I ask.

He gives me an odd look. "It's just water from the kitchen."

He leaves.

The Beaumonts never got their own things. None of the wolves of Redcedar Hollow did if they could get a wolfless to get it for them. And they sure as hell never brought me anything.

I stare at the food.

"Eat it," Eva says again. "It's good. And Dr. Bennett insists."

Mechanically, I lean over and spoon soup into my mouth. It hits my tongue and melts, buttery and hot and perfect. I swallow, and I can feel the heat move all the way down into my stomach. I can't remember the last time I ate something this good.

Abruptly, there's a sound of surprise from outside the door. "Wait! With respect, Lady—"

"I will see her!" A woman's voice comes from outside, imperious and shrill. "Get out of my way!"

"Damn it." Eva rises and turns toward the door. Her stance is wide, the set of her shoulders determined, like she's about to catch a boulder rolling down a hill.

A woman bursts into the room. The tall redheaded guard—Parker, I think—chases her. But the new person is impossibly fast for a woman in what looks like her early fifties wearing needle-thin high heels.

The woman stops in front of Eva. She's tall and slender, with a sleek black bob that suits her high cheekbones. Her clothes—an expensive sweater and impeccably tailored pants—are black. Her lips are red. Her jewelry is rubies and moonstones, all large and glittering.

"Claudia," Eva says. There's a warning in her voice.

"He's *my* son," the woman hisses. "No matter how much you try to steal him, he's mine. I will see this girl he is determined to throw our pack's future away for."

She shoves past Eva. Even though they look the same age and Eva is more solid and not wearing heels, Eva stumbles when Claudia shoulders her. Parker has to rush to catch her.

Claudia sweeps to the side of the bed, crosses her arms beneath her breasts, and looks at me as if she smells something abjectly foul. "You!" She wavers a little on her feet.

It's morning. Is she drunk?

"You—" She steps back, eyes as wide as if she's seen a ghost. Then she shakes herself, the sneer returning to her crimson lips.

"You!" she says for a third time. Her thoughts seem to have finally caught up to her. When she speaks, there's a slight slur to her words. "S-still in his bed, are you, you little slut? Selenite. You will never be good enough for my son!"

She darts forward too fast for me to dodge. There's a loud crack, then a burst of pain as she slaps me across the face.

## Nine

### *SELENE*

"Claudia!" Eva gasps.

Pain ricochets through my cheek. I press my hand to the spot. It stings, and warm wetness seeps between my fingers. She split the skin. Probably one of her gaudy rings.

This morning has been a confusing sea of emotions, and I've been adrift. But this? This is familiar. This I know how to handle.

I drop my eyes. Not because I'm afraid, though plenty of the wolves in Redcedar Hollow think I'm spineless, but because if I look at her now, she'll see my rage.

I know wolves like this, who hurt those weaker than them with impunity. It offends them when the "weak" don't take it lying down. That we feel anything besides fear, sadness, or helplessness. If we dare to feel angry, it just makes things worse.

As drunk as Claudia is, I can feel a shocking amount of power in her. She has Alpha blood nearly as strong as her son's. There's no way I'll ever be a physical match for her.

All that passes through my mind in an instant. My eyes bore into the comforter. "I didn't ask to be here. If you have a problem with me, you can take it up with the Alpha."

"Claudia!" Eva hisses again.

Parker hauls her back. There's concern on her face, like Eva might really get hurt if she goes against Claudia. With Eva behind her, Parker tries to grab Claudia, but the woman swings at her. Parker dodges, and Claudia lurches toward me again, bracing her hands on the bed.

"Do you think you can dismiss me?" She grabs my wrist and jerks me out of the bed, yanking me around like a rag doll. Her strength is shocking, even for a werewolf. The black tips of her slightly extended claws dig into my arm.

Parker grabs Claudia's shoulder, but her eyes go to the claws that are threatening to break my skin. "Lady Darrow, you need to calm down."

She ignores Parker and shakes me. "Selenite. Wolfless, are you?"

"It's Selene," I say.

Power washes over the room. Suddenly, there's a deadly snarl, and Claudia is yanked away from me.

Killian has a cup of water in one hand and his mother's arm in the other. She writhes and whimpers. "Ow! Killian, you're hurting me."

It's daylight, but his eyes flash that pale sickly yellow for an instant. He releases her, and Claudia stumbles. Parker catches her, then shoves her onto her feet. Killian stalks over and leans down into Claudia's face. There's a bestial depth to his growl I feel in my stomach when he says, "Lay a hand on her again and I will tear it off."

Oh. My.

"Killian!" Claudia shrieks in despair.

"Lieutenant, show my mother out."

Parker's grin is feral. "Gladly, Alpha."

Claudia continues to shriek for Killian, but he ignores her as Parker drags her out the door and away.

Killian sets the water down on the bedside table. Then he closes his eyes, curls his hands into fists, and breathes in, then out. "Eva. Are you all right?"

"Of course."

"Of course," Killian huffs a humorless laugh. Then he opens his eyes and looks at me. I've still got my hand pressed to my cheek, which has started to throb in time with my heartbeat.

"I'm going to give you two a minute," Eva says.

I straighten, alarmed. "You could stay—"

Eva comes over and grasps my hand. Hers is warm, weathered, and strong. "He's all right. You can take him."

I look at the angry large man towering over me and decide that Eva is nice but out of her mind.

She's also out the door.

"There's no excuse for my mother," Killian says. "I apologize on her behalf."

I scoff. His gaze sharpens on me. "What?"

"Why would you apologize for her? Why do you care?" The words are shoutier than I intended.

He stalks toward me. I flinch, but instead of striking me like his mother did, he takes my face in his hands. Gently, he eases my fingers away from the slice on my cheek.

When he sees the blood, he growls. The sound resonates in my chest, and I shiver.

It's only partly fear.

Whatever it is that pulls me toward him isn't better since last night. It's worse. I am drowning in him.

Killian takes a napkin, dips it in the water he brought, and cleans the blood from my face. I think that will be all, but he cups my jaw in both hands. He tilts my head up and lowers his face to mine. My balance wavers, and I catch myself against his chest. His heart beats beneath my palms, unsteady. He drops his eyes to mine, and I notice how dark and long his lashes are. That there are flecks of deeper brown in his topaz irises. Beautiful.

"I care," he whispers, sending another shiver through me, "because you are under my protection. As long as you're here, no one is allowed to hurt you."

Then he presses his lips to my cheek. The cut isn't deep, and I immediately feel the tingling coolness as my skin heals. He pulls back, then presses a second kiss to the spot.

His hands drop to my shoulders, big and heavy. I turn my face and tilt my head back, and he presses another kiss lower on my cheek. My fingers curl in the soft fabric of his sweater, and his arms slide down my back. His lips move to my jaw, then to my neck. Heat unfurls low in my belly, and god, I want his hands on my skin. I want his lips on my neck. I *want*.

He kisses his way back up my neck and along my jaw to my cheek. He brushes the corner of my mouth, then hesitates.

He's so close. So, so close, but he starts to pull away.

No.

I take his face in my hands and pull his mouth to mine. My fingertips brush the softness of his dark hair, my palms splay over his rough, stubbled jaw.

This time, I steal his sounds—a groan of desire rather than a gasp of surprise.

His arms come around me, and he lifts me like I weigh nothing as we devour each other. My legs wrap around his waist, my arms around his neck. His biting kisses are everything. His strength is everywhere. Whatever emptiness is inside me aches less when he molds me to him like this, and I want—

What am I doing?

I gasp and break the kiss. Killian pulls back at the same time and practically dumps me on the bed. We both pant, pulling in heaving breaths. My mind scrambles, trying to figure out what just happened. How it happened. Where the tide pulled me under.

"Don't touch me," I say. Then, accusatory, "You kissed me again."

Killian barks a laugh. There's no humor in it. I wonder if there's ever humor in his laughter. "*You* kissed *me.*"

"You kissed me the first time," I snap. "This is your fault."

"I was half out of my mind when I kissed you the first time. How does that make this my fault?"

"If you hadn't done it then, I wouldn't have wanted to do it now."

"That explains everything. You're right. It's my fault."

"That's very grown up of you to admit, Alpha."

Killian rubs a hand over his face and groans, then paces away from the bed before pacing back again. He points at the soup, and now it's his turn to sound accusatory. "Eat."

Steam is still rising from the bowl. The bread is still warm. "I was trying to, but your mother attacked me."

"I won't let it happen again."

I sit down and scoot to the edge of the bed, glaring with narrowed eyes until he takes two steps back. "We'll see."

I am starving, so I eat. As I do, he and I watch each other.

I bite back the urge to snap at him not to look at me. We've already bickered enough. If we keep going, I might kiss him again, and I can't. This is Killian Darrow, the monster of Shattered Moon. This is Jackson's killer. He said it himself.

But I am having serious problems reconciling knowing who Killian is and what he's done with feeling it. If I asked him what happened that night, would he tell me? Maybe hearing it in graphic detail from the murderer's perspective would help.

But I'm not ready for that on top of everything else, and I have a nagging fear that even hearing the details from his own lips won't work. Every time I try to think clearly, logic gets pushed out by the sheer force of his physical presence.

God or fates or whatever else, I've never experienced anything like that kiss, and he was just as desperate. At least whatever is doing this to me has got him too.

Maybe his curse is contagious and this is how it begins. With terrible, all-consuming lust.

Killian remains silent until I finish eating. When the food is gone, he gestures across the room to two overstuffed chairs set on either side of a table in front of a fireplace.

Seeing no other option, I rise, then go to sit. Killian follows and drops the blanket from the bed on my lap without a word. I open my mouth, then close it again. I don't know what to say or how to react. People don't do things for me.

But it's not like he did it nicely. In fact, I'm pretty sure he's just as irritated with me as I am with him right now.

Do I have a reason? Yes. Because my treacherous body wants him to do unspeakable things to me and, given who he is, that is bad and stupid and wrong.

I watch the way the muscles of his broad back move beneath his sweater as he kneels and lights a fire—something else that's normally my job—and admire the lines of him. The breadth of his shoulders, the curve of his neck, the way he tapers from shoulders to hips. I remember how big his body feels compared to mine. The strength in his arms, his chest.

He rises and sits in the other chair, and I'm grateful for the table between us.

The fire crackles. The blanket is warm. Outside, the winter day is pale gray. This moment would be cozy if I weren't sitting here with a man who wants to use me. And whom I would like to use. In a different way, sure, but one that's equally as objectifying.

I play with the soft blanket on my lap and firmly turn my thoughts away from his body. "Thank you for saving my brother."

A crease forms between Killian's brows. "I'm glad he showed up on the new moon."

We both sit in silence, with what could have been hanging in the air. My eyes catch on a leather cord wrapped around his wrist multiple times. A heart-shaped locket is dangling from it.

"What are you, Selene? A spy? Or the bait in a trap?" He sounds contemplative, not angry.

The shift in topic throws me off. I have no deflection prepared for this, so my answer is more honest than I intended. "I could be either."

Killian tilts his head, chin still in his palm, and says, "Hm."

"It seems unlikely I'd be a spy since my parents thought you'd kill me."

"Maybe they didn't."

"You've killed every other adult wolf from Redcedar Hollow who's crossed into your territory."

"They didn't have the same ... impact you did. An impact that's still unexplained."

"If Sofia finds some hidden family with bloodline magic in my past, let me know."

For a long moment, there's no sound but the crackling fire. He stares into it, and I sneak the opportunity to study his profile. Angular jaw, scarred cheek, thoughtful eyes. He's shaved, but the hint of a five o'clock shadow remains.

My parents and Bianca are underestimating him. I've known him for less than a day, but it's obvious he's more complex and far more intelligent than they give him credit for.

Killian turns and catches me looking at him. It sends a thrill through me, but I don't look away.

"The treaty." He drops the words in my lap like stones.

I raise a brow. "What about it?"

"I gather you object to being 'claimed.' Do you want me to send you back and demand your sister instead?"

"Maybe I'd like you to demand my sister and set me free."

He absently draws his middle finger across the gleaming wooden surface of the table between us, making small circles. "You'd rather be a refugee of the Steel Alliance than the Alpha Lady of Shattered Moon?"

I scoff, but I can't take my eyes off that circling finger. "You have to be an Alpha blood to be an Alpha Lady. I don't even have a wolf."

"Mate-consort of the Alpha, then. You don't want that?"

I pause just an instant too long. I hate that his words hit home. "What if I said I don't?"

"If you mean it, maybe you go free."

"And Finn?"

"Goes with you."

"And you continue to martyr yourself for your pack, cursed forever?"

His finger stops circling. We stare at each other. Once again, I'm sinking into the depths of those topaz eyes.

He wins because I'm the first to break the tension by breaking the silence. "You won't set me free. We both know it. You'll make me your mate-consort whether either of us wants it or not because I'm less dangerous than Bianca and you seem to be willing to trade power for security. What do you really want from me, Alpha Darrow?"

Now it's his turn to pause. "I want you to call me by my name."

"Is it not 'Darrow'?" I say sweetly. I swear I see one corner of his mouth quirk upward, and another thrill goes through me. What would he look like if he really, truly smiled?

Internally, I shake myself. He is—if not my enemy—my opposition. The fact that my body has decided it yearns for his like the earth for spring is a problem. I can't let myself daydream about his smiles. I can't let myself fall into the trap of trusting him just because I want him.

"I prefer 'Killian,'" he says.

"How informal."

"We're going to be married."

"Are we? I'd like to know what your pack thinks about that."

"Is there someone waiting for you back at Redcedar Hollow, Selene?"

"Yes. Two dozen wolfless who need protection from my parents." The words kill whatever lightness there was in the mood. I pull the blanket up to my chin like a shield. "Come on. You don't want a wolfless mate. You want to find a real ally. Some Alpha you trust so your pack can have an Alpha Pair."

His eyes bore into mine. "Selene. I *want* a wolfless mate."

Frustration sharpens my tone. "Why? Why would you hamstring yourself like that?"

Killian toys with the locket he wears around his wrist. His eyes are distant. I don't think he realizes he's doing it. "I made a promise once that I'd never mate bond again. I intend to keep it."

So that was what that exchange at the gate with Maddox meant.

*You said you'd find a way out of it. You swore to him. To me. To Grace. You said you would honor my sister's memory!*

"I'm a way for you to keep your promise to your dead mate and the treaty," I say.

"Yes."

My cheeks heat, but I have to ask. "What about succession? Heirs?"

An expression I can't exactly read crosses Killian's face. "I want Maddox to be my heir."

My brow furrows. "Maddox? He's, what, five years younger than you?"

"Seven." Killian shrugs one shoulder. But when I think about it, having an heir close to his own age makes sense. With the curse and the level of violence Killian faces on a daily basis, he's probably gone years assuming he could die at any time.

"So there would be no expectation for us to ... make ... heirs?"

Killian's eyes are as hot as molten gold on mine, but then he tears his gaze from me. He leans forward, elbows braced on his knees, hands clasped so hard between them, his knuckles go white. "No. I ..." He exhales through his teeth. "The curse means I need to be careful of ... extreme emotion."

"Extreme passion?"

His eyes are hot on mine again. "Any emotion."

"You seemed fine a few minutes ago. Have you tried?"

He knuckles his eyes and sits back. "Trust me."

"So no?"

He growls, but it's low and more irritated than angry. "Do you want to be the woman to find out?"

We stare at each other.

Killian's expression goes suddenly serious, his tone almost pleading. "Selene, you can't forget who I am. Don't let your guard down."

"Don't worry, Alpha Darrow. I haven't."

But I have. The fact that he's the one reminding me not to is sobering.

Then he arches his back and rolls his shoulders, and I nearly forget again.

"You're right that I have no choice," he says. "But I still want you to agree to this. I'd rather work with you than in spite of you. You seem practical. I think this arrangement can be mutually beneficial."

"Yes. I am practical." It's my turn to stare into the flames. "What would I have to do?"

"It depends. You can help me with the day-to-day running of the pack or not. If you have something that interests you, you can pursue it. The only required parts are that we are legally married and you appear with me at events. I've already announced your presence to the pack, but I want to have an official dinner for our engagement in two weeks, on the next new moon. Then there's the Conclave. If you're with me, I can actually go myself for once."

I clear my throat. "At the Conclave, the leaders of packs can propose laws, correct?" I ask, even though I already know.

"Correct."

"Would that include wolfless mate-consorts?"

Killian considers me. "There hasn't been one before, but I'd say it does."

Excitement grows in me, a trembling, determined thing. "What if I wanted to propose a law that forbids the forced servitude of wolfless?"

Killian raises a brow. "I'd say you might be surprised how many packs will support you."

"Then why hasn't someone done something before?"

He turns over his hands, studying them, and bares his teeth, like this is an argument he's had a thousand times. "Tradition."

The word is a slap. I bite back deep bitterness. "You could have changed my life. You could've changed hundreds of lives."

He looks up at me, regret written across his face. "If I'd been able to actually attend for the last five years, I would have."

"What were you going to do this year? You're hosting."

"They didn't give me a choice. I would've gone during the day and kept myself on an extremely short leash."

I look into the flames again. All my life, I've watched my Alphas play games of power. I've been an outsider to that game, or a pawn. Expendable.

My parents changed that when they traded my life for Bianca's to goad Killian into an act of war. No longer a pawn but a queen. A piece worth something, but still a piece. Powerless except when I'm moved around by someone else's hand.

Killian's offer will change that. He's going to put me in a position to play the game.

That thought gives me pause. As much as I'm afraid for the wolfless of Redcedar Hollow and my own future, power repulses and terrifies me. No good ever comes from having it. It corrupts. It makes you stop seeing other people as people, and if you don't, it kills you. Jackson and Bianca are both evidence of that in their own ways. He was kind, and he died. She loved me one day, then she didn't.

I'd rather die dangling from that oak tree than become like her.

So much to gain, nothing to lose. Except my sense of self.

And Killian. What do I do about him? Even knowing what he is, just being in the same room makes my head spin and my body heat. He's as dangerous as the fire I stare into and so much more likely to kill me.

It's wrong to get a thrill from that. It makes me a terrible person. But I never claimed to be good, even if I want to do what's right.

"I'll do it," I say, running my fingers across my lips, still sensitive from his kiss. "But I want one more thing in return."

# Ten

## SELENE

I lean toward him, drawn by his quiet, raw intensity, and nod to a table in front of the wall of windows that holds a translucent statue as tall as my hand.

"Swear a blood oath you'll never exile Finn from your pack."

Some people still worship a god or gods, but since the Waking, some worship the fates. Weave Readers—the fates' equivalent to priests or pastors—promise they're real, though I don't know whether they're any more likely than gods to answer prayers.

Many wolves worship the Fate of the Moon, often depicted as a middle-aged woman with long hair and the moon phases in a glowing band across her forehead. She can be whatever race, whatever body type, as long as she has the moon phases, wolves at her side, and an expression of compassionate wisdom on her face.

"Swear he'll always have a place here," I continue. "And give him everything he needs, including an education and enough money to make his way if he chooses to leave when he's older. Swear that you'll be good to him, and make sure this pack treats him well, even if he turns out to be wolfless."

Killian stares at me for a long moment. Just when I think he'll refuse, he says, "That's it?"

That's it? I just asked him for a whole life.

76

Killian rises from his seat, moves toward me, and crouches in front of my chair. His proximity makes it hard to breathe, especially when he lifts a hand to my jaw and traces my cheek. His gold-brown eyes are soft, and so is his voice.

"You have me under your thumb, Selene. You could ask for anything. Money. Impossibly expensive gifts. Influence. Magic favors from my allies. But this is what you want? Everything for Finn, everything for the wolfless, and nothing for you?"

"Yes."

He frowns, and it occurs to me that he's so used to people using him for favors that he probably finds selflessness suspicious.

"I'll make your deal. But if you betray me to Redcedar Hollow or if it even looks like you're running back to them, I promise, I will kill you."

Ah, there's the Alpha assholery I've been waiting for. "If Redcedar Hollow ever get their hands on me, Alpha Darrow, I'm already dead. I won't leave. That's my promise." I hold out my hand. "So we're agreed?"

He takes my hand. Despite the unease that lingers between us, his touch is as electric as it was last night. "Agreed."

One word. That's how easy it is for him to change a life.

Killian walks to the small table where the statue of the moon fate is sitting on a square of cloth. There's a collection of offerings around it— a white moonstone that shimmers blue, a few acorns and leaves, and a polished steel bowl partially filled with water.

I trail behind him and tilt my head. I've never seen a statue like this one. I thought it was quartz, but from the wear on her features, the stone is something softer and cloudy instead of clear.

Killian grows the claw on his right forefinger long and slashes it over his left palm. The shallow cut wells with blood. He makes a fist, squeezing a few drops in. Even though it's day, the light pouring in from outside seems to dim.

"I, Killian Darrow, swear on my blood and my life that I will never exile Finn Beaumont from my pack. That he'll be cared for. That I will raise him and give him everything he requires. That I will be good to him, and so will my pack, regardless of his nature."

His blood plinks into the water and swirls beneath the surface like smoke. Blue light the same color as the flash in the moonstone bursts from the heart of the statue. There's a great pressure in the room for an instant, then it's gone.

He and I exchange glances. Whether oaths like this are actually witnessed by the fates or just react to our own magic, I couldn't say. There are no terrible consequences if he breaks it, as far as I know, but this kind of oath is something wolves take seriously.

He doesn't ask me to swear a similar oath, and I don't offer.

"What kind of stone is that statue carved from?" I ask. "It's not moonstone. It shouldn't have flashed."

He looks down absently. "No. I think it's selenite. It was here when I reclaimed the castle, along with a few other things."

Suddenly, my whole body is gripped as if in a giant, icy fist. A cold breath brushes my ear. I exhale, and it turns to mist.

*Selenite, there are things you must know ...*

As abruptly as it gripped me, the feeling releases. My whole body trembles. I move on shaking legs back to the chair, sink into it, and hang on, staring at the statue.

What ...?

Killian doesn't notice. He's looking out the window, into the gray sky. From here, the wintery hills stretch out into a point, the silver lake looping around and then away to the east.

I'm still trying to figure out what I just experienced when Killian turns away from the view and crosses the room to a dresser with a small wooden box on top. He opens the lid and pulls something out, then approaches, takes my hand, and pulls me from the chair.

With a grim look on his face, he holds up a string of moonstone beads, each the size of half a pea. They're white except when they catch the light and flash that iridescent blue. A small crescent moon pendant in white gold hangs from the center. Three tiny rubies glimmer darkly at its center and points. Moonstone blue and ruby are the colors of Shattered Moon.

"What's this?"

"Something else that was found here. It could be an engagement present, if you'll wear it. Unless it reminds you too much of other things."

He means the servant collar. I'm shocked he'd think that deeply about what would or wouldn't make me uncomfortable.

I examine the necklace. It is short, but it won't wrap tight like the collar did. And it's pretty. I wonder who it belonged to. "No. I like it."

"Turn around."

I turn. Killian brushes my short hair to one side, then lowers the necklace in front of me. His fingers whisper tortuously lightly against my skin as he connects the clasp.

What would happen if I turned and kissed him again?

Before I can, he finishes and steps away. I turn back to face him, and he spends so long taking me in that his gaze becomes as weighty as a touch. "You look ..." He clears his throat. "It suits you."

"Thank you."

There's silence between us again, and I fight the urge to reach across the space between us. Not for any lust-filled reason, just to hold him and be held by him.

That's a worse idea than ripping off his clothes and begging him to take me. Lust for Killian is one thing. Being emotionally vulnerable to him is another.

"Now what?" I finally ask.

As if I've snapped him out of a daze, Killian shakes his head. "Now I take care of a few things, you relax, Dr. Bennett checks on you again, and I'll see you tonight." There's resignation in his tone, not excitement, but I understand why. Despite the way I want him—no, because of it—I feel the same way about sharing a bed. Resigned.

As if he can't resist one more touch, he leans in and kisses me on the forehead before he leaves. "We'll be in the woods, just in case things go wrong."

~

## KILLIAN

Leaving her is like leaving behind part of my own flesh. I don't like the feeling, and I don't trust it.

A few hours later, the pack healer comes down the hall from the direction of my apartment. I've been standing in the open doorway of my office, leaning against the frame and staring vaguely toward my rooms for ten minutes. When Dr. Bennett sees me, I straighten and gesture him into my office.

"Alpha," Josiah Bennett smiles, and I shake his hand. "Ms. Beaumont is looking good today. I was able to get the blood samples you wanted, so I'll get those on their way to Fall Line. The lady just needs food and rest. And care. You look concerned. Why?"

He sits in a chair, and I lean on my desk and fold my arms. "Have you ever heard of wolfless forming a mate bond?"

The doctor frowns. "No, can't say that I have."

"So there's no way a wolfless can have a fated mate?" I know this answer, but it's the only reason I can think of to explain the hold Selene has on me. The way I want her.

"Not that I've heard of." Dr. Bennett lifts bushy brows and gives me a once-over. "Is there a reason you ask?"

I rub my jaw, considering. "There's something between Selene and me. It's ... strong."

Bennett pulls a comically sympathetic face. "Well, Alpha, she's a beautiful woman who will be even lovelier when we get her back in good health. And if I'm not mistaken, it's been a long time."

It has been a long time. Longer than anyone knows. I drop my face into my hands and rub my eyes. "Right. It just seems ... mutual."

The doctor chuckles. "You're a handsome man, Killian. Maybe it's been a while for the lady too."

"Okay. Thank you, Doctor. I won't take up any more of your time."

CLOSE TO SUNSET, I find Selene in Eva's apartment, where Finn is staying until we figure out something more permanent. I wait in the hall while she says goodbye. Just seeing her lifts some weight from me, and it's torture, after the hours away from her, to keep my distance, to not embrace this woman I've known for only a day.

I hope Dr. Bennett is right that we're just two touch-starved people who suddenly find themselves thrown into close proximity.

It can't be anything else.

The thought of the endless nights stretching out in front of me, close to Selene but never close enough, makes me wonder whether this is worth it. Maybe I should let the curse have me.

I won't sleep either way.

I'm glad Selene stayed on the upper floor with Eva today. The wolves of Shattered Moon didn't take the announcement of a wolfless as my potential mate-consort as well as I'd hoped, and there have been whispers and muttering everywhere. Deacon and Sofia are doing damage control, though not without Deacon tersely saying that he told me so.

If I could tell the pack about the curse and the impact Selene has on it, they'd understand why I need to be with her. But I can't because I can't risk others finding out. My allies might think I'm too unstable, and my enemies would realize I'm vulnerable in certain ways—like that I have no idea who I'm killing until it's over.

Selene and Finn take a long time to say goodbye, but I don't deprive them of it—if things go wrong tonight, it will be the last time they see each other at all.

WE TAKE a four-wheeler down one of the overgrown old roads. Cold air wraps around us. Night is on its way.

We're cutting it close.

Selene's arms are around my waist, her body pressed to my back. When the sun gets close to the horizon, she slides her hands beneath my shirt and splays them against my abdomen. Need surges through my blood with vicious heat, and I grit my teeth. It takes everything I have not to crash every time she moves or curls her fingers.

It's been a long time since I was intimate with anyone. Years. Almost seven, despite it being only five since Grace's death. I didn't think I was missing anything before Selene. Now having her hands on me is killing me.

It doesn't matter how much I want her. Like I told her, strong emotions, passion, anything that makes me lose control is off the table.

But could letting go be safe with her?

If we gave in, would this need become more bearable?

*Selene, I'm cursed and responsible for your brother's death, but every time you cross my mind, it's like I've stuck a tent pole down my pants. If we could fuck to see if that gets rid of the problem, I'd appreciate it.*

I curse, glad she can't see my face or hear me over the roar of the four-wheeler's engine.

What if we did give in?

If we did, the only time I'd trust myself would be on the day of the new moon, and that is a long two weeks away. It's also the night of the dinner in her honor, when she'll officially be presented to the pack as my fiancée.

We arrive at the shelter just as the last slivers of sun disappear over the horizon. The monster stirs. Hunger stabs into my stomach, and pain lances through the back of my skull. I sling the bag over my shoulder and reach for her hand.

Selene hurries to take it, twining her fingers in mine. Her hand is cold despite the fact that she's bundled in several layers. Immediately, the pressure in my gut and the pain in my head subside. The relief is so overwhelming, I don't know whether I'll ever get used to it.

The sunset catches my eye. Without thinking, I slow down and take in the bands of saturated hot orange that fade up into pink, pale gold, and then blue. Even broken by the trees, it's beautiful.

Selene pauses at my side. "It's been a long time since you got to just look at a sunset, hasn't it?"

"Yeah."

"Were you into that kind of thing before? Sunsets and stargazing?"

"I was 'into' taking a minute away from the chaos sometimes, yeah."

I start to move, but she squeezes my hand. "Take your minute, Alpha. We have time."

She's right. We do have time.

"Come on." She tugs me up the hill.

At the top, we find a clear spot where we can see for miles. We stand in silence, and for the first time in five years, I watch the red sun sink. I watch the orange sky fade to gold and then deep, dark blue.

I don't have to dread what comes when the last sliver of light disappears. Not as long as she's by my side.

I exhale as it goes and wait, Selene's hand tight in mine.

The curse doesn't claim me.

When I look down at her, silver swirls like stars beneath her skin.

I have never wanted to kiss anyone so badly. But this time, it wouldn't be out of lust. It would be because I want to kiss the woman who gave me back sunsets.

I can't let myself. I don't get to feel these things anymore. I don't get to be close.

I tear my eyes away. "Thank you."

She shrugs, but I swear a smile lifts the corners of her mouth. It's barely there, but it's enough to know a real one would devastate me.

"It's just a sunset. We'll have a lot of them."

We will. And a lot of nights sharing a bed that will follow. I bite back a groan and lead her downhill to the base of a limestone bluff, to a cave opening that's been walled up with logs like a cabin.

"What is this?" she asks.

I lead her forward, pause, scent, and listen for anything that might have found this place and be lurking inside. When there's nothing, I push open the heavy wooden door. "This is where I stay when I can't go home."

Inside, it's cold and dark as pitch. I drop the bag and reach in with my free hand, finding my striking rod by feel. Then I push up my sleeve and guide her so that she's holding onto my arm. Her elusive scent immediately fills the space, goes to my head. "I need both my hands."

She doesn't protest. Moving slowly so that I don't jostle her and break contact, I feel around until I find what I'm looking for, then go to my knees and strike sparks from the rod.

A tiny flame jumps to life inside a clay oven built into the cave wall. Soon the fire I laid the last time I was here catches and bursts into life, casting a flickering glow over the rest of the space. When I'm confident it's lit, I move to the lantern on one of the shelves carved into the stone and light it as well. Then a second and a third, until the small cave is as brightly lit as any home.

Selene makes a noise of surprise. I try to see this place through her eyes.

It's cozy, I think. The wall that covers the mouth of the cave is made of horizontal logs stuffed with mud and moss to keep out the chill, forming a room that's about ten feet wide and fifteen feet long. I've hollowed out nooks in the rock walls for shelves, and there's a wide natural platform a few inches higher than my knees that holds a simple stuffed mattress heaped with blankets to form a decent-sized bed. The other furniture consists of a small, battered table, a single chair, and a chest made of reclaimed wood.

The most important part of the shelter is the stove. I built it into a natural ventilation shaft using clay and stone, and when it gets going, it heats this place well in the winter months. Every time I leave, I lay out logs and kindling for a new fire. There's a pile of firewood next to it and a larger pile covered with a tarp outside. The only thing this place lacks is running water, but there is a spring nearby. It bubbles up out of the ground not far from here, so it's clean enough to drink from.

"Did someone build this place for you?" she asks.

"I built it."

Her lips part in surprise, and it kills me not to taste her again.

*Remember what you are. Remember what you've done.*

Selene clears her throat. "Do you have whatever you were going to tie our hands with? That might be a good place to start, just so we don't accidentally let go."

In answer, I reach into my bag and fish out a roll of elastic bandage. It worked last night; it will work again.

Selene gives me a tight little smile. "Good choice."

We move to the bed where we can easily sit side by side, both of us pretending the air between us isn't so charged that it's a miracle we don't get struck by lightning. I pull back my sleeve, and she makes a sound when she sees my arm.

A rough network of scars runs over my skin. They range in size from raised, jagged large lines to pale white marks that are barely visible.

"What happened?" she asks, eyes big.

I shrug. "Other wolves. Howlers. People who crossed the man I used to work for."

"Who's that?"

"Marcus Vandran."

"The warlord of the Fall Line Protectorate?"

"Yes. I helped him get where he is, and he helped me get where I am."

Selene lifts a brow. "I see."

She rolls up her sleeve, revealing scars of her own. I point to a wide, shiny streak. "What's that?"

She grimaces at me.

"I told you mine," I say.

Selene huffs a breath and says, "One of the wolfless overcooked the steaks on Bianca's birthday—well-done instead of medium rare. I told her it was me. She told me she'd make sure I knew what well-done felt like."

Rage rips through me. The beast pushes against his confinement, whispering loudly in my mind, *Breakthemkillthembleedthemeatthem.*

I growl, and I don't stop until I feel Selene squeezing my arm. She peers up into my face, a carefully controlled neutral expression on hers.

She's afraid.

I focus on the light inside her, pulling it into me through our connected hands, and chase the monster back into the dark. Quietly, I say, "I don't think things would have worked between your sister and me."

It takes both of us passing the elastic roll over and under our arms, but soon the bandage is secure. Our forearms are crossed, our hands pressed together from wrist to palm, our fingers left free to move. I made sure to secure the arm without Grace's locket so the pendant wouldn't dig into our wrists all night.

We're joined only by our arms. Our hands. The touch shouldn't feel intimate, but it does.

"Comfortable?" I ask when the silence gets too loud.

She wiggles her fingers. "Perfect."

I stoke the fire and put out the lanterns. We got ready for bed before we left the pack house, so there's nothing to do but go to sleep.

Remembering her struggle last night, I flip down the blankets before she can climb in. "Take the side by the wall."

"Why?"

"Because." I want to be between her and the door. Not because I think something will break in. Nothing ever has before. But in case. "I'm used to sleeping on this side."

"Okay." She lies down, and I pull up the covers around us.

I've been exhausted for years. Last night, I was asleep within seconds. Tonight, her maddening not-scent surrounds me. Wolfish instinct says if I just roll toward her, if I press my face into her hair or against the warm, soft skin of her neck and breathe her in, I'll finally figure out what it is about her that drives me to the edge of control.

But I don't do that. Instead, I grip the blankets with my free hand, close my eyes, and count my breaths, in and out.

*One. Two. Three.*

I reach an impossibly high number before I finally fall asleep.

# *Eleven*

## SELENE

I can't deny my growing fascination with the Alpha of Shattered Moon.

The morning after our second night, he makes me breakfast on his little stove. It's just eggs and bacon from a cooler he brought, but I can count on one hand the number of times someone has cooked for me in the last decade.

An Alpha blood has *never* cooked for me.

The moonstone beads of the necklace Killian gave me are smooth and satisfying to roll between my fingers, and it's quickly becoming a habit. Something to do with my hands while I think. I toy with it as I watch him cook—the way the muscles move in his forearms, the competence of his sure large hands. He's mesmerizing.

We return to the pack house and head for his apartment, and I notice I'm getting a few looks from wolves in the hallways. They aren't exactly welcoming.

"Do they know why I'm here?" Walking among the Shattered Moon wolves without Killian's hand in mine leaves me feeling exposed. I keep my fists balled and my arms folded tight against my chest to stop myself from reaching for him.

It's odd, too, because I'm used to having to dodge out of the way of anyone coming toward me in the hall. But they part for Killian like water around a stone.

"I told them what they need to know yesterday. That I retrieved you from Redcedar Hollow, you're the daughter of the Alphas, and I'm taking you as my mate."

"And I'm wolfless?"

Killian hesitates, then nods.

"How did they react to that?"

"Shattered Moon has been through a hard five years, but we've been through it together. They'll adjust."

My lips press into a wry smile. "Of course."

We reach his apartment. I sit on the couch, my knees hugged to my chest, while Killian showers. Parker and Zev are here too. Zev makes small talk, asking me about the people I've left behind. He's down-to-earth with a self-deprecating sense of humor, and I appreciate how easy it is to talk to him. Parker barely speaks, but when she does, it's always some witty, acerbic observation.

Killian emerges a few minutes later. He wears another dark sweater that emphasizes his shoulders, clings to his broad back, and cuts just right over his waist and down to his hips. His sleeves are pushed back like they always are, once again revealing the muscles and veins in his forearms. His damp black hair brushed away from his face so the ends curl against his neck. Warm topaz eyes fix on me, and my heart thuds as he stalks toward me.

But then he pulls up short several feet away and stuffs his hands into the pockets of his black pants. "I have to work."

I stand and pull the soft sleeves of my shirt over my hands. "Oh. What should I do?"

"I thought you could rest." He gestures at the shelves that line the living room. They're filled with books and what I realize are movies. He's got a television as well, which is a rare thing in the last few decades. "It doesn't sound like your family made your life easy. Take some time to do whatever you want."

"Is Finn ... has the school day already started?"

"I think so."

"Oh." I have no idea what to do with myself. I look at the books, the movies. "I'm sure I'll figure it out."

"I'll make sure Eva brings him straight here after school," Killian says. He glances at Parker. "Parker is going to stay with you."

A guard to keep me safe or to keep an eye on me?

"Okay. Thanks."

He looks like he wants to step toward me. The lusty part of me wants him to, but the rest of me is grateful when he doesn't.

"I'll see you tonight." Killian gestures at Zev, and then he's gone.

~

He comes back just before sunset, and we go to the cave again. I battle my lust. We make awkward conversation. Then we sleep.

That night, I have strange dreams; when I wake up, I can't remember them, but I know I was afraid.

~

"Selene! I drew this in school!" Finn bursts through the door. He holds up a picture that has got to be Killian in hybrid form. It looks like a drowned weasel in tight black pants.

"*Wow*. That is gorgeous, Rocket. Let's hang it right in the middle of his fridge. But you colored yesterday. I thought you guys were supposed to make playdough today?"

"Caretaker Ms. Callie is sick, and we had Caretaker Ms. Noelle instead. She's only been in the pack two years, and she's new at teaching. She got the days mixed up."

"I see."

I get to see Finn every day after school, but because sunset comes so early at this time of year, it's never for long enough. I miss spending time with him but not enough to deprive him of the friends he's making and the fun he's having while finally, really learning.

~

During the day, I haunt the castle like a ghost, with Parker trailing behind. The lanky lieutenant doesn't talk much, but when she does, it's with that annoyed humor I appreciate.

The feeling of déjà vu I had on that first night doesn't go away. If anything, it gets worse. As if I've always known this place, I discover the communal pack areas. The massive kitchens, the great hall where the pack eats and holds events, the library, the infirmary, music rooms, and even a game room. Most are located on the first floor except the library, which takes up three floors in a tower on the southwestern side of the castle.

I also find a hall almost hidden behind the grand staircase in the foyer that apparently leads to an entire empty subterranean wing of the castle. The entrance is covered with a tarp, but the echoes of familiarity are there, stronger than ever.

I peer around the edge of the tarp. The hall is only about twenty-five feet long before it dips down a short flight of stairs and disappears from view, so there's not much to see except dust and debris. Some of the windows are broken and boarded up, the walls partially burned down to bare stone. A few doors on this level remain intact, including one right inside that leads beneath the foyer's stairs. A tarnished plaque beside it reads, *Servants' Hall.* The scent of ancient ash swirls to my nose. I blink, and I swear I see it as if it's one of the halls upstairs. Wide with regularly spaced arches and lanterns that hang between. Except instead of marble, the floor is plush carpet.

"Not down there," Parker says. "It's not safe."

I roll the beads of my necklace between my fingers and mess with the little crescent moon. "What is it?"

"Old servants' rooms through the first door right there. Bane's personal wing down below. The explosion that killed him took out part of it, and a lot of the interior burned. Killian meant to fix it, but then—" She waves her hand in a sweeping gesture I assume encompasses his curse and everything to do with it.

I take one last look, then reluctantly release the tarp and walk away.

As is becoming our habit, Killian and I get ready for bed, bind our hands together, and talk about our days for a few minutes before falling asleep.

I'm still waiting for the other shoe to drop, for Killian to turn into a violent man who matches the beast. For him to be an Alpha like every other Alpha I've ever known.

It hasn't happened.

We lie on our pillows facing each other, bound hands between us, fingers intertwined. It's still awkward, but after nearly a week, it's slowly getting easier.

"It's our second to last night out here," Killian says. "We've proven you keep the curse away, so the day after tomorrow, you and I can start sleeping in the pack house. The new moon and our engagement dinner are in a little more than a week. Sofia is getting you a dress. She'll bring samples so you can pick something out."

I tense. "All right."

"Do you have any questions?"

*Why do I feel like I know this entire place? Why can't I stop thinking about you while you're gone and craving you while you're here?*

"No."

Killian covers a yawn with the back of his hand. My gaze catches on his fingers. I'm a sucker for men's hands, and his are perfect. Strong and lean and slightly callused. The memory of those hands on my face when he kissed me makes me ache. I hoped this desire for him would fade, but as the days pass, it's only getting worse.

Again, mentally, I know that those are the hands that ended my brother's life. But I just don't feel the connection between Killian and Jackson's death. Sooner or later, that is going to get me into trouble.

"All right. Goodnight, Selene."

"Goodnight."

THE NEXT DAY, probably because Parker tattles about how bored I'm getting, Sofia takes pity on me and assigns me a shift to help in the kitchen or with cleaning, depending on the day. Everyone in the pack without an "official" job has a shift. Having something to do helps, even if the people I work with mostly ignore or side-eye me. But since everyone takes a turn, it still doesn't take up much time.

Luckily, Eva invites me to sit in on Finn's classes in the schoolhouse as well. The school is a small building separate from the pack house but within the compound walls. I snatch the chance to spend more time with my brother.

Shattered Moon has about a thousand wolves, but not all of them live at the pack house. Of those who do, around seventy are under the age of eighteen. Finn is seven, but he's in the class of eight- to ten-year-olds because he's a little advanced, which makes me proud.

As it turns out, it's a good thing I show up that day. The substitute caretaker, Ms. Noelle, smacks her hand to her mouth as soon as she walks into the classroom, then turns and runs out. Eva follows her and discovers she's also got whatever illness Ms. Callie has.

So I walk Finn's class through reading a book about wild things, and then a few classes combine in the building's kitchen to make cookies. Since the Waking and the Wars of Power, ingredients like sugar and chocolate aren't impossible to come by, but they are an uncommon treat.

That same day, I find the piano in Killian's suite of rooms.

I've been hesitant to explore his space. Alphas, by definition, are territorial, and there's still a level of unspoken mistrust between us. But I've poked around everywhere else, and I think he might not mind.

The first door I open leads to a cozy music room with a shiny black baby grand piano inside. Though the room is small, its single window is large. Unlike the cool tones of the rest of Killian's apartment, the floor here has a plush cream carpet, and the paper is a sunny yellow with a pretty floral motif. There's even a padded nook in the window perfect for reading.

I am instantly in love.

I've always been enchanted by music. I sing lullabies to Finn, and at Redcedar Hollow, we would sing in the kitchen or the garden to pass the time. Bianca has a piano, of course. She got it because of a whim she had when she was ten, but she never plays it. She backhanded me for touching it once.

No one will do that here.

Still, I creep close on silent feet, as if my sister might jump out from behind a corner and yank my hair hard enough to make my scalp bleed or shriek for her personal guards to smack me around.

Slowly, I slide onto the bench.

"Oh," I breathe as I reverently touch the keys. I press one down, and a note shivers through the air. It doesn't sound out of tune, though I'm not the most qualified person to say.

Warmth swells in my chest.

I am going to learn to make music.

~

"LADY SELENE," says an older woman who dips her head to me as she passes me.

A couple of days after I discovered the piano, Parker and I are walking through the hall on the first floor on our way to lunch. Sofia has encouraged me to be more visible to the pack before the dinner where Killian will officially announce our engagement.

I barely remember to nod back, then whisper, "Lady?" to Parker, who walks at my side.

She gives me a wry look. "You're about to become mate-consort to a wildly rich man and the most powerful Alpha in a generation. What did you think your title would be?"

"I don't know. I didn't think about it at all." A group of younger wolves wearing the same combat uniforms as Parker passes.

My eyes catch on a twenty-year-old guy in the group. Golden-skinned with straight dark hair falling over intense eyes and a narrow, straight nose. His features hint at both European and East Asian ancestry. There are black hoops in his ears, black rings on his fingers. The looping lines of black tattoos disappear into the sleeves of his fitted black T-shirt and curl up his neck from the collar. Everything about his lean body is coiled to spring.

It's not strange to see a wolf with tattoos, piercings, and jewelry. Those things are common enough among the wolves of Shattered Moon —definitely more than among the regimented, straight-laced soldiers of Redcedar Hollow.

What is strange, however, is the instant tug of connection I feel, and the fact that I know who this is, even before his eyes catch mine—black-ringed gold irises that fade into pools of deep violet.

Maddox. He stares at me for a long moment before he breaks his gaze away.

"Wolfless bitch," one of the young men with him sneers as they pass.

A woman titters. "Seriously. If he had to invite Redcedar Hollow into his bed, I can't believe he let them get away with sending her instead of the sister who'd actually benefit us."

There's a snarl and not one flash of movement but two.

Parker has body-slammed the male to the floor, and Maddox has the female wolf pinned against a wall by her throat.

"What did you just say about the Alpha?" Maddox snarls. Violence radiates off him like heat from a lit oven. The woman whimpers and squirms. He's not cutting off her air, but he's not being gentle either.

Parker goes down to one knee and leans over the man she flipped right over her shoulder onto his back. "Talk shit about Lady Selene again, Hudson, and I'll pull your dick out through your throat."

"S-sorry, Lieutenant," he stammers. "Y-yes, Lieutenant!"

Parker lets him up, and he flees. Maddox still has the woman pinned. All of Parker's attention is suddenly on him. "Maddox. Stand down. Let Leah go."

Maddox leans into the other woman, whose eyes are wide with fear. A sound like distant thunder fills the hall.

It's Maddox, growling.

"Soldier!" Parker snaps.

He's going to do something stupid. I don't know how I know, but I feel it.

I move to his side and put my hand on his shoulder. Alpha aura radiates off him. It's different from Killian's. His is a tide. Maddox's is heat from an open flame—intense, burning, and destructive.

"Let her go."

"She insulted you and the Alpha."

"Then let me speak for myself."

With a soft snarl, Maddox takes a step back and inclines his head to me. I don't know how to read what's in his eyes before he turns and stalks down the hall.

I return my attention to the young female wolf, Leah. All of her friends have abandoned her, and it's just Parker and me in the hall with her now. The girl has long reddish-brown hair, a scattering of freckles, and suspicious hazel eyes. She's taller than me. Even though every wolf-less instinct I have screams that I'm not allowed to stand up to a "true" wolf, that she'll turn on me, that the rest of the pack will justify the use of force to punish me, I refuse to back down.

I lean close, lift my chin, and tilt my head to one side. "Leah, right? You think you want my sister as your Alpha Lady?"

The younger woman glares at me. "It's nothing personal. I've just heard she's strong."

"Strong?" I smile tightly. "Yes. Bianca is strong. Strong enough that I couldn't stop her from locking me in a shed one night when I was four-teen and she was fifteen. It was February. She left me there overnight. I almost froze to death. Why? Because the boy she liked told her she was tainted because she shares blood with a wolfless."

Leah blanches.

"She's so strong," I continue, "she used to show it by tying rabbit pelts to a wolfless she chose at random, then taking them to the woods and telling them to run. She called it a 'training exercise.' Do you want to know who she was training?"

Leah swallows.

"The strongest, most violent wolves in our pack. They chased us. They caught us. Sometimes we survived. Sometimes we didn't."

I point to four parallel claw marks that drag around my forearm, then pull the collar of my sweater aside and show a healed bite mark on my right shoulder. "She personally led a hunt for me four times. I was lucky."

I step back. "I'm sorry I don't have the kind of strength you're looking for."

Parker lets out a low whistle. Leah hustles away.

Parker gestures toward the great hall. "Still in the mood for lunch?"

I hug myself with one arm and roll the beads of my moonstone necklace between the fingers of my other hand. I've been telling myself his pack won't accept me, but having it shoved in my face leaves me feeling unpleasant and unsettled.

"I think I'll eat upstairs today."

# Twelve

## KILLIAN

"I'm telling you, she's a spy!"

I pinch the bridge of my nose and toy idly with the top letter on a mountain of correspondence. There's always so much to do, I can never catch up. "There's no evidence of that, Deacon."

"She's a Beaumont," my Beta insists. He sits in the chair across my desk, and we've been going back and forth for twenty minutes. Twenty minutes I don't have because it's winter and my day spans only the short hours from sunrise to sunset.

I both crave and dread those long, dark hours alone with Selene.

"They sent her to die. You don't send in a spy if you think they're going to be killed before they can do any spying." I hold up a hand, preempting his next words. "I'm not going around with you about this again."

"Redcedar Hollow has increased their patrols along our border."

"Probably because they expect retaliation for deceiving me." They deserve it, but I'm sick of bloodshed.

"Frank Beaumont sent a demand for the boy."

My blood chills. I stand. "For Finn?"

Deacon nods.

"Shit." I sit down again. "Tell me what he said."

95

The Beta sighs and shakes his head. "I suppose 'demand' is too strong a word. He sent a message as a father asking for his son, not an Alpha commanding the return of his heir."

I exhale, but I'm not relieved. "How does he even know Finn is here?"

"Like I was saying, we must have a spy."

"Or he's guessing," I retort. "Because Selene would never betray her brother."

There's a knock on the door. "Enter."

Zev comes in and sees Deacon, then I feel the pressure against my mind that means he wants to speak to me through the pack tie. I allow it. I'm in the habit of keeping my mind to myself when I'm working.

*"Alpha, there's been an incident with Selene and a few younger wolves. Apparently, it happened yesterday. I just found out."*

"Beta Jones," I say, "you're dismissed. Zev, tell me everything."

I MEET SELENE AT SUNSET, but for the first time, we're staying in the castle. After a week without any effect from the curse, I'm ready to sleep inside, in a real bed.

Selene is quiet tonight. She was quiet last night too, and now I know why.

I get to the apartment a little before sunset, leaving myself free to eat dinner with Selene and get ready for bed. I wonder whether she'll bring up the incident with Leah and Hudson, but she doesn't.

When she comes into the living room, my mouth goes dry.

Usually, Selene sleeps in sweats so big that she's drowning in them, but it's much warmer in here than it is outside.

Tonight, most of her short, pale hair is pulled up into a tiny bun at the top of her head, leaving the rest to brush the base of her neck. She wears a silky, lacy tank top with thick straps that clings to her and bares a strip of skin above a pair of drawstring flannel pants. The pajamas are a pale rose color that suits her and brings out the pink in her cheeks. She's been here only days, but rest and full meals have softened the harshest of her edges. The skin beneath her eyes no longer looks bruised. If I met her in the woods now, I wouldn't wonder whether she were a wandering ghost.

There's a starburst of pain in the back of my head, and my stomach lurches. Selene, apparently recognizing whatever she sees on my face, holds out her hand. I take it. The pain and nausea ebb.

After a week of full sleep, I'm not ready to fall into bed as soon as the sun sets, and it doesn't look like she is either.

"So ... if we don't just go to sleep, what is there to do?" she asks.

There are so many things I can think of. All of them involve taking off the rest of our clothes, especially now that we can do those things in my bed.

"Killian?"

"Uh ..." I haven't had enough spare time to worry about filling it in years. "There are movies? Or books?"

"Do you have any games? Cards, maybe? Or even just some paper and a pen."

"What can we do with paper and a pen?"

She grins. "Oh, Alpha. I don't think you've ever had to be resourceful to entertain yourself, and it shows."

Five minutes later, we're seated at the dining room table with a pad of paper between us. We've also gathered a worn box of playing cards, a stack of books, and a box of snacks from the kitchen downstairs that Eva made Maddox deliver. I think about offering Selene something to drink, but I don't mix alcohol with the curse.

Selene chews thoughtfully on a slice of cheese and makes a grid of small dots. She draws a line between two of them, then hands the pen to me. "Connect two dots. The line has to be vertical or horizontal. When you complete a box, you put your initials in it. The person with the most boxes at the end wins."

I frown and pick up a handful of dried apple slices. For the sake of this, we've left our hands unbound. Instead, we've each rolled up one leg of our pants and extended our legs beneath the table, then wrapped them together with bandages a few inches above the ankle where they cross. "It's a strategy game."

"It is. Make your move, Alpha."

I do. Then she takes her turn. Before I realize it, an hour has passed and full dark has fallen outside the wall of windows. Selene draws a line that closes two boxes at once and puts her initial in both with a wolfish grin. "And with that, I believe I win."

I frown at the paper. "We should count again."

"We've counted twice. I beat you."

"By one!"

She laughs, and I'm struck by the beauty that humor brings to her face.

"We can play again," she says.

I want to. I loved watching her, her free leg pulled up to her chest, her arm around her knee as she glowered at the paper, deep in thought, then grinned wickedly before she made each mark. But I've put off this conversation long enough.

"There are some things we need to discuss. Nothing bad, and nothing has changed about our arrangement, but I wanted to let you know that your father sent a message asking for Finn."

All the joy falls from her face. "When?"

"Today."

"You waited this long to tell me?!"

"Only because nothing changed. I said no. I made you a promise, and I'm keeping it."

Selene sits back in her chair and rubs her face. "What if he pushes you?"

"I'll push back."

She presses her lips into a thin line and looks to one side. She doesn't believe me, but there's nothing I can do to change that. Only time can.

I fold my arms and lean back as well. "You didn't tell me about what happened with Hudson and Leah."

That gets her attention. "Who told you?"

"Maddox told Eva. Eva told Zev. Zev told me."

She frowns. "Eva told Zev?"

I know what she's asking, but that is nobody's business but theirs. Zev has been pining for years, and I'm fairly certain Eva wants him too. She claims she's too busy, but the truth is she thinks she's too old for Zev, who is ten years her junior. "I send him with her when she wants to go foraging in the woods. They talk."

Selene raises a brow but lets it drop. "Parker handled it. And Maddox. He's ..."

I hear her unspoken words and scowl. "Yeah. I know."

"He's the one you're making your heir?"

"I've known him since he was a kid. He has it in him."

"He's strong," Selene says. "I felt his power. I didn't know the children of wolfless could be that strong."

"They can. Eva isn't his biological mother, but Asher and Grace were powerful too."

"She's not Maddox's biological mother?"

I sigh and lean back, considering how much of Maddox and Eva's story to tell. None of it is a secret, really. "Her mate was named Gideon. His best friend was a witch—I don't know what his name was, but Maddox was that man's son by a werewolf woman from an old family. She was in some kind of danger. The witch handed Maddox over to Eva and Gideon when he was about a year old and said he'd come back. He never did."

A sad look crosses Selene's face. "Poor kid."

"Yeah. Though he doesn't remember them. Eva and Gideon are the only parents he's ever known."

"Did he have biological siblings?"

"No idea." I shrug. "None that Eva ever told me about. Or him."

I yawn and press the back of my hand to my mouth to cover it. When I open my eyes, Selene seems to be intently studying my hand. When I let it fall, she blushes. "I think I'm finally tired. We should sleep."

We change the binding so our hands are clasped together, climb the stairs, and get into my bed. It's twice the size of the mattress on the rock platform inside the cave and far more comfortable.

We settle in. We're quiet, but neither of us is sleeping.

It's different, being inside. It feels less like I need to be aware of every sound, every scent. But that just means all that awareness shifts to her. In this soft bed, it's so easy to imagine pulling her under me, exploring every inch of her, discovering what it takes to make her whimper my name.

But it's also easy to imagine falling asleep with her curled against my side, her head on my chest. Sex would be one thing, but even after just a week I crave more, and that's dangerous.

"What did you do to those two wolves?" she asks suddenly, startling me from the fantasies that have my body going hard. "Leah and Hudson?"

"Extra cleaning shifts. Extra time on the training field."

I might have also scared the shit out of them and threatened to exile them, but I don't tell her that.

Selene's thumb moves over mine, absently stroking, and I go still. Abruptly, the movement stops.

"Um. Sorry. Goodnight, Killian."

I close my eyes and try to get my body to calm down. "Goodnight, Selene."

~

# SELENE

A few nights after we start sleeping in the pack house, my dreams finally take shape. I'm running through the forest. Everything is huge, or else I'm small. I'm looking for someone who abandoned me.

"Mama!"

Suddenly, there's a hooded figure in front of me. Relief swells as I reach for them.

Relief turns to terror as the figure whirls and drives a dagger into my left shoulder. Pain burns through me, fire in my veins flaring out to consume the rest of my body. I scream and try to pull away, but I can't move.

"Selene!" A male voice. It means safety, but I can't get to it. The fear is too strong. My heart is going to beat right out of my body.

Then a strong arm is around me, pulling me against a hard chest. A hand strokes over my back, cradles my head. "Wake up. It's a dream."

Just as the terrible vision fades, I swear I hear a voice. The same one from that moment with Killian and the statue of the Fate of the Moon.

*"There are things you must see ... "*

Then I'm awake, held close. Safe. My heart is racing, but Killian's is steady beneath my ear. I curl against him and, for a long moment, just breathe while he strokes his big hand soothingly over my back.

"You okay?" he murmurs.

"Yeah. Just a nightmare."

"You want to talk about it?"

I flex my fingers against his chest. "No."

We stay like that for too long. The way he's holding me, I could tilt my chin up just an inch or two. That's all it would take for our lips to meet. To let his heat and hunger drive out the last of the fear.

Killian is still, his breathing so tightly controlled, and I know he's fighting the same urge.

I've spent ten or more nights by his side now, and this isn't getting better. I'm so tired of resisting this need. I can't spend every night of the rest of my life like this, especially when I know he feels it too.

As I finally fall back to sleep, I think maybe I should stop trying so hard.

Maybe we should just let go.

## KILLIAN

I want to know her better. The thought plagues me all day, making it hard to focus on work.

Even if our marriage is one of political convenience, even if I'm still not sure I can trust someone from Redcedar Hollow, I want to know her.

I can't escape how much I like Selene Beaumont.

No one has ever captured my attention this way. Not even Grace.

I touch my pocket, as if the gift I had the pack smith make for her might've climbed out and run off. It hasn't.

"She's going to like it," Zev says as we climb the stairs.

"Maybe. I don't know about the design."

Zev chuckles. "She will."

We reach my apartment, and I head inside. Zev, as always, stays behind at the door.

When I walk in, I hear music. It's hesitant, and there are a few missed notes, but there's a natural musicality to the sound that has potential.

Sometimes Sofia comes to the music room and plays, but it doesn't sound like her. Frowning, I head upstairs and stand in the open doorway of the small music room.

Selene is sitting on the piano bench, leaning forward, pressing one elegant finger to a page of sheet music as she reads notes out loud to herself before she fits her fingers on the keys and starts to play the old folk song again.

The sound hits my soul. Music is another thing I haven't had time for in five years, and I admit—I've avoided this room in particular.

I must make a sound because Selene hits a dissonant chord, then turns to look at me with those frost eyes so wide that I can see the smoky ring all the way around her irises. She looks nervous, like I'm about to shout at her.

The opposite. When I speak, my voice is low and rough. "Don't stop on my account."

Color floods her pale cheeks. "I'm sorry. I don't mean to be noisy."

I cross to her and see she has her fingers arranged just slightly wrong on the keys. "You aren't noisy. You're practicing. Try it like this."

I lean down and slide my hands over hers, adjusting, then pressing down. Music drifts around us as I move her fingers to the next chord and press down again. Her body is warm in my arms, her face so close. This is torture. I've behaved myself, but being around her isn't making the desire go away. It just keeps getting worse.

I have to remember who I am and what I've done to her.

I pull back.

"Wait." Selene grabs my wrist. Her irises have all but disappeared behind wide pupils. "I—Can you show me again?"

The air between us is electric. Hesitantly, I lean down and open my hands over hers again. I play slowly, reposition, and play another chord.

Then Selene turns her face into me and nuzzles my neck. Awareness jolts through every nerve in my body. I close my eyes as she slides her hands from beneath mine, and I continue to play the song from memory.

My mind may have forgotten the music, but my hands haven't. I'm only half-aware of the way it's flowing from my fingertips when Selene shifts and presses her lips against my neck.

"Selene ..." There are reasons we haven't done this since the first day. Good reasons. But when her teeth scrape my skin, they fly from my mind.

I turn to her, the last notes of the song fading as I claim her mouth.

It's been more than a week, and I am starving. Dying. I straddle the piano bench and pull her against me. Her hands go into my hair, tangling and tugging my face down. Her lips part, and I take what she's offering me. I lift her, drag her onto my lap so her legs are around my waist. I'm already hard, my erection straining against my zipper. She rocks against me, and I swear I see fucking stars.

I turn, pressing her against the piano and moving to kiss down her neck. I palm one small breast through her sweater and groan when she gasps and arches against me. Her hands slam down on the keys, sending up a discordant burst of sound.

She tugs my hair and pulls my head back, bringing her lips back to mine with a growl of satisfaction deep in her throat that just about breaks any control I have left. I press her against the piano, and we hit several more harsh notes before she pulls back, breath ragged.

I stop when she does, my eyes drawn to her neck as her throat bobs. She shifts her weight, and the movement grinds her against me. I suck in a breath through my teeth, and she moans, but more in resignation than in pleasure.

"I should ask you to put me down."

"You probably should." But she hasn't, so I hold on to her. I have felt off all week. Empty. This finally feels right, even though I know it's very wrong.

She swallows again. "It's early. Did you come looking for me because you need to talk to me?"

I stroke my thumbs over her waist, stupidly nervous. "I wanted to ask you something."

"What is it?"

"I ... want you to have dinner with me. Down by the spring. Tomorrow is the last day before the engagement dinner. It's supposed to be warm for this time of year, and clear. I used to like to look at the stars ..."

I'm an idiot. This is a stupid, cheesy idea. She'll hate it.

"I would love that." She smiles, and the genuine happiness in it makes my heart pound.

"You would?"

She grins wider. "Yes, Killian. I would."

If I don't let her go, I'm going to start kissing her again. I stand and let her slide to her feet, then pull her gift from my pocket and place it in her hand.

It's a pocketknife. The hilt is carved bone with the phases of the moon on it. When she opens it, the steel edge gleams with a layer of silver.

"What's this for?" she asks, some of the humor fleeing.

"In case you ever need it. Don't hesitate."

She turns it over in her hand, slips it into her pocket, then gently kisses my cheek. "Thank you."

## SELENE

Killian leaves the room that morning before I wake up. I pull on what's becoming my usual outfit here—a soft, oversized sweater, jeans, and boots I can tromp around in the forest in if I want to. I slip the knife he gave me into my pocket, reassured by its small weight.

When Parker doesn't show up, I poke my head out of the apartment door. "Where's Lieutenant Costa?" I ask Wes Bennett, the guard on duty. Killian's personal guards are different from the mass of pack soldiers that train out in the yard with Beta Jones every day, and I've mostly learned their names. "I was hoping to go on a walk."

"Getting security locked down for your dinner that's coming up." Wes looks like he's Maddox's age. I'm pretty sure he's the son of the pack healer, Josiah Bennett. He's got the same calm demeanor and the same shape to his dark brown eyes. "She said you should be okay on your own. Just don't leave the area right around the castle grounds."

"Thanks." Relieved, I grab my coat and head outside. It's been a long time since I walked alone in the woods, and with the dinner coming up, I want to think. Doing a lap around the pack house just outside the walls and then standing on the cliff and staring mindlessly at the lake for a while will be perfect.

It's strange, walking around without Parker, but I also feel less visible, especially with a knit cap tugged low over my pale hair.

There's something so freeing about being in the forest alone. I breathe in the scent of dry leaves and sleeping earth and grin as I make my way through the trees, well within sight of the wall that surrounds the castle. The forest here is healthy and old, so there isn't much undergrowth beneath the spreading branches of ancient white oaks and short-leaf pine. I keep an eye out for anything I might be able to forage. There's always something, even in the dead middle of January.

I'm about halfway through my walk when the wind shifts, and my body freezes before my brain catches up.

A wolf's scent is on the wind. It's not one I know, and it's very, very close.

When I look into the trees, a pair of eyes looks back at me. They're the same bright blue as the cold spring that emerges from the base of the cliff below the pack house.

I take in the rest of the wolf, who is huge and chocolate brown. Iron bands close around my chest. I don't recognize him from Shattered Moon, but I don't know every wolf here.

Instinct shouts to back away, but I hold off. The wolf doesn't attack. Instead, he unfurls slowly from his crouched hunting stance. He stretches and yawns, showing me his teeth, his claws digging into the dark earth.

They're ... metal? Silver?

Then the wolf turns and trots away.

My heart races. When I'm sure he's gone, I sprint for the castle.

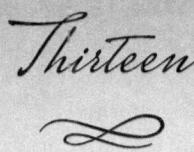

# Thirteen

## SELENE

I don't tell anyone about the strange wolf. For him to have come that close to the pack house, he has to be part of Shattered Moon—just some guard or something. I had to be mistaken about his claws.

Killian and I wait until it's fully dark to head out. He has a basket and an armful of blankets. I have a lantern. We leave the pack house and walk through the woods, eventually coming to an old wooden staircase that winds down the side of the cliff to the shore of the spring. The lake isn't far, glimmering softly. The night is peaceful and lovely, with only the quiet sounds of small forest creatures skittering in the leaves or the occasional call of a barred owl to break the silence.

I, however, am feeling anything but peaceful. Ever since our kiss on the piano bench, there's been a feeling of inevitability about whatever is between Killian and me.

The last two weeks have been a dream. One that's slowly eased me into the idea that I could have some semblance of a future here. With him. It's absurd because two weeks is only two weeks, but in that period, thanks to the long winter nights, we've spent more time together than most people do over the course of a few months.

It takes both of us to lay out the blankets and get everything set up. We eat the dinner the kitchen packed, which is just leftover roasted chicken on thick slices of bread, and then lie back to look at the stars through the dark, lacy frame of the leafless branches.

There are two thick blankets beneath us and two on top, but that doesn't stop me from shivering. When he notices, Killian tugs me close. I slide over until I'm pressed against his side and lay my head in the crook of his shoulder, and he laces his fingers through mine.

"You used to do this?" I ask, breaking the unbearable silence.

"Yeah. My whole life. I spent a lot of time outside as a kid. Claudia ... she wasn't the most nurturing mother. I didn't like to go home. When I was twelve, I met Asher, and after that, it wasn't so bad. I spent a lot of time at the Quinns'."

"Oh." It's fascinating, the way our lives have run almost opposite to each other. As a young child, I was treated mostly fine, but my life became hell at thirteen. Killian's started hellish and got better around that time. Until the curse, I suppose.

Gently, he rubs his thumb across my knuckles. We've been so careful not to do this kind of thing that the light scrape of his skin draws my entire focus. Back and forth in a way that would be soothing if I didn't already feel like being near him, surrounded by him, was about to make me spontaneously combust.

He turns my hand over, eases my palm open, and traces the lines with a finger, circling around, moving across the center, then brushing the sensitive skin on the inside of my wrist. Even just this simple touch has heat pooling, my body aching. All I can do is hold my breath while he takes his time stroking my hand, my wrist, and finally, the inside of my elbow, back and forth, up and down.

My whole world narrows to his fingers, to where he'll touch next. Then I discover that my own fingers are right where his shirt ends. Because we're lying down, it's pulled up a little, exposing a finger's width of smooth skin.

I start my own back and forth across his abdomen, and Killian's breath catches. He continues up my arm to my shoulder, and I gently tug up his shirt so I can explore the ridges and planes of his lean stomach, then down to his waistband.

My chin tilts up, his down. I close my eyes. Our lips are so close. Neither of us speaks. I've gotten used to wanting him, but this—acting on it—feels forbidden. It's like as long as neither of us breaks the silence, we don't have to face the reality of who we are and what we're doing.

Then, apparently, Killian is done resisting. He bumps his nose into mine, then moves in and kisses me. The stroking along my arm stops as he wraps his hand around my bicep instead and pulls me on top of him, arranging me so that I straddle him, my aching center pressed against where he's already impressively hard.

I moan, flexing my hips against him by instinct. He deepens the kiss and slides his hands down to grab my ass, pulling me tight to him as he moves against me. A needy, delicious pleasure builds between my legs. I lift myself enough to pull Killian's shirt up so I can run greedy hands over his abs, the strong muscles of his chest. He kisses along my jaw to my ear, and goosebumps shoot across my skin as his teeth close on the outer shell.

He finds the hem of my sweater and slips his hands underneath, exploring my waist, my ribs, and then beneath my bra, cupping my breasts. I cry out as his thumbs brush across my nipples. We grind our hips together faster, harder. There's nothing in the world but this moment and Killian, his mouth and his hands and his hard, beautiful body.

I make a noise of protest as he flips us onto our sides, but it dies on my lips when he flicks open the button on my jeans and undoes the zipper. His fingers dip below the waistband to palm my ass.

"Take them off," I whimper, wiggling my hips. "I want you to touch me."

Killian swears again, then helps me out of my jeans and panties. He arranges me so my head is pillowed on his arm, then slips his hand down my stomach, then lower, until he cups my sex. I gasp and have the strongest urge to bite down on something. Being touched by him like this is beyond anything I've ever dreamed of experiencing.

I lift one knee, opening for him. He takes the invitation and curls a finger, teasing my entrance, circling it, stretching it. Then he drags his finger up, slicking the wetness up to my clit. I'm so desperate, so ready, that just a touch makes me cry out. He captures my mouth, quieting my sounds as he gently circles and strokes.

"Fuck, Selene. You feel so good."

The desire in his voice undoes me. I open wider for him, jerking my hips against his hand, searching for release. He strokes back to my entrance and slips one finger, then another, deep inside me. He pulls them partway out, then pushes them back in, rhythmically, deeply finger fucking me.

I can no longer control the sounds spilling out of me. I love this. I love the feeling of him inside me. I want more, to be claimed by him. To have him buried so deep inside me, I can't tell where I end and he begins. His fingers, his cock, his teeth in my skin. I want to be possessed by him in a way that has nothing to do with ownership and everything to do with mindless, glorious sex with someone so good, so meant for me, there will never be anyone else.

"Killian!" I'm so close I want to scream.

"Open your eyes, Selene. Look at me."

I obey. Immediately, I'm captured in luminescent topaz.

"Look at me when you come," he commands. "I want to see you go over the edge and know it's because of me."

He thrusts his fingers deep and grinds the heel of his palm against my aching clit, and I break. I shatter into a thousand shining pieces. I scream into the diamond sky, pinned and captured by his eyes. Just when I think it's over, he curls his fingers and rolls his palm against my clit, and I break again. He keeps me going until I'm a boneless, whimpering mess. And still, when he withdraws his fingers from me, bringing them to his lips to taste me while still looking into my eyes, I feel the loss so keenly and deeply that I would absolutely tear off his pants and climb on top of him if I could move.

But I can't. It's all I can do to lie there and breathe while I recover from the most mind-melting moment of my life. He hooks a leg over me and pulls me close, his erection pressing against my stomach.

Curiously sated and yet not sated at all, I stroke my hand over his side and down to palm him over his pants. He hisses in a breath.

"I want to touch you," I whisper.

The muscles in Killian's jaw flex, and his wolf flashes topaz in his eyes. "That's not a good idea."

So far, I've seen no signs of the pale yellow in his eyes that signifies the curse taking him over. "I think we can at least test it and see," I tease.

Killian groans, and his head falls back as I rub up and down his length.

Suddenly, he freezes and grabs my wrist. His head snaps to the side. Then I'm on my back and he's over me, his chest rumbling with a growl. Not in a sexy way. In a predatory, protective "back off" way.

I hear it then. A big body moving between the trees. I scramble to pull up my pants, and Killian moves so he's crouched between me and the sound. I kneel, pressed against his back. There's nothing to see but the dark.

Then a pair of eyes as bright blue as the spring at the base of the cliff luminesces among the trees, and the shadow of a huge wolf in hybrid form moves toward us.

"Breaking your promise," the stranger growls. "Right out in the middle of the woods. Unprotected. Alone. I told you I'd come back. You should've believed me."

My heart pounds, adrenaline and fear chill my blood. "Who is that?" I whisper.

Killian doesn't respond. At least not to me. "She's not my mate."

A scoff. "Fuck off, Killian. She screamed your name so loud they heard it forty miles away at the other end of the lake."

Heat floods my cheeks.

"I promised you I wouldn't take a mate, not that I'd be eternally celibate," Killian snarls.

"I know what tomorrow is, you bastard," the stranger retorts. "I know what you're announcing."

"Then you know why too, don't you?" Killian says.

"Do you think I give a fuck that Redcedar Hollow backed you into a corner?"

"You should care. Eva and Maddox are still part of this pack, and Fia and Zev and everyone you used to care about."

A beat of silence answers. The blue eyes draw nearer.

The tide of Killian's Alpha aura rises. "That's close enough."

The spring-blue eyes dart down to meet mine, and I know where I've seen them.

This is the brown wolf with metal claws from earlier today.

"Do you know why your brother is dead?" he asks.

My whole body turns to ice. "What do you know about my brother?"

"Asher." There's a warning in Killian's voice I don't like.

"Do you know why?" the stranger—Asher—asks again.

Asher. Maddox's brother. Eva's son.

Grace's brother.

"I know Killian did it," I say, trying to keep my cool.

A growled chuckle rumbles from the dark. "Oh, yeah? What did he tell you, that it was negotiations gone wrong?"

That was what my parents said, that the attack on Jackson was unprovoked, a result of talks going against Shattered Moon. But I know

now Grace and Jackson died because of the curse. Killian wasn't in control.

Before I can respond, Asher continues. "Or did he tell you the truth? That he thought my sister was having an affair with Jackson—something she would *never* fucking do—and that, in true Bane fashion, he murdered them in a jealous rage?"

Killian freezes.

My heart plummets.

"That's not why," I say. I rise. So does Killian, keeping between me and the other wolf.

"It's not?" Asher laughs, and the sound is cruel. "That's strange, because I'm the one who found him standing over their bodies. My sister's heart was ripped from her chest. And your brother?" Asher's voice turns glacial. "He was partially eaten. Did Killian tell you that?"

Nausea turns my stomach. "What?"

"Leave, Asher," Killian's voice is low and as rough as the busted gravel road we walked to get here. "Get out of my territory."

Asher snaps his teeth. "You can't exile me, *Alpha*; I already went rogue."

Even if Killian did exile Asher, it wouldn't stop him from coming into Shattered Moon territory. There's no magic that keeps exiled wolves away, only fear of being killed if they return. A fear Asher clearly lacks.

"Killian, it's ... It's fine. It's not true." I say it like I can force him to repeat the words by the power of my will alone. Why won't he say it wasn't jealousy? Why won't he say he didn't eat Jackson's body? God, I feel sick.

There's only a sliver of moon in the sky, but it's enough to flash white on Asher's toothy, wicked, wolfish smile. "Whoops. Looks like she won't be screaming your name again any time soon. At least not because she let you touch her."

Then there's a ripple of power and a hint of smoke as Asher drops to all fours, shifts into his full wolf form, and trots away.

Killian stands there. I lean against his back. His heart thuds against my ear too fast. After a long minute, when I assume his wolf senses have told him Asher is truly gone, he turns back toward me, but it's like he doesn't see me.

"We need to get back to the pack house."

"Killian."

He bends and tosses things into the basket one-handed, closes it, then starts kicking the blankets into a pile.

"Killian!" I jerk on his hand. He finally looks at me.

There's so much guilt in those honey-colored eyes. That's when I know.

"He's right, isn't he? You killed Jackson and Grace because she was cheating on you with him. And you ... you ate ..." I taste bile. "I thought it was because of the curse."

"It was."

"So she wasn't cheating on you? You did kill her by accident." I hear the desperation in my own voice.

He doesn't answer.

I let this monster touch me. I let him put his fingers inside me. I assumed he was a victim, but this ... now it feels like murder.

Even so, I take a breath. I reach for calm. "Please, explain it to me. I want to understand."

He ate Jackson. I've kissed him on that mouth. I've had his tongue down my throat. I press a hand over my lips to stifle a gag.

A growl rumbles through him. "There's nothing to explain."

"Killian—

"Leave it, Selene!" he roars.

I jerk back in fear.

Yellow flashes in his eyes. His clothes rip, popping at the seams as his body blurs and shifts and grows. The cold scent of eldritch magic sours the air.

"No!" He lurches forward. His hands have already become claws. They gouge into my arm as he grabs me.

I cry out at the slicing pain, but I've endured worse from people I trusted more. I hold still and wait until the change reverses. Until he's standing there in ripped clothes, his chest heaving, just a man again.

My jaw is tight. It's hard to get out the words, but I do. "You're right, Alpha. It's not my business. We should get back to the pack house."

"Your arm. I can—"

"Leave it."

Killian starts to speak but stops. He gathers the blankets, and we return to the castle in silence.

Of all the nights since I came to Shattered Moon, this one is the longest.

# Fourteen

*New Moon*

## SELENE

When I wake up on the morning we're to be officially engaged, Killian is nowhere to be seen.

I toy with the moonstone necklace he gave me. Then I take it off. I curl up in the bed.

Sometime later today, Sofia is going to show up with a team from the pack who've volunteered to help me get ready.

I suppose I'll just lie here until then.

But with nothing to occupy my mind, dark thoughts devour it.

I let Killian touch me, and he is a murderer. A liar. He tore Grace's heart out, and he consumed my brother's flesh.

Downstairs in the apartment, there's the faint sound of the door opening and closing. The low sound of Parker speaking to someone. Is it Killian? My stomach knots with a terrible mixture of disgust and dread.

There's a light tap on the door. When it opens, it's not Killian. It's Eva.

"Hello, sweetheart." She sits in the chair by the bed. "Parker says you had a rough night."

106

"Rough? Yeah." I bark a humorless laugh. I want to shout at her that Killian is a murderer, but Eva must know. Or … doesn't she?

Does she have any idea that the Alpha she loves like a son murdered her daughter in a jealous rage and not because of the curse?

I open my mouth to tell her, then pause.

What if Eva doesn't know about the infidelity?

I will never know Grace, but I won't betray her or hurt Eva by telling on the dead. I may just now hate Killian the way I should have before, but Eva doesn't deserve that grief.

If she would even believe me. And without Killian confirming or denying anything, I don't even know for sure whether Grace cheated or whether he only thought she did.

Eva takes my hand. "Today is supposed to be a fun day. Don't stay in here. Come with me to class. Finn would love to see you."

Finn. What if Killian gets so angry at me, he takes it out on the only brother I have left? If he got angry enough at Grace to tear out her heart, it's more than possible. Should I send him away? If I did, I'm not sure I'd ever see him again. Where would he go?

I have no answers, only worry. Lately, I've been spending so much time with Killian, I've hardly seen Finn. I have a sudden need to be around my brother's sweet innocence. Besides, if I'm at the school, I won't be here if Killian comes back.

I force a smile. "I'd love to sit in on class again."

I get up, get dressed, and trail after Eva to the classroom. She's right —Finn is happy to see me, and I'm rewarded with his giant grin. I help with a paper and scissors craft, slowly unwinding as Eva, the other care-takers, and I laugh at the antics of the pack children.

Finally, craft time is over. The kids have a snack. When Eva declares it's time for a lesson, I tuck myself into the back corner of the room, perching on a stool next to a low set of bookshelves.

A few more classes file in, and Eva stands in front of a combined group of kids aged about six to twelve. They sit in a semicircle on a worn, brightly colored rug, completely enchanted as Eva spins history into a drama that has them hanging on every word.

"Once upon a time, there was no magic. No one knows why. Some people say the Earth passed through a wibbly spot in space or through the shadow of a star. For hundreds of years, humans thought the world without magic was normal, but they were wrong. Now we know it for what it was: the Quiet. A time when magic slept and most, but not all, of humanity forgot how things were supposed to be.

"Then one day, magic came back. We call that day the Waking because humanity woke up and remembered what we are. The supernatural aspects reappeared. Werewolves, witches, sirens, elemental mages, nature-touched—all kinds of humans heard the song of magic in their blood.

"But the Waking caused trouble. Humans, who were already divided, used these new differences as another reason to hate each other. The Wars of Power began. They didn't end for fifty years, and when they were over, the world wasn't the same.

"All over the planet, things changed as magic settled. Mountains shifted. Fissures opened. Forests came alive. The eldritch walked the land again. In truth, no one really knows if the return of magic woke up the eldritch or if magic returned because they were the ones who stopped dreaming."

Eva goes on, talking about how different the world is as the children listen with rapt attention. For their sake, she skips over how bloody the Wars of Power were, the fact that millions died, countries fell, and cities burned. For the most part, the Wars were fought between mundane humans and the aspected. To this day, I'm not sure whether anyone can say for certain who won.

Now most mundane humans cluster in protectorates like Fall Line or large cities that survived, like Chicago, New York, and St. Louis, though some have carved out their own pieces of the world. Many indigenous tribes returned to their ancestral lands. River pirates, crime families, and religious cults have also laid claim to certain areas.

As for the aspected, we live in environments as varied as we are. Some—certain kinds of witches, vampires, seraphs—prefer the cities. Chicago, protected by the Steel Alliance, is home to large populations of every kind of human. Others of us—those whose aspects are more primal—took to the wilderness or newly empty rural places after the Wars. Shifters. Sirens. Nature-touched like dryads, naiads, and sylphs.

When the fae emerged from newly opened portals to the Realms in the middle of the Wars, it took only a few interactions for humans of all kinds to decide to leave the Rocky Mountains to them. They're ancient, and their magic makes ours look like a match against a bonfire. They would probably rule us all, but if they stay in our world too long, pure fae wither and die.

I'm so lost in my own thoughts that I almost miss it when Eva says a name that's been in the back of my thoughts for weeks now: Alaric Bane.

I straighten. Her voice has turned serious, and now she's holding a book open in front of her. "Alaric Bane, the man who called himself the Alpha King, was born during the Wars of Power and rose to prominence in a world torn apart. Some people who knew him say he conquered like he did because he wanted to put things back together, unite wolves, and keep them safe.

"Other people don't think so. There are more werewolves than there are any other kind of aspected except witches, and we're very strong. We make good soldiers. Those people say Alaric Bane wanted to make a werewolf army big enough to take over everything.

"We all agree on one thing, though: in his time, he was the most powerful Alpha the world had seen.

"Bane used his terrible power to subjugate every wolf he came across and built a kingdom centered in a place that was easy to defend and hard to get to. A place where the land is ancient and magic is strong: this very place we're sitting right now."

The children *oooh*.

Eva nods. "He built this very castle and crowned himself king. He called his pack Conqueror's Moon and united tens of thousands of werewolves into an army that no one could defeat. For years, his power grew. More and more packs and other Aspected fell to him."

A little boy with light brown skin and a fiercely focused expression lifts his hand. "Oh! Except for the Great Lakes! The Steel Alliance is there!"

Eva nods. "Correct. They couldn't beat him, but he couldn't take them over, either."

I'm using the bookshelf next to me like an armrest, moving my fingers absently over the glossy wooden top. When I look down at my hand, I notice a copy of the same book Eva is reading from, *The Rise of Conqueror's Moon*.

"Conquest wasn't the only thing Alaric Bane wanted," Eva continues. "He had two other obsessions. The first was legacy—he wanted people to remember him. He wanted to feel like he left his mark on the world. For that reason, Bane had lots and lots of children. Most were full werewolves, but many of them had a mother of a different aspect."

I study the book. The cover is a picture of Alaric Bane when he was young. He stands on an outcropping of stone surrounded by the forest, staring down at the photographer with shadowed eyes.

I've seen pictures of the man before but never studied them. I study him now, looking for Killian in the despot's face. It shouldn't be hard. They're both murderers, after all. Like father, like son.

... I don't find him.

Bane's hair is dark and long, worn in a warrior's topknot at the back of his head. Faded hazel eyes gleam beneath heavy brows. The color is nothing like Killian's, but I already know he has Claudia's topaz eyes. Bane's skin is also porcelain-pale and cool-toned versus Killian's warmer fairness.

Coloring isn't the biggest difference, though. It's the shape of his features that really throws me off. They're so different from Killian's on a basic structural level. Bane's forehead is broader, his brows heavier, his face shorter, his nose narrow and pronounced. There is something about the arrangement of it all that tugs on me like I've seen it before, but definitely not in Killian.

I've stared at his face so much these last few weeks, I see him when I close my eyes. I would know.

The longer I study Bane's features, the more I frown. The Alpha of Shattered Moon gets a healthy amount of his looks from his mother, but he and Bane don't look related at all.

Disconcerted, I scoot the book away with my fingertips and focus on the lesson again.

A fair-skinned little blonde girl with dimples waves her hand in the air, excitedly bouncing even though she's seated. "I know, I know what happens next! He *ate* them all! Except Alpha Darrow! Lady Claudia ran away and hid him, and he's the only one that survived!"

My stomach lurches. I always thought the part of the story about Bane devouring his own children was an exaggeration. But given what I now know about Killian ... maybe it wasn't.

Eva gives the little girl a dry look. "Cecily, did Michael tell you that?"

She bounces again, a wide grin splitting her face. "Yeah!"

Eva scowls at one of the older boys, who shrugs sheepishly. "He did not eat his children. But at some point, living on through them wasn't enough. Bane wanted to be immortal and never die."

The children *oooh* again.

Having recaptured their attention, Eva gestures grandly at a picture hanging from the whiteboard. It's an antlered, shadowy creature that looks as if it's made of earth and smoke, with glowing yellow eyes. Humanoid, but it's impossible to tell whether it's male or female or whether sex is even something that applies to its kind.

"Most believe he went to one of the highest eldritch, Old Scratch, for forbidden magic. Scratch told him that if he wanted to live forever, he had to consume his children's power. Yes, 'consume' means 'eat,' sort of. But their power, Cecily. Not the children."

"But—" the little girl interrupts.

"No," Eva cuts her off.

"Okay," Cecily says, sounding contrite. Then she bounces again. "But it's true our Alpha is the only one of his kids to live, right? He's like a superhero!"

To my surprise, a strange expression crosses Eva's face. She pauses, looks like she's thinking, then says, "He is like a superhero, but I think that's just because he's himself."

The kids don't notice that Eva sidestepped saying directly that Killian is Alaric Bane's son, but I do.

"One by one, his children began to disappear, from the ones in their twenties to the ones still in their mothers' bellies. Then, twenty years ago, when he was at the very height of his power, Alaric Bane died in this very castle. Most people agree that mothers of the children he'd murdered decided they'd had enough. At least half a dozen of them came together to kill him. But because of the powerful magical explosion, no bodies were left. No one knows exactly who they were."

Her retelling sounds accurate to me. I've heard from my father that they found the remains of Alaric Bane and the women who finally took him down splattered in bloody chunks all over the ruins down that tarped-off staircase.

I have to admit, the fallout of Bane's death fascinates me even more than his life because it has impacted me directly. It almost threw this part of the world into a second round of the Wars of Power. Wolves turned on each other. Thousands went rogue or made new packs, like my father and Redcedar Hollow.

There's a knock at the door, and everyone in the room turns to look as the Beta pops his head in. He scans the room, and I'm startled when his eyes land on me. "Ms. Beaumont. I've been looking for you. Can I have a word?"

I nod, wave to Finn, and warily follow Beta Jones out of the classroom. He smiles tightly but doesn't say anything until we're out of the school, walking on the grounds.

"How do you find Shattered Moon, Ms. Beaumont?"

"It's been very different." Hearing "Ms. Beaumont" jars me a little, as everyone else I've interacted with in the last two weeks calls me "Selene" or "Lady Selene."

He raises a brow and folds his hands behind him as we walk along the base of the wall. It's a gray day. The ground is wet, and the sky spits cold, light rain. "A diplomatic answer."

"Two weeks is hardly time to form a real opinion." I smile to soften the words.

"Time enough to form an opinion of the Alpha," he counters.

I force my smile to remain in place. Soft, not strained. What's between Killian and me isn't Deacon Jones's business unless things get so bad it somehow impacts our ability to fulfill the terms of the treaty. I can't speak for the Alpha, but sharing a bed with a monster—while not exactly an experience I've relished—isn't worse than some things I've lived through. At this moment, the treaty is in no danger from me not doing my part. "Not quite, Beta Jones. I learn things about him that shift my perspective every day."

He grunts, apparently amused, but then his mood fades into one that's more serious. "Have you heard from your former Alphas? Been contacted by your old pack at all?"

I let out a startled laugh. "No. My family and I aren't close. Anyone I'd want to speak to is wolfless and not allowed to contact me."

He's watching me like he's waiting for me to slip. To reveal that I'm … what? A spy, maybe? Jones can watch all he likes. I'm no spy.

"Why are we having this conversation right now?" I ask.

"Alpha Darrow told you about your father's request to have the boy sent back?"

I can't hide my reaction to this. My eyes snap to his, and my voice is too sharp. "Yes. Why? Has my father said anything else?"

Jones shrugs and frowns as if in thought. "Not that I know of. I just wasn't sure if you'd heard."

"How very thoughtful of you." We're passing through the pack's orchard, and I watch a blue jay dart from one leafless apple tree to another.

I'm aware the Beta doesn't approve of me, and it doesn't escape my notice that he's ambushing me with information he knows would have upset me had Killian not told me first. Maybe I could believe his concern is genuine if I tried, but I don't.

Everything about this conversation, down to pulling me out of Finn's class instead of scheduling a time to speak to me, is an attempt to throw me off. Deacon Jones knows what he's doing. He didn't expect I would be able to see it.

*Play the game.*

"You're in charge of pack security, aren't you, Beta?" I ask, though I already know.

"Of course."

"Perfect. If Redcedar Hollow contacts me, you're the first person I'll come to ..."

As I say it, my eyes catch on something. A bird in the twisted heights of a shortleaf pine just over the wall. Though there are still working phone lines in some places, pigeons, doves, and crows raised by green witches or sylphs are the most reliable way to send messages.

I swear I just saw a mourning dove with a stripe of Redcedar Hollow green painted across its leg.

I step toward the wall and squint to try to get a better look, but the bird flutters away.

Beta Jones moves to my side and follows my gaze, tilting his head. "Did you see something, Ms. Beaumont?"

"No." I shake my head because I can't have seen a Redcedar Hollow bird here. "No. I just didn't sleep well last night."

The Beta looks at the sky. "Well. It's getting on in the day. I have things to do, and you should go get ready for dinner. It's a big night."

He walks away, and I'm left wondering why those words sounded so ominous.

## Fifteen

### SELENE

The dress is iridescent plum silk that shimmers into black. The cut is deceptively simple—a V in the front that plunges between my breasts, a deeper V in the back. Beneath the bodice that hugs me like a second skin, the fabric pours into an opulent floor-length skirt full enough to nearly hide the thigh-high slit on the right side. Black open-toed ankle boots with peekaboo cutouts and spike heels click on the tiled floor of Killian's huge master bathroom as I step back and study myself in the mirror, checking that the dress hides what I want it to hide.

It does, thank goodness. The puckered pink skin of the never-healing wound on my left shoulder is completely covered.

Once I've reassured myself the old scar won't be seen, I actually look at myself. The deep color of the silk against my ghost-pale skin is startling. Usually, I'm not a fan of wearing something that highlights my colorlessness. But tonight, I feel like a star that floated down from the heavens with a piece of midnight sky as my dress.

I've never worn anything like this. Never had anything as artful as the subtle, smoky lavender makeup on my face, my cheeks and brow bones highlighted in silvery white. I thought any color on my skin would make me look like a clown, but Jessica, the woman Sofia sent to help me get ready, knows exactly what she's doing.

I almost look like I'm ready for this, even though I'm not.

I spent so many nights helping Bianca get ready for events, then attending them as a server. Tonight, the dinner is in my honor. Half of me feels like I'm obligated to find that fact pretentious and ridiculous. After a lifetime as a servant, it's uncomfortable to have something so huge centered on me. I keep having to tell myself it's part of being mate-consort. Part of the Alpha game.

But the other half of me—the half that has always wanted to be able to go to balls in pretty dresses—is excited. This dinner is Killian showing the people in attendance that he accepts his wolfless future mate. He wants this union.

At least, he wants it on the surface.

I thought I did too. Last night changed everything, but in the end, my personal feelings about Killian don't matter. I made a deal for Finn's future and peace between our packs. I will embrace this.

So instead of pushing down the feeling of being thrilled to get made up, wear the expensive dress, and be fussed over, I set it free.

"Thank goodness you've put some meat on your bones in the last couple of weeks," Sofia says as she looks me over.

I blush but turn so I can see my back in the mirror and agree. My face is less sunken, my ribs less prominent. I still have a ways to go, but I look healthier than I did.

I look pretty.

Will Killian think so?

I exile the thought, tossing it into the dark with the memory of his touch, the press of his lips on my heated skin, what it felt like to break apart while he held me.

Killian is a murderer. I have to stop wanting him.

I wish that didn't feel so completely impossible.

## KILLIAN

Selene is getting ready in my apartment, so I get dressed in my office.

I know she doesn't want to see me.

At least tonight is the new moon. When the dinner is over, she'll be free from me for the evening.

A familiar tiredness has settled over me. I didn't really sleep. As soon as the sun came up, I was in the woods, searching for Asher. I caught his scent and followed it long enough to discover he's been here for a couple of days, circling the castle, avoiding patrols. He's clever. I was able to track him because we grew up together and I know his tricks, but there's something different about him now. The path his trail takes, a subtle difference in his scent. It put me on edge.

Where has he been for the last half-decade and what has he been doing?

Eventually, I lost him. I don't know whether he's still here or whether he considers what he did good enough, and now he's gone.

I doubt it. He's still bent on revenge for Grace, and I'm tempted to let him have it. But only if he takes it out on me, not Selene.

And, god, is he in for a surprise if he kills me.

I finish getting ready in the bathroom attached to my office and head downstairs. The banquet is being held in the castle's great hall. Sofia is determined to arrange a dramatic entrance for Selene, which means I need to get there first.

The foyer of Shattered Moon's pack house is two stories high, with a wide crystal chandelier salvaged from the time of Alaric Bane that hangs from the center of the ceiling. On the right, a grand staircase sweeps up to an open area on the second level. Directly in front of me, two sets of heavy wooden double doors are flung open, leading into the great hall.

When I enter, the massive multipurpose room is already crammed full of hundreds of people, all here to see her. Us. Though after last night ...

I just hope she shows up.

The great hall is as tall as the foyer, with windows that face out over the cliff to the green-gold ribbon of the lake and forested hills that roll all the way to the horizon. There are half a dozen smaller chandeliers in this room, spaced equally down its length, each one set between exposed beams that curve up to support the lofty ceiling like arching ribs. The setting sun hits at just the right angle to blaze through the windows and free a thousand rainbows from the chandeliers' teardrop crystals while shrouding the corners of the room in shadow.

Though this castle was built after the Waking, it evokes the feeling of ages. The weight of tradition. That weight thickens the air and is made heavier by the tension hanging over the crowd. Despite the work both Sofia and I have done over the last two weeks to convince the wolves of Shattered Moon, and despite Selene being present among them, many—especially Deacon's soldiers—are still angry about her being wolfless.

Too bad for them.

Aside from my pack, there are a handful of local faction leaders present. Solitary green witches, naiad families who serve the lake and the local rivers, representatives from the nearby sovereign villages of the Osage nation, and the leaders of two rogue factions that hold territory to the south and west of us.

And there, leaning against a wall in the back, surrounded by soldiers in high-collared navy blue coats, are Warlord Marcus Vandran and Warden First Arcanist Eli Whitlock, who rules the Protectorate territory called Rowan Ridge.

Arcanists are not a type of aspected; arcanism is a field of study. A scientific approach to magic. Most arcanists are mundane humans, like Whitlock, though many come from one of the seraph families. Whitlock is one of the few who has taken his study far enough to perform his own magic.

Every Aspected has their own scent, from the smoke of a werewolves to the iron tang of vampires to the ancient, wild fragrance of the fae. Whitlock is human to the bone, but sometimes I catch something around him. The earthy scent of pure magic that's both like and unlike the fae. Likely, it comes from his laboratory. But it lingers on him, even when it seems it shouldn't, dusty and deep.

I frown slightly when I see the two of them. Vandran has an open invitation to Shattered Moon, but I have no idea what he's doing here. He didn't tell me he was coming.

My old mentor catches my eye and grins. He's much the same as when I met him a decade ago, broad and barrel-chested, but now he has silver at his temples and has aged into his roughhewn good looks. He might be all human, but he's bigger than every wolf in the pack except Zev, and it's easy for him and me to make eye contact over a sea of heads.

I'm deeply curious about the samples of Selene's blood that I sent to Fall Line. But if I go over there, Whitlock is going to start going on in that deep, honeyed drawl of his about his latest research, and he won't stop until the night is over.

I glance at the windows and note the position of the sun. Selene will be here soon, and I need to be where Sofia told me to be. Still, I can't risk insulting Vandran. He's the reason I'm an Alpha at all.

I start toward them, but as I do, Vandran jerks his head toward the dais as if to say, *Get on with your business; we'll talk later.*

Thank goodness.

I don't have to push my way through the crowd—I release the mental dam holding my power back by a fraction and let them feel my approach.

They part, and I make my way to the dais where the high table sits, unimpeded and unhurried. As I pass through the crowd, their whispers lap against me in insistent little waves.

"... she's probably some kind of spy ..."

"Did you hear how she handled Leah?"

"... out of his mind? To agree to take an impotent Redcedar Hollow servant-princess ...?"

"... so kind to the children."

"No good will come of it."

"... smart too. She was in the library and recommended me just the book ..."

"...never have an Alpha pair. We'll never be as strong as we could be."

I press my mouth into a thin line and keep walking.

Deacon Jones waits like a gargoyle on the dais stairs. Beyond him, my mother is already at the high table. She shoots daggers at me with her eyeballs, likely because I've neglected to spend time with her lately. Or because I threatened to rip off her hand when she slapped Selene.

The only time I've seen her since, she sniffed and told me I really am my father's son. I swear if she didn't know Grace's secret—and if Eva didn't insist I be kind to her—I would've exiled the harpy years ago.

Sofia is already seated, as are several of the dozen pack council members. My Gamma looks eagerly toward the door, and I know it's because her mate will arrive when Selene does.

I climb the stairs and come level with Deacon, who is standing rigidly with his arms folded across his chest. As always, his high-collared military suit with its blue and crimson detailing is crisp, and as usual, at least lately, disapproval is rolling off him in waves. I feel like a traitor king about to face justice at the hands of his steward.

"There's still time to renounce this match and demand the other sister," Deacon mutters. No preamble, no greeting. That's my Beta.

"Now is not the time."

"They tried to goad you into violence. If not for the effect she has on you—"

"If not for the effect she has on me, their attempt to bring the Conclave down on us would've worked."

Deacon's square jaw moves like he's grinding his teeth. He speaks into my mind. *"This is a mistake, Alpha. I'm telling you, she's a spy, and without a mate bond, you'll have no way of knowing it. At least with the sister, you could mate bond and keep an eye on her that way."*

"Selene isn't a spy," I reply coolly. I've had almost no problems with Deacon for five years. I don't know why the older man has decided to become a nuisance now. *"And bonded wolves sneak around all the time with their mates none the wiser."*

*"I found evidence she's sending information on our pack back to Redcedar Hollow,"* Deacon shoots back.

My adrenaline spikes.

*"That's impossible."* There's no way anyone could've predicted Selene would survive her first night with me, and because of that, I've trusted her. She knows about the curse, about its particulars, when it affects me and when it doesn't. She knows where my cave shelter is, where I rest when I'm most vulnerable. Redcedar Hollow can't learn any of that. If they do, Shattered Moon will become exponentially harder to defend. *"What evidence?"*

He surreptitiously produces something from his pocket. At first, I think it's a curled twig. Then I see it's a bird's foot. Green paint slashes across the knobbled skin of its talons.

A low growl vibrates my chest. I take the claw and turn it over. The scent isn't one of our birds.

Deacon holds out a small scroll of paper and says, *"I found a cache of notes in a hollow tree not far outside the wall. It's correspondence between her and the Redcedar Alphas. Wes Bennett will confirm she's gone out into the woods unsupervised."*

I take the paper and unroll it. It simply reads, *Report received.* A scent lingers on the message, but it's too vague and buried in Deacon's soapy, minty smell for me to confirm or deny whether it's Selene's. I can't get a read on hers even when she's in my arms, shuddering with pleasure and crying my name.

I crumple the note in my fist. *"What do the other messages say?"*

*"Mostly the same, or they're in code. We're working to decipher it."*

*"There's no evidence Selene is the one sending and receiving these."* Though if she isn't, we have a bigger problem because there's a spy in my pack I haven't identified.

*"It's her,"* Deacon insists. *"She'll spring some kind of trap for you*

*sooner or later. Don't let your guard down. If you insist on going through with tonight, watch her every move."*

I hold back the desire to snarl at my Beta in front of the entire pack and say, *"I have no plans to let down my guard. You're dismissed, Beta. Go sit down."*

Deacon inclines his head. *"Of course, Alpha. As you wish."*

I run my thumb over the crumpled paper.

Could the spy be Selene?

No. She'd never tell her parents that Finn is alive.

A sudden hush falls over the hundreds of wolves packed into the great hall, and I look up.

Opposite the dais is a staircase that sweeps down from the gallery above.

Selene is standing at the top of the stairs. Suddenly, my lungs are clamped in a vise. My world narrows only to her.

I have no words. She's ... perfect. Elegant. Beautiful. Ethereal. The Fate of the Moon made flesh.

I had her in my arms last night. I had her writhing against me. Her hands stroking me. I had her panting in my ear. I thought we could make this relationship work, even if I didn't know what making it work would look like.

Asher's little show ended that. Now it's like we're on opposite sides of glass, and I'm afraid she'll never let me touch her again except to keep the beast at bay and politely take her hand on nights like tonight.

I wish I could tell her the truth.

Selene starts down the stairs. Parker and Zev walk a little behind her and to either side, an honor guard.

I step forward to meet her, but Sofia preempts me without even moving from her seat at the long table. *"Don't. They doubt her. If you go to her, it will look like you think she needs your protection to walk among them."*

My eyes find Sofia's. She's been my friend for years. I trust her judgment, but I don't know about this. *"I want to show them I'm with her."*

*"Then show them when she gets to you,"* Sofia responds.

*"What if she's nervous?"*

*"She is nervous,"* says my Gamma, *"But she knows they're watching her. This was her idea. She's a clever woman, Alpha."*

She is clever. But is this a show for the pack, or is it that she can't stand my touch and wants to avoid it for as long as possible?

Selene reaches the floor of the great hall and pauses, looking around. If she's nervous, she shows no sign of it. Her mouth is curved in a small, welcoming smile, and she looks relaxed, serene.

For a moment, I'm afraid they won't part for her the way they did for me. But then they do, drawing back. The movement creates a direct path to the dais.

To me.

Selene walks between them, her pace calm and unhurried. When her eyes find mine, they don't let me go. My heart thuds as she draws closer, and I resist going to her for as long as I can, but by the time she's near the steps, I forget restraint and move to meet her.

I'm afraid she'll pull back, but she lifts one elegant hand, and I take it. With the other, she picks up the skirt of her dress and lifts it just high enough to walk up the steps.

She doesn't pull away from my touch. I wonder whether she was able to put last night aside. I hope so. If she asks me about Grace and Jackson, I can't give her the answers she wants.

We reach the top of the stairs, and I scan the crowd, including the high table. While everyone else is focused on Selene, Deacon is standing with Vandran and Whitlock, whom he's known for years. The three old men whisper to each other, but their eyes go to me when the pack falls silent.

"Wolves of Shattered Moon." I intone in a carrying voice, "I present Lady Selene Beaumont of the Redcedar Hollow Pack, daughter of the Alpha Pair and my intended mate-consort."

I wait for polite applause. Whispers rustle through the crowd, then fade into a deep, awkward silence.

No one claps.

No one looks happy.

## Sixteen

### SELENE

My eyes sweep the crowd. Killian seems startled at their lack of reaction. Of course, he is. No matter how terrible things are for him, he's always been handsome, powerful, an Alpha. But I'm not surprised by their reaction at all.

*Play the game.*

I step forward and duck my head, remembering at the last minute not to go into the deep bow of a pack servant. Then I raise my gaze to them and speak.

"All my life, I was taught Shattered Moon is my enemy. Yet here I stand, having discovered that what I believed isn't the same as what is true.

"I'll be honest with you: I know I'm not what you expected. I can't be the Alpha many of you hoped would strengthen you as warriors. But all the strength I do have, all the wisdom, all the care, all of my time is yours. I will be an asset, even without Alpha magic. I have no pack but Shattered Moon, no people but you. I am honored to be among wolves who put so much faith in their Alpha's choice. I will strive to be worthy of it, and you."

There's silence again. My heart climbs into my throat. It seems to stretch forever.

Then someone in the back starts to clap. From where I stand a little above the crowd, I watch as the rest slowly raise their hands and begin to applaud as well. It's not a roar. It doesn't last forever. Not everyone participates. At the high table alone, Lady Darrow, Beta Jones, and a few pack council members stand stone-faced.

But enough of the pack seem tentatively accepting. Some are curious. A few even smile.

For now, I'll take it. I'm not sure I'll win them with time, but I will do my best to keep the promises I just made.

"Lady Selene," Killian says again, gesturing to me. He dips his hand into a pocket, pulls out a box, and opens it.

There's a ring inside. It's white gold, the swirling metal set with a large oval cut red diamond in the center. Two teardrop-shaped moonstones frame the diamond top and bottom, with two more small round moonstones on each side. Two crescent moons nestle among the stones, facing opposite directions. The moons were cast to look cracked.

Killian captures my hand in his, and electricity floods my body before I can regain control. He gives me a grim smile as he slides the ring onto my outstretched finger. Then he raises my hand to his lips, pressing a gentle kiss along the back of my knuckles.

My lips part. My knees melt.

Even knowing what I know about him, my body remains a traitor. I barely register that people are clapping again as he announces our wedding will take place one month from tonight.

Then he leads me to the long high table, and we sit at the center, with me to his right, as if he is a king and I'm already a queen.

Unfortunately, that means Claudia is seated on my other side. She seems content to speak to everyone but me, which is wonderful as far as I'm concerned. I haven't seen her since that slap, and I would love to continue to pretend she doesn't exist.

Then dinner is served.

The food is good. I know it is—I helped Sofia plan the menu and source all of it. Even so, I hardly taste it. The banquet passes with dizzying quickness. I'm too aware of my seat at this table, the conversation that buzzes around me, the fact that I'm being watched by powerful people who never would have cared about me before.

But mostly, I'm too aware of Killian. The way he looks in that black suit. The heat that I swear I can feel radiating from him even now. The topaz gaze that slides my way beneath thick, dark lashes when he thinks I'm not looking.

I just have to get through the next few hours I'm expected to be at his side. He doesn't need me tonight. When he's gone, the air won't be so charged. I'll be able to breathe. To think.

My gaze falls on two wolves at the high table I don't know. One is a fair-skinned, redheaded man with a large beard, the other a woman with dark brown skin and long micro braids swept into a complex updo.

"Grayson Fischer and Fatima Martinez," Killian says quietly. "Each head two large rogue factions that border our lands."

Reluctantly, I tilt my head toward him so he knows I'm listening.

Killian leans closer, and I shiver as his warm breath brushes the shell of my ear. "Fatima's group is large, neutral. They're good allies and neighbors. Grayson's is small and volatile, constantly on the move."

"They're groups of rogues," I say quietly. "Not packs?"

"No. They don't believe in pack hierarchies."

"Are they not Alphas?"

"Fatima is, and plenty of Alpha blood wolves run with her."

I study the two rogues, my interest piqued. "I'd like to speak with them. If we can get the council to pass a law that frees the wolfless, do you think they might help me find a place for the Redcedar Hollow wolves who want to stay in the area but don't want to live in packs?"

"Mm," Killian hums into my ear, and I shiver again. "I can't speak for them, but they might be amenable."

I turn toward him, which is a mistake. His face is barely an inch from mine. His eyes go dark, and his gaze slides languidly to my lips.

It would be so easy to forget last night, to lean forward and kiss him. I want to kiss him like I want to breathe. "Maybe ... you could arrange something for me. For later."

"Mm." This hum is a low rumble that sends heat everywhere. He's still staring at my lips.

All I have to do is lean forward. All I have to do is forget.

But I can't.

"Oh, dear!"

Something wet splashes across my front. Dark red wine between by breasts and on my lap, discoloring the purple of the dress. The scent of red wine slaps me in the face.

Next to me, Claudia presses a hand to her lips. "Oh, *no*! I'm so clumsy."

"Mother," Killian snaps.

"I'm sure it was an accident," says Beta Jones, who's sitting across from us, a smirk playing around his mouth.

I force a pleasant smile, glad that Sofia and I chose this color. Below the dais, no one seems to have noticed. People are finishing their meals. They're moving tables. A small group of musicians has begun to play softly. Still, Claudia's little stunt has caught some attention. Everyone at the high table is looking at me.

"It's all right," I insist. I rise, clamping down on anger and embarrassment with the brutal efficiency of a lifetime of practice.

Feel nothing. Not yet. Not until I'm away from the weight of all of their eyes. I just have to keep this doll-like smile pasted on my face. "I'll go clean up."

Killian starts to say something, but I don't want to hear it. I can't look at him.

Is it any wonder he turned out to be a killer, with a mother so cruel and a father so terrible?

Tears burn behind my eyes. More people are looking now.

Maybe I'm not ready to play this game, after all.

"It will just take a minute to get cleaned up," I say, unable to keep an edge completely out of my voice. "Please excuse me."

I leave the table, making a beeline for a door that leads into one of the back halls and the bathroom a little ways down. Behind me, I hear Killian lay into his mother. His words are too low to hear, but her shrill response isn't.

"What?" she whines. "Are you going to *tear my hand off*, Killian? I didn't touch her. It was an accident!"

The light in the bathroom is harsh and fluorescent after the chandeliers of the great hall. I blink against it, and the tears still threaten to fall as I pat down the dress with a dry towel, then blot it with a damp cloth, then a dry towel again.

It takes ten minutes or longer, but the fabric is dark, and I've taken care of Bianca's expensive clothes most of my life. Soon enough, there's hardly a noticeable spot at all.

By that time, I've mostly gathered myself. I've even managed not to cry. I look into the mirror and straighten my hair.

I'm a little surprised at the woman who gazes back at me. I don't look like the wounded wolfless my evil future mother-in-law just dumped wine on. I appear calm and confident despite the emotions roiling beneath the surface. Just like an Alpha would.

"Okay," I whisper, lifting my chin and nodding to myself. "Okay. It wasn't that bad, actually. I can do this. I've got this."

Feeling a little better, I step into the darkness of the hallway.

The lights are out. The door to the great hall is closed.

Something is wrong.

A cold scent drifts through the air. Dusty and ancient, like Killian when the curse claims him. Like eldritch magic.

Something behind me lets out a low, animalistic growl.

# KILLIAN

I bare my teeth, lean across Selene's empty chair, and grab my mother by the arm.

*"This is the second time you've crossed Selene,"* I say into her mind. *"Do it again, and I'll exile you."*

Her eyes go wide.

"You wouldn't dare!" she hisses. Then her expression turns sly. "Don't forget what I know, Killian."

Disgust floods me. She knows my secrets. Eva wants me to be kind to her.

Tonight, I'm not in the mood to care. *"Try me, Claudia. Clean up your act, or I'm sending you on a one-way trip back to the Free Cities."*

Not that I can make her stay there. In fact, I'm fairly certain Claudia exiled would be far more of a thorn in my side than Claudia at least partially under my control. But, god, it would be satisfying, throwing her out.

There's a tap on my shoulder. My mother plasters a simpering smile across her face at whoever it is.

Vandran stands beside my chair. I hide a grimace when I see he's not alone—Whitlock is behind him.

The arcanist is one of those rail-thin old men who look like time sucked all the fat from under his skin, though his gray eyes are sharp as ever. His white hair and short beard are impeccably neat, as is his military coat in Rowan Ridge gray accented in Fall Line navy and gold. The coat is cut long, down to his calves, and belts at his narrow waist, robe-like.

Heavy rings glitter on his knobby fingers, each a different metal paired with a different gaudy stone. There's a green star sapphire surrounded by silver scrollwork, a moonstone carved in the shape of a howling wolf, a ludicrous amethyst on a fat gold band, a huge ovular black stone that shines yellow, a pointed ruby that could easily put out someone's eye, an opal cut as round as a pearl on a ridiculously thin band that seems to be made of polished bone, among others.

"Killian. You seem preoccupied." Vandran's smile is easy and crinkles the corners of his dark eyes. "Did I catch you at a bad time? I'd like to talk."

"Of course not. It's an honor to have you here." I rise from my chair and give my mother a flat look. She smiles archly at the warlord. To his credit, he doesn't even look at her.

With a last glance at the door where Selene disappeared, I follow Vandran off to one side. Whitlock slips into my vacated chair and strikes up a conversation with my mother. As we walk away, I hear him begin to wax poetic about some arcane thing or another and her laugh, high and girlish, in response. I cringe.

Vandran and I wind our way through the crowd. The banquet is turning into a party, as planned. It's good for the pack to get together, play music, and dance. We move to the back wall to be out of the way.

"I saw you speaking to Deacon. Everything all right?" I ask.

Vandran chuckles. "We had a bet on whether or not Lysander could pull off an information heist—Deacon knows him from way back. I said the dreamwalker couldn't do it. Deacon had faith. He was right. Never doubt a faeblood. There's a reason they're outlawed by their own people. His abilities are unmatched. I should have known. You've met the man, have you not?"

I have. He's a half-fae bastard of House Oneiros, the fae house of dreams. The man is a dreamwalker who uses his magic to stalk, steal knowledge, and, on occasion, kill remotely. We met a couple of years ago, when I was visiting Dominion Reach, Vandran's stronghold on the Atlantic coast. Lysander was an alcohol-soaked piece of shit with no loyalty back then, and I assume he's the same now.

When I founded Shattered Moon, security was a high priority. I hired an entire coven of witches to ring my territory with ward stones, but even those wouldn't keep out the fae. Fae magic, eldritch magic, and human magic are three different things.

I searched for a long time for a way to protect my pack from him. On this continent, the fae enter and leave our world almost exclusively through doors hidden throughout the Rockies. Almost no one bothers to ward against them this far east.

As luck would have it, the answer finally found me in the form of Rohan Mehta, a Chicago-based traveling dealer of antiques and magical artifacts. He knew of a witch who studied fae magic and commissioned them to create a second set of ward stones for me, specifically to protect against the dream thief.

I cover my distaste with an easy grin. "Always glad to hear my Beta is a winner, but I assume that's not why you came all the way here in person. It's a long journey from Fall Line."

"Ah. Yes." Vandran sighs. "I can't lie; I'm worried about you, Killian. Deacon told me what Redcedar Hollow did and about the girl. I wanted to get a look at her for myself."

I shrug one shoulder. "Selene is harmless. She doesn't even have a wolf."

But is she? Who is responsible for sending that messenger bird?

"Did Warden Whitlock test the blood I sent you?" I ask.

"Yes, and you were right. There's something odd about her. Does she really quiet the beast?"

My heartbeat picks up. "Yes. I haven't lost control for two weeks. I've actually been able to sleep. It's been ... good."

It was more than good until last night.

Surprise flares in Vandran's eyes. "What does she say when you ask her how she does it?"

"She doesn't know. Sofia suspects some bloodline magic but hasn't been able to find anything in the Beaumonts' genealogy that explains it."

Vandran crosses his arms over his broad chest and leans against the wall, brows furrowed. "You don't find that suspicious?"

The hair on the back of my neck prickles. Something feels abruptly off. I glance around and see Selene isn't back yet. I scan the room for Parker. Sofia is just leading the tall redhead out onto the floor for a dance.

I reach out to Parker through the pack tie. *"Selene still isn't back. I hate to disrupt your marital bliss, but please check on her."*

Parker shoots me a glare across the room, then murmurs something to Sofia. She's on the opposite end of the great hall, but she starts toward the closed door out to the hallway.

Closed? We usually leave the doors open for airflow during events like this. Was it closed before?

"Killian," Vandran's sharpened tone snags my attention. "You don't find this whole thing suspicious?"

Oh, right. "How can it be suspicious when they sent her to die? They wanted me to kill her so the Conclave would send soldiers to help them crush us."

Vandran scowls. "And you're carrying on with this farce anyway? Bowing to Frank and Delilah Beaumont's bullshit?"

"You're a member of the Conclave. You know how they are. What choice do I have?"

"Keep her around if you have to, but demand the other daughter. Don't waste yourself on some wolfless."

I frown. I have a sudden, intense dislike for this conversation. "Be careful, old friend," I say softly. "You know I don't appreciate being told who to be with."

Vandran gives me an unamused look from his lazy position against the wall. "I do recall that."

He thought I was wasting myself on Grace too. The only fight we've ever had was when he demanded I put her aside and take some powerful Alpha Pair's daughter as a mate instead.

But would Selene prefer it if I demanded Bianca, now that she thinks what she does? If I insisted on having her older sister, I could let Selene go. She deserves to live a life she chooses.

Across the room, Parker's path is blocked by a group of younger wolves all clumped together who start to dance. She starts to push her way through, then shakes her head, backs up, and walks around them.

Vandran keeps pushing. "You've got your head up your ass if you think Beaumont will keep his side of things. He's still coming for you, and then he'll be back to harassing my trade caravans. A wolfless former pack servant isn't going to cut it. You need the other daughter, and then you need to kill Frank and Delilah." He lowers his voice. "Like we talked about when I gave you the money to build this pack."

"What about this do you not understand?" I snap. "I've done what you wanted me to—I've built a pack to be Fall Line's ally. I'm sorry if it isn't a werewolf army tens of thousands strong like Conqueror's Moon. Shit happened, and all I want now is to protect what I have. We've been searching for a solution for the curse for years. I find Selene, and you want me to get rid of her? With all due respect, I'm not the one with my head up my ass."

He lifts his chin. Not many men can loom over me, but Warlord Vandran comes close. "Be reasonable, boy."

"You helped me rise, but I paid you back with interest. You're not pack, and I am not a boy."

*Breakthemkillthem* ... The monster seethes, wild, just beneath the surface. I grit my teeth, ball my fists, and take a breath to force it back down. Which I can, but only because it's the new moon.

Vandran must see the monster in my eyes because he blanches and holds his hands up in a gesture of surrender. He's seen the curse in action exactly once, and he left that interaction lucky to be alive. Some of his soldiers weren't as lucky as him.

"All right, Killian. I'm sorry. I didn't mean anything by it. I'm just worried about you."

I kick the last vestiges of the beast into the dark and rub my temples. "I have to be free of this, Marcus. Once I am, I'll let her go if she wants to go. Then we can talk about going after Redcedar Hollow. *If* you can keep the Conclave off my back. After all this time, they still think I'm gunning to become my father."

Vandran sighs and puts a hand on my shoulder. "You leave the Conclave to me. As for a cure, Whitlock and his protégé Tristan Evans have both isolated some interesting things in her blood. Studying it more will help. We'll figure it out soon. Who knows, maybe you won't even need her."

My gut wrenches, as if the very core of my being rejects the idea of not needing Selene.

I ignore the feeling. I hate being at odds with Vandran. He's been like a father to me, given me everything. Without him, I'd still be a rogue. Likely drunk or dead in some back alley of a nameless Free City village.

I press the heels of my palms into my eyes. "All right. Thank you." Then I think of something. "Have you heard anything about Asher? Where he's been for the last five years?"

The warlord rescued us from the Free Cities at the same time. When we were seventeen, we tried to rob one of his warehouses for food and supplies. We got caught. Instead of killing us, he saw our potential and brought us into his orbit. He had us trained by Gage Hagan, a gruff old wolf people called the Warlord's Blade. Asher was set to take the old man's place as Vandran's personal assassin and fixer until it was decided we'd create Shattered Moon, instead.

Vandran's eyes dart to where Whitlock is speaking to my mother, then he frowns and shakes his head. "Quinn? No. Haven't seen him in years."

Across the room, Parker has finally reached the door.

Vandran rubs his chin thoughtfully. "Have you ever considered Redcedar Hollow might be the source of your curse?"

That pulls my attention back to him. I scoff. "You think they wanted to make me into the uncontrollable weapon that killed Jackson Beaumont and then the rest of their people by the dozens?"

Vandran chuckles. "It sounds ridiculous when you say it like that. But what if they didn't know what they were doing? What if they meant it to have one effect but it had another?"

"And then what? They went back to the high eldritch who gave it to them and modified it so Selene makes it go dormant?"

"Went back?" Vandran says absently. His brow furrows, and he looks thoughtful. "You know, I could take her with me. I'd give her a nice little house on the beach. All she'd have to do is be available for Whitlock and his people for research. If we don't have a full cure for you soon, I'll bring her back. But don't make her your mate. Not when there are other, better options."

"Bianca Beaumont is in no way—"

*"Alpha,"* Parker says through the pack tie in a voice that's far too calm. *"The door to the hallway is locked, and I smell blood."*

# Seventeen

## SELENE

The growl reaches out of the shadows and runs chill fingers down my back. Adrenaline spikes. Slowly, I turn.

It's too dark. I can't see.

I exhale. The sound is suspended in silence. Then my eyes adjust. About four and a half feet off the ground drifts a pair of sickly yellow irises.

Claws scrape. Acting purely on instinct, I throw myself forward and to the side and hit the cold marble floor on my stomach. A seam somewhere on my bodice pops. The air leaves my body in a rush.

Whatever is in the hall with me crashes into the wall and snarls. It sounds huge.

*Bang! Bang! Bang! Crash!* The door to the great hall flies open.

"Selene!" It's Parker's voice, but I'm frozen in place with fear.

With the door open, light spills into the hall. It half-illuminates a warped version of a huge wolf just a few feet in front of me. At first, I have the wild thought that it's Killian. There's something wrong with it in the same way something is wrong with the monstrous version of his hybrid form. It's too stretched, too ragged, its gray fur patchy. Its eyes that same sickly yellow.

But I *know* it isn't him. I can't explain how.

The wolf moves, limping, turning away from the wall it just crashed into and toward me. Its entire flank seems to be covered in dark, seeping blood, like it's already been in a fight.

"Shit!"

I hear footsteps and know Parker is charging straight for us. The illumination from the great hall dims, and I risk a glance behind. People are crowding the door to peer out, blocking the precious light.

Parker barrels toward me as the wolf lines up for another charge. Shreds of clothing explode as she leaps and bursts into the form of a rangy gray wolf. She lands on all fours, not even breaking her stride.

My attacker leaps. So does Parker. I throw myself out of the way as they meet in an explosion of snarls and snapping teeth. The wounded beast is bigger than her by a head, but it's lanky and sickly. Parker's momentum carries them into the dark. There's a slam, the sound of plaster cracking, and a yelp. I run to the bathroom door, throw it open, then flip on the light.

The tile floor is illuminated by a cone of harsh fluorescence. Parker is lying dazed on the floor. The monster wolf snarls down at her. The wall above her has a huge wolf-sized dent in it, as if the beast threw her into it.

"Parker!" I turn to the people standing at the door, just watching. "Somebody help us!"

Parker doesn't move, but the creature turns back to me, yellow eyes glowing. Beneath the smoky scent of werewolf magic is that eldritch scent of dust, age, and cold stone.

I move back, but the wolf leaps, claws catching in the hem of my skirt. I let out a cry of fear and pain as it wrenches at the same time as I try to run. I fall to the side and land hard on my elbow.

The creature looms over me. Its lips curl back. Saliva drips in strings from its jaws. My heart climbs into my throat, and I can't breathe around it.

Then the air in the hall is split by a deep, reverberating howl that could crack the bones of the earth. The monstrous wolf turns just in time to be lifted off its feet and flung so far that it disappears into shadow. There's a crash, then a yelp.

A new figure stands above me, a silhouette of a wolf in hybrid form, huge and black with silver-tipped fur. He looks down at me, topaz eyes flashing.

"Killian," I whisper.

He reaches down with one clawed hand and draws me to my feet. My fingers press into the warm fur that covers his abdomen. Then he flings me to the side just before the other wolf comes careening out of the dark. It tackles him, flattening Killian onto his back and sending them both sliding across the floor.

I lurch forward, reaching like I can do something, but another furry body interposes itself between me and the snarling beasts. It's Parker, back on her feet. She leans her huge body against me, pressing me into the wall as she bares her teeth in the direction of the fight.

There's the sickening, crackling pop of snapping bone and tendon, then silence. For a heartbeat, everything is still and dark.

The hallway lights finally flicker on, illuminating everything in perfect detail as Killian rises from the tangle of gray and black fur and drops the broken body of the dead wolf to the floor. Its entire torso is twisted, as if he took his massive hands and tried to wring it in half.

The wolf is lying with its jaws open, tongue lolling, and mouth leaking blood that matches the crimson of the wound on its side. White is already filming its sightless eyes.

He killed it. Just like that. Efficient. Ruthless.

Is that how he killed Jackson?

"K-Killian." My voice catches. He's covered in blood, and there's gore smeared all over the floor and spattered on the wall. A trail of it leads down the hall, likely where the monster came from. But how did it get in? Why was it injured before it got here?

Killian turns. Sees me. Then he snarls at Parker.

She drops her ears and tail, scampering out of the way as the huge wolf man stalks forward and yanks me against his chest.

I stand as still as stone while he wraps his arms around me. I can't stop picturing my brother. It's been five years, and sometimes it's hard to remember his face at all anymore, but now I can see it. His blond hair smeared with blood. His eyes sightless.

If Jackson was with Grace, I bet he was in human form when he died.

Did Killian twist him like that? Break his neck before he started feasting on him?

"We're going upstairs," Killian says. He issues no commands, but Parker and Zev fall into step behind us. We pass through the great hall.

The useless wolves who observed the fight and did nothing crowd us, but then Sofia, Eva, and Deacon Jones are there, keeping people away.

Neither Killian nor I speak all the way up to his rooms. Killian opens the door and steps through. Parker and Zev stay outside. The sweet-smoky smell of wolf magic fills the air as he shifts down into his human form, the expensive suit he was wearing hanging from him in tatters.

He closes his eyes and breathes in, then wrinkles his nose.

I run my hands nervously over my beautiful dress. A side seam has popped, and there's a rip along the hem of the skirt where the wolf dug his claws in. "What?"

"That wolf was poisoned with howler venom. I can still smell it." He pauses, his eyes going distant in a way that tells me he's speaking to someone—or several someones—over the pack tie. "Vandran and Dr. Bennett have the body. They're looking into it."

"Who was the wolf?"

"I don't know," Killian says. "He's not Shattered Moon. Did you recognize him?"

"No."

"It's likely he was a rogue."

"There were leaders of rogue factions here tonight," I say slowly.

Killian's jaw tightens, and his eyes go unfocused again. "Deacon is questioning them now. They're supposed to be allies, but if they broke the peace ..."

I'm already shaking my head. "That doesn't make sense. The rogues don't have any motive to attack me. But it is convenient for this to happen on a night when they're here. Someone from the pack, on the other hand—"

Suddenly, I have all of Killian's attention.

He steps forward, backing me up until I'm pressed against one of the floor-to-ceiling windows with nothing but frigid glass and the black void of night behind me. "No one in this pack would break the treaty by attacking you. They know what the consequences would be."

I press my bare back against the frozen glass, grounding myself in the sharp cold. Tremors run through my muscles, a lingering aftereffect of being attacked below. That clinging fear and the way he's invading my space make my voice sharp. "You saw them tonight, Killian. At least half of them don't want me here."

He tilts his head, the picture of Alpha arrogance. "They may not, but Shattered Moon is loyal to me."

I recoil at his words, then bite back. "They're loyal to you because you're strong. So many of them want you to be like your father."

Killian rumbles with a warning growl. "Or maybe you staged this."

"Me?" I laugh incredulously and shove him. He doesn't move.

Our truce didn't feel fragile before last night, but now it's cracking beneath us like fracturing glass. I want to be calm, but I'm so afraid. So angry.

I can't believe I trusted this murderer, this monster. I can't believe I let my guard down. Let him touch me. I can't believe I wanted him so desperately.

No. *Want* him, even now.

"Oh, yes," I snap. "I captured a rogue wolf, left it out for howlers to infect—but saved it before it could get ripped to shreds, don't forget that part—hid it somewhere, then let it in here and conspired to get your mother to dump wine on me so I could die in a dark hallway outside a bathroom!"

"Even infected with howler venom, it was one wolf. You know what Parker is capable of. What I am capable of. There's no way you expected to die tonight."

I throw my hands in the air. "How would I have managed to get it here?"

He braces his hands on the window on either side of me and leans down, his face inches from mine. "Who says you acted alone? An attack like this is a perfect way for Redcedar Hollow to sow unrest. To make me paranoid." He pauses, then says ominously, "I know about the birds."

I scrunch my nose. "What birds?"

He produces the foot of a dead bird from his pocket. It's banded with green paint.

My nose scrunch deepens. "Have you had that in your pocket all night?"

"My Beta handed it to me right before dinner. He told me about the messages."

"What messages?"

"There's no way it could be anyone else, Selene. This pack hasn't taken in a new wolf in over a year except you and Finn, and I don't think a seven-year-old is capable of espionage on this level."

I ball my hands into fists, my vision going red. "Or maybe you did it because you think they're more likely to send you Bianca if I'm dead and they have no other option! Maybe you want to be in an Alpha Pair, after all."

"Yes," he snarls, "that's exactly why I saved your life."

"Parker saved my life." I retort. "Maybe you were just saving her. After all, she's pack. I'm the enemy."

I know Killian saved me. I don't care. He's being an ass.

"Do you know how many people I have telling me to get rid of you?" he shouts.

I hate how I can't take my eyes off him, even now. That anger only heightens the magnetic pull, only makes it more impossible to tear my eyes away. I press my hand against his chest as if I'm strong enough to keep him at any kind of distance. The heat of his bare skin sears my palm through his torn shirt.

"Do you think that scares me?" I ask through gritted teeth. "I've spent my *life* waiting to be thrown away."

He's trembling now. There's rage in his eyes. I've never seen him angry like this. Arrogant like this.

Here they are, the cracks. Here are his true colors. The shoe I've been waiting to be crushed by when it drops.

Here is Jackson's killer. Grace's murderer.

Killian's heart races beneath my palm, but I am suddenly chillingly calm.

I go up on my tiptoes and whisper against his ear, "Do you want to hurt me, Alpha? Go ahead. I always knew you would. I've been waiting for you to gut me the way you gutted her. To see if you have a taste for me the way you did my brother. I'm sure your father would be proud."

I indicate the locket around his wrist. "I'm sorry I don't have any jewelry you can add to your trophy collection. You can have this if you want." I lift my hand and gesture to the worn, knotted blue-and-purple friendship bracelet Finn gave me.

Killian's eyes are wide and wild. For an instant, I'm sure I've done it. Found who he is at his core and unleashed it. He raises his hands and grips my face, and his touch is not gentle.

I wait for him to move. Grow his claws and slit my throat. Wrench my neck and break it.

Instead, he studies my face. The scar through his brow and lip is stark against his skin. Strands of black hair have tumbled over the faceted depths of his honey-brown eyes. The rage drains away, replaced by something wounded and desperate. When he speaks, the words are quiet, not cruel. It only makes them cut deeper.

"You weren't what I asked for. You were never what I wanted."

He releases me, then turns and stalks out of the apartment, slamming the door behind him.

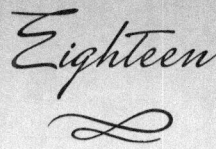

## Eighteen

### KILLIAN

That night, I go into the forest. For the first time, I wish the curse would take me. But even the monster's madness wouldn't silence her words.

*I've been waiting for you to gut me the way you gutted her. To see if you have a taste for me the way you did my brother. I'm sure your father would be proud.*

She's clever, and, god, she can be cruel. I gave her cruelty back. I tell myself she deserves it. But still, my heart beats for her. My mind clings to her.

Maybe Vandran was right—maybe this is all a plan by Redcedar Hollow and I'm just too dense to see how it all comes together. Maybe she's working some kind of love or lust spell on me. Plenty of witches are willing to sell them in the arcane black markets that can be found in the underbelly of any decent-sized town.

Paired with Deacon's birds, it makes too much sense.

She tricked me, and like a fool, I let her.

The one thing I lack is definitive proof she's a spy. If I find evidence I think the Conclave would accept, I will kill her.

The next day, when I drag myself to my office, no progress has been made in discovering who let the infected rogue into the pack house. Deacon argues to keep holding the rogue leaders, but Selene was right about one thing—they have no motive. Even if they wanted to strike some kind of blow against me, they're both smarter than to do it that way. I command Deacon to release them.

For the next week, I search for answers during the day. I find places Redcedar Hollow has made incursions on the border and flag them for my Beta and his soldiers to check. I don't find any more messenger birds, and no one is able to decipher the coded messages.

At night, I let the curse take me. It's a relief to let the monster consume me.

*I've been waiting for you to gut me the way you gutted her.*

If she knew the truth about what happened to Grace and Jackson, would it change things?

It's a secret I've kept for five years—Grace's secret. I'm not going to tell anyone now, especially not Selene when she is likely my enemy.

I do not sleep.

A week after the pack dinner, I catch the scent of howlers.

Howlers are low eldritch native to the Ozarks. Some legends say they're humans whose blood awoke to magic with werewolf aspect but whose minds couldn't handle it. Or that they're guardians of the land bent on avenging the destruction of the old forests and old ways. Whatever their origin, they're the size of a bear, with red eyes and horns that twist back over their broad heads. Their heavy jaws are filled with teeth coated in saliva that's deadly venomous. If the venom doesn't kill us outright, it drives us mad like the rogue that got into my pack house.

Very few things can easily kill adult werewolves. Howlers were made for it. I can't allow them on my land.

I stalk the monsters. At the same time, I look for signs that other wolves have captured one or somehow made contact. That rogue was bitten somehow, though he could've been injected.

I find nothing.

I spend nights cursed, hunting. Days throwing myself into pack business, ignoring Sofia and Eva when they ask whether I've seen Selene. Ignoring Zev's blunt questions and Parker's sarcastic comments.

During the rare times I am in bed in the cave, it feels empty. I dream of Selene, our fingers intertwined, her soft breathing easing me into sleep.

My longing doesn't matter. I'll marry her for the sake of the treaty. Otherwise, she and I are done.

## SELENE

*You were never what I wanted.*

Without Killian, my sleep is troubled. I'm running. Something horrible is chasing me, but it doesn't have a face or a name. I try to cry out, but I can't. Over and over again during that first week, I have the same dream.

He doesn't come back to his apartment. He doesn't even attempt to see me, which is good. I don't want to see him.

I've lost my appetite for wandering, though that blocked-off hallway beneath the foyer stairs still haunts me. The lukewarm reception from the pack at our engagement dinner stays in my mind, as does the crowd at the door during the rogue's attack. Not helping, just watching.

Will I ever be accepted anywhere?

"Selene, why are you sad?" Finn asks one evening after school.

We're making dinner together. Since Killian stopped coming here, I moved Finn in with me. I sleep in the Alpha's bed, and my brother stays in the guest bedroom. I fully have my brother back. In that way, at least, I'm happy.

I pat beneath my eyes with my sleeves. "I'm not sad, Rocket; it's just the onions."

He scowls at me. "You are sad. You miss Alpha Killian."

"The Alpha and I have a deal. That's all. We're not friends."

"But what if I need to tell him a secret?" Finn protests.

"What secret?" I demand.

Finn's brows pull together in a familiar stubborn expression. "A *secret*, Selene."

I crouch to his level and take my brother by the shoulders. His bright brown eyes are partially hidden by a tumble of curls. The innocent look on his face tugs at my heart. "He's dangerous, Finn. Okay? Promise me you won't go near him. He's hurt people in our family before. You aren't safe with him. Never forget that."

His eyes go wide. He doesn't know that Killian murdered Jackson—he was two when our elder brother died. I'm not ready to tell him, but I should.

"Okay," he says quietly. "I promise."

~

WHEN FINN IS IN SCHOOL, I throw myself into learning the piano. Day in, day out. I have Finn, music, books, movies, and Killian's scent for company. Eva visits, as do Sofia and Parker, but I find it hard to connect with them now. I notice that Maddox has taken Zev's place outside the door, I assume because Zev is always with Killian.

Maybe Killian hopes Maddox will lose his volatile temper and do the job of killing me for him. Joke's on him—Maddox seems to be calmer around me. I actually start to feel safe in his presence.

Days pass until I don't know how long it's been since I've seen the Alpha of Shattered Moon except in my less troubled, much sexier dreams.

I try not to remember those dreams as I sit in the music room one afternoon, picking half-heartedly at the piano. The song is difficult, and I lose my patience and hit a dissonant chord harder than I need to.

"What the hell is this noise?"

I hit another sour chord as I whirl, knocking sheet music everywhere. Killian's mother stands in the doorway draped in black like a fashionable bat, lips red, wine glass in hand.

"Claudia. What are you doing here?"

It's Parker's day off and Maddox's shift to train with Deacon. Claudia probably knew that. She must have chosen today and intimidated whichever of the younger wolf guards is at the apartment door.

The perfectly put-together older woman throws her black shawl over her shoulder and scoffs. "I'm his mother. What are *you* doing here? He wouldn't want you in this room."

I gesture at the piano. "Teaching myself to play."

She laughs, the sound delicate and completely fake. "Oh, dear. I thought you'd fallen and hit your face on the keys. Grace was a much better player."

Ice forms in my stomach. "Grace?"

"Oh, yes. This room was hers. So was the piano."

Killian has seen me playing this. He's kissed me at this piano. "He didn't say anything."

A tinkling laugh. "Darling, why would he share anything important like that with you?"

Since Killian disappeared, I've been so off balance. Claudia has barely pushed, and I feel knocked off my feet. I hate it. I hate her.

"I think you should go," I say.

Claudia smirks. "You're such a pathetic little thing. No wonder he no longer wants you."

Exasperated, I ask, "Do you play or something? If you'd like a turn—"

She scoffs. "I'm no more the entertainment than I am the help. Unlike you." She takes a sip of her wine and a step closer. "Certainly, now that you've been here long enough to see what an embarrassment you are—and to see how objectionable my son finds your presence—you'll consider leaving."

"I ... what? I can't leave." God, I wish I could leave. So many times, I've convinced myself it might be possible, only to come back to reality hard and realize I have no choice but to stay here. "That will violate the treaty."

She tuts. "We can figure something out. If I met with your sister, I'm sure I could convince her to take her rightful place."

Bile rises in my throat at the thought of Bianca anywhere near Killian.

No matter what has happened between Killian and me or what he's done, I'd never be that cruel.

"Killian has no interest in Bianca."

Claudia laughs that fates-awful laugh again. "Oh, sweetheart. You think because he screwed you a couple of times, you mean something to him?" She does a fake little pout. "You're desperate to cling to your new, elevated position, I get it, but it's *so* hard to watch. Please, put us all out of our misery."

"We aren't having sex."

"Whatever you say." The obnoxious laugh again. She moves to the window, throws back a gulp of wine, and looks out over the lake and forest. "No one will blame you for leaving, Selenite. Killian won't either. He's simply too much of a gentleman to tell you he wants you gone, just like the rest of us."

*Selene*, I think, but I don't give her the satisfaction of correcting her out loud. Sarcasm dripping from every word, I say, "A gentleman, is he? I guess he's not much like his father, after all."

Claudia sips wine and snorts. "Oh, no, he's very much like his father."

"Alaric Bane was a gentleman?" I ask incredulously.

"Alaric Bane? No, his father—" Claudia wheels toward me, her eyes suddenly wide.

She stalks over and jabs a finger at my chest. "Listen to me, you little gold digger, I'm offering you a chance to leave. Killian is out there sleeping in the dirt rather than with you. Do the decent thing and get out of here. He doesn't want you. A mother knows these things."

I tell myself Killian preferring dirt to me is fine. But whether I care where he sleeps or not, I still can't leave. I won't put Shattered Moon in danger like that, even if most of the pack doesn't like me, and I will die before I let Bianca get her claws into Killian.

*Play the game.* I tap my lips with a finger and pretend to be confused. "His mother? How strange. Eva hasn't said a thing."

Claudia's face contorts in a rictus of feral rage. The air electrifies with Alpha magic, and I realize my mistake. Killian didn't just get his immense power from his father. Claudia is *strong* in Alpha magic. Strong and drunk.

"I am his mother!" she snarls. Needlelike claws slide out from her fingers in a liquid motion, and she lunges at me.

I stumble over the piano bench as I try to escape. I have to get to the door, to the guard. But my foot catches, and I fall painfully. My shoulder slams into the piano and my hip into the ground. I throw an arm up to shield my face and cover my eyes. "No!"

Feverish heat flashes through my body. It feels like my blood is boiling away. The old wound in my shoulder flares like it's on fire, skin searing. I scream.

*Slam! Crash!* Claudia lets out a sound that's part howl, part shriek.

I lower my arm and gasp. Claudia Darrow has been thrown into the wall. I don't mean against it—I mean into it, breaking a hole in the sheetrock. When I look down at my hands, silver light swirls beneath my skin, then subsides.

My gut lurches. My hand trembles. "What the hell? What the *hell*?"

Claudia clambers out of the wall. Her goblet is shattered and her shawl shiny with wet spots. Red spatters the carpet, and I don't know whether it's wine or blood. White dust covers her black clothes and streaks her face and hair.

"What did you just do to me?" she howls. "You're no wolfless. You're a liar. A spy. Why did Frank and Delilah send you here?!"

Fear wraps icy fingers around my lungs. "They didn't send me!"

"*Liar!*" Her eyes blaze with topaz fire, so like Killian's but devoid of warmth. "I am going to tell my son, and he is going to kill you!"

# Nineteen

## SELENE

For days after, I wait for Killian to come to the apartment, to accuse me of using some kind of strange magic against his mother, to end me.

*I've been waiting for you to gut me the way you gutted her.*

*You were never what I wanted.*

He doesn't come back. He just lets me sit in the silence with the echo of our words.

As far as psychological torture goes, it's worse than anything Bianca has ever done. Which, I suppose, I should expect from someone like him.

Sometimes I think about what he said about birds and messages. He had that talon, but anyone can kill a bird and splash its leg with green paint. He said he got it from Deacon Jones. It's easy to imagine the Beta setting me up, but it seems impossible he'd go so far that it would threaten Killian's ability to stick to the terms of the treaty.

If the Alpha of Shattered Moon executes me as a spy, I'm sure the pretend outrage of my family will be something to behold.

In reality, they haven't contacted me since I've been here. I expected blackmail long before now, and their silence has put me on edge. They are never not up to something, which means some plot is in the works.

Maybe they *did* send the bird.

My run-in with Claudia pisses me off, and I decide to redouble my efforts to get to know the pack. I do indulge in Finn, music, movies, and books. But I also make more of a point to see Eva and the others, to be downstairs among the wolves of Shattered Moon.

I start to make friends, but deep down, my efforts feel like a farce. Impermanent. Like Killian is going to show up and tell me the wedding is off at any moment. That I'm exiled, and all of my efforts are a waste.

But he doesn't, and the ceremony drags closer. Sofia has me trying on dresses, approving menus, and giving my opinion on flower arrangements.

"Sofia, I don't even know if this is happening!" I throw down a stack of papers on the dining room table one afternoon and pace to the windows. It's almost sunset. If I watch, will I see him walking into the woods for the night?

Sofia and Parker, who's taken to hanging out inside the apartment when her mate is here, exchange glances. They look genuinely confused. "What? The wedding?"

"Yes! I'm sure you've noticed things are not going well between Killian and me."

"The wedding is happening," Parker says. "If it doesn't, the Conclave will end Shattered Moon. Half this pack might be old bastards and young assholes who are angry Killian's not going to relive his father's glory days, but Killian will grind himself into dust to protect them. Even if it means marrying you."

Sofia elbows her mate. Parker rubs her ribs. "What?"

I run a hand through my hair and force myself to breathe. It's getting longer, and several silvery strands fall into my face. The last time I looked in the mirror, I noticed how rounded my cheeks have become, how I can no longer count my ribs. I'm still pale with strange eyes, but for the first time, I like what I see.

"The wedding is happening," Sofia insists.

I wish I could believe her.

~

*Full Moon*

# KILLIAN

Claws part the air, whistling toward me. I lean back and turn my head. They whiff a bare half inch past my ear. Maddox, in his silver hybrid form, snarls and cuts upward with his other claw, just like I knew he would. I've already dropped my shoulder and pivoted out of reach. Maddox misses again.

Sofia's voice sounds in my head. She stands several yards beyond the white-painted sparring circle with her arms folded across her chest. *"The kid is out of control. You need to shift. He's going to kill you."*

"If he does," I toss back at Sofia, *"thank him for me."*

*"Not funny."*

I'm not trying to be funny. It's been two weeks since the dinner. Tonight is the full moon. I haven't seen Selene. I haven't found out how the wolf got in. I haven't found any evidence of another spy, which means it's more than likely her.

Even so, knowing she's here and not seeing her hollows me out with a living emptiness. The ache is a constant, almost physical thing. I've considered clawing my own head open to make it go away.

For the millionth time, I remind myself that except for a contract, she and I are over.

Maddox charges, eyes on fire with rage. Slash, slash, slash. On the last one, his claws skim my bare chest, leaving shallow, parallel lines that sting for a few seconds before they begin to heal.

Sweat chills on my forehead, chest, and back. Winter air rasps in my lungs. Maddox and I have been going at this for an hour. Him in hybrid form, me as a human. We started out sparring alone in an obscure corner of the clear field where the pack trains. Slowly, more and more have gathered, watching us.

They've kept their distance despite the fact that I've remained human. Even from here, I smell their fear. They've seen me lose control before, though they don't know about the curse. They think I'm like Maddox.

Maddox isn't cursed, but there's blood madness in some wolves. A reckless letting go at the edge of man and beast that calls to some, especially those who experienced violence, trauma, or loss at a young age. Before Eva and Gideon Quinn took him in, Maddox knew that kind of loss. When I killed Grace and Asher left, he knew it again.

He does need this extra training, and that training has to be with me because I'm the only person I'm absolutely certain he can't kill.

*"Killian."* Sofia's mental voice is sharp. *"This is ridiculous. Just talk to her instead of letting Maddox tear the shit out of you."*

*"She's not wrong."* Zev has no Alpha blood, so he has no hybrid form. Instead, he's a pale gray wolf nearly the size of a horse who sits at Sofia's side. His mouth is open, tongue lolling out in a doggy grin.

They don't know about Asher's visit or the truth of Grace's and Jackson's deaths. They don't understand the extent of the rift between Selene and me and haven't accepted that it's one I will never cross.

*"I'll talk to Selene as soon as you talk to Eva,"* I say privately to Zev.

He snarls.

The pack tie is both complex and intuitive. Any wolf in the pack can speak to any other, or any number of others together. Any wolf can also isolate so that mental messages—except for mine—can't reach them.

Sofia, Zev, Parker, and I have a small group that I'm almost always open to. If I could add Eva to it, I would.

I duck below Maddox's snapping jaws, then bait him into charging me. He falls for it. I'm on one side of him now, and he's still moving forward. I raise my knee, trip him, and slam the heel of my palm into his upper back.

The younger wolf smashes into the ground. Inside the sparring circle, the grass is worn away to dirt laced with shards of flint that constantly work their way up from the ground in this region. Maddox's claws gouge the earth, and he roars. He puts on an extra burst of speed and spins back toward me. Power radiates from him like a bonfire.

Sofia is right; I've pushed him too far.

"Maddox. Enough."

He launches at me again. Snap, slash, slash, snap. More stinging red lines appear on my body.

My wolf surges. The monster stirs in its wake. I clamp down on the curse but give in to the wolf. Power explodes through my body. Between one slash and the next, I go from a man who stands just over six feet tall to a hybrid who stands over seven.

I catch Maddox's wrist in my clawed hand and snarl in a low, menacing voice filled with power, *"Enough."*

Maddox's blazing eyes catch mine, and the realization that he's as tall as me hits like a blow to the gut. If he had a pack to draw from, if he weren't part of mine, if he had more experience, he would be as powerful as me.

But I do have a pack, and I am his Alpha, and I have no fucking patience for this. I flare my aura and crush his will beneath mine.

Maddox yelps and falls to one knee like a puppet with its strings cut. Madness leaves his eyes. He drops his hybrid form, shrinking into his lean, tattooed human body. His chest heaves. He doesn't look at me.

"Are you all right?" I ask.

"I'm fine, liar." He spits on the ground at my feet.

"Maddox!" Sofia barks.

The younger wolf has been angry since he realized I'm going through with the wedding to Selene. Not angry at her—only at me. In the last couple of weeks, he's gone from defending my actions to goading me.

I've been patient because he's Grace's brother. He's allowed to be upset. But today, I'm too tired; I've been on edge too long.

I snap.

I grab the younger man by the throat and haul him into the air. He yipes and claws at my hand. The curse bubbles and whispers, caressing the back of my mind, louder than it should be during the day.

*Breakthemkillthembleedthem* ...

Maddox's pulse beats beneath my palm. His blood rushes hot through his vulnerable neck. It would just take one twitch. One bite. I could tear out his throat. His blood would flow hot over my hand. I could rend him. I could tear out his still-beating heart and consume it.

Maddox's eyes go wide, and he gags. He claws and kicks, but he's human now.

Zev leaps in front of Sofia, who's trying to get to me, screaming, "Killian! Stop!"

Horror streams through the pack tie from the wolves who are here witnessing this.

Let them see me for the monster I truly am.

After all, Selene does.

*Yesssss* ... the monster hisses inside me. It feels different. Louder, stronger. It wants this. It is *hungry*, and so am I.

A memory flashes through my mind. Maddox is seven. Asher and I are fourteen. We shift into full wolf form, toss Maddox onto my back, and take off into the woods. Their father, Gideon, was long gone, and

Asher and I did our best to make sure Maddox never felt like he was missing out on anything.

We used to bring him on all of our excursions, sometimes staying out in the forest for days at a time. Sometimes Grace would come with us, sometimes she didn't. Maddox is my brother in spirit, if not in blood. That's the only thing that gives me the strength to break through the growing yellow fog in my head.

It's the only thing that saves his life.

I drag Maddox close and snarl into his face. "Don't disrespect me again."

I throw him aside. He flies ten feet, lands on the ground, and rolls. He's up in a flash, but Zev blocks him, and Sofia hisses, "Stand down, Maddox."

I stalk away, the pack parting for me. Fear is sharp in the air.

I have to get out of here before they see the way I'm shaking.

Selene was right to believe I'd gut her one day. More and more, a breaking feels inevitable. If I actually find evidence of her betrayal ...

She would be safer if I sent her away. If she's a spy, so would the pack.

Sending her to Fall Line suddenly feels like the answer to every problem I have.

I was used to being alone before her. I'll get used to it again.

Vandran said he'd treat her well, and I trust him.

# Twenty

## SELENE

The day of the full moon, I decide to visit Finn at school again. It's become my favorite way to interact with the pack over the last week. Unlike some of their parents, the kids don't look at me like I might pull a bunch of Redcedar Hollow soldiers out of my pockets and set them loose on Shattered Moon.

I cross the cold grounds to the school building, enter, walk down the long hall to Finn's classroom, then knock on the door and stick my head in. The kids chorus a greeting, and I wave to them.

Eva walks over. She looks concerned. "Hey, Selene. Did Finn forget something? How is he?"

I blink. "How is he?"

Eva tilts her head, confusion on her face. "Yes. He wasn't feeling well. I had Noelle take him up to Killian's apartment."

My heart drops into my stomach. "What do you mean, he wasn't feeling well? Who's Noelle?"

Eva's brow furrows. "She's one of the newer caretakers. Callie has been sick a few times lately, and Noelle substitutes for her."

"Right. I remember Finn mentioning that. He's with someone named Noelle?" In the month I've been here, I've met almost all of Shattered Moon's wolves, but I've never met a Noelle.

The fear that Redcedar Hollow is up to something, that I'm missing something, rears its head and seeps cold into my veins. They were supposed to come after me, not Finn. *Me.*

I fight for calm. I'm being paranoid. It's probably fine. "I haven't seen him. When did you send him up?"

When horror dawns on Eva's face, I realize it is not fine. "Just barely. You should have passed them coming across the yard."

The cold in my veins crystallizes to stabbing ice. I push away from the door. "No, I didn't see them at all."

Noelle. Who is Noelle? Finn talked about her, but have I seen her?

Then I remember. She came into the classroom one day but immediately turned around, saying she was sick. In fact, she'd clapped a hand over her face as soon as she saw me.

What if that wasn't because she was sick but because she recognized me and knew I would recognize her?

The room spins.

The way the grounds are set up, there is no way I could've missed them. Not if this Noelle woman was really bringing Finn to me. Not unless she took him in the opposite direction, toward the woods.

Why take a sick little boy toward the woods?

Birds. Messages. A Redcedar Hollow spy. Not me but someone who's been here for years.

"You need to check on Callie," I say to Eva. "I don't think she's sick. I think she's been poisoned. I think Noelle has been trying to poison her for two weeks."

I'm leaping to conclusions. I could be so completely wrong, but instinct screams at me. Finn is gone, but why take him? To reclaim him? To draw me out? I know my father wanted him back, but I've heard nothing about it recently.

Or have they taken him to draw out Killian?

If I go after Finn, I'm walking right back into their hands. Bianca's hands.

It doesn't matter. I don't care whether he's bait or who they're fishing for.

I turn and run.

"Selene, wait! Let me find someone to tell Killian! You can't go alone!" Eva shouts behind me.

I ignore her. Killian won't help. Maybe before our fight, but not now.

And if Redcedar Hollow is after him ... it's better he doesn't help.

If anything happens to me, he can always demand Bianca.

Besides, Killian is probably deep in the forest doing whatever he does. It's only been a few minutes since Finn was taken, and neither Eva or I—or any of the children, who are too young to have their wolves—can call for help over the pack tie. By the time we grab someone, explain things, wait for them to explain to Killian, then wait for him to show up, it will be too late.

The door to the schoolhouse slams behind me. I run across the yard, darting between garden beds and through the bare orchard. My mind races just as fast.

How would I take Finn if I were an agent of Redcedar Hollow? Noelle, or whatever her name really is, won't think she's being followed yet. She must have either threatened Finn so he'd lie about being sick or given him something so he'd appear sick. If I hadn't come looking for him, the lie would have bought her three or four hours.

The border with Redcedar Hollow is twenty miles from here—half a day's easy, loping run in full werewolf form. A three or four-hour lead would give her plenty of time to get there, but she won't be able to cover as much ground carrying or dragging Finn.

If she has an Alpha hybrid form, she could carry him and run nearly as fast as someone in full wolf form, but I don't think my parents would risk an Alpha blood on a long-term assignment in Shattered Moon. They'd consider that person expendable. Given my parents' beliefs, that should mean she's a regular wolf.

Which in turn means she's probably making her way through the woods, carrying or dragging my brother, as a human. Even if they're meeting someone, the rendezvous will probably be close to the border to minimize their chance of discovery.

Maybe I can catch them. Maybe there's time.

I stumble as I run out of the gate, my chest heaving, and look wildly around. I stand on the gravel road that leads out from the pack house. Everything is still except the tiny birds with gray backs and white bellies foraging among fallen leaves.

There's no sign of Finn. No sign of anyone.

I close my eyes and ground myself, reaching out to catch any fleeting sense of my brother's location that I can. Just like the night Finn escaped and Redcedar Hollow recaptured me, there's the sensation of rushing through the forest. Cold wind blows. I inhale and ... *there*. I feel him!

But he's moving too fast.

I pause for a single second.

I promised Killian he'd never find me running toward Redcedar Hollow. If he finds out …

I scoff. He probably won't even care.

~

## KILLIAN

"You're making the right choice," Deacon says.

I stand at my office window, looking out over the grounds toward the forest. It's just after noon. The sky is pale gray and overcast. We've had a few snowstorms, but it's getting into the ugly part of winter when everything is cold and miserable, and it feels like spring will never come.

"Am I?" I ask absently.

"Yes. We can hide the fact that she's not here until the Conclave, at least. In the meantime, we send emissaries to Redcedar Hollow and start talks to get the sister you were supposed to have in the first place. Vandran said he'll have someone from Dominion Reach collect the wolfless girl in a week."

"She's a woman, and her name is Selene."

This is the answer. Why does it feel like the stupidest thing I've ever done?

Images flash through my mind. Selene wrapped in a blanket, tossing words back and forth with me in front of a fire. Selene as she slept, a few strands of pale hair spilling over her face. Selene in that midnight sky dress, coming down the stairs in the great hall. Selene clinging to me, arching against me, begging for me to touch her on a blanket in the woods.

"Alpha," Deacon says sharply. "Are you closed off from the pack tie?"

Guiltily, I turn toward him. I've kept myself closed off more than I should lately. "I wanted to be able to focus while I sparred with Maddox this morning, and I haven't opened myself to it yet. Why?"

Deacon bares his teeth. "Because I just got a message from one of the caretakers at the school, who says it's from Eva. The boy isn't in class, and Selene was spotted heading into the woods in the direction of Redcedar Hollow."

The bottom drops out of my stomach.

"The Preceptor said this? Eva said this?"

"Yes, Alpha." His mouth draws down in a frown. "I'm afraid every-thing we suspected is real. Selene knows we're closing in, and she's making a run for it."

I should have listened to Deacon and Vandran. I should've known she'd betray me.

I tear from the office without bothering to explain to my Beta where I'm going. Zev and Parker are standing outside. Color is high on Parker's cheeks, and she's breathing like she ran here.

"Alpha," she says, "I've been trying to reach you. Selene said she was just going down to the school—"

"I heard," I snarl. "You two, with me."

"Alpha, what's going on?" Zev asks. Parker must not have told him yet.

"Selene is running, and I'm not going to let her escape."

"Escape?" Parker says. "Alpha—"

"With me," I command.

It's just after noon, but the curse bubbles beneath the surface, the wild, bloody urge to rip and tear and kill without inhibition turning my senses sharp and making me snap and snarl as I burst from the pack house and shift into hybrid form. In seconds, I'm through the gate, then I'm racing through the woods.

I catch her scent, distinct for being strangely indistinct, and I am on her trail.

*"Alpha."* Zev's voice in my mind is even as he and Parker pace me in their full wolf forms. I can tell from his tone he wants me to remain calm, but I am not fucking calm. I've spent these two weeks loathing myself. Two weeks fucking pining for her.

She never cared. She never wanted anything but to betray me. Asher's appearance, his story, it was a convenient excuse for her to put distance between us.

Now she's running. This is proof. This is betrayal.

I won't let her get away with it.

~

## SELENE

It's beyond difficult, running through the woods when there is no path. None of the ground is even. The earth rises and falls in hills and hollows, rocky bluffs, creeks, and unexpected ravines.

Even in the dead of winter, vines and dried plants reach up to twine around my feet and trip me. Some of the dirt is unexpectedly soft. Some is muddy and slippery with the misting rain that permeates the air at this time of year. It turns the trees into a blue-gray backdrop against golden stands of waist-high grass, the deep green of the redcedars, and the burnt orange leaves that still cling to some oak trees.

For a long time, I don't see any sign of a trail. I think I've lost them—I've lost Finn—forever. But then I spy broken branches. Bent, dead grass stalks. Two bald, muddy streaks broken through the leaf litter where someone small planted their feet and had to be dragged.

I nearly weep in relief when I spot the tread of Finn's shoes a few paces later. I'm on the right track.

I'm so bent on finding him, I don't hear the pursuers coming from behind. Not until there's a bone-shaking snarl and something massive and impossibly strong slams me into the cold, wet ground.

"I warned you, Selene," a deep voice I haven't heard for two weeks snarls against my ear. "But you betrayed me, and now I have to kill you."

## KILLIAN

A pale streak darts through the trees ahead. I know it's her. I'd know her in the dark. In mist. In the dreams I chase her through during my too-short hours of sleep. I will always know her.

Selene doesn't shriek as she goes down, only grunts in surprise, landing on her stomach with my claws braced on either side of her head. I lean down and growl against one ear.

"I warned you, Selene. But you betrayed me, and now I have to kill you."

She flips onto her back to face me. Her eyes are wide with fear, but it's gone in an instant, replaced with a perfect dead-eyed mask.

I forgot how beautiful she is, even like this. Fuck me.

"Get off of me, Killian."

157

That dead-eyed look pulls me up short. I rise and shift into a man, then turn to the other two. "Tell the Beta—"

Parker growls, and I look toward Selene just to see her running again.

No. Fuck no.

"Stop." I throw all my Alpha power into the word, letting magic burst from me in a wave that makes Zev and Parker whimper and shudder. Whether she's wolfless or not, an Alpha command that strong should freeze Selene in her tracks. Drop her to her knees.

But she just keeps running.

What the hell?

With a growl that sounds more like the beast than I care to admit, I'm after her. She's got a few seconds' head start. She's dressed in good shoes. I'm barefoot. Half-naked.

I catch her in less than ten strides, wrap my arm around her waist, and slam her against the nearest tree. Her head whips back. I put my free hand behind it. Bark digs into the back as her head impacts my palm. I curl my fingers into her soft silver hair and force her to look at me.

"Where the hell are you going?" I snarl.

That rage I keep catching glimpses of flashes in her eyes. Not fire. Ice.

It's been so long since I've been close to her. So long since I've touched her. That look that makes me want to do something insane. Test her, press against her, trap her body between me and this tree, and kiss her until she's weak-kneed. Drive her as mad as the nights spent by her side, then alone, longing for her, have driven me.

It makes me want to drop to my knees, beg her forgiveness, and tell her everything.

"I'm going to get Finn," she snaps.

Confusion throws cold water over my rage. "Finn?"

I glance around. If Selene is running, Finn should be here. I scent him faintly, but he's not with her.

Only the smallest curl of Selene's lip mars the perfection of her face. "You were right, Alpha. You had a spy in your ranks. Someone from Redcedar Hollow you failed to uncover. But not me. A woman named Noelle. She took Finn from the classroom. Back to *them*."

The fear in that last word devastates me, and I say the stupidest possible thing. "You swore you wouldn't go to them."

"You swore you'd protect him," she retorts. "You claimed he was pack. Said he was yours."

I search her face. I don't know what I see. *"Parker, the boy is missing?"*

*"Yes, Alpha. I thought you knew that. I thought that's why we were out here chasing her."*

Shit.

I trust Parker with my life. If she says Finn is missing, he's missing, but why?

This is a trap. But for whom?

Eva would've told her caretaker to include this in her message to Deacon. Did he make it sound like Selene was running away on purpose? Would he go that far, knowing I might kill her, because he thinks it's best for the pack?

I know the answer, and I don't like it.

Selene sags against the tree. "Kill me if you need to, but Finn is innocent. Please, no matter what, bring him back. You promised."

Trust her, don't trust her. A trap for me, a trap for her. Miscommunication and spies. Finn's kidnapping could be bait, or it could be Frank Beaumont deciding he's not willing to let the boy go, after all.

Either way, he's missing. She's not betraying me. And she's right; I promised.

Gently, I release Selene. "I'll find him. Go back to the pack house. You and I have things to resolve."

Shock widens those uncanny eyes so that the dark rings around her irises show all the way around. "I-it might still be a trap." Her words tumble over each other. "I don't know if Noelle is working alone or with someone or where they're meeting. I don't know if it will be on your land or theirs. I don't—why are you doing this? Why do you believe me?"

"I protect what's mine." The fact that he's Beaumont blood could mean trouble with the Conclave. Frank has the stronger claim to Finn, and if he cared to send someone after the boy, he might care enough to fight for him legally. But Finn disavowed his former pack, which is any wolf's right to do except an Alpha's. I took him in, and I swore an oath.

I shift into my hybrid form, my body growing, muscles rippling, senses sharpening.

Selene pushes away from the tree. "I'm not going back. I'm coming with you! I have a way of finding him."

My gut twists into a knot at the thought of her running into a fight with no experience, no way to defend herself. "No."

"But, Killian!"

I ignore her, gesture at Zev and Parker, and take off. If she can't keep up, she'll turn back. There's plenty of daylight left, but I want to move fast.

We're too far from the pack house to wait for help, but I send a message to Deacon over the pack tie and command him to send every soldier we have into the woods, either as reinforcements or to patrol and make sure this isn't a distraction for something bigger.

*"You were wrong, Beta. She wasn't running. Next time you give me information, you'd better be certain it's right."*

*"What happened to her?"* my Beta asks.

*"She'll be in the woods. Have someone take her home."*

*"You can't go after the boy, Killian,"* Deacon says. *"Crossing into Redcedar Hollow land will violate the treaty."*

*"The Beaumonts violated it first,"* I bite back. *"Finn is part of Shattered Moon. Redcedar Hollow gave him and Selene up, and I claimed them. They are* mine.*"*

*"It's a trap, and you're walking right into it."*

*"So be it, as long as I walk out with the boy."*

# Twenty-One

## KILLIAN

It takes longer than I want to find him. Whoever she is, Noelle is clever. She backtracks through a few streams, and we lose the scent. That loss costs us almost two hours. By the time we're back on the trail, the sun is sinking dangerously low. Anger over being tricked and worry about time make me rush.

Deacon was right; it's a trap, and we run right into it.

There's a place where a ravine intersects the territory border between Redcedar Hollow and Shattered Moon. Noelle's and Finn's scents lead down into it. I pause, but then the tang of iron hits my nose.

Blood. Finn's blood splashed on some of the leaves right where the hills crease into the ravine. A child's sobs rend the air.

"No! No! No! Not you! Leave me alone! Selene! Selene!"

It's Finn. The sound of his pain eradicates coherent thought. I charge in with Parker and Zev at my heels.

I barely notice when I leave my land and cross onto theirs.

One second we're careening along the bottom of the ravine, and the next we're bottlenecked. Four wolves in front of us, four behind. More snarl from above. Even though I still hear Finn, none of them are him or Noelle.

A shadow passes over us, and something heavy drops from above. Suddenly, I can't move.

161

They're nets. Weighted nets loaded with burning, energy-sucking silver.

We fight as the wolves surrounding us stand back and watch the silver do its work. There's so much woven into the fibers that Zev and Parker collapse in under a minute. They whimper as I continue to tear at it and the wolves watching us laugh. Poisonous fire lances through my muscles and my head, sapping my strength, until even I can't stand it.

I fall to my hands and knees. The more I move, the more tangled in the silver-threaded net I become.

I was expecting a trap but not this. There's so much silver. I don't understand how they got it here.

Leaves crunch under someone's feet, and Finn's crying gets louder. A woman comes around a bend in the rock wall. A tall, rangy female with white-tipped gray fur in Alpha hybrid form. Finn struggles in her grasp.

When the woman sees me, she throws her head back and cackles in delight.

"You actually showed up. I can't believe it. You really can't stand the idea of Frank having his kid back, can you?" She grins, her teeth gleaming bloody in the red light of the coming sunset.

I force my thoughts to move through the debilitating pain. "Who are you?"

She dumps Finn on the ground and sashays closer. "Harper Lloyd. A Beta of Redcedar Hollow. We've met."

She's right. She was at the treaty negotiations. I would've recognized her sooner if not for the silver making it feel like needles are being driven into my brain.

"We have a treaty," I growl. "You're breaking it."

She laughs and shrugs one shoulder. "What are you going to do? Tell the Conclave? They're not here." She ambles over and crouches in front of me. "Noelle was only ever supposed to feed us general information. Now we have you. Incredible."

"Yeah, you have me. So let these two go, and the boy."

She scoffs. "And leave me without hostages to control the son of Alaric Bane? The most bloodthirsty Alpha in the world? Yeah, no."

There's a snap and a snarl behind me, then a woman's voice shouting, "Let me through!"

Selene appears flanked by one full wolf and one Alpha hybrid. For an instant, it seems like she's in on this, and my vision goes red. There's no way she could have found Finn this quickly unless she knew where they'd be.

Then Selene sees Harper and stops. Her pale cheeks turn white as snow.

If I thought I'd seen Selene afraid before now, I was wrong. *This is* fear. She's gone still. Silent. I'm not sure she's even breathing. She's like a cornered rabbit, hoping that if she doesn't move, the wolf won't attack.

"B-Beta," Selene says. Her voice is a rasp.

"Selene!" At Harper's side, Finn jumps to his feet and tries to run to her.

Harper trips him, and he goes sprawling right in front of me. I lunge, but one of the big Redcedar Hollow hybrids has the net. He yanks me back. I'm so weak, he slams me to the ground.

Zev tries to get up, but the rust-colored hybrid snaps a kick into his ribs and they crack. When Parker tries to rise, he smacks her across the side of her head with a clawed slap that splits her face. She yelps. Blood gushes. I'm not sure whether she still has her right eye.

"Stop!" I roar.

Every single Redcedar Hollow wolf spasms as if an electric current is jolting through them, but that's all. Since they're bonded to another Alpha, my power over them is limited. Maybe I could overcome it, but not while I'm bound by so much silver.

The Redcedar Hollow Beta smirks at me. "Damn. This net really does work."

She rises and looks at Selene. "Your parents are fucking pissed that you ruined their plans."

"Tragic," Selene says so dryly that it almost disguises her fear. She never takes her eyes off Finn. "We aren't part of Redcedar Hollow anymore. You're in violation of the treaty my parents signed. Release Alpha Darrow and the other two, and give me my brother back."

Harper's lupine lips curl back, revealing long, sharp teeth. "You aren't in a position to demand things, wolfless." She gives Selene an appraising once-over. "You don't look as scrawny as you did last time I saw you."

"Amazing what being allowed to eat enough can do," Selene retorts.

"Hm," Harper says, as if she isn't convinced. "Listen, Selene. For once, you're not on my list. I'm here for the Alpha and the boy. You've had a shitty go of things, and I never really thought that was fair. I won't drag you back to the Hollow. You walk away from this. Go north, or east. You don't need to be tied to this monster. You don't have to worry about the kid—your dad really does want him. You can be one thousand percent free."

Selene is scanning the top of the ravine. Her eyes catch on something, but when Harper says "free," Selene's eyes snap to the Beta. She looks like she's considering the woman's offer. "Free?"

"Yeah."

"Give me my brother."

Harper scoffs. "Or I guess be a stupid hero and I'll just kill you."

"Come on, Harper," Selene's voice takes on a coaxing tone, and it could be delirium, but I swear I see silver luminesce beneath her skin. "You were never as evil as Bianca. You've got the real prize right there in that net. Give me Finn, and I'll leave. You won't hear from me again."

I growl. I may not believe Selene is a spy or that she was in on this, but by her own admission, she is practical. I know who she loves, and it isn't the monster she believes murdered Jackson Beaumont and desecrated his corpse.

If she can walk out of this ravine with only one person, I know who it will be. Hell, if she can walk out of here with three people, it will be Finn, Parker, and Zev. I won't make the list.

Selene may not have set this trap, but she's walked right into what she wants—a chance to be rid of me.

"You know what will happen if you take Finn back," Selene continues. "You know what my mother will do."

Harper looks around at the other wolves. Something seems to pass between them. Then, slowly, a smile creeps across her face. "Okay. You want him? Take him. You have until I'm done with Darrow. Then, for old times' sake, we get to hunt you down. Remember that? Training?"

Selene exhales slowly. "I remember."

"Do we have a deal?"

"Yes." No hesitation. Not even for a second.

I try to wrap my failing brain around it as Selene walks over and crouches in front of me. "Did you hear that, you evil bastard?" she hisses, leaning forward with her hands buried in the leaf litter to glare into my face. "I get to be free."

"Traitor," Parker snarls weakly. The silver is really getting to all of us now. I'm nauseated and ready to collapse. Parker and Zev are lying on their sides, breathing shallowly.

I look into Selene's beautiful, icy eyes and feel nothing but numb, like the moment between a deep slice of a sharp blade and the pain.

"Then be free," I murmur.

I can't stop myself. I have to touch her one last time. My claws catch in the net, and the silver blisters and burns my skin, but I slide my fingers through and brush her face. In hybrid form, my hands are less sensitive, but I remember how soft she is. How warm. "I hope you find what you're looking for."

Something passes across Selene's face, then disappears. She sits back on her haunches. "Let Finn walk to the mouth of the ravine."

"Sure." Harper lets Finn go.

"Selene!" Finn cries. He runs over to her as soon as Harper releases him and throws his arms around his sister. My heart twists. I don't know how I ever thought that I or Shattered Moon would mean a fraction as much to her as he does.

She probably loved Jackson the same.

We were never going to work.

Selene's careful mask wavers again. She leans into Finn's embrace, then says, "Walk past me to the end of the ravine. I'll be there in just a second, okay? Get ready to run as fast as you can."

Finn throws a look at me. "But Alpha Killian—"

Selene's face crumples for a moment. She breathes out harshly and says, "Remember the last time I told you to run on without me? How everything turned out okay?"

Finn nods.

"Everything will be okay this time too."

I can tell she doesn't believe what she's saying, but Finn obeys.

"Looks like you got what you wanted," I say softly.

She finally looks at me then, eyes fierce. She leans forward again, hands buried in the leaf litter. They move, and something in her grip clicks. "I haven't even begun to get what I want."

Harper makes an impatient noise. "Go on, Selene. Get moving. When I chase you down, I want a challenge, for once."

The wolves around us start to move. Incautious. Confident. They know they've won.

Selene tugs the silver net toward her, pulling it tight with one bare hand. It leaves angry welts, but because she's wolfless, it doesn't knock her on her ass.

Then she raises the pocketknife I gifted her from among the leaves and slashes. The blade is razor sharp. It slices a long gash clean through the silver-laced net.

Our eyes lock. Shock robs me of one, then two precious seconds while everyone in the ravine absorbs what just happened.

"Go, Killian," she whispers.

She isn't running. She isn't taking her freedom.

With the last of my strength, I burst through the net, twist around, and claw out the throat of the hybrid closest to me.

"Grab Finn and run," I snarl.

Selene obeys, sprinting toward the mouth of the ravine, where Finn has already disappeared. She's out of sight in seconds, beyond the curve in the ravine's walls.

I can't follow. Zev and Parker aren't free, and I won't leave them.

Four Redcedar Hollow soldiers in full wolf form converge on me. One leaps and sinks its teeth into my shoulder. Two go for my legs. The last for my throat.

I dodge the throat strike, slice and disembowel the one aiming for my shoulder, kick one aiming for my legs, then grab the other in both hands and throw it so hard into the wall of the ravine that stone cracks and little pebbles come rattling down.

The one I kicked rolls several feet down the ravine, then cracks into an exposed boulder and doesn't move. I grab the wolf that initially went for my throat, pull it close as if to embrace it, then jerk its head sharply to the side.

It goes still.

I let it slide from my arms to the ground.

*Breakthemkillthembleedthemeatthem.*

Violence makes my instincts twist and writhe. The sun is sinking, and the curse is so close to the surface. There's no time to think, only move.

The next wolves attack in a blur of motion. Just as quickly as the first group, two are dead, one is dying, and one is lying at my feet, unconscious.

*Breakthemkillthembleedthemeatthem.*

This is how easy killing is. This is why, when they tell me I'm violent, that I'm my father's son, I know they're right.

This is why I can't let anyone get close to me.

The wolves I dazed come for me again just as I move to rip the silver net from Zev and Parker. This time, the enemy soldiers attack from either side of me. I underestimate the impact of touching the silver and hit one knee. One of the wolves clamps its teeth into my arm, tearing at flesh, and I howl.

Just as I get the net off my friends, a blow slams into the side of my head, sending me falling to one side.

The Beta has joined the fray.

I don't have a chance to recover before Harper leaps on me and drives her claws deep into my side, just below my ribs, sending pain searing through my body. I stagger to my feet, but she jumps back as I swipe, then dodges behind me and rakes her claws down my back from shoulder to hip, slicing deep.

First there's numbness, then there's pain and the wet warmth of bleeding.

Too much blood too fast. I hit my knees again and don't have the strength to rise.

The monster boils beneath the surface. Yellow fog begins to roll across my mind.

I've always wondered whether the curse would let me die. It seems like I'm about to find out.

The Beta of Redcedar Hollow looms over me and grins. She has no idea what she's done.

"I'm going to rip out your throat, take your pack, and give it to my Alphas. This war is over."

My breath whistles. I can't inhale all the way. Life streams out of me. I feel the biting cold of death.

*Breakthemkillthembleedthemeatthem.*

There's no hope for Parker and Zev, but, gods or fates, let Selene and Finn be far enough away. Let them escape.

Then a voice rings out through the sunset, coming from above. "The war is already over. That's what the treaty was for, you dumb bitch."

Both Harper and I look up in time to see a massive boulder teeter over the edge of the ravine.

It falls right on top of Harper. Bones crunch. She screams, pinned beneath it. She's not dead, but her torso is mostly crushed. She won't be walking out of here.

The yellow fog flickers, but it doesn't fade completely. Instead, darkness rises in its place.

Harper's scream is the last thing I hear before I black out.

# Twenty-Two

## SELENE

I make Finn drag away the silver net. Since he's a kid and wolves don't get their magic until puberty, silver doesn't affect him yet. Then I make him wait with Parker. She's catching her breath on a nearby mossy boulder, her face a mess of red.

Zev looks just as bad as she does, but he's tending to Killian, who's lying unconscious on the ground. He's lost so much blood.

"Will he make it?" I ask.

Zev looks haunted but nods. "Yeah." The bodies of the Redcedar Hollow wolves are all around us. Harper wheezes, not yet gone. I keep my gaze fixed on Killian and Zev. Seeing Harper—one of Bianca's cronies and my worst childhood tormentors—has been bad enough. I don't want to know whether I recognize any of the others.

Zev jerks his head toward the sky, which is rapidly darkening. "Once he wakes up, we're fucked."

"Don't worry about that. I just need to do one thing first."

I go to where Harper lies dying. Blood foams at her mouth. She will have already told my parents what happened here today through the pack tie.

I sit on the ground close enough to talk but out of her reach. "This was an act of war. You tell them I said that. Tell them I'll make sure the Conclave knows."

She laughs, which turns into a wracking cough that splatters blood everywhere. "I don't know what you're talking about. I acted alone. Completely unsanctioned by my Alphas. In fact, you'll find dozens of wolves who will testify that I was on the verge of going completely rogue."

Anger crackles through me. I bare my teeth. "No one will believe them. They'll know."

She laugh-coughs again. "They'll know, but they won't care. Of anyone alive, Selene, you should know there's no such thing as justice. Only strength."

She props herself on an elbow and stage whispers, "Your parents really don't have a clue, you know. They want to sit and wait. Bianca is the one pushing us forward. She's the future of the pack. Once she's in charge, it's over for Shattered Moon and for you."

"Maybe. But you won't be there to see it." The hilt of the knife Killian gave me is smooth and warm in my hand. I flip it around and, with the practiced ease that comes from years of slaughtering chickens, pigs, and rabbits, grip Harper by the chin, pull her head back, and cut her throat.

Blood gushes over my hand. I make a sound, drop the knife, and have to scramble in the bloody mud to pick it up again.

I have never killed a person before.

I can't tell yet whether I'm freaking out or whether I feel nothing at all.

"Selene!" Zev calls, voice urgent.

I run to Killian. Zev has sweatpants on. He's pulled an extra shirt out of the satchel he carries and torn it up to bandage the worst of Killian's wounds.

Now a tremor runs through Killian's body. He's still hybrid, silver-tipped dark fur stretched over miles of taut, strong muscle. Another tremor runs through him. I drop to my knees and take his hand, pressing the rough pad of his palm to mine.

"Don't lose yourself," I whisper fiercely.

I can't believe what he did for me tonight. He could have let Finn go. It would've been easier.

Instead, he kept his promise.

What do you do with a man who kills one brother but saves another?

I look where Finn is helping Parker mop up her face. Thankfully, she still has both eyes, but she and Zev both are going to have some gnarly scars. We need to get them all to Dr. Bennett. Even more urgently, we need to get off Redcedar Hollow land and away from here.

We crossed their border; I don't trust them not to cross ours.

"Can someone come get us?" I ask, holding tightly to Killian's hand.

Zev nods. "Killian summoned them after we parted ways with you. Warriors are coming here to guard the border, and Sofia is bringing a van to meet us on the nearest road, if they can get through the overgrowth. But we need to move. Redcedar Hollow might have people stationed closer to here than the soldiers in their pack house."

It's the most words I've ever heard the man say at once.

"Selene!" Parker must be settled because Finn runs over and throws himself at me. I catch him with one arm, still making sure I don't let go of Killian, and squeeze him to me, breathing him in. Cookies and sweat and dirt.

"Finn, you did so well. You were so brave."

He leans back from me and sniffs, swiping his arm across his nose. He and I had a brief reunion at the top of the cliff when I snuck up there, desperate to find a way to help. These hills are full of cracked limestone cliffs like the ones that make up the walls of the ravine. A strong, long branch and a loose stone hanging half-over the edge of the bluff were all I needed.

Harper is gone. One bully down.

"I don't feel brave," Finn whispers. "I was scared, and everyone is hurt. I'm still scared."

I clear brown curls from his dirt-streaked face. "Brave is being afraid and doing it anyway," I say.

He nods. "You always tell me. I remember."

Parker appears with a T-shirt bandage wrapped around her head. "Let's get out of here."

I've never heard her worried instead of irritated before. It's enough to get me on my feet. I take Finn's hand. Zev hefts Killian with my other hand still in his.

"All right. Let's go."

The next twenty minutes are a hellish walk through the increasingly dark woods. Every twig snap, every whisper of breeze seems like it has to be Redcedar Hollow catching up to us. The night is freezing, and Finn is tired, and soon I've got him on one hip despite the fact that I've run farther today than I ever have, and he's more than half my size.

When I almost trip and drop Finn and lose my grip on Killian, Parker comes and takes Finn from me.

Finally, we stumble out onto a busted old road. Winter grasses have popped through the cracks. Saplings have grown up through the holes in some places. Relief just about overwhelms me when I see the beat-up old pack SUV there waiting for us with Sofia behind the wheel. She jumps out and wraps Parker in her arms. Sofia tries to examine her mate's wounds, but Parker won't let her.

"We'll take care of it at home."

We pile into the SUV. Parker is in the passenger seat with Finn on her lap, Zev crammed all the way in the back, and Killian and I are in the middle.

Killian wakes up on the ride. I know when he does because his fingers tighten around mine. Then he shrinks down into his human form. He lets out a breath and leans his head back against the seat, exposing the long, strong line of his neck.

"Finn?" he whispers.

"We saved him," I say.

The car bumps along. He doesn't open his eyes. "She offered you everything. You could've left. You might have gotten away."

His voice is low. I doubt the others can hear him over the rumble of the car, though they are wolves, so maybe they can.

"Maybe I could have."

"Why didn't you?"

"I didn't want to."

It's not a real answer, but his hand tightens on mine, and I squeeze back.

I don't feel like I actually breathe until we're inside the walls of the pack compound, then pulling up to the castle. Killian insists he can walk inside. Zev throws one of the Alpha's arms over his shoulder and helps him because Killian is wrong.

The whole time, his other hand is grasped in mine. Neither of us lets go. I don't think it's just because we can't.

Half an hour later, I touch Finn's sleeping face and whisper, "Good night." Eva has him in her arms, and she waves to both of us as she takes Finn to her apartment to sleep. Killian and I take turns cleaning up, like the very first night when he brought me in from the cold.

It's strange and awkward to stand and hold someone's hand with your back to them while they shower off, then you do, but we manage.

Dr. Bennett, who has already taken care of Parker and Zev at Killian's insistence, comes to see him. Killian is medicated with herbs and Alpha saliva, then stitched. His wounds, like Parker's, are deep, but he should be recovered from them within a couple of hours.

The doctor declares that what we both need is rest, then leaves.

Just like the first night, Killian and I are alone in his room, holding hands.

As we sit on the bed, I wonder randomly whether Claudia ever told him what I did. There's still a gaping hole in the music room wall, but he hasn't been here to see it.

That power would've been nice to have during the confrontation with Harper. I still don't know what it was or whether I'll ever figure it out. Right now, I'm just relieved we all lived.

"You saved Finn," I whisper.

"We saved him."

"I didn't kill eight wolves." Eight, but not Noelle. She disappeared.

"Zev said you killed the Beta. Are you all right?"

I exhale raggedly. "How can you ask me that? How can you be worried about my feelings after the way we left things?"

He shrugs and lets his head fall back. He sounds so tired. "I don't know, Selene. I've tried, but I can't not worry about you. I can't not care."

My jaw trembles. Tears prick the backs of my eyes. "I hated it. Killing her. I don't want to do it again. But if I have to, I will."

"You won't have to."

"You don't know that. Do you still think I'm a spy?"

"No."

"Do you have the binding for our hands?"

Killian finally looks at me. His topaz eyes are unreadable. He's got a few bandages wrapped around his torso and some clean sweatpants on, but his chest is still bare. The expanse of scarred skin taut over lean muscle is a lot to take in, so I look down at our joined hands instead.

"Nightstand," he says.

I can reach over to the nightstand and retrieve the beige roll of self-adhesive bandage.

"Same way as usual?" I ask.

He gives the bandages a weary look. "We don't have to do this, Selene."

"Yes, we do. If I let go, you'll go on a rampage. This is our only option for tonight."

He tenses. "I can stay up in a chair by the bed. That's an option."

I scoff. "How many more things about tonight will be the same as the first one, do you think? You're not sitting up in a damn chair. You saved my brother."

"Does that make up for what I did to the other one?"

I go still, then look up at him. All of the wanting, the aching, the emptiness of two weeks without him hits me, and despite his words, all I want is to fall into his arms. "You want to talk about this now?"

"No, I want you to rest. I'll—"

"I swear if you bring up that damn chair again, Killian, I will stab you with my knife."

He grunts a humorless laugh. "Okay."

I close my eyes and try to ground myself. "Tell me what happened to Jackson. When Asher confronted us in the woods, you didn't actually say."

His hand tightens convulsively around mine. He's quiet for a long moment. Then, as if he's finally putting down a heavy weight, he says, "That's because I don't want Asher to know. I don't want anyone in Grace's family to know."

Surprise and anticipation prickle over my skin. "Know what?"

Killian is silent for so long, I wonder whether he'll answer. Then he says, "Asher is wrong. Grace was 'cheating' on me. I knew, and I didn't care. We were never really more than friends."

# Twenty-Three

## SELENE

E verything in me is strung tight, waiting to hear what he'll say next. "Never more than friends? I thought you loved her."

"I did. Deeply. But not romantically. I chose Grace as my mate because I trusted her. Vandran kept talking about how powerful I was going to be. I'd been around the Warlord of the Fall Line Protectorate long enough that I knew I was about to be surrounded by people who only wanted things from me, just like he is. People I couldn't trust. Grace agreed to marry me and be my mate so I'd have someone to watch my back. We did sleep together a few times, and it was fun, but there was never anything there but deep mutual affection."

His words wash over me, hard to grasp. Hard to place within the history I thought I knew. "I don't understand. If you weren't jealous, what happened with Grace and Jackson?"

Killian licks his lips. "Your brother came to Shattered Moon on a 'diplomatic' visit from your parents, which really meant he'd come to deliver a handful of veiled threats. While he was here, he and Grace discovered they were fated mates."

I press a hand to my mouth. "But you two had already marked each other."

"True, but mate bonds can be broken. Everything about mate bonds

177

is relatively straightforward. With a fated mate or someone you've already marked, you just ... say it. Accept them or reject them. Though rejecting a mate bond does have physical consequences. The only challenging part is that you have to mean it with your whole soul."

"I still don't understand. If you weren't jealous, then it was the curse, wasn't it?" Relief washes over me. "Eva doesn't know about Grace and Jackson. Asher thought you had assumed the wrong thing. Her family doesn't believe she would have cheated on you."

"I don't know if you can call it cheating if she had my full support."

"But it was the curse? That's how they died."

He hesitates, and for a moment, it feels like there's something else. But then he nods. "Yeah. It was the curse. And what Asher said I did to Jackson's body ... I didn't. I need you to know, even cursed, I've never done that."

"Then why did he say it?" Asher claimed Killian ate parts of Jackson after killing him, something that is unspeakable among wolves.

Killian hesitates. "It was...there was a lot of gore."

I flinch. Even so, hearing he didn't actually consume my brother is a massive relief.

I toss the bandages aside. Killian watches them like he's confused as to why they're suddenly on the floor. "What are you doing?"

He's not wearing a shirt. I'm in only a loose T-shirt and shorts with a comfortable sports bra underneath. "Could you sleep on your right side?"

Killian hesitates, then nods.

I could make tonight as puritanical as every other night has been except for our ill-fated picnic. But the bald truth is, I'm exhausted, he smells incredible, and I've never been held, not really, not even by Sam, the wolfless at Redcedar Hollow I had a fling with.

I want to know what it feels like. I want to know what it feels like for it to be Killian.

"You won't say anything to Eva?" he asks. "Or Maddox? Or Asher, if that bastard ever shows his face again?"

"He tried to ruin this. He almost succeeded."

Killian just shrugs. I can see what Grace meant to him in the concern on his face.

This conversation is a double-edged sword. On the one hand, he didn't murder Jackson in cold blood. On the other, it stings, realizing how much he loved her, even though he claims they were only ever friends.

I wonder what it's like to have this man love you that much. "Your secret is mine. I won't tell."

Carefully, maintaining contact with him with one hand, then the other, I pull off the baggy shirt.

Killian's breath goes ragged when I toss it to the side. His eyes rake down my body. Desire darkens his gaze. But then his brows pinch and anger flashes in his eyes. He touches my shoulder, then my ribs, with impossibly gentle fingers.

I'm confused until I realize he's touching my scars. In all the times we've been close, I've never been this exposed.

"Who did this to you?" he growls.

My cheeks flush. "Bianca. My parents. The pack." My body is covered in a lifetime of scars.

What with the banked rage in his eyes, I'm glad the thick strap of the sports bra covers the worst one—the puckered old pink injury in my shoulder from my father. I can't remember when he gave it to me exactly, but I'm pretty sure it was just after I discovered I was wolfless. The only other time I ever tried to escape.

That ominous rumbling starts in Killian's chest. I put a hand over his heart. It beats steadily beneath my palm. "Stand down, Alpha. It's over."

It's a lie. I'll have to face my family and former pack again as soon as next month at the Conclave. I take a calming breath and tell myself it will be fine.

Killian doesn't miss my reaction. "Is it?"

"Yes," I insist, even though it's still a lie. Some hurt is never finished.

"I won't let them touch you. Never again." Killian's eyes are dark, his voice possessive. Heat flares in my belly, embers sparking into flame.

He pushes silvery hair out of my eyes and hooks it behind my ear, and, god, I have missed him.

I press his hand against my cheek, holding him there, uncertain when lust turned into this aching longing just to be near him. "I'm sorry for what I said after our engagement dinner." About Grace and waiting for him to gut me. "It was cruel. I can't—" My throat closes over my words. "I'm sorry."

He caresses my cheek with his thumb, and I lean into his touch.

"I'm sorry I made you afraid enough to say it. That I didn't talk to you about the spy. That I didn't tell you the truth about Grace sooner. And for what I said."

"Thank you, but all of that is still no excuse for me to say what I did."

He traces his fingers lightly over the scars on my arm, sending goosebumps racing over my skin. "Fear this deep"—his touch moves to another set of scars on my ribs—"this old"—another scar along the base of my neck—"this proven isn't an excuse. It's a reason."

He captures my hand and presses my fingers to a raised white line that slashes from the base of his neck over his collarbone to his chest. "I would know."

He would. This scar is one of hundreds. A lifetime of survival written on his flesh in the same language it's written on mine.

I make my voice light. "Well. We should sleep. Tomorrow, things are back to normal, right? The way they were the first two weeks?"

He shakes his head. "No."

Fear and shock zing from my stomach to my chest. "No?"

He dips his head, coming close. "I'm not doing this anymore. I'm not pretending I don't care."

Then he presses his lips to mine.

It begins as a gentle exploration. Maybe because we're both worn out, Killian thinks it's going to stay that way.

No, thank you.

I open my mouth, inviting him in. He takes the invitation, his tongue brushing mine, his teeth nipping my lower lip before he deepens the kiss. Heat blossoms in my core. I let out a startled squeal as he lifts me, manhandling me into his lap, then turning my body so I straddle him.

"Killian," I breathe.

His fingers trail lines of fire down my neck, then lower, between my breasts and over my racing heart. He flattens his palms against my back, shifting so our bodies press together. I sink against him and discover he's already hard. His erection presses against my center right where I want it, impossibly good. I make helpless, breathy little sounds.

"You didn't have to save me," he whispers. His eyes search mine. "You could have run with Finn. You could've been free. Give me the real reason why."

"You could have refused to go after him. Why didn't you?"

"I protect what's mine," he says, his voice rough.

"So do I."

Our mouths find each other, and nothing has ever been as right as this. I skim my hands over his back, noting that the slashes seem to be almost healed. He had that deep wound in his side, too, which could take a little longer to be completely better. He's strong, but I want to be careful.

I slide my fingers over hot skin and hard muscle, up to his shoulders and the back of his neck, and into his soft, dark hair. He makes a low sound of pleasure and leans into my touch. I trail kisses along his jaw and down his neck, his stubble scratchy against my lips.

He moves his hand down, over my back, rough skin caressing my stomach before his fingers dip into the waistband of my shorts.

I'm not wearing anything underneath. He makes another sound of pleasure as he realizes it, then slides his hands fully beneath the fabric to grip my ass. I rock against him as he kisses me again.

Then he's picking me up and laying me on the soft bed, his body covering mine. His breath catches in a little wince of pain.

"Killian—"

"Worth it," he says against my mouth. His hand trails over my sports bra, and I gasp as he palms my breast through the fabric, sweeping his thumb in circles around my pebbled nipple. He kisses down my neck and chest, down my bare abdomen. Need twists tighter in my core as he strokes, kisses, sucks until I'm panting and writhing beneath him.

Finally, he pushes up the fabric of my bra and closes his mouth over one aching peak. I cry out and arch against him, searching for friction. But he puts one big hand on my stomach and presses me down, making me lie there and take what he gives me until I'm practically sobbing with pleasure and want.

He sits back, and his hands move over my legs, then underneath, stroking the sensitive skin behind my knees, then caressing back up my thighs. He hooks his fingers in the waistband of my shorts. I lift my hips, and he pulls them down and off. Then he's over me, kissing my belly, the lines of my hips, down to the juncture of my thighs.

Killian mutters a few filthy curses as he takes my ankle in his big hand and lifts my leg over his shoulder, opening me to him. He kisses my inner thigh with a pleased hum. "You're perfect."

I feel exposed. Vulnerable. With any other person, I would hate it.

But with him, some unseen force overrides common sense, tempting me to trust him. Promising me I'm safe as long as he's there.

Then his mouth is on me, and I don't think at all.

His tongue is first, circling my clit, lazy and languid, like he has all the time in the world. He spreads me, then tilts his head to get a better angle and closes his lips over the sensitive place. I throw my head back and cry out, fisting my hands in the sheets.

He devours my pussy as voraciously as he did my mouth. It's so unspeakably good to be touched by him like this again. He slides one finger, then a second deep into my heat, penetrating me, stretching me, filling me.

I feel possessed by him. Claimed. Utterly his in a way I've never wanted or even known I could be. I want to fight against it, but my mind is too hellbent on reveling in every sensation. Anticipation winds through my limbs, arches my back, curls my fingers into his hair. I need this. Him. Almost. I'm so close. I'm so close. I'm—

"Killian!" I break and drown beneath a killing wave of pleasure, the orgasm shattering me like I'm made of brittle glass. Just when I think it will end, he crooks his fingers and strokes a place deep inside me that has me screaming and coming all over again.

When the ecstasy fades, I am a puddle of boneless, satisfied jelly that I think used to be a person.

Killian does that pleased hum again and pulls back, one hand wrapped around my hip. Then he moves up to the pillow, his skin sliding against mine. He wraps his arms around me, tangles our legs, then carefully rolls to his uninjured side and tucks my head beneath his chin.

It takes a long time for my brain to function properly again. Back at Redcedar Hollow, I understood sex and liked it well enough when I had it, but this ... it's not the same.

"That was really good."

"Good. That was the goal."

I huff an incredulous laugh at how matter-of-fact he is when he just melted all of me. "I'll be sure to give you full marks on your approval survey, Alpha."

"Approval survey?"

"Yeah, I heard that's something you liberated, free-thinking packs that treat all wolves like people have."

He chuckles. "I'll get Sofia on it."

I would also like to get on it.

I pull back from him just enough to trail my hand down his chest, down his stomach. He watches me, luminescent topaz irises bare rings around his pupils like two miniature solar eclipses. He's not wearing anything but soft gray sweatpants, and when I press my palm against him, he bucks into my hand.

I love it. I want it. I want to watch this perfect man, this powerful Alpha, utterly lose control as I unravel him as thoroughly as he unraveled me. But when I reach for his waistband, he traps my hand against the hard plane of his stomach.

I look up at him, surprised.

Roughly, Killian says, "It's enough."

I grind against him and watch the muscles in his jaw flex and his eyes close as he fights for control.

"It's clearly not," I tease.

He doesn't smile. Instead, he pulls my hand away from him and strokes my cheek. "I told you. Strong emotion can trigger the curse. I don't trust myself, and I refuse to hurt you."

He's serious about this. "That's not fair."

This time, I'm rewarded with the smallest, most tender of smiles. This all feels so new, so fragile, that I find myself memorizing it in case I never see it again.

"I've survived less-fair things." He brushes a kiss across my lips. "We should sleep."

"Do we need to bind our arms?"

Killian's eyes wander down my naked body. "Not if you stay like this. I won't let go."

He's a monster. My enemy. The son of a tyrant everyone swears he wants to become.

But I have never felt this safe.

I settle against him, our bare chests pressed together. "Good?"

His arm flexes, and he pulls me flush against him. He buries his face in my hair and inhales. Our fingers intertwine.

"Good," he whispers.

～

## *KILLIAN*

Nothing between us is the same. For once, things seem ... okay.

An ache settles beneath my ribs. I told her I didn't want to pretend, and I don't. But there are some things that haven't changed. That can never change.

Some secrets I can keep because Selene has no wolf.

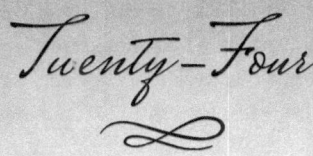

*Twenty-Four*

*New Moon*

## KILLIAN

The afternoon before my second wedding, I sit on a wooden bench in the pack graveyard. My elbows are on my knees, and I toy with the worn leather cord wrapped around my wrist multiple times. Overhead, the clouds send down little flurries of snow that hint at a bigger storm to come.

The pack graveyard sits on a rise a little ways from the castle. It's tucked in a small bowl of land next to the high wall with its own narrow wrought iron gate to the forest beyond. Muted light slants across the gravestones, filtering through the spreading branches of the ancient oaks that surround it in a protective ring. Separated from the bustle of the castle as it is, the air here feels weighty. Sacred.

It's been two weeks since we saved Finn. Two weeks of restful days, evenings with him and Selene, like we're a family, and nights doing everything I can to make Selene come harder than I did the night before

It's been easy to convince myself that these moments of peace aren't as delicate as a thin crust of perfect snow over churned mud.

It will be fine. In a few hours, I'll be in the great hall, and Selene will be mine in name. Mine, even if we can never mate bond.

Mine, even though it's as dangerous as ever for anyone to be close to me.

I lean forward and brush snow off the gravestone I sit beside. "I'm trying to keep my promise to Asher. And to you."

Silence answers me. Grace's headstone is pink granite speckled with blue and shimmering with flecks of quartz. It's one of dozens in this quiet, oak-shrouded hollow, most left here from my father's time.

It's not a lie. It doesn't matter whether all I can see in my mind are Selene's uncanny too-big eyes. Doesn't matter whether my memories are consumed with her taste. With the feel of her body. The sounds she makes when I make her come. The slow insanity of not letting myself have what I crave because I fear the curse.

Tonight, though, it's at its weakest. I can be with her and she'll be safe.

I think. I wish I could be sure, but she doesn't want to wait.

*Here lies Grace Quinn-Darrow, Alpha Lady of Shattered Moon.* The dates on the stone show that she was twenty when she died. So fucking young. Barely grown. Gone.

I grip the locket, squeezing hard so that the frigid metal bites into my flesh, like the pain can absolve me of Grace's death. But it can't. Nothing can.

"We deserved more than two years," I whisper. "You deserved more. God, I fucking miss you. I'm sorry."

The graveyard is one of the few places with a gate on the outer wall. I've come here every day for the last two weeks, left it open to the woods, and waited.

Asher hasn't returned. He hasn't been reckless enough to leave a scent I can track either. He's better than he was when he left. More careful. More highly trained.

I'm not the only one who's changed in the last five years.

The distant sounds of Deacon drilling the pack hit my ears, and I smell the faint scent of food for tonight being prepared in the kitchen. I've gotten so used to keeping my distance from all of them. So used to being exhausted. To being hunted within my own mind. Being with Selene has returned a feeling of normalcy I thought I'd never have again. I could lie and say that's why I enjoy her company. Why I already care so damn much.

"I'm keeping my promise," I say again. "I can't take her as a mate."

But I'm not keeping it at all in any way that matters, and the closer

184

the wedding gets, the more I feel for Selene, the more that knowledge eats away at me.

Peals of children's laughter break the silence. I stand so I can see down to the castle. Despite the snow, kids are darting around the yard near the school, playing some game with the younger caretakers.

A smile plays across my lips. "Remember when we first came here? There were four kids in the pack. They couldn't play outside because the walls were broken and it was too dangerous."

"It's still dangerous. You should keep this shit closed. Anyone could just wander in."

I'm on my feet in an instant, turning, knowing who'll be there.

Asher.

The setting sun casts the space below the wall in deep shadow. Like that night weeks ago, at first, I see only his eyes, blue in the dark.

Then my former best friend and Beta emerges.

The last time I saw Asher in his human form, both of us were twenty-two. Five years have changed him. He's no longer coltishly lanky but honed and lean. His skin is bronzed, like he spends all his time outside. The wicked smile that had people falling all over themselves when we were teens remains, but it's taken on a razor-edge of cruelty. He doesn't walk; he stalks. As if when I knew him he was domesticated and has since gone feral.

But he's not all different. He still keeps his hands stuffed into his pockets, his chestnut brown hair still falls into eyes as blue as his mother's, and his father's sword, its hilt wrapped in braided red leather, is still in the same place on his hip, where he's worn it since before I ever knew him.

Power courses through me, the involuntary reaction of one Alpha being confronted with another Alpha who's strong enough to pose a threat.

I move between him and the path through the graveyard that leads to the rest of Shattered Moon.

He shakes the hair out of his face and gives me that shit-eating grin I know so well, but unlike when we were younger, it doesn't reach his eyes. "Did you think I left?"

"I hoped, but I know you better than that."

"Oh, yeah?" Asher moves too casually to the bench and sits. I keep my position between him and my pack, but his eyes don't leave his sister's tombstone. His throat works, and he finally takes his hands from his pockets. He runs his fingers over the top of the stone. "Hey, Gracie."

The words are a broken whisper I'm not supposed to hear.

"It's a political alliance, Asher. The Conclave forced me into it. Selene didn't ask for it."

"Right. I thought that might be true, but then I heard a rumor you've got her screaming your name at night once again. She changed her mind about fucking a wife-killing cannibal, I guess." His hand still rests on top of his sister's tombstone, his thumb running back and forth over the polished granite.

I'd ask who he's been talking to, but I know it's Maddox. He always idolized his older brother. If he caught Asher's scent, he wouldn't rest until he found him. What I want to know is when and how Maddox did it without me knowing and how he tracked Asher when I couldn't.

I'm going to have to remove him from Selene's guards.

"She's wolfless. I'm not taking a mate because she can't form a mate bond. She was a servant at Redcedar Hollow. Fuck, Ash, the way they treated her ..." I stop. I'm talking too much.

Asher pauses. Then he finally looks at me. "Is that going to save her when you snap?"

I blanch. Asher still doesn't know about the curse. Maddox is the only person who knows that he's had contact with. If his younger brother tried to tell him, Asher clearly didn't believe him.

Asher rises and walks toward me. Casual. Easy. He stops a few feet away and looks beyond me toward the pack house. His eyes scan the castle, the grounds. "You need your alliance to keep my mom and brother safe? Fine. Marry her. But if you care about her at all, Killian, send her away."

"Asher—"

I don't see him move, but suddenly, his sword is in his hand, the blade pressed against my throat. The silver hisses and burns. "Do you want her alive?" he snarls. "Or do you want to see her guts dragged out all over the snow like my sister's?"

The blade cuts. Warm blood oozes from my neck.

Asher's eyes go distant, and he looks over my shoulder toward the wall, like he's seeing something. I look, but there's nothing there.

He nods, as if now he's agreeing with the unseen person, then leans in, merciless. "You don't deserve happiness when you took Grace's. Send this one away, or she dies. Probably by your hand, but if not, by mine.

At least if it's me, she won't fucking suffer. But you will. You have no idea how many times I've already killed you."

"Alpha!"

It's a child's voice. Little footsteps crunch through the snow. At the realization that one of the kids is coming, my aura flares, smashing against Asher's. I feel his give, like a single dent in a steel shield. He staggers back and hits the stone wall hard enough to make him grunt.

"Stay away from my pack."

Asher straightens, brushes dust from his jacket, and gives me that unfeeling version of his old smile. "You've got two days before I start hunting," he says as he turns away. "Enjoy your honeymoon."

Then he's gone. I swipe my hand across the cut on my neck. It burns, and it isn't healing. Fucking steelborn and his silver-edged sword. He didn't even give me the chance to tell him what I'm planning, just ran his own mouth. Typical.

"Alpha!"

When I turn, Finn stands just a few feet beyond the bench next to Grace's grave. "Are you okay? I can run and get help!"

I lift the collar of my black coat and wipe at the blood. I'm probably just smearing it, making it worse. "No, Finn. I'm okay."

"Who was that?" His brown eyes are huge.

I go down on a knee so I'm eye to eye with him. "Just someone I used to know. You shouldn't be over here. You know it's not safe to be alone by me."

Finn looks mutinous. "Selene is alone by you all the time!"

I let out a humorless laugh and rub my face. "Selene is grown up. And she's different."

Finn shifts from foot to foot. He's got a piece of paper clutched in his hands. He ducks his head and begins to shuffle away. "Okay. S-sorry —I—sorry."

I should let him run from me. I know it's better for him to be afraid, but he thinks I don't want him here, and I hate that. "Wait. What do you have?"

"I wanted to give you a present. To say thank you for when you saved my life."

Something hard lodges between my throat and chest, making it hard to speak. My brow furrows in confusion. "Present?"

"I made it in school today." He takes a cautious step toward me and thrusts out the paper in his hand.

It's folded in half like a card. The front has a crayon drawing of three stick figures. One is short with curly brown hair, and one is a little taller with hair outlined in black and colored in white. The last one is tall, almost giant compared to the other two, with dark hair and all-black clothing.

I run my thumb over the page. "Is this ...?"

Finn pokes at the picture, suddenly excited. "This is me, and this is Selene, and this is you. We're all happy because you saved us, and you're happy because Selene helped you fight and saved you!"

Words catch in my throat. The card is made of the cheap paper the kids use for coloring, and there's something lumpy folded inside.

I open it to reveal a string made of knotted threads like the bracelets he and Selene both wear. His in bright primary colors, hers in cool jewel tones. This one is so huge, Finn could probably wear it as a necklace. It's blue, crimson, and white—the colors of Shattered Moon—threaded with the same brighter red as his bracelet and purple as hers.

The card reads, *Thank you for helping my big sister and me! We are so happy! Thank you for letting us stay! We love our new pack!*

Underneath the words, which are only a little misspelled, is a drawing of a crescent moon with the bottom breaking into pieces. It's the crest of Shattered Moon.

Holy shit.

I've interacted with Finn several times and eaten dinner with him nearly every night for the last couple of weeks, but we've always had someone else as a buffer. I've never spoken to him alone.

I understand suddenly, sharply, why Selene is so determined to protect him.

With numb fingers, I pluck the colorful threads from behind the tape, doing my best not to tear the paper. "What's this?"

"Friendship bracelet." Finn's cheeks are red. He won't meet my gaze, but he thrusts his wrist out so I can see his. "I made them for me and Selene when we were ... before. Caretaker Miss Callie got me some threads and said I can make more during craft time. I wanted to give the first one to you."

My chest feels like it's in a vise. First Selene puts cracks in my walls, and now Finn demolishes them.

I want to break the Alphas of Redcedar Hollow for making them suffer.

"I'll wear it," I say.

When I try to wrap the bracelet around my wrist and fail, Finn shuffles forward and ties the knot for me.

"If you do it like this," he says as he ties one end, then the other, "it will slide big and small, so it can grow with you when you shift."

Holy shit, I am undone. "Thank you."

There are more footsteps in the snow, and I glance up to see Eva striding between headstones. "Killian, of course you're out—oh! Finn. There you are! Miss Callie was going out of her mind looking for you. All the other kids just went inside for hot chocolate. Then it's time to get ready for the big ceremony!"

"Chocolate?" Finn's dark eyes brighten. He pats my arm and says, "Thanks, Alpha. I'll see you later!" Then he dashes off past Eva, through the garden, and through the door that leads to the pack house's kitchen.

I rise and rub the bracelet on my wrist, unable to look at Eva. She suddenly moves forward, puts a hand under my chin, and pushes it up. She touches the blood welling from the cut, then rubs it between her fingers as she lets out a curse with a harsh breath. "That boy paid you a second visit, did he?"

"He came to tell me he intends on holding me to my promise," I say.

She rolls her eyes. "Maddox told me as much. Apparently, he can't be bothered to visit his mother. He knows I'd knock some sense into him if he did."

"Eva—"

"Stop, Killian. We both know what you're about to say."

I let out a brief, helpless laugh. Eva always did have a way of cutting through bullshit. Grace was the same. "And we both know I'm right. He's right. I'm too close to her. It's dangerous. If we keep doing this night after night for years, something will go wrong. One night, the bindings will come loose, or we'll forget them—"

"What do you think you're going to do, Killian? Send her away?"

I'm silent.

Eva makes a sound of disgust and throws her hands into the air. "You claimed her as a mate. You made her promises."

"On paper, for the sake of the treaty. It's political."

"You and Grace were political," Eva snaps. "You were friends who married for the sake of convenience, and it was silly. Both of you wanted out within six months. You and Selene are something else."

"I—" I blink. "You knew that? About me and Grace?"

"Killian, I am her mother. And I practically raised you from twelve to seventeen for all the good it did."

Her words cut sharper than Asher's blade, and I have no defense. "I promised."

Eva snorts. "I reject your promise, Killian Darrow. Grace was mine more than she was ever yours. I don't blame you for what happened, and neither would she."

She takes my face in her soft hands. "Asher is her brother. I am her mother. *I* get to say when you are forgiven, and I say you never did anything wrong. You didn't kill my daughter. Whoever put this curse on you did."

She's said it before, so many times. And like so many times before, it tears me open and makes me bleed because she doesn't know all of it. Even if she guesses that Grace wanted to end our relationship, she doesn't know about Grace and Jackson Beaumont, and she doesn't know what happened the night they died.

If I hadn't convinced Grace to be my mate, she would be alive. But she was. Our minds and souls bonded, connected. No distance could've protected her from me. No walls. No weapons. Not even her brothers could have saved her.

I gently pull Eva's hands away. "That doesn't make Selene any safer than it made Grace."

"Killian—"

I shake my head and look toward the pack house. The sun is almost down. Tonight is the new moon. Tonight, she can be safe and mine.

"One night," I say. "Then he's right. I have to send her away. Vandran made me an offer last month. I almost took him up on it a couple of weeks ago. This time, she's going."

# Twenty-Five

## SELENE

I stand at the top of the stairs that descend into the great hall, just like I did a month ago. It's February, and outside the wide windows, the new moon darkness is flecked with pure white puffs of falling snow. It picked up after sunset, and the castle and grounds are covered in a thick blanket of white.

The great hall has been plunged into shadow and candlelight. What's visible in the light from the glowing centerpieces is swathed in black, crimson, white, and iridescent moonstone blue.

Instead of a few long tables, the room is scattered with dozens of smaller round ones. They're draped with black tablecloths and dripping with richly scented hothouse flowers that came all the way from a green witch near St. Louis.

More candles are bordering a stage on one side where musicians are waiting, and two lines of candelabras as tall as I am are lining an aisle from the bottom of the stairs to the dais where the high table usually sits.

There, in front of a cluster of three pack Elders, Killian is waiting for me.

We're really doing this.

I am getting married.

To Killian.

There's an impatient huff at my side and a tug on my arm as the musicians start to play. I glare at Deacon Jones. I didn't want the Beta to escort me down the aisle any more than he wanted to do it. After what Killian told me about the "miscommunication" they had the day Finn was taken, I don't trust him at all. But his position demands he take a certain place in pack ceremonies, so here we are.

"Are you going to run?" Jones growls under his breath when I don't move.

"You wish."

We start down the stairs as the musicians start to play. It's a string quartet from Chicago, brought here at Killian's insistence. The cost was astronomical, but he didn't bat an eye.

I gather my skirts in the same hand that is holding a flawless bouquet of deep purple-blue roses, then step down carefully. If I trip, I don't trust Jones to catch me.

Sofia's team has done their work again. My dress is moon-pale silver silk that clings to my body, showing off my newly filled-in curves. It shimmers with seed-sized moonstone beads and flecks of red diamond that swirl in patterns embroidered in black. The delicate lace neckline is high in the front and plunges in the back. I wear the moonstone ring Killian gave me, but I've traded the simple beaded crescent moon neck-lace for a jeweled black gold chain set with red diamonds that hangs down my back, suspending a heavy moonstone pendant that depicts the crest of the Shattered Moon Pack. Sheer lace sleeves cling to my arms all the way down past the first knuckles of my fingers. My hair, which has been curled into loose waves, is crowned by a circlet of more moon-stone, red diamond, and black gold.

It's not the first time that I've worn a wedding dress recently. Maybe that's why I can't shake the feeling that this must be a prank, despite the perfection of the last two weeks.

My fragile alliance with Killian has grown into something I don't know whether I can ever be without. I've always survived by having as little as possible to lose, but now I have so much, it frightens me.

I could see Bianca pulling something like this. Let me go. Let me believe I'm free for a precious six weeks. Then, at the last second, pull it all out from under me.

Is that what's happening here? Am I about to be humiliated?

For several wild seconds, I'm sure that's exactly what's happening. I forget how to breathe. I press a hand to my stomach.

Then there's movement by the dais—Killian turning to look at me. Even from here, I feel the weight of his gaze. It's comforting, like being buried under just the right amount of heavy blankets on a cool night.

Music swells as we reach the bottom of the stairs. I release my skirt, hold the sweet-smelling bouquet in front of me, and pace down the aisle of candles on Deacon Jones's arm. The silk train whispers behind me. In the candlelight, the silver dress shimmers like magic.

I cling to the sight of Killian, tall and dark and waiting for me with delicious hunger in his topaz eyes. One corner of his mouth turns up in a smile, and I try not to realize that little smile is all I want to look at for the rest of my life.

"Selene!"

Finn waves at me from his seat at a front table, and I grin and wave back with the flowers in my hand.

"You're so pretty!" he whisper-yells. The wolves around him chuckle.

"Thanks, Rocket." I toss him the flowers, and he catches them with a delighted giggle.

Deacon stops at the steps to the dais. Killian reaches down for me, his hand grasping mine as he helps me up those final two steps.

His rain and cedar scent surrounds me, and as soon as our hands meet, calm washes over me.

This is right. We are *right*, despite how it happened.

"You're beautiful," he whispers.

I give him a crooked smile and move a strand of dark hair out of his face. He's perfect in his black suit, even if I prefer those sweaters he always wears with their sleeves pushed up. "So are you."

The three pack Elders who serve on the Council—the Weave Reader, the Lore Keeper, and Eva, as Preceptor—are standing in a loose triangle before us. Diya Singh, the Weave Reader, is in front. She's holding an ancient-looking large book. Eva and the Lore Keeper, Oscar Grayhorse, are standing behind and to either side of her.

Killian captures my other hand and brings it to his lips, pressing a soft kiss against my knuckles. Tonight, there are no whispers from the pack. Or if there are, I'm too wrapped up in this moment to hear them.

I scan the audience.

"Who are you looking for?" he murmurs.

"Your mother," I whisper back. "I want to make sure you gave her white wine tonight."

He laughs quietly. "She's in the back. Parker is making sure she behaves."

"What about howler-mad wolves?"

"Not invited."

"Pack and allies," intones Weave Reader Singh. The woman has to be at least a hundred years old. Her dark skin is as wrinkled as crumpled paper and her once-black hair now white shot through with only a few dark streaks. "We gather for the mating. While others may dance with different partners, wolves mate true."

"Wolves mate true," the audience echoes.

Killian's fingers tighten on mine, and I feel something. A simmering in the air around us. Waves of warm prickles roll down my arms and back. The wretched old injury in my left shoulder burns. I swear I smell the smoke of wolf magic. Faint but present.

I blink, confused. From the way Killian's dark brows furrow, he senses it too.

There shouldn't be magic around us. Not when I'm wolfless. A mating ceremony like this draws magic from both wolf souls taking part in it. With only one wolf, the ceremony is like a human wedding—a legal formality.

The Weave Reader doesn't stop, though, and none of the other council or senior pack members seated at the tables nearby seem to notice whatever is happening between Killian and me.

My heartbeat drums in my ears as the call and answer portion of the ceremony ends and the Weave Reader turns her gaze on us and us alone.

"Lady Selene Beaumont, do you receive this man into your heart as your mate? Will you be his comfort, his love, his support, and his first protector all the rest of your days?"

This is it. My final moment to turn back.

I have no desire to.

"I will."

The feeling of the magic twines around me, around where my hands join with Killian's, tightening.

"Alpha Killian Darrow, do you receive this woman into your heart as your mate? Will you be her comfort, her love, her support, and her first protector all the rest of your days?"

I look up at him and smile.

And Killian ...

He hesitates.

It's just for an instant, but I see it. Something uncertain flickers in his eyes. Something that says he doesn't actually want to do this.

"I will," Killian says. The words are quick, and maybe no one else heard or saw what I did. Maybe I was wrong.

The Weave Reader says, "To whom will you offer your blood? The old gods, the new, or the Fate of the Moon?"

"The fate," Killian says.

The Weave Reader nods. "Offer your blood to the Fate of the Moon as a seal on your promise."

She steps aside, and Killian and I move to the statue. This one is larger and carved of white marble, used as a pack shrine instead of the little selenite statue in his bedroom. A large mirrored bowl filled with water sits at its feet.

I keep looking at his face, searching for the confidence I've suddenly lost in this, but he won't meet my eyes.

He grows a claw and holds out a hand for mine. Now I hesitate.

That makes him look at me, and in that look, I see something even more startling than hesitation.

Tenderness and something deeper. Something that makes my heart break and mend all at the same time.

"Selene," he whispers, his hand still out to me. His sleeve has pulled back, and I notice Grace's locket is gone. It's the first time I've seen him without it, ever.

Heart suddenly hammering, I place my hand in his. Killian pricks the tip of my ring finger with a claw, then does the same to his own. Together, we let blood drip into the mirrored bowl.

Like when he swore his oath to me, there's a flash of moonstone blue and the sting of power. It surges between us, and even though there should be nothing, I have the faintest feeling of being bound.

Weave Reader Singh interrupts my thoughts. "Killian and Selene, you are mates."

As simple as that, it's done.

If I had a wolf, we might perform the marking in front of everyone else. Sometimes, when the mating is politically important, couples do that, biting each other chastely on the wrist or shoulder in front of the pack.

Most of the time, though, mating ceremonies look like this. Either the marking has already happened or the couple does it in private. If I had to choose, I'd do it in private. It's supposed to be … an intense physical experience.

I'll never know. I'll never have that with him.

There's a little more to the ceremony. Because Killian is an Alpha, we both swear another oath to serve the pack. I'm afraid to look out at the crowd as I say the words. A month ago, they hated me enough that someone we still haven't found made an attempt on my life.

But in the last month, I've tried to make a more concerted effort to be among them. Since making up with Killian, I've been able to do more, like sit in on council meetings. Aside from that, I've worked with Sofia on the practical logistics that come with running a pack and had at least two meals a day in the great hall where anyone could approach me.

I've made headway. Mostly with the parents of the children Finn is friends with. But I think it's something. As the days have passed, I've heard fewer whispers in the halls. More people have greeted me with a smile.

When I do finally look up, nervous that they're all going to be glaring at me, I'm surprised.

While it's easy to tell not all of them love me, there are a lot of smiles. So many more than I anticipated.

I smile back.

I can do this. It's going to be okay.

After all the vows are made, Killian leads me to the open area of the great hall just in front of the staircase. The musicians begin to play softly, and my heart jumps into my throat as he pulls me against him for a dance.

"You were perfect," he whispers against my ear.

I close my eyes. Goosebumps race across my skin at his closeness, and I breathe him in. My husband. As close to a mate as he can be. "Thank you. So were you."

He laughs a little. His hand is heavy on the small of my back, and he presses me even closer.

"We could leave now," I say abruptly. It's the new moon, and he's promised me tonight is the night we can finally have actual sex—something I've been looking forward to with great anticipation.

Killian's laugh is so abrupt, so genuine, that I find myself grinning too. His lips graze my forehead. "Sofia will murder us if we leave before the dinner you two planned."

I huff. "They're going to have us at dinner every night after this."

The song is ending, so maybe it's my imagination that Killian suddenly goes tense. "Right."

Since he refuses to escape the reception, we stand and greet an endless line of people while the rest of the pack dances. After a while, food is brought out. The lights come up, and Killian and I join the pack council and other senior members at the high table that's been brought back to the dais.

My feet ache, and I'm more than happy to sit next to Killian, eat, and listen to the way he moves the conversation around us.

Killian isn't shy, and he isn't exactly quiet. He just doesn't say anything unless he has something to say. But over the last weeks, I've noticed that he's good with people. A word here, an offhand comment there, and he can keep things easy and conversation flowing in a way that feels effortless.

I know he thinks he's a monster, that the curse is something he deserves for being born the son of the worst tyrant since the Waking, but he's wrong. Killian is brilliant, diplomatic, compassionate, and humorous when I least expect it. He's a good Alpha.

Maybe together, we can figure out the curse and set him free.

There's a tap on my shoulder. I turn and try not to flinch as Claudia leans over from the seat next to me.

"Selene, sweetheart." She pulls a box from somewhere beneath her chair. "In honor of your new position, I wanted to give you a gift."

I feel Killian's attention shift to us. His voice is a low, warning growl. "Mother?"

"Oh, calm down, Son. It's just a present."

Claudia hands me the box. It's about eight inches square and an inch or two deep, like one that might contain a heavy necklace.

"Thank you, Lady Darrow." Warily, I lift the lid.

At first, I think that's exactly what she's given me—a choker-style necklace woven of fine wire. Then I recognize the thing in the box for what it is.

A bejeweled servant collar.

My hands go numb. There's rushing in my ears. The world is far away.

Beside me, Killian growls again. Power ripples from him in angry waves, intensifying by the instant. I wonder whether he'll exile her the way he's threatened to.

That would be satisfying.

Without thinking, I put a hand on his knee and curve my lips into something smile-shaped. Everything in me wants to curl up, but I'm not a pawn anymore.

Killian's hand slides over mine, warm and rough, squeezing tight, shaking with rage. For some reason, knowing he's this angry dulls the razor edge on my nerves. He's ready to defend me, but I'm capable of defending myself.

I'm not the half-starved wolfless woman Claudia has slapped, attacked, and insulted.

I am Lady Selene Beaumont, Mate-Consort of the Alpha of Shattered Moon.

I reach into the box and take the delicate jewel and wire confection in both hands. Claudia's expression is one of cruel glee, but it fades to confusion as I display the collar for everyone to see.

"Oh, Lady Darrow! It's perfect," I gush. "What an intriguing choice. You've taken a symbol of resilience, endurance, and strength— qualities I've relied upon my entire life—and elevated it to an art piece. You have truly outdone yourself. Thank you."

A beat of silence follows. I allow my voice to sharpen, but my smile never falters as my eyes bore into hers. "I will not forget this."

Tension at the table draws as fine and taut as the wires that make up the collar. Gently, I place it back in the box, slide the bottom into the lid at an angle like it's a display case, and turn it around. The hateful thing gleams in the glittering light from the chandeliers.

Claudia makes a strangled sound. "Darling, you should put that away, don't you think?"

"*Darling*," I laugh lightly as I fold my hands on my lap. "Why wouldn't I want to display exactly what you think of Killian's choice to the rest of the pack?"

Claudia's eyes bug out, her expression apoplectic.

I allow my smile to turn into a delicate frown and draw my brows together in feigned confusion. "Unless I've made a mistake. Is there a different reason behind the gift you'd like to explain?"

Killian, who has lifted his wineglass to his lips, sets the glass down and coughs like he's choking. I gasp in pretend alarm. "My love! Are you all right? Did something go down wrong?"

His eyes go dark, and suddenly, the air is charged.

Oh, god. I called him "love."

Yes, I was laying it on thick. But if I don't, I might put Claudia through a wall again.

"Love." In front of everyone, when it's not even something I've let myself think in the depths of my own mind.

Shit.

He swipes a napkin from the table to wipe red wine from his lips. Heat blazes in his topaz eyes. "Everything is fine, *love*." His voice is dark, velvet, possessive. A thrill goes through me.

Well. I asked for that.

"Is there something you'd like to explain about the meaning of your gift, Mother?" Killian asks casually. He leans back and sips his wine, taking my hand again beneath the table.

Claudia's face goes white as chalk. She pushes her chair back and throws her napkin down on the table. "Not at all. It's exactly as she said. A gift to remind her of her—what was it, dear? Resilience, endurance, and strength. She'll need them for what comes next."

Killian narrows his eyes at her.

"What comes next?" I ask, amused.

Claudia's smile is the evilest I've ever seen. "You know, for the day after tomorrow, when he sends you away. Warlord Vandran is *so* looking forward to having you at Fall Line. He told me all about it."

She rises from her chair, blows me a kiss, and leaves, her black dress clinging to her as she slinks off.

There's no way. There's no way.

Blood rushes in my ears. I look at Killian.

But I know. I see it in his face.

"I see." I rise from the table. Slow. Deliberate. I am shaking. Half the council is staring at me. News of what Claudia said will spread through the pack like wildfire. It probably is, even now, over the pack tie.

I force a smile onto my face. "I think I've had too much to drink."

My wine glass sits on the table, full and untouched.

Killian rises too. "Selene, I can explain—"

Explain. Not deny.

"Are you sending me away?" I whisper too low for anyone else to hear.

He swallows. "It's for the best."

"No." The word is abrupt. Harsh.

"I was going to tell you—"

"It's all right, Alpha. I've heard what I need to hear."

I pick up the box with the jeweled collar, lift my skirts, and leave the table. My vision has narrowed to a tight tunnel. I need to escape. A door. Any door. I have to get out of here.

Around me, the pack tie is doing its work. The whispers rise.

I leave the dais with as much decorum as I can. Killian is already coming after me, but he stops when the Beta says something that grabs his attention.

Deacon Jones and I may never be friends, but at this moment, I'm grateful for him.

"Lady Selene."

I look up. Somehow, I'm by the wall, near one of several sets of French doors that lead out into the dark, snowy gardens.

Maddox is there. He's the one who spoke. There's a strange expression on his face. Sadness?

Of course, sadness. Killian is his brother-in-law, and Maddox just had to watch him marry another woman.

Maddox glances over my shoulder. Killian has shaken the Beta and is coming down the steps to the dais, but Maddox and I are in an area swathed in shadow, and I don't think he's seen us. Maddox jerks his head toward the French doors. "I'll cover for you."

"Thank you," I murmur.

I flee out the door and into the pitch-dark, snow-shrouded night.

# Twenty-Six

## SELENE

I run out onto a stone patio that leads down a short set of stairs to the gardens. The stupidity of fleeing outside is immediately apparent as my feet sink into several inches of icy, wet snow in shoes that are barely more than crimson straps with attached heels.

My breath plumes into the night. My fingers are already going numb where they clutch the collar in its box. I'm shivering. But if I go back into the ballroom, I'll come face-to-face with Killian. I can't. Not in front of everyone. Not while the betrayal is still fresh and bleeding.

The small door that leads into the kitchen from the garden isn't far. I can go there and sneak up some old servants' stairs to the top floor. I don't know what I'll do after that. Grab clothes and Finn and run maybe. Since he's planning on sending me somewhere anyway.

He didn't even ask. I married a man who doesn't even respect me enough to ask.

I cling to the stone railing as I make my way down the stairs, slipping a little. Only when I feel the cold sharpen on my face do I realize I'm crying.

"Stupid, arrogant, asshole Alpha. He's just like them."

The French doors swing open, and Killian steps into the night. "Selene!"

I hit the snowy ground and run. Melting snow burns my feet as I take off along the side of the castle, heading south.

Running from him is just as stupid as coming outside in the first place. He's bigger than me. Faster. He's not wearing ridiculous shoes.

He's on me so fast. His arms wrap around my waist, and he lifts me from the ground. I kick and jab backward with my elbows. He grunts when I connect but doesn't let me go.

"Selene, stop!"

"No! You're sending me away to Fall Line, and you didn't even ask! You said you care about me, but you lied. You don't even respect me. I should have known it was another Alpha lie!"

"Selene." He sets me down and spins me to face him but keeps my body locked against his. "I only decided this afternoon. I was going to talk to you about it tonight. We haven't had a chance—"

"You *decided*?" I yank the collar out, toss the box aside, and bring it up to my neck. My fingers are already too cold to feel the clasp, and I struggle to close it.

"What the fuck are you doing?" Killian snarls.

"I'm remembering my place, Alpha. Since you're the one who gets to make decisions for me."

"Selene—"

"Don't bullshit me, Killian. Your mother knew, and I didn't! Clearly, this is who you think I am. You're the Alpha, and I'm just here to serve at your convenience."

"Fuck that." He tears the collar from around my neck and rips the thin strands of precious metal apart in his hands. Jewels pop and go flying, scattering into the snow.

Watching that collar get shredded does something to me on such a visceral level that I'm shocked into silence. When all that's left is a tangled, mangled knot of broken wires, he tosses that over his shoulder too.

He drags me close and drops his forehead against mine. "Asher is back. I saw him today. I told you I promised him that I'd never take a mate again, but I never told you what he promised me. If I don't send you away in two days, he's going to kill you."

I scoff and smack him on the shoulder, seconds from breaking down into incomprehensible sobs. I can't stop seeing him rip that collar apart. He's so close, but he still doesn't get that making choices to protect me is still making choices for me. It takes away my agency and makes me feel like the helpless servant I used to be.

"How? How is he going to get past your whole army, Zev, Parker, Maddox, and you? I thought I was safe at Shattered Moon!"

"Asher will wait years if he has to, stalking you from a distance until he sees his chance. The only way to protect you from him would be to lock you up inside the castle, and even then, it just takes one guard leaving their post, one person making a mistake. I won't let you live like a prisoner, Selene."

"You don't get to choose for me!"

"This isn't something you would choose!"

I'm shocked into silence for a second time.

More quietly, he says, "I will make sure you get everything you want. You want Finn to be the richest kid on this side of the world with every opportunity at his fingertips? I will make it happen. You want a law presented to the Conclave to mandate the wolfless are free? I'll do it. I'll do whatever you want. But Asher is right; no matter what we do, no matter how many precautions we take, one day, it won't be enough."

His voice breaks. "Please. I don't want your blood on my hands I barely held on after Grace. I won't survive if I come back to myself one morning and it's you."

He sounds so desperate, something in me cracks. I hit my fist against his shoulder again, the gesture helpless, hopeless. "There has to be a way to break the curse. We'll think of it. And Asher ..."

I don't know what to say about that short of suggesting Killian murder his best friend and Eva's son, which I won't do.

His hands tighten on my hips. Still broken, he says, "I've been trying for five years."

I bare my teeth and grab his face, forcing him to look at me. "You and I have both lived our lives for other people. For once, I want to live for me. You are my chance at happiness, Killian. I haven't come this far to lose it now. I'm not going anywhere."

I pull him down and kiss him. His entire body shudders, and he wraps his arms all the way around me, pulling me against him, lifting me clear of the snow. His hands go to my ass, and I hike the skirts of my dress to wrap my legs around his waist. He stumbles a few steps, and then he's got me pressed against the frigid castle wall.

The contrast between the cold and his heat makes me gasp and arch against him. He flexes his hips, grinding into me, sending spirals of pleasure spinning up from my core into my belly, my chest.

I've had Killian's hands on me enough in the last two weeks that my body responds instantly in anticipation of pleasure. My nipples peak and my panties dampen, my skin sensitive to every kiss, lick, nip. He's held back, never letting himself find release because he was afraid of the curse.

Tonight, I'm going to push him over the edge of control. I'm going to know what it feels like to have him inside of me. This isn't where I planned on it happening, but I don't care.

"Say it," I growl. "Say you aren't sending me away."

"Selene ..." He angles kisses down my jaw and neck, then down onto my collarbone. One big hand palms my breast through the fabric, and I moan.

"Say it."

"I won't—" He hooks his fingers on the neckline and pulls the dress down over my left shoulder before I think to stop him. Killian's heated eyes catch on my exposed skin. Before I can move to cover it, he stops me. "You're hurt."

I look down at the permanent wound on my left shoulder. It's a livid line of pinkish red that looks worse because of the cold. "It's old. My father gave it to me the night I tried to escape when I was thirteen."

His dark brows furrow. "It never healed? Did anyone ever look at it?"

I laugh and can't help the bitterness in it. "I was never first in line for the pack healer. No time to be a medical mystery when there are chores to be done."

"Your parents didn't offer—?"

"Did my parents or Bianca ever offer to lick it and heal me?" I laugh again. "No."

"You could've asked for Dr. Bennett to look at it."

That brings me up short. I'm so used to the wound, and not used to being cared for. "I ... that never occurred to me."

"Of course." Killian rolls his eyes, huffs a laugh, and bends to where the scar starts along the top of my left breast. His breath mists warm against my skin, and then ...

His tongue.

I'm fighting back a moan when he pulls away and makes a face.

Oh, my god. "Do I taste bad?"

He lifts his thumb and drags it along his tongue. His brows furrow. "Selene, there's silver in this wound."

"There's ... what?"

"Hold on to me."

The revelation has barely started to rock the foundation of my world when he curves his finger into a claw and slices into me, opening the cut. I cry out in pain, then his claw retracts. There's a sliver of silver on it. It looks like the tip of a knife no longer than my pinky nail.

Power shifts around us, gathering, swirling, rising in a wave.

Then it crashes into me, and the world goes white.

# Twenty-Seven

## SELENE

I'm engulfed in pain unlike anything I've ever felt. Like blood returning to a limb that's been asleep so long, I forgot it ever had feeling. It's in my head, my chest, my stomach, my thighs, my hands. I make a sound somewhere between a gasp and a scream as my body bucks.

"Shit. Selene?" Even though I can feel Killian's heat against my front, the cold stone of the castle against my back, his voice is far away.

"Make it stop," I whimper. Tears stream down my face. I try to run from the pain, fight it, push it away. Nothing works. I can't separate my mind from the agony. It's so close, so everywhere. "It hurts, please, it hurts."

Dimly, I'm aware when Killian scoops me into his arms and starts running. I writhe, as if contorting my body into some other position might bring relief.

Something in me breaks free, hurtling from the depths, ascending to burst through the surface. I inhale to sob, and abruptly, Killian's scent is *everywhere*.

Before, he smelled good. Now, when I breathe in, the scent paints a vivid picture of a rainy early-spring night with cedar trees swaying in the breeze. Not just spring—March, when it's newest. The night is sharp with the just-warming earth and the smell of new green things barely poking out of the dirt. Snow fell yesterday, but it won't fall again. That is what Killian smells like.

He smells like *mine*.

A sound breaks from my throat. Snarl, growl, howl of triumph.

*I. Am. Free.*

There's a feeling of being lowered so quickly, I wonder whether he dropped me. Then there's snow, wet and burning cold against my skin. Sharp bursts of pain ricochet through me as bones pop and snap and flesh crawls and fur sprouts and my body is remade. There's something around me, too tight. Then hands grasp the fabric of my wedding dress and rip, and I burst free.

I scramble to all four of my silver-furred feet and shake hard. The snow is cold but no longer burning. The moonless night is bright just from the light of the stars. Like having a veil ripped from my eyes, a filter from my nose, pillows from my ears, I see and smell and hear *everything*.

I am a wolf. I am whole.

I throw my head back and howl.

Killian falls to his knees in front of me. He stretches out a hand, and I still as he makes contact with my muzzle. I sniff and then yip excitedly.

*Mate.*

We've been struggling so hard to figure things out this whole time, wondering why we were so incredibly drawn to each other. This is why. The silver in my shoulder kept me from shifting, but now that I can, I know.

I do have a wolf, and I have a fated mate.

It's Killian.

He takes my muzzle in both hands and strokes my fur, and I can see that he knows too. His wolf is in his eyes, and he's on the edge of control. "It's you," he whispers. "It's been you this whole time."

I reach out my mind and try to speak with him, but I can't. There's something missing.

I whimper and cast my mind out further, searching, running along some kind of psychic web, driven by instinct. I run into a wall. Or, not a wall, because it's flexible. It bends around me. It feels right. Like home. Like not being alone.

*"Pack?"* I whisper.

Killian's eyes go wide. The force I feel hesitates. It feels on the verge of rejecting me, then it says, in his voice, *"Yes."*

He leans down and presses his forehead to mine. A connection shoots between us, and all of a sudden, I'm brought into a web so all-encompassing, so intimate, I forget what it was ever like to be alone. But before I can reach out, the mind that wrapped itself around me softly pulls me away to my own, separate space. It's gentle, but I whine at the separation from the others.

*"For now. Just for now, you're so new,"* the voice in my mind reassures. Killian's voice. I believe him because he smells like he is mine.

*"We're fated,"* I say.

*"I know."* He pulls me to him. His fingers curl in my ruff. He's shaking.

*"Run with me,"* I plead. Vaguely, I remember there are complications. But none of that matters anymore because I have a wolf, and I was always meant to be Killian's, and he was always meant to be mine.

Killian rises. For a long moment, I'm not sure what he's going to do.

Then he shrugs out of his jacket and lets it fall on the snow. His hands move down his chest as he unbuttons his shirt. Then he strips out of his pants. His form blurs.

Then he's standing next to me, a black wolf with silver-tipped fur who's so big that my head only comes to his shoulder.

He stands still while I sniff all around him. Yes. My Alpha, my mate. I yip with excitement, pounce around him, nip at his muzzle, and then take off. Snow flies around me as I stretch my legs and body and *run*.

For a heartbeat, he stands there. Then he's after me.

I cover the ground between the castle and the wall that surrounds the grounds in seconds. Joy explodes inside me as I pivot and take off along the inside of the wall, my feet beating the earth in time with my pounding heart.

I've almost come all the way around to where the wall meets the cliff over the spring when Killian catches me. He tackles me, and I fall and roll along the ground. The big black-furred wolf huffs in a way that sounds exactly like a laugh, and I jump up again. His mouth is open, tongue lolling out in a doggy grin. I stretch my front legs out in front of me, wag my tail, and pounce.

We roll through the snow together, nipping and playing, jumping up to run and chase and catch each other again.

It's the most perfect hour of my life.

Finally, the cold creeps in through my feet, and our play slows. Killian leads me in through a back door that's been modified so it can be opened by wolves. It leads to a small mudroom then into the locker rooms where the pack soldiers change to train. It's not unheard of for wolves to come in this way after a run, so there are cubbies filled with sweatpants and T-shirts in all sizes.

He shifts back, pulls on pants, and then waits patiently, talking me through my first intentional shift. I become human again lying on my side on the cold tile floor, tired and weak. Killian strokes my hair, my back. He's grinning at me.

"You got it on the first try. Perfect. You are perfect."

"I feel like I was hit by a train."

"You've had silver in your body for over a decade. Give yourself time. Your strength will continue to grow as you heal."

He hands me clothes. I pull on the pants and T-shirt. Then I rise, wrap my arms around his neck, and kiss him.

Kissing Killian has always been electric—as if, even repressed by silver in my system, our bond couldn't be completely masked. But that was just a little static spark, like crossing a carpeted floor in socks and getting jump scared by a doorknob.

But this, now? This is lightning. It's thunder. It's the whole goddamn storm.

*I have a wolf. I have a mate. Killian is my mate.*

*We are meant to be.*

He lifts me without breaking the kiss. With most of the pack either still at the reception or in bed, Killian and I are able to stumble through the halls, kissing and touching each other, without being seen.

Though, to be honest, maybe we were. Maybe when we fell to the floor laughing, right in the middle of the hallway, and I rolled on top of him and he cupped my ass with one hand and the back of my head with the other, his tongue delving into my mouth as he angled me for the deepest possible kiss, we were right in the center of a crowd of people and I just had no idea.

All that matters is him.

We make it to the Alpha suite. I think there are guards outside, but I'm not sure. He lifts me like a bride—because I am one—and carries me across the threshold, all the way up the stairs. We literally tumble into bed, and I am so lost in the bright haze of sensations that is his body against mine.

He slides his knee up, parting my thighs, shifting so that his erection presses right where I ache. I hate the clothes between us. My fingers curl into false claws that I rake down his back. I ride the edge of control, feral. I want him panting for me. Groaning my name. I want to turn him over and straddle him and fuck him until we both shatter into oblivion.

*Mine.* I have a wolf. I have a mate. Killian Darrow, Alpha of the Shattered Moon Pack, belongs to me.

I push, and Killian sits up, bracing his back against the headboard. I climb onto his lap and straddle him just like I wanted. He holds my waist, his eyes half-closed as I grind against him, searching for friction. I take his mouth, then work my way down his jaw.

He smells like heaven. He tastes divine. His stubble scratches my lips, but the almost pain just makes it all the sweeter. His head falls back, his hands working up and down my sides, then finally sliding all the way down to cup my backside and pull me more tightly against him, just like I want.

My name is a breath on his lips. He changes the angle, deepening the kiss. I grind against him, frustrated with the need that has been building and building and building for six entire weeks.

He pulls back. His wolf is luminous in his eyes. "Tell me you want this. Me, even cursed. Be sure."

"I'm sure," I whisper, desperate, pressing my hand against the small of his back to get him closer—which has about as much effect as me trying to move a boulder. "I want you, Killian. I see you, and I want you."

A shudder runs through his body. "If you change your mind ..."

"I won't. Keep going. Touch me."

He laughs wickedly, then he rolls so that he's on top of me. He settles his weight between my legs and braces himself on his elbows, bearing his weight so that I'm pinned beneath him but can still breathe easily. I whimper and open my legs, then slide my palms down and grab his ass with both hands.

"Fuck." He presses his hips against me. His breath is hot on my skin as he nips and kisses my jaw.

"I don't think we need this." He bites one side of my shirt and grips the other side in one hand, then tears it completely open, baring my breasts to him. His thumb traces over one peaked nipple, and I jerk against him.

My whole world narrows to him, to us, to his body and mine as he bends and takes my nipple in his mouth, torturing me with tongue and teeth. His hand finds my other breast, massaging it, then pinching my other nipple and rolling it between his fingers.

The skin of his chest and abdomen is hot against mine. The contact makes me feel drunk. I want to chase this aching agony he has woken in me all the way to the end.

His fingers stroke down to my waistband and slip beneath, pushing the sweatpants—the only thing I have on—downward.

"I have waited so long for this," I whisper.

He lifts himself from me just enough to drag the pants down my legs. Then they're gone, and I think he might have flung them across the room.

His hand moves down my stomach. I trap it against my belly, intertwine our fingers, then shift my body in a way that encourages him to flip over onto his back.

"We've done this," I say. "I want to touch you."

He hesitates, exhales, and rolls so that he's lying on his back.

Finally, he is mine.

I kneel at his side and take my time exploring the shape of his jaw, the rough, stubbled skin of his cheek, and the strong lines of his neck while he shifts restlessly. I trail my fingers over his chest, his stomach, touching and exploring everywhere. Then, I wrap them gently around his shaft.

Killian's breath catches. He whispers my name, and I feel powerful in a way I never have before. I trace the shape of him, listening to every quiet sound he makes, loving the way he rocks his hips up into my grip.

When his breathing goes harsh, I straddle his hips and press my sex against him, sending shocks of pleasure through my own body as I grind against him. He pushes into a sitting position, his back braced against the headboard. He touches me and kisses me until I'm right at the edge, until a few more movements will send me over.

I shift until I can feel him against my entrance, then sigh with satisfaction as I press down and he slips inside me. I'm so slick, there's no resistance.

I ease onto him, and he fills me so completely, I almost come right then. Partially because he feels so good, partially because it's Killian and we're finally doing this.

He's taken so much care, shown so much restraint. His body is covered in a fine sheen of sweat, and his jaw and neck muscles work as he fights to stay completely still.

I roll my hips, and Killian's eyes blaze bright topaz around pupils blown so wide with need that they once again remind me of a solar eclipse.

"Fuck me, Killian. For once, I want you to let go."

He makes a sound like an animal, and then suddenly, I'm beneath him. He lifts me just enough to stuff a pillow beneath the small of my back, changing the angle of our connection. His fingers dig bruisingly into my hips, but I like the bite of pain.

He ravages my mouth, then thrusts deep, fast, and hard. I cry out, my hands splaying over his back, moving down to his hips. Just feeling the strength in the motion almost makes me come again.

He drops his head to my breast, sucking one nipple into his mouth and pinching the other like he did before. Electricity shoots straight to my center, and suddenly, I'm right back on the edge. Just feeling him touch me, just knowing his cock is buried deep between my legs.

The orgasm crashes into me, so huge and shocking that I scream his name. Pleasure ripples through my body over and over, drowning me in waves of bliss that tear animal noises from my throat.

Killian comes when I do, slamming deep and moaning my name as he empties himself inside me.

There's a feeling right where my heart beats. Something that's empty, waiting, half. Something that could be whole if I could only have him.

I bite back a whimper as I realize what it is. A nascent mate bond only waiting for Killian and me to mark each other to complete it.

He moans, and the sound is so undone, it also undoes me. I lick and suck and bite at his neck, all the way down to the place where it meets his shoulder. An instinct is growing inside me.

Killian is mine. I need to mark him. I find just the right place at the base of his neck and try it out with a sharp nip from my teeth. Killian gasps and bucks up against me, and then—

"No!" His whisper is hoarse. He pulls out of me and away. The distance makes me growl and snap my teeth.

Killian's chest heaves, and he laughs raggedly. His hair is a mess, his eyes heavy. "No," he repeats. "Selene. I can do everything—we can do anything—but you can't mark me."

The words are ice water splashed on my face. The primal instinct that grabbed hold of my body recedes, leaving me weak and shaking. I'm sated from our lovemaking, but on a deeper level, I'm profoundly unsatisfied. I'm also confused. He means what he's saying. I can ... sense it.

There's a tenuous connection between us that gives me a vague impression of his emotions, and he's dead serious.

"What do you mean, I can't mark you? We're fated, Killian. We can do this. *Really* do it. Maybe I'm not an Alpha, but with a normal mate bond, we'll still strengthen the pack. To have found each other at all ... it's so rare."

A real mate bond. My heart lurches. My whole life, a mate bond has been a level of closeness with another person I could only fantasize about.

"No." He says the word with a cold finality that's like sliding that bit of silver right back into my skin. "Nothing that happened tonight changes what I promised. You and I are exactly what we were before."

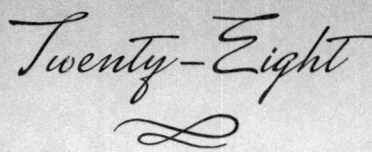

## SELENE

I slide off the bed. His scent is still getting to me, clouding my mind. Desire is already pulsing through me again, tangled up in that unsatisfied, soul-deep need I don't know how to fill.

"Why are you doing this?" I ask, unable to keep my voice from shaking.

Killian's back is against the headboard, the covers rumpled around his hips. He draws up his knees and rests his forearms on them, his head in his hands. "I have no choice."

I understand why he's afraid. I can't even say he's wrong. But I am so tired of him unilaterally making decisions.

"Fine," I say casually. "Then I guess we have no other option."

I close my eyes.

If he doesn't want to be my mate, we need to reject the bond.

## KILLIAN

Selene's wolf is beautiful. Pure silver, like moonlight. Elegant. Lithe. As soon as I pulled the tip of that blade from her shoulder, her strange, vague scent blossomed into the full, heady burst of waterlilies floating on a clear pond. Of the earth on a cool summer night when the forest is in full bloom.

I knew instantly that she was mine.

I ran with her through the night, wild with her joy. I wanted her before, but now, every second I don't have her, it feels like parts of me sublimate into nothing. If I can't claim her, mark her, have her by my side forever, it will eat away at me until I'm gone.

But now, as I lean against the headboard and watch her there, standing naked just beyond the edge of the bed, I know I would rather disappear under the weight of my own agony than risk her life.

Suddenly, something shifts inside my chest. A gaping wound that deepens with each breath. An incompleteness that feels like being torn in two.

Selene has her eyes closed and a look of concentration on her face.

She's rejecting the mate bond.

"No!" I lunge at her, grab her, pull her close. "Stop."

She opens those pale, dark-ringed eyes and scowls. "Let me go. This is the only choice you've left me with."

A stabbing cold goes through my chest.

"Stop!" I'm desperate. I throw some of my Alpha aura into the command.

Selene raises a brow at me. The ice stabs again. Now that she has a wolf and I've brought her into my pack, she shouldn't be able to ignore an order from me. But she does.

Pain crosses her face. What she's doing is hurting her as much as it is me, but she screws her face into a look of determination.

"Selene, please."

"Please?" She shoves away from me, goes to a dresser, and begins frantically pulling on clothes. The empty place in my chest throbs. "No. You don't get to make choices for me. You said you care, you act like you want me, but you keep pushing me away!"

With a whole bond, we'll have access to each other's minds, feelings, and general physical locations. Even with it incomplete, I can feel the anger seeping off of her. Worse, the heartbreak.

I pull on the sweatpants. I thought I could keep some secrets, but I can't let Selene think I'm making this choice because I don't care about her when it's completely the opposite.

"I had to kill Grace."

"The curse killed Grace," she snaps. "Stop being a martyr."

"No, I did." I run my hand through my hair. I've kept this secret—Grace's secret—for five years. "I had to because she killed your brother. She's the one who desecrated his corpse. And she wasn't done; she was already hunting for more."

Selene folds her arms and glares at me. I see her chin tremble. "Explain."

I don't want to explain. I want to pull her back into bed and kiss her. I want to make love to her while I still can.

I sit on the edge of the bed. She stalks toward me. "You said you killed Jackson."

"No. I said I'm responsible for his death."

"Semantics." She slashes a hand through the air. "I'm so sick of this, Killian. Give me the truth. All of it. Now."

I rub my eyes. "That night, Grace was out with Jackson. I knew it, and I didn't care. We'd already made plans to break our bond. But they were seen. Hagan, the wolf who trained Asher and me, told Vandrar, who told me. I went to warn them to go somewhere more private. I'd been fighting the worst headache of my life all day, but I thought it was stress. I found them as the moon rose ... and the curse tried to take me for the first time. I knew I was losing myself, and I fought back the fog. I was able to hold onto a sliver of control."

My jaw clenches, and it takes effort to recount what happened next. "While I was fighting it off, the curse seeped through the mate bond and took Grace. Before I knew what was happening, she'd shifted into something that wasn't her and torn out Jackson's throat. While he was lying there on the ground, she opened him up and—"

Selene presses a hand over her mouth. Bile rises in my throat as the memory plays back in my mind. "Alpha commands to stop didn't work. I was still inside her mind. The creature she became knew there were others nearby—that our pack was nearby. She started toward the castle with the intention of doing to our people what she had just done to her own fated mate. I had to protect the pack, so I killed her. After, I no longer had the strength to fight. It was all the curse needed to take root in me."

Confusion clouds Selene's night-frost eyes. "But the curse was going to force Grace to hunt the pack. You protect them, even when it has you."

Muscles in my jaw flex, and I nod. "I burned through every ounce of willpower I had to force the monster into the woods. Grace wasn't strong enough to do it, but I was. And I've kept it out there, hunting only my enemies, for five years."

Selene moves to the bed and sits beside me. "You think if we actually mate bond, the curse will infect me."

"I know it will."

She scoffs. "You don't, though. I have magic that keeps it away. It might not be able to cross to me."

"Selene, I would lay down my life for you. I would find a way to hand you the moon and stars. But even if it's torture to live like this, craving you for the rest of my life, I won't mark you. A partial bond is better than nothing at all."

Selene makes me happy—more than happy, she makes me feel whole. Content. A mate bond with her would give me such indescribable peace.

But I am the cursed son of Alaric Bane. I don't get to be at peace.

I pull her onto my lap, and she lets me. I wrap my arms around her and bury my face against her neck, inhaling the scent of her hair. If every breath of mine inhales her scent for the rest of my life, it won't be enough. "I just want to protect you. I can't see you become what she did."

She leans her head against my shoulder. "You didn't tell me any of this."

"It didn't matter when you didn't have a wolf."

"You were protecting Grace again. Like the infidelity. You don't want her family to know what she did to Jackson."

I close my eyes because, of course, Selene immediately understands. "Yes."

"Fuck," she whispers.

"Yeah. Fuck."

"Killian?"

"Yeah?"

"I won't reject the mate bond, and you're not sending me away."

I swallow. "You're choosing the most difficult path, Selene."

"Is it, if at least we get to be together?"

"It's selfish of me to put you in danger."

"No. It's selfish of you to try to save yourself from what you'll go through if you hurt me when the curse is active. It's selfish of you to strip away my agency because you don't want to grieve again, with zero thought at all for the grief I will feel if you force me to leave. What's *un*selfish would be for you to recognize that the choice between physical safety and the emotional pain of being separated from you is mine. I get to decide how to live my life, and I choose to live it with you, so shut up and be with me."

I open my mouth to respond, but I'm having a hard time wrapping my brain around her words.

I think she's right, and I don't like it. "Asher is still a problem."

"Come to bed," she commands, ignoring me. She rises from my lap and crawls beneath the covers. I follow, pull her against me so her back is to my front, and drape my arm over her waist. She wiggles her ass until it's firmly planted against my groin. I start to get hard.

"That's interesting," she murmurs, wiggling again.

I grab her hip and growl, "Stop, or neither of us will sleep."

She flips over and hooks her leg over mine, her arm around my neck, then snuggles close and kisses me.

"Okay, Husband." She grins. "Mate. Let's not sleep."

*Bang! Bang! Bang!*

I'm suddenly, savagely awake. Outside, the sky is pale with dawn. I tighten my arms around Selene.

"What?" I snarl.

Selene tries to sit up. "Who is that?"

"It's Deacon," comes my Beta's voice from the other side of the door.

I groan, roll on top of Selene, and kiss her neck. "Leave it. He'll go away."

Selene laughs and kisses my forehead, then pushes me off her. She pulls the covers up to her chin and calls, "Come in."

Deacon does. I have no idea what he was expecting, but when he sees us in bed, his brows draw down over his eyes.

"This better be good," I growl. "I cleared my schedule today."

"I wouldn't call it good, but it is important." He glances at Selene, then does a double take.

I am about to do something that would require me to find a new Beta for the second time when I realize why he's staring.

Her scent is all over this room. He can tell she's not wolfless anymore.

"There are things the pack needs to be filled in on," I say casually, though I have no idea how to explain that even though Selene isn't wolf-less, we won't be completing the mate bond. "Why the hell are you pounding on my door when it's my fucking honeymoon? And stop staring at my mate." I bite out the last words with a sting of Alpha power.

Deacon jerks his gaze away from Selene and drops it to the ground. "Apologies, Alpha. The Alpha Lord and Lady of Redcedar Hollow are here under a peace flag from the Conclave. So is their daughter, Bianca."

"What?!" Selene whispers.

Terror murmurs across our vestigial connection. She scrambles up and starts throwing on clothes.

I rise slowly until I loom over my Beta. "Why did you let them into my pack house?"

Deacon Jones is not a small man, not a weak wolf, but he cowers from me. "Th-they're here under the supervision of Conclave representatives. They said it's time for you to honor the treaty. They've brought you their daughter as a mate."

I laugh and gesture at Selene, who is dressed now. She's clutching the hem of her oversized sweater. She's gone very, very still.

"I have taken their daughter as a mate," I say.

Deacon visibly swallows. "That's the problem, Alpha. They claim you misunderstood their 'gesture' when they left Selene on Shattered Moon land. As she was a servant, it was within their rights to send Ms. Beaumont as a proxy for you to marry in Bianca's name. They claim Selene is not their blood at all, not the daughter of the Alphas of Redcedar Hollow. Warlord Vandran sent his arcanist to help you, but unfortunately ... Whitlock says the blood tests you had him run prove them right."

# Twenty-Nine

## SELENE

Killian is *angry*. Angrier than I've ever seen him. A few weeks ago, that anger would have scared me. Now it's a shield I can hide behind, one that will allow me to think. Or at least it would if Deacon's announcement hadn't left my head spinning.

*Not* their daughter? This is the most insane con my parents have ever tried to pull. I am a Beaumont. Since Marcus Vandran is the person Killian trusts most in the world after Eva and Sofia, I have to assume they tricked him.

After Killian orders Deacon out and gets dressed, he's ready to storm the foyer where the drama of the Beaumonts' arrival is apparently unfolding. Rage boils off him in waves. Outside the windows, last night's snowstorm is back. His unbridled fury stands in intense contrast to the slow drift of the thick, soft flakes.

I feel sick, but one of us has to keep their wits about them. I touch Killian's arm. "Killian, you have to calm down."

His topaz eyes flash bright with his wolf. "No. I will not have them denouncing my mate in her home or pulling their bullshit in mine. They're leaving right the fuck now." He grips my hips, pulls me against him, and kisses me deeply.

I take his face in my hands and force him to look at me. I wish I could show him the fear that has taken root inside my chest because it's too old, too much a part of me to explain it in words. "Don't underestimate them. If they came here, it's because they already know they can win."

He grips my wrists, his thumbs stroking back and forth over my skin, inhaling deeply once, then again, then a third time, and I realize he's breathing me in, using my scent to calm himself.

I wrap my arms around his neck, standing on tiptoe until he bends and kisses me again. He fists his hands in the back of my shirt and holds me so tight that I can barely breathe, like he can imprint his body on mine. Like his life depends on it.

Six weeks. Six weeks, and he's this deep under my skin. Six weeks, and he has fundamentally altered the core of everything I am.

How did I live for the last seven years with him so close but never knowing he was here?

"Can you have Deacon tell them to leave?" I ask.

Another deep breath, then he intertwines our fingers. "No. If Frank and Delilah came in person, I have to meet them in person."

Foreboding washes over me. "Don't go. Stay up here with me."

A smile curves one side of his lips, and he knuckles a few fallen silver strands behind my ear. "Don't worry, love. You are mine. We're fated. I married you, not a proxy. Nothing can take what we have away. Do you want to stay up here?"

"No." I take his hand. He's so confident, but he doesn't know them like I do. I have to protect him in any way I can. "If you're going, so am I."

I let him lead me from his suite of rooms. We collect Parker, Zev, Maddox, and some of the guards as we go, and I assume Killian called for them through the pack tie—something I'm part of now but still in that separate space for some reason. I'll have to ask about it soon.

Maddox keeps looking at me out of the corner of his eye, but I barely have the presence of mind to notice. Especially because everyone else is staring at me too.

They can smell that I'm no longer wolfless.

"Selene," Parker murmurs. "Do you have something to share?"

"There was silver embedded in an old wound in my shoulder," I say, my voice low. "It's been there as long as I can remember. It kept me from shifting."

I swear I got that wound from my father when I was thirteen. But now ...

The wolves around us exchange glances.

"How did it get there?" Maddox asks sharply.

I have a flash of memory so vivid, it stops me in my tracks.

The forest is dark and huge, and I'm so tired of running.

*Mama!*

*Be brave, baby. If you have no wolf, he can never find you.*

Then that same voice, more recent.

*Selenite, there are things you must know …*

My breathing goes harsh. I've never remembered anything like that before.

Did freeing my wolf free some old memory associated with it too?

But how is that possible if I was a child and wolves don't emerge until we're in our teens?

"Selene?" Killian waits for me. He lifts my hand, kisses my knuckles. "You can wait upstairs. You don't have to see them."

"No." I clutch his hand. The foreboding looms larger. I don't want to be separated from him.

"But she has a wolf—" one of the guards starts.

A growl rumbles from Killian. "Focus. The Beaumonts first."

The whole conversation feels distant. The last time I saw Bianca, I was in a cell in the Redcedar Hollow pack dungeons. She delivered drugged food and a kick to my ribs that knocked the wind from me.

My family traded my life for conquest. My parents, at least, did it with a sense of cold practicality. But Bianca reveled in my suffering.

When we were children, she coddled me like a little doll. I didn't notice the way she treated people she saw as less than her. Then I had no wolf—or so we thought—and she took it as a personal betrayal. She made my life hell.

I feel suddenly dizzy and feverish. A mistreated child should be more afraid of their parents, right?

But the person I fear most is my sister. And what did Harper say before I killed her?

*Bianca is the one pushing us forward. She's the future of the pack. Once she's in charge, it's over for Shattered Moon and for you.*

We reach the gallery above the foyer. Near the wall, there's a place where someone standing upstairs can look down, see who has arrived, and not be seen.

I press my back to the wall and look down, and there they are.

My family stands with Deacon Jones and another man I recognize as

Marcus Vandran's arcanist, Warden Eli Whitlock. Redcedar Hollow and Fall Line soldiers are arrayed around them.

My sister looks the same—a towering Amazon with a perfect body, ballad-worthy face, apple green eyes, and thick, curled honey-blond locks that brush her waist even though her hair is pulled into a high ponytail. She's wearing combat clothes in shades of gray and black with high black boots and a cropped jacket in Redcedar Hollow's signature dark green.

My mother looks like her, but smaller, more severe, and older in that stretched, subtly surgical way. She had to travel all the way to Chicago for those surgeries—the largest cities are the only places they can do them anymore.

My mother is wearing a flattering black dress that nips in at her waist with a belt. A green coat is draping her shoulders, though her arms aren't in the sleeves. She has a green bag in one hand and pushes up over-sized dark sunglasses with the other, emphasizing her sharp, perfectly manicured crimson nails.

*They claim Selene isn't their blood at all.*

Bianca looks so much like her, and Jackson was a perfect mix of my mother and father. Even Finn has the stubborn set of my father's jaw.

I look for myself in Delilah Beaumont's face and find nothing, just like there was nothing of Killian in Alaric Bane.

My father wears a more formal version of pack combat gear. If Bianca is dressed like a soldier, he's dressed like a general: dark pants, a black button-up shirt, and a military-style coat with a high collar that just has hints of green at the wrists and throat.

I search his weathered face and don't find myself there either.

This is insane. If I weren't theirs, I would know.

Their presence sparks a visceral fear inside me. A weight presses down on my chest. A quiet whimper works its way up my throat. I shake my hand free of Killian's and back up into the hall. Back, back, not looking, seeking shadows where I'll be safe.

I hit a wall, and I close my eyes, my heart slamming against my ribs.

This is so stupid. I lived with them my entire life. I faced them every day. Why am I having a panic attack?

*Because I have so much more to lose. I know what it's like to be happy. I know what it's like to be free. I let myself believe the suffering had ended.*

I shove the heels of my hands into my eyes until I see dancing lights and try to get enough air, try to think, but I can't, I can't, I—

There's warmth around me, and I open my eyes to see Killian. He's standing between me and the world, one hand braced on the wall over my head. He wraps the other around my waist and tugs me close so I'm braced against his solid chest. I don't have to say anything, don't have to explain.

He kisses the top of my head. "Don't be afraid. We're going to handle this, and then I'm going to take you right back up to that bedroom, and we are going to start our honeymoon."

I curl my fingers into his shirt and muffle a sob against his chest. *"I have a terrible feeling,"* I say through my little part of the pack tie that connects me only to him.

He tilts my chin up to kiss me softly. His eyes capture me like they always do, a warm honey brown that's filled with so much understanding, so much kindness, so much care. *"We'll be quick."*

I hold that moment with him. Memorize it. His eyes, the way he holds me, the way it feels to be close to him, because I can't shake the fear it's our last.

"Are you ready?" he murmurs.

"Yes." I'm not, but I won't let my family see how weak they make me.

"They told you so many lies, Selene. Remember who you are."

"The wife of an Alpha, who has a wolf after all?" I ask dryly.

He gives me an odd look. "No. A stubborn, observant, wickedly intelligent woman who can run circles around all of them on your worst day."

I kiss him again. I want to believe him. I want to believe that the woman he sees in me matters. But the most stubborn, observant, intelligent person in the world can't do a thing against a strong, violent enemy who catches them by surprise.

Killian takes my hand, and we move through the gallery to the top of the stairs, his guards in formation behind us.

Silence falls among the wolves in the foyer as Killian and I pause at the top of the stairs. My parents and Whitlock are dressed so formally, I wish I'd put on something nicer than the soft sweater and comfortable jeans.

We descend the stairs. Deacon Jones leans toward my father, exchanging words I can't hear. The two of them look much too friendly for comfort. Killian must feel the same because he snarls softly, and his power rises in a prickling tide.

Despite his irritation, when we meet my parents in the center of the room, Killian's tone is cordial. "Alpha Beaumont. You've taken us by surprise. How can I help my new ally? I see you've brought others from the Conclave."

Now that we're on the ground level, I see others who were hidden from view when we were standing in the gallery. People I don't recognize and who aren't wolves. They stand behind the Redcedar Hollow soldiers and off to one side, but I catch their scents in eddies of air and marvel at how much stronger my senses have become.

One of the men has the spicy scent of witch magic about him. Another woman, tall with bark-brown hair and serious, wise eyes, has the unmistakable presence of the nature-touched, like a whiff of pure, wild outdoor air with a hint of petrichor.

Killian nods to them, composed, even though I swear I feel a faint sense of confusion and surprise through the wispy connection of our incomplete bond. When he looks at Whitlock, that confusion deepens. *"Whatever is going on, whatever the tests said about your blood, Vandran didn't warn me."*

The pit in my stomach grows heavy, hard, and cold. Sofia appears and comes to stand beside us, her arms folded across her chest. Her eyes flick to Killian's, and I assume she says something through the pack tie. Whatever it is makes Killian tighten his grip on my hand.

I don't see Eva, and I'm sharply relieved that wherever she has Finn, he's safe.

My mother steps forward, her green coat sweeping around her like a cloak. She gives Killian a cursory dip of her head—the bare minimum respect owed an Alpha in his own pack house.

"Alpha Darrow. Forgive us for springing this on you, but we wanted to be sure we caught you at home."

Killian has angled his body so that he's almost between me and my family, but it doesn't help now that they're so close. I catch their scents and feel the blood drain from my face. All the sick, hateful, terrifying things they make me feel come rushing back, and I *remember*.

This harrowing fear used to be my norm. I felt it all the time, a low, grinding awareness always at the back of my mind. Now I'm right back in that state, aware, afraid, helpless, like these last six weeks in Shattered Moon never happened.

"You've caught us, then. With help." Killian casts an expressionless glance at Deacon Jones. Then he addresses the members of the

Conclave. "Forgive me for not being ready; we weren't expecting you until next month."

"We're not staying. Just popping over to make sure everyone holds up all bargains made," says the man who smells like rich, expensive spices. He's tall and fair-skinned with neatly cut light brown hair and eyes that flash a deep, multifaceted purple, a telltale sign of witch blood.

"I certainly have, even when others have acted in bad faith." Killian's gaze passes mildly over my parents, then Bianca.

My eyes catch on my sister. She's wearing a gaudy large necklace with a pendant of black stone that flashes yellow in the morning light slanting in through the foyer windows. Bianca is also wearing thick black bracelets with carved obsidian beads as big as the top part of my thumb and earrings to match. Usually she has better taste.

I make a face. I hope someone rips her earrings out.

Maybe it will be me.

Then Killian's and Bianca's eyes lock. His gaze lingers on her, and it seems like he has to tear himself away. He seems shaken.

What the hell?

"Why ... why have you come?" Killian asks.

Terror bottoms out my stomach as Bianca flashes her teeth at me in a horrible parody of a smile. She's let her canines grow long.

When I look up at Killian, he's still staring at her.

The truth hits me with sudden, horrible clarity.

It doesn't matter what we do here.

Somehow, Killian and I have already lost.

"We're here for you, of course, Alpha." Bianca's voice is as honeyed as the color of her hair, a thick, sensuous purr that always gets her what she wants. "There's been a misunderstanding, I'm afraid. You're standing next to the wrong woman. I was always meant to be your mate."

# Thirty

## SELENE

Killian tugs me closer. His eyes go to my mother's. In a wolf pack with an Alpha Pair, it's most often the Alpha Lady who makes decisions on where the pack should go, which bargains should be struck, which treaties honored. It's the job of the Alpha Lord to make sure everyone else falls in line.

"I'm standing next to the woman you sent. The one I claimed. The daughter of the Alpha Pair of Redcedar Hollow."

My mother pulls her sunglasses from her face with elegant, crimson-nailed fingers, and her eyes flick to me. There's such hatred there, I flinch.

"Oh, dear," she says in her dry, bored voice. "You think this weak little bitch is mine?"

It's like the world hiccups, slipping on its axis. My brows pinch together. "Mother?"

Delilah Beaumont flips the sunglasses closed and stows them in a pocket. "I'm so sorry, Alpha Darrow. As we've said, there was a mistake. Bianca wasn't quite ready to make the transition from Redcedar Hollow to Shattered Moon yet, so we sent a servant in place of our daughter so the treaty could be honored while still giving her time to adjust. My mate and I only share one living child," her mouth twists bitterly, "and that is my daughter, Bianca. Selene was never more than a stand-in."

My vision tunnels. I step toward my mother without thinking. "You're lying."

Two giant soldiers from Redcedar Hollow move in to block my way, which makes Maddox and Parker jump in front of me. There are snarls and growls all around.

My father waves a hand, his voice bored. "Stand down, stand down."

The two Redcedar Hollow guards obey. Only when they move do Maddox and Parker follow suit.

"My lady isn't a liar," my father says in his low, sophisticated drawl. "Twenty years ago, a rogue woman on the run came to me and asked me to take in her pup and raise her as my own. Out of the goodness of my heart, I agreed. But Selene is fully grown, and the lie has gone on long enough. Especially now that she's trying to steal Bianca's place. She knew she was to be a proxy. She lied and whored her way into your heart, Alpha Darrow, and for that I deeply apologize."

I grab Killian's arm with both hands as he lunges forward, and soldiers are suddenly leaping between all of us again. Yellow flashes in Killian's eyes.

*"Don't let him provoke you,"* I plead.

Killian's voice takes on the gravel of a wolf partway through transformation. "Speak of my wife that way again, and I'll tear your fucking head off and feed it to yours."

The Shattered Moon wolves who have gathered to watch the scene erupt into whispers. All the work I've done trying to get them to trust me has been half-undone in an instant. I feel like I've been stabbed in the stomach.

"My true daughter, Bianca, will be your mate," my mother—is she my mother?—declares. "The treaty is clear. You were to marry the daughter of the Alpha Pair of Redcedar Hollow, and that is Bianca. It's really very simple, you see?"

"I married Selene Beaumont," Killian growls.

My mother raises one perfect eyebrow. In a drawl well-matched to my father's, she says, "That person doesn't exist."

"Alpha Darrow." A new voice, deep and smooth with an aristocratic drawl, cuts across the room, and the crowd parts for Warden Whitlock. Killian nods to his guards, and they allow the arcanist to approach.

Whitlock reaches our side and lowers his voice to whisper in Killian's ear. His voice is low and sonorous. "Unfortunately, our blood tests show that Selene is indeed not a Beaumont. The Alphas of Redcedar Hollow requested the presence of the Conclave because the treaty is clear. Our warlord sends his condolences and says he'll help in any way he can, but if you reject Bianca and continue your relationship with Selene, the Beaumonts will be within their rights to bring the joint forces of the Conclave down on Shattered Moon."

No. No, no, no. This can't be happening.

Bianca lifts a brow and flashes that predator's smile again. "You should encourage him to make the right choice, Selene."

I bare my teeth. My wolf rises. I know it must lengthen my canines and flash in my eyes because Bianca's go wide. She looks me over as if seeing me for the first time and whispers, "What?"

"This is all pointless," Killian says. "I married Selene by name. We sealed the ceremony with her blood and mine. There was no mention of Bianca. Nothing was done by proxy."

The man who smells like spice shrugs one shoulder. "Technicalities, really, Alpha. The Conclave has a vested interest in seeing the treaty honored. We're more than happy to allow the marriage papers to be edited in light of the misunderstanding."

"No!" I snarl.

Just like that, their eyes are all on me.

"Selene," Bianca's voice is silky over the silence. "Did the Beta happen to tell you why else we're here? We were *so* happy when Beta Jones recovered Finn for Daddy."

Finn? No. He's here. He's safe. He has to be with Eva.

But when I look around, then up at the pack of children leaning through the railings of the balcony, I see Eva, and I don't see him. My father's expression is smug. But it's my mother's scowl that truly confirms the truth of Bianca's words.

"Jones," Killian snarls.

"No! Where have you taken him?" My cry echoes from the walls and ceiling of the foyer at the same time as Killian's.

Killian lunges for Deacon, but the Beta jumps behind my parents and their guards.

"I should have exiled you weeks ago!" Killian barks.

"Don't be so quick, Alpha," Bianca says smoothly. "Selene, you should know that all of the wolfless of Redcedar Hollow say hello. In fact, Noelle is with them right now. I'm keeping in touch with her over the pack tie. I'm sure they're *dying* to hear what you and Killian do here."

Killian goes still. The muscles in his jaw work. He's never met the wolfless I consider my true family, but he knows I love them, and apparently, that alone is enough to pull him up short. "What do you want?"

"Simple, like I said," my mother replies. "Selene is not our daughter. Bianca is. She'll take her rightful place at your side."

I laugh without humor. "So when you thought being with Killian was a death sentence, you sent me. But now that you know it's not, you want your power. Or you want Bianca close to Killian so she can murder him in his sleep. Good luck with that."

"I refuse to believe that Selene isn't your daughter," Killian says.

Whitlock sighs and gives Killian a deeply sympathetic look. "I knew it would come to this. It's why I'm here. His Excellency the Warlord wanted to make sure the proper procedures were observed." The old man digs in a black bag at his waist and produces a knife with a blade of rippling black metal and a vial. From another pocket, he produces a small clear bottle with golden liquid inside.

He gestures at one of the Conclave members. "High Priest Erebos, if you would? I've brought supplies. We'll perform the test."

"What is this?" I demand.

"It's a familial test," Killian says, his voice low and terse. "I saw it done when I worked for Vandran." He switches to speaking in my mind and says, *"To confirm the identity of ... hostages. You and your parents each give blood. A drop of the gold liquid goes in. If you're related, it turns gold. If not, it turns transparent."*

*"Hostages?"* I stare up at him. *"What did Vandran have you do?"*

Killian looks away.

The witch man—apparently a High Priest, which is one of the titles of a coven head—takes the items from Whitlock. He examines the components, turning them over, sniffing them. He takes out a small bell and strikes it against each. They flash white.

"What was that?" I ask.

"He just cleansed them of any existing energy or spell, ensuring I didn't leave any lingering magic on them," Whitlock says. He speaks with a bored, academic inflection, then nods to a few others in the crowd. "The other witches here can confirm that's what happened if you'd like. Every party must be satisfied that things are aboveboard."

Killian demands confirmation, and a few other witches come forward and confirm the components are clean.

"Alphas," Erebos says.

As one, my parents hold out their hands. He nicks their fingertips, drawing welling drops of crimson that plink into the vial. Then he turns to me.

Killian stands between the High Priest and me. He doesn't move.

I shelter behind him, my brain still whirling. I don't remember another life. If I were brought to Redcedar Hollow twenty years ago, I would have been four. Plenty old enough to remember. If I had another mother, I would remember her too.

But there are the dreams. The visions. The voice I've been hearing since I first came to Shattered Moon.

*He'll never find you.*

Being a Beaumont is all I've ever known.

What if they're telling the truth?

Who am I?

Gently, I push Killian aside. Or at least I put a hand on his arm and say, "Let it be done." In his mind, I say, *"We have no choice."*

*"I'll force them to leave. I'll kill them if I have to."*

*"Then the Conclave will destroy Shattered Moon and you sentence the rest of the pack to death."*

Reluctantly, Killian stands aside, but he glares unabashedly at Erebos as the man raises a knife to my outstretched hand and pricks my finger. The High Priest flashes Killian a look out of the corner of his eye as he does it. He masks it well, but I can tell Killian's looming presence makes him nervous.

Erebos gently squeezes, and my blood falls into the vial as well. Then he unscrews the dropper lid from the golden liquid and trickles one drop into the vial with the blood.

I hold my breath. I wait for the rest of the liquid in the vial to turn gold.

Instead, it goes crystal clear.

"I am sorry," Erebos murmurs, an expression that could be real sympathy on his face. Then he turns and lifts it, showing the rest of the room. "Selene is not the child of Delilah and Frank Beaumont."

All the air goes out of the world. I can see the moment it hits Killian too, the way they've maneuvered us. Everything that's at stake.

When the Alphas of Redcedar Hollow pick a fight, it's because they know they've already won. Every single time except one: when they started a pack war with a young Alpha they thought was weak and disguised that war as vengeance for their dead son. An Alpha who held them off, almost on his own, for five long years.

Killian didn't even win their war. He forced them into a tie. One they've already tried to cheat their way out of once. But he thwarted them there too. He keeps beating them.

Only then do I realize how deep their hatred of Killian must go.

They have Finn.

They have the wolfless.

They have the terms of the treaty on their side.

If we don't do what they say, everyone and everything Killian and I love will be crushed. We might survive. We might be able to stay together. But the cost ...

There's a low sound, like distant thunder. A terrible electricity crackles in the air. I catch the smell of eldritch magic, ancient and cold.

"I won't let you do this." Killian's eyes have gone yellow. Through our incomplete bond, I feel the curse surge inside him. His aura turns jagged and sharp-edged.

"Killian, no!"

I reach for him. We're jammed into the foyer. If he somehow calls on the curse take him now, he'll kill us all.

Can he? I don't know. The way he fights it, I doubt he's ever tried.

Before I can grab him, Bianca steps forward, lays a hand on his cheek, and whispers, "Be still."

There's a strange burst. Like the inverse of light coming from somewhere behind my eyes. Something in the vicinity of my heart shifts, like a door slamming.

The magic of the curse winks out.

I cry out and grab Killian's hand. "What did you do?"

But when my mate, my husband, looks at me again, there's no warmth or kindness, no care in his topaz eyes. They're as cold and faceted as cut gemstone.

Slowly, he withdraws his hand from mine, then takes Bianca's and pulls it to his lips, kissing the back of her knuckles. He bows to my parents.

"It will be my pleasure to honor the treaty."

Then those blank eyes find me. "Beta Jones, throw this woman into the old servants' rooms and find a collar. She's going to pay for the lies she told."

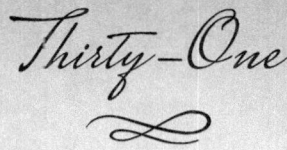

## Thirty-One

### SELENE

"**K**illian!"

I reach for him, but he pulls away. Beta Jones gestures, and two pack soldiers I don't know grab my arms bruisingly hard and drag me back. They're taking me toward that tarp-covered hallway that leads to the never-repaired old wing of the castle. Alaric Bane's wing.

"Killian, what are you doing?!" Eva is above us in the gallery, leaning over the railing.

He doesn't even look at her.

Parker, Zev, and Sofia all move toward me.

"Back away," Killian snarls, releasing a shockwave of Alpha power.

It's like they've been hit by a train. They don't just stop; they go flying backward.

Maddox watches it all with his arms folded across his chest, his gold-violet eyes impassively searching Killian's face. But when Eva rushes down the stairs and tries to approach, her son wraps an arm around her waist and forces his struggling mother behind him. "Mom, stay back."

I fight with everything I have, kicking and throwing my weight, but even with the new strength of a full werewolf slowly creeping into my body, I can't shake the soldiers who are carrying me between them.

"Killian!" I reach through the incomplete mate bond, pressing toward him with all my strength.

He shakes his head, blinks, and looks at me. For an instant, I see horror in his eyes. "Selene ..."

Bianca moves between us, breaking our eye contact, and the moment is shattered. She touches his cheek again, and he lifts his hand to press it close, just like he's done dozens of times with mine.

"No!" I reach out to him through the pack tie he set up between us, one that's isolated from everyone except him. *"Killian!"*

It's like running face-first into a wall. I can't get through. He's closed me off, and I have no access to anyone else.

The soldiers tear down the tarp and drag me into the broken old hallway. They shoulder open the smaller door just inside, then throw me into the narrow, dark space beyond.

"Wait!" I leap to my feet and desperately try to throw power behind my words the way I did when I flung Claudia across the piano room.

The soldiers slam the door so close to my face, it nearly breaks my nose. There's the heavy thump of a bolt being slid into place. When I try the handle, it doesn't move.

"No!" I smash my body into the heavy wood, pound my fists against it.

Forty-five minutes ago, I was asleep in bed next to my mate. My husband. The man I realize too late that I love. That I have loved in small, growing pieces since he knelt at my feet in the forest and looked at me like I was a goddess.

There's only silence outside. Either the soldiers are gone or they refuse to answer.

My breathing ragged, I press my back to the door and face the pitch-black hall, fighting the urge to collapse in a heap and sob. My eyes adjust, and I see dim lines of light at intervals beneath what must be doors leading off the hallway I find myself trapped in.

"Okay. It's okay," I whisper, trying not to give in to the vivid image of the ghost of an evil, long-dead Alpha king stalking me through the dark.

I move to the closest line of light and feel around at doorknob level until my fingers brush metal, then grasp and turn. The door swings open to reveal a tiny cubicle of a room with a moth-eaten, dust-covered cot that barely fits inside. There are hooks on the walls—presumably for clothes—and a narrow chest of drawers jammed in next to the head of the bed. I can stretch out my arms and span the width of the space with my palms pressed flat against the walls.

It's worse than Redcedar Hollow. Smaller, danker. It smells like mothballs, mildew, and subtle rot. No surprise, since it hasn't been occupied in twenty years. I move the two steps it takes to get to the back of the room and the tiny window. Even when I climb on the cot, it's too high for me to see anything outside except an iron-gray sky and silent, swirling snow.

I exhale all at once. Tears burn the backs of my eyes still, but I refuse to let them fall.

I knew it would all be ripped from me.

*Twenty years ago, a rogue woman on the run came to me and asked me to take in her pup and raise her as my own.*

If I'm not a Beaumont, who am I?

There's that strange flash, pain and fear half-remembered. The voice. I touch my shoulder where the old wound was, then pull my sweater aside and look.

Without the silver, the wound is gone. Only a crescent-shaped mark bisected with a jagged white scar remains.

I turn toward the light, trying to see it better. The moon-shaped mark doesn't look like it's from the injury. It looks natural, like a birthmark hidden for years by puckered pink skin.

I roll my shoulder. There's no pain. Not even a twinge.

Just one more way everything has changed.

I give myself one minute to grapple with it all. To shatter. To rage and finally cry. Then I pull on the practicality that got me through the last decade of my life like a well-worn coat, dry my eyes, and get to work.

I go back into the hallway. The first thing I do is open all of the doors so that the weak light from the windows can stream in. I find a small communal bathroom about halfway down the hall and a stairwell that winds both up and down at the end.

Surprised, I explore. Both directions lead to more servants' rooms. There are only two floors up from here but several floors down. The lower floors don't have windows. Each floor has at least one bathroom. When I try the faucets and flush the toilets, I find that the bathrooms on the bottommost floor and the floor above mine work. The sink spits out brown water at first, but it goes clear after it runs for several minutes. So I have free access to water and toilets. That's a relief.

There have to be at least a hundred servants' rooms in this forgotten little area. But as much as I search, I don't find another way out.

I collect the few useful things I find in the empty rooms—extra blankets and pillows, a few dusty but otherwise clean towels, a second thin mattress —take them to the room I've chosen, and make it as comfortable as I can.

Then I wrap one of the threadbare blankets around my shoulders, return to the heavy wooden door that leads into the ruined hallway, and sink to the cold stone floor, my back to the wall. With my heightened wolf senses, I listen for any movement outside.

If I'm going to escape, I need to know whether or not there are guards.

With nothing else to do, I close my eyes and have no choice but to internalize the events of the morning for real.

I'm worried about Finn to the point of being sick, but my mind is taken up with Killian.

Bianca quieted the curse. *How?* Maybe I missed it in the brightness of the foyer, but I didn't see any lights beneath her skin. If it is bloodline magic and we aren't related, she shouldn't be able to do it.

But as soon as she touched him, his eyes ... I shudder at the memory of his beautiful, warm eyes gone dead and cold when he looked at me.

For a moment, I wrestle with my former beliefs. Part of me, an old part, screams that I never should have trusted an Alpha. That what happened in the foyer happened because Killian saw the writing on the wall, saw the chance to save his own skin, gain more power, and strengthen his pack, and took it.

Not long ago, that part of me would have drowned out everything else, and any tenderness I had for Killian would've festered and turned to hate, no second chances, no questions asked.

But I know him. The man he is beyond the curse, beyond the Alpha power he was given by a lucky combination of DNA.

Oddly, I hear Claudia's voice in my memory, slurred with wine.

*"No one will blame you for leaving, Selenite. Killian won't either. He's simply too much of a gentleman to tell you he wants you gone, just like the rest of us."*

*"A gentleman, is he? I guess he's not much like his father, after all."*

*"Hm? Oh, no, he's very much like his father."*

*"Alaric Bane was a gentleman?"*

*"Alaric Bane? No, his father—"*

I was too distracted to think much of it at the time, but what if she was going to say his father was someone else? Eva hesitated to call Bane Killian's father too.

Killian not being Bane's son isn't a thought I would've entertained before today. But I'm not a Beaumont, so who knows? Maybe no one's parents are who they think they are.

What a terrible joke.

I sit there for hours, until my thoughts are well-worn circular ruts. Hunger claws delicately at my guts, the first harbinger of a familiar old ache.

I rise and go back to the first room I walked into. With the extra mattress and the heap of blankets I gathered, it won't be the worst place I've ever slept in. Still, I fold several of the extra blankets and hide them in various other rooms. If Bianca comes in and thinks I'm too comfortable, she'll take them from me.

My stomach prickles with a more insistent hunger. I am not looking forward to adjusting to going without food again.

God, I hope they're feeding Finn. And Killian ... my stomach curdles at what Bianca did, somehow. Is it another curse? Magical mind control?

My poor love, so terrified of losing control as the monster. Now she's brought that nightmare to him even when he's a man.

But Killian knows how to fight. For five years, he's kept the beast from doing its worst. Maybe he can fight this too.

I shiver and hug myself. We didn't tell anyone we were fated. Even though Killian has blocked me from speaking to him on the pack tie, he hasn't rejected our mate bond. If Bianca is controlling him and she finds out about it, she will absolutely force him to.

Whatever she's done to him, it hasn't compelled him to tell her yet, so maybe he does have some control.

It's a tiny thread of hope, but I hold on to it.

I've curled up with just enough of the thin blankets not to shiver when I hear the snick of the bolt being drawn on the main door. I rise as someone enters my room, unwilling to be caught lying down. I brace myself for Bianca.

It's Claudia.

I let out a sigh that probably sounds irritated but is mostly relieved. It's like expecting to face down a bear and finding a yapping little dog. "Claudia. What?"

Killian's mother stands in the doorway in her signature impeccable black, red lips curved in a smirk. "I'll let your rudeness go this time,

Selene, since you're finally back where you belong. I knew it would happen sooner or later."

"Right." I angle around her to see out the hall door.

Two pack soldiers stand just visible on either side. Whether they came to escort Claudia or were there the whole time and just preternaturally silent, I have no idea.

Bolting would be useless. I move back to the bed, drop onto it, and massage my temples. I was able to bide my time at Redcedar Hollow for eleven years. I can be patient again. But what will happen to Killian and Finn in the meantime? What will happen to the Shattered Moon Pack?

"Please leave me alone, Claudia."

She stalks into my space. "That's *Lady Darrow* to you," she hisses. Her power fills the space like a tide. Like Killian's.

Claudia is *strong*. I'm not sure why so many people don't take her seriously as an Alpha, even one whose power is subservient to Killian's. Can't they tell?

Then I remember how much time she spends drunk and sneaking around, listening in for tidbits she can use for blackmail, and being generally heinous company.

I can't take her seriously either.

I shrug in response to her. Maybe she'll shift. Maybe she'll tear me to pieces, but I doubt it. "If you don't like how I speak to you, the door is behind you."

"You arrogant little bitch!"

"I'm serious, Claudia. I can see you came here to gloat. Okay, you did it. You see me in the circumstances you think I deserve. You were right all along. Now I want to sleep. Go away."

I pull up my blanket, ready to lie down again. Claudia rips it off me. "You're not going to take this moment from me. You deserve this. You're back where you belong, where your whore mother always belonged—"

Her eyes flare. We both go very, very still. She clamps her mouth shut and releases my blanket. She starts to back out of the room.

I stand. "Excuse me?"

Claudia knows my mother. Claudia knows who I am.

She has *always known* who I am.

It's no wonder Killian keeps her around instead of exiling her. She knows everything, but she's got the secret-keeping capacity of a leaky sieve.

When I first came here, I thought she hated me and thought me unworthy because I was wolfless. Now I suspect it was something else. I suspect Claudia has always known who my real mother is, and for some reason, she hates her.

I don't care how strong she is; I lunge for her and grab her wrist, careful to be quiet and not draw the attention of the guards. "First you make me question who Killian's father is, now you know my mother? Tell me what you know, Claudia!" I whisper.

"Shut up!" she hisses, trying to wrench from my grasp. "You let me go, or I will have them come in here and kill you!"

She throws power into the command. As strong as she is, I should be sucked under by it, especially now that we're in the same pack and I've been made a servant. But instead of sinking, I float, never once going under.

What is happening to me?

I jerk her wrist, pulling her closer. She's taller than me, but she stumbles. "You said something about my mother. My real mother. Who is she?"

Claudia shoves me, but she doesn't anticipate my slowly increasing strength. "I was talking about Delilah!" she whisper-shrieks.

"You weren't, or you wouldn't be panicking now." It won't be long before the guards pick up on the commotion and come in here. I have to get her to tell me. I have to know.

Claudia's lips curl into a sneer. "You're just like her. You act all sweet to get the attention of the most powerful man in the room, then hog it all for yourself. That's how I knew from the beginning I'd hate you. That you could never be good enough for my son!"

"Who am I just like?" I demand.

Claudia tries again to jerk her hand free. "Fuck you!"

I snarl. Heat prickles inside me, the warmth of the silver light times a thousand, the same feeling I had when I threw her into a wall. Magic saturates my words as I command, "Tell me whatever secret it is you're keeping!"

"Killian is not Alaric Bane's son!" Claudia blurts.

We both freeze. All other thoughts are driven from my mind. I'm so shocked, I release her. "What?"

I was right. I was *right*.

Claudia twists, looks out into the hall. We both wait.

The two guards continue their low conversation, completely undisturbed.

"Killian isn't Bane's son," she repeats, the words clearly spilling out against her will. "I lied. When Vandran dragged him and that Quinn boy back home that night and threatened us ... I'd already been saying he was Bane's for years. I never thought they'd be so stupid, stealing from Marcus Vandran. I lied to save my son's life, and they believed me because they knew I used to be part of Conqueror's Moon." Her eyes sharpen. "Bane had so many children, and without his body, there was no way to do a familial test. It was so easy. Vandran wanted to believe."

"But Eva knows, doesn't she? That's why you hate her, too. She's the only one who can threaten your fake status as the mother of the only surviving child of Alaric Bane." The hate in her eyes tells me I'm right, so I demand, "Who is Killian's real father?"

Her lips tremble, and her eyes are glassy and horrified. She presses her hand to her mouth and shakes her head. "You ... you made me tell you."

Then, before I can say anything else, move, or even get a hold on my thoughts, she runs from the room. "Guards! She's attacking me! She's insane! Lock the door!"

"No, wait!" I shout.

But as soon as Claudia is out the door, they slam it and almost break my nose again.

"Damn it," I whisper into the darkness. "What about me? Who am I?"

# Thirty-Two

## SELENE

I try to reach Killian through the pack tie again. I'm desperate to tell him what his mother said. I'm also desperate to know what Claudia knows about my true parents. But when I try to touch Killian's mind, it's like running into a wall again, except now it's made of rubble. The pack tie isn't gone, but it's damaged in a way that it wasn't before.

What did Bianca make him do?

I retreat into my own thoughts and a thousand questions, which are all I have for company.

If Claudia knew my mother, does that mean my mother was also part of Shattered Moon?

Is that why I keep having déjà vu and that dreamlike sense of knowing the castle? Was I born here?

If Alaric Bane isn't Killian's father, who is?

Will it change how he sees himself to know the Alpha King's violence isn't his legacy?

Will it change things for the Beaumonts if they know he doesn't have the connection to Bane that Dad—Frank—covets so very much?

I obsess over it all until I fall into a fitful sleep. No one brings me dinner.

Thankfully, no one brings a collar either.

AT FIRST, I think the woman in the dream is me.

She stands with her back to me at the edge of a pool of bright blue water, and I recognize the spring that bubbles up from below the cliff beneath the pack house. She's tall and ghostly pale. It seems like she's silvery and glowing from the light of the moon, but that isn't it. There's no moon in the sky.

All of the silver light is coming from her, swirling in slow whorls beneath her skin.

Then she turns, and I realize I'm not seeing myself. This woman's hair is longer. It leans more to pale gold than silver. She's a few years older than me.

Her mouth moves. Whispers echo to me in confused, rippling waves, overlapping and tangling together.

It's the voice I keep hearing in visions and dreams.

*... there are things you must know.*

*... must ...*

*He'll never find you now ...*

*... something ...*

*... find you ...*

*... find ...*

Then her eyes blaze white, and suddenly, the voice is clear. A rune appears, burning bright in the air between us, silver and sharp as wolf's teeth.

*Find it, Selenite. There is something you must see.*

Selenite.

That's what Claudia called me. More than once.

She didn't just know my mother. She knew *me*.

The shock of it tears me from the dream with a gasp. I shoot up, looking wildly around the room, expecting to see the woman because I feel her presence surrounding me.

I'm alone.

I DON'T KNOW when I fall asleep again, but I'm woken by a crash that has me sitting up for a second time. I roll out of bed into a crouch, ready to run, as if, by instinct, I know who has come to visit me. As if I can sense the oppressive weight of her nearness. But there is no running. No escaping.

Bianca looms in my doorway.

Without preamble, she lunges, grabs me by the hair, throws me to the floor, and kicks me in the ribs. Pain explodes along them, terrible and familiar.

I have returned to hell.

She kicks again. I grunt at the impact and curl into myself. Without the silver in my shoulder, I'm still growing stronger, just like Killian said I would. It doesn't hurt as much as it would have even last night, but there's still pain.

The kicks stop. Bianca drops into a crouch next to me and strokes my hair.

"Did you miss me, little sister?" she purrs. "I told Momma and Daddy you would."

I bare my teeth but remain curled up. "Where's Finn?"

She laughs. I *hate* her laugh. I hate how light and infectious it must be to people who don't know her for the evil demon hellspawn she is.

Her fingers are almost soothing against the top of my head. She grabs my face and tilts my chin up, examining me. "It looks like they've been letting you eat everything in sight, little piggy. Don't worry. I'll make sure you only get what you deserve again."

"What did you do to Killian?" I hate the tears in my voice just as much as I hate her laugh. No matter how much I want to, I refuse to let them fall.

Her smile turns indulgent. "I made him mine. Last night, in his bed. We marked each other."

"Liar," I hiss. The pack tie is damaged, but the wispy threads that dance between his soul and mine are unchanged. If he marked someone else, it would break his bond with me. And that's aside from the fact that anyone who bonds with Killian will share his curse.

Bianca's eyes narrow. "How would you know whether or not I'm lying about that, Selene?"

Dread settles in my stomach at my mistake. My mind whirs, searching for an excuse, a distraction, a way to protect him and keep her from marking him as long as possible. I could tell her about the curse, but something holds me back. She has some kind of power over him— she showed it yesterday when she calmed him.

But having that power means she might already know about the curse. If that's the case, how much does she know? Can she break it? If they mate bond, would it even affect her?

I have to keep her from marking him for as long as I can. Not just because I want to protect Killian, but because if they become an Alpha Pair, his strength will magnify Bianca's. I can't allow that to happen. For my sake, for the wolfless, and for everyone she'll terrorize if she gets what she wants.

And then I know exactly what to do.

Bianca loves one thing more than torturing me, and that is torturing me in front of as many witnesses as possible. The more important, the better. She's also just intelligent enough to think she's smarter than everyone else and cunning enough to assume she can tell when she's being tricked. I've used those things against her in the past, and I do so again now.

I let my voice drop into a shaking whisper. It's not hard; I am on the verge of tears. I just let it show. "With the Conclave coming, I thought ... No. You wouldn't humiliate us like that." I breathe out as if in relief. "If it's done, it's done. It's good to know even you aren't that cruel."

The silence is suffocating.

Bianca scoffs. She doesn't say anything right away, but I can practically hear the wheels turning in her brain. She sees the chance I've presented to her. She won't let it pass.

Her hand splays over my head. She stops caressing and instead digs her nails into my scalp. "What a brilliant idea, Selene."

I struggle to sit up. "You said it was done!"

She shrugs one shoulder. "Maybe it wasn't."

"No! You can't!"

She backhands me so hard I spin around and fall onto the cot. My cheek throbs, and there's blood in my mouth. I can already feel the bruise forming under my eye. She grabs me by the hair again and yanks back, forcing me to look into her poisonous green eyes. "Don't you ever tell me what I can't do."

She throws me down and stands. "Now, if you want to see *my* brother again, get your ass up, get in the kitchen, and make my coffee. We'll leave the door to the servants' hall unlocked, but if you run, Finn gets the punishment I would've given you. Do you understand?"

Will Frank let that happen? I'm not sure. I don't think he will, but I can't risk it. "Yes."

"From now on, I'd better have breakfast the way I like it in the

Alpha suite every day by sunrise, or I'll beat the fucking shit out of you. Or Finn. Or maybe I'll make you watch what I can get Killian to do to me. All of those punishments sound like fun."

I sob and struggle to stand. She kicks the back of my knee with her thick-soled black boot, sending me sprawling onto the cot one more time before she laughs and sashays to the door. "I've missed you, Selene. You always were my favorite."

Then she's gone.

I lay there until I'm certain. Until the door slams. The lock doesn't click.

Then I roll onto my side, press both hands over my mouth, and smother a laugh. It's hysterical. Tears fall over my hands, but I laugh all the same.

I did it.

I bought Killian a month before she marks him.

My wounds are already healing. I'm not even dazed by her attack.

Bianca thinks she's dealing with the old me. My parents believe they are too. They pay so little attention to me, I'm not even sure whether any of them but Bianca has noticed I'm not wolfless, and apparently, she's just going to ignore the change.

That's her mistake. I'm not who I was. Not at all.

I am not going to let them get away with this.

When I get ahold of myself again, I begin to plan. The first thing to do is continue to allow Bianca to believe I'm completely under her thumb. The second, to make contact with Sofia, Parker, Zev, and Eva. It should be possible if I'm not going to be confined in this dank hallway. Maybe I'll contact Maddox too. I'm feeling some of his unhinged anger myself right now.

The third thing to do is to find out where they're holding Finn. The fourth, to figure out what hold Bianca has over Killian and find a way to set him free.

Taming my feral smile into an expression of fear and subservience, I rise and go to make my "sister" her coffee.

❀

*February - March 106 WW*

# KILLIAN

There are whispers in the fog. There's blood in the darkness. After five years of no rest, I thought I knew what it meant to be worn down to the bone.

I didn't. Only now, after fighting a losing war against Bianca's control for what feels like an eternity of days and nights, do I know what it is to be exhausted. At first, I think Whitlock will take news to Vandran and they'll do something. But whatever happened that first day, when Bianca's control was strongest, Whitlock must not have noticed anything.

Help isn't coming.

I'm so tired. I just want it to end. But every time I think about rolling over and giving up the scrap of control I've kept from Bianca, I remember Selene's scars.

I know what will happen to my pack if I stay down now. So no matter how much it hurts, no matter how badly it grinds me down, I keep getting up. I keep fighting.

Bianca's mind control is a finicky thing. In my lucid times, I quickly discover that I have a decent amount of minor autonomy unless I have a direct command to be silent or still.

She can command me to do certain things with my magic—like ravage the pack tie just enough to keep Shattered Moon intact but prevent me from communicating mentally.

However, she's not strong enough to compel me to sleep with her or use my Alpha aura against my will. One thing I manage to keep for myself, as well, is the knowledge that Selene is my fated mate. Bianca hasn't commanded me to mark her or to take her mark either. I come out of the fog once to hear her planning and realize she has some brilliant idea to do it in front of the Conclave.

I laugh in her face. "Do it. See what happens to people I share a mate bond with."

Bianca looks confused, then she laughs right back. "Oh, honey. Do you think your curse will pass to me? It won't. I'm protected against it."

My last thought before the fog rises again is to wonder, panicked, how she knows.

She keeps trying to control my aura. The last time, I fight the command so hard that I almost pass out. Interestingly, so does she. Her face turns red, then white. I get the sense I'm not fighting Bianca directly, but something deeper, older. Something that drags its claws along my brain.

It feels like my original curse. Which Bianca, conveniently, can hold back. She doesn't have to touch me. As long as I'm under her control, the monster never comes for me.

I notice, as well, that every time Bianca really has to pit her will against mine, she clutches the giant black gemstone around her neck. Its sickly yellow sheen reminds me of the fog.

When I first suspect the stone is the source of the curse, I make the mistake of lunging for it right away. Bianca commands me to break two of my own fingers after that, then doesn't call for Dr. Bennett until the bones are healed enough that he has to rebreak them for them to heal straight.

How long ago was that now? The fog makes it so I can't keep track. I don't know.

The worst days are the first ones, when Frank and Delilah are still at Shattered Moon. They want to hurry things along by forcing me into an Alpha challenge with Bianca. She refuses. She doesn't just want the pack —she wants me. The most powerful Alpha in a generation. The son of Alaric Bane.

Despite this, I put up enough of a fight that they do discuss murdering me. But even if they succeeded, leadership of the pack would go to my designated heir, which follows a strict hierarchy that's been bound into wolf bones and blood since the first of our kind.

"Who is your heir?" Delilah demands.

Frank scoffs. "It's his Beta. Who else would it be?"

"Is that true, Killian?" Bianca says in her purr. "Is your Beta your pack heir? You haven't named another?"

"Yes," I say in a voice like gravel, grateful I never officially named Maddox my successor.

"Jones would be much easier to kill or control," Delilah says.

Bianca sneers. "Don't be disgusting, Momma. Deacon Jones is ancient."

"He's ten years younger than me," Delilah barks.

"I said what I said," Bianca snips back. "Besides, Jones's Alpha blood is weak. He can barely shift into a hybrid form."

"Don't forget," I grind out, forcing the words even though it feels like I'm trying to breathe and speak underwater, "you still have to kill me first."

They make faces, as if an insect they'd smashed just resurrected and learned to speak.

That statement is all I bother to add. After that, the conversation devolves into another vicious argument between Bianca and her parents. I let the fog take me.

If only they knew.

I can't lie to them if Bianca commands me not to. But even though he thinks he is, Deacon Jones is not my heir.

That position belongs to my original Beta.

Asher Quinn.

He left the pack, but I never exiled him. I never severed the connection all the way.

God, I want to see his face if they succeed at killing me and he suddenly has all of Shattered Moon inside his head and on his shoulders. He may have my capacity, but he's got enough Alpha magic to handle ten times the number of wolves in Shattered Moon without a problem.

He'd try to raise me from the dead just to kill me again.

Soon after that, Bianca forces me to accept her into the pack using a similar method she used to get me to trash the communication facet of the pack tie.

Unfortunately for her, ancient wolf magic forces me to follow certain protocols, thwarting her. I have a Beta and a Gamma, which means the most senior position she can take in the hierarchy is below theirs—equivalent to the wolves who sit on the pack council.

Bianca doesn't like it when people are above her in power, and she goes to great lengths to ensure there are as few strong Alpha bloods near her or me as possible. She bans Sofia from my presence, demotes Maddox, and nearly exiles my mother—a fact that sends Claudia into raging fits—but once again, the compulsion's power can go only so far. She can't force me to get rid of anyone, so I fight back just to spite her.

Luckily for my mother, there's a more interesting target for Bianca's jealousy and ambition: her own parents. From the moment I'm under her control, Bianca wants them gone.

I disappear into the fog for what feels like a long time before it peels back again.

At first, as always, I become aware of the gaping hole in my chest where Selene should be. The pain of being parted from her for so long, knowing that they've got her trapped somewhere below, living out the nightmare of her old life, would be enough to send me to my knees if I could control my own body.

But I'm not in control. I'm standing off to one side, quietly looking out a window, because the Beaumonts treat me like furniture.

"I can handle it, Momma," Bianca snarls. "I'm going to be Alpha Lady of this pack. I'm ready. I don't need you."

"Don't you?" Delilah's voice is cool and condescending.

"You can't even challenge him. This isn't how this was supposed to work," Frank says.

"*You* shouldn't have fucked with the eldritch," Bianca retorts. "I told you to demand a witch. Their magic isn't this goddamned finicky."

"A witch couldn't control him," Delilah snaps back. "Besides, why would they risk it when they know what works?"

My body goes cold.

Once, Vandran suggested that the curse was the Beaumonts' attempt at mind control gone wrong. Their first-ever attempt to take over Shattered Moon.

It sounds like he was right. I suspected when Bianca told me she was immune, but wasn't positive.

Now, after five long years, I know beyond a doubt who cursed me, and it's the stupidest answer it could be. These idiots wanted power, made some crossroads bargain, and got fucked over by some half-baked high eldritch curse. Their greed is responsible not just for Grace's death and my suffering but also for the death of their own goddamned son, Jackson.

This time, the argument turns vicious, ending with Delilah and Bianca shifting and slashing at each other and Frank having to pull them apart. They destroy a table and send cracks spiderwebbing through the nearly indestructible glass of a window.

After that fight, Frank and Delilah leave. My pack is completely at Bianca's mercy.

Time slips by. The moon wanes, goes dark, and waxes again.

The longer I'm without Selene, the more it feels like I'm being starved.

I love her. I need her. If the absence of her sharp tongue, sharper wit, and cautious smile has taught me anything, it's that. I never could have sent her away.

The revelation makes everything so much harder.

Bianca rarely lets me leave the apartment except as her puppet to attend meetings that involve planning for the Conclave. She doesn't let me speak to anyone.

Once, after one of several attempts I make on her life when her control slips, she lets me see Selene. My mate is down a long hall, scrubbing the marble floors on her hands and knees. She's dressed in ill-fitting old clothes. Her short silvery hair is pulled back and twisted into a small bun that's halfway to falling apart. The weight she'd started to gain has fallen from her face.

I think Bianca planned on having me hurt Selene as punishment for trying to kill her.

Instead, that moment is the closest I come to throwing off her control. Four Redcedar Hollow wolves who "joined" Shattered Moon have to wrestle me back to my rooms, and Bianca has to grip my face in her hands and fight tooth and nail to shove me back into the fog.

It's the first time I've seen fear in her eyes.

I try again after that, every single day. I have to save Selene. To avenge Grace. To stop my pack from falling into Bianca's grasp.

I can't.

Fighting means that I fall into the fog less. That I have to be mentally present in Bianca's company more.

It's torture, but I keep trying.

A week before the Conclave—which Bianca has been busy planning —I'm standing in the dining room of my suite of apartments looking over the forest and the lake. I can hear Bianca behind me, talking to the traitor, Deacon Jones. She's forbidden me from killing him, but as I listen to his voice, my claws slide out on their own accord.

One day, I will rip him apart.

The door opens and closes. Deacon is gone. Suddenly, Bianca's arms are around my waist.

I gather my will, resist her control, and push her away.

So damn tired.

She laughs, then orders, "Sit."

Without my say, my body moves to a chair.

"Good boy," Bianca purrs.

"What did Jones want?" I grate.

Bianca pulls out a chair next to mine and turns it to face me. She sits, crosses her long legs, and sighs. "You have a howler problem, Alpha Darrow. At least three packs are hunting the northern border of your land."

Howlers? There were traces of them weeks ago, and there was that rogue poisoned with howler venom, but nothing ever came of it.

It must have been the Beaumonts, and Deacon must have helped them.

I try to rise, but the compulsion won't allow it. "Let me go, Bianca. If you don't let me take care of this, dozens of wolves in Shattered Moon and Redcedar Hollow will die. Let me defend my pack."

She purses her lips in a thoughtful moue. "Don't you mean *our* pack, dearest? I am your wife."

I bare my teeth but ignore the remark. She keeps insisting my marriage to Selene was a proxy marriage.

"Let me go," I say again. "I'll take my best fighters and clear them out. The Conclave is coming up. If they hear we have eldritch stalking my territory, they won't come. Is that what you want?"

She glares at me. "The Conclave is happening as planned, Killian. You can be sure of that."

"Then I need to take care of this."

*Let me*, I beg inside my own head. *Let me be alone with my people. I will find a way to end you.*

That, or I could end myself, I realize. Against that many howlers, it's definitely a possibility.

For as long as I've been under Bianca's control, I've fought against the idea of ending my own life. I don't want to give up. I don't want to leave Selene or my family. But the longer this goes on, the more I realize it might be my only way out. I'm a hard motherfucker to kill. I don't even think jumping off the cliff outside the pack house would do it.

But three packs of howlers?

Yeah. That could kill me. Even as the beast. Then the pack would belong to Asher, and who even knows where he's gone? The important thing is, he's out of their control, and he's a vengeful bastard. He might succeed at getting rid of the Beaumonts where I failed.

If I go on this hunt and manage to get myself killed, I'll never see Selene again. I won't have a chance to say goodbye. It hurts so much that it's like plunging my claws into my own chest and eviscerating my own heart.

But with me gone, Asher won't hurt Selene. He'll take care of the pack, and he'll take care of her.

I want to keep fighting. But if I can't ... my death might be for the best. And not because I'm wallowing in self-pity this time. Because, like my mate, I'm being practical.

*Sorry, Asher. But also, fuck you.*

Bianca toys with the black pendant at her throat. The light catches in it, and it gleams yellow. I've wondered for weeks now whether there's a distance limit to its power, which is another reason I want to get away from her, even if I have to fight howlers to do it.

I keep my voice light. "It's just howlers."

She scoffs. "*Just* howlers?"

I scoff back, more myself than I've been in a long time. "You're the heir of Redcedar Hollow. You, of all people, should know how good I am at killing. Let me do this. I'll clear them out, and you can host the Conclave."

Finally, Bianca nods. Then she leans forward, eyes narrowed. "In case you're wondering if this means you might get outside of my range of influence, Killian, hear this: if you aren't back every morning by the time the sun rises, I won't hurt Selene ... I'll kill Finn in front of her. And I'll make sure she knows it's your fault."

My gorge rises, but it doesn't change my half-formed plan. If I die, she has no reason to make Selene hate me. If I'm dead, Finn will be safe.

"Sunrise." I nod. "That will give me the time I need."

*Selene. I wish I could say goodbye.*

# *Thirty-Three*

## SELENE

"We confirmed it. Finn is in that church," Parker whispers.

My breath catches in my throat. "You're sure?"

We're in one of the bathrooms on a lower floor. It's the easiest place to meet without the wolves Bianca brought with her from Redcedar Hollow—or one of the traitors, like Deacon Jones—finding us.

If anyone walks in, I dive into a stall and pretend to be cleaning a toilet.

These last few weeks have been a lot of this—meeting the few people I trust in secret. Making plans. Every night, I dream of the woman I think might be my mother. Every night, she tells me there's something I have to see. She shows me a rune.

Last night, she showed me a dark hallway. I think I know where it is, but I haven't been brave enough to go there.

Once, I caught sight of Killian at a distance. I was scrubbing a floor.

I wanted to chase him but stopped cold when I saw all the soldiers around him and Bianca on his arm.

That moment was like twisting a knife. I am so miserable without him.

I am not a killer, but I will kill her for doing this to him, to me, and to Shattered Moon.

Parker blows out a breath. "We're sure."

I blink back sudden tears, grateful for the volatile young half-wolf. "Tell Maddox I owe him everything."

Maddox has spent the last two weeks "scouting" the howler packs. It was my idea, and Sofia suggested it to Deacon.

But instead of scouting, Maddox took Finn's toothbrush to one of the green witches who lives on pack land to the south. She's apparently not a fan of wolves, but she tolerates him. Sofia gave him an exorbitant amount of pack trade credit to bribe her, and it worked since Shattered Moon is basically her only supplier of things she can't grow herself.

The witch taught him a tracking spell and a spell to cover his scent. He doesn't know much about that side of his heritage, but he was able to execute both well enough. Between the tracking spell and his nose, he chased Finn's trail up to an old church in an abandoned town on the northeastern corner of Redcedar Hollow land and discovered Noelle going in and out. Noelle, who, according to Sophia, has had a crush on Maddox since she arrived here. He's been getting close to her. She must have finally slipped up enough for him to lay eyes on Finn.

"When can we get him?" I ask. The Conclave is soon. I can't protect the wolfless of Redcedar Hollow from here, but I might be able to free Finn. Once we have him, we'll try to break Bianca's hold on Killian.

I just have to pray that without Bianca's inciting presence at Redcedar Hollow, my parents won't be cruel enough to take their anger out on their own wolfless.

Parker shrugs. "Needs to be soon."

I nod. "Bianca's been distracted with planning for the Conclave. I don't want to cut it too close. We should do it tomorrow. Tell the others."

Parker slips out of the bathroom. I wait several minutes, then follow. I have more "chores" to do, but the more I keep my head down, the less I'm supervised.

If I'm going to see what the woman in my dreams wants to show me, I need to do it now.

I return to the now-familiar hall beneath the foyer stairs where the servants' quarters are, keeping my eyes down as I pass some of Bianca's loyalist guards. As far as they know, I'm just going back to my tiny room and lumpy cot.

They don't follow. Which is good because I don't go to my room. Instead, I face down the dark hall that used to be blocked by tarps.

I remember Parker's warning that the area is dangerous and I shouldn't go in there. But I can't shake the feeling that I remember this place.

When I'm sure no one is watching, I slip into the shadowed ruin and down the stairs.

Alaric Bane's old wing is carved down into the living limestone of the cliff. I descend a short set of stairs that takes me out of sight of anyone above. This hallway looks a lot like the ones on the upper floors —wide marble mosaic floors, torch-like sconces, and hanging lanterns between columned sections. Weak winter sun streams in through dirty windows that look out over the sleeping land and lake.

Then I see it in my mind's eye, like a vision. As it is now, but clean, the walls unburned and unbroken. As if it were larger or I were smaller.

I take a grounding breath. Like I do when I'm locating Finn. I release conscious thought and go where my feet tell me to go.

At first, they take me to the wrong place. At the end of one of the long, twisting halls, a wide set of double doors hangs from their hinges. Beyond them is a massive bedroom with black walls and heavy, richly-made furniture. A wide chandelier of intertwined antlers hangs from the ceiling.

In the center of the room sits the biggest bed I've seen, the covers thrown back as if someone was just roused and might momentarily return. I could believe it if not for the thick layer of dust over everything.

There's a terrible weight to this place. A darkness of hungry ghosts that are lying in wait.

But not for me. If I could guess, I would say they were waiting for vengeance against a despot king who will never return.

This isn't where I need to be. I turn, and my eyes catch on a smaller door that also hangs off its hinges. Drawn like a magnet to a lodestone I move to the threshold and stop just short of the door.

This room is a fraction of the size of the other, though it's still large and richly furnished. The walls are a cool twilight purple, the chandelier smaller, made of pale gold that drips with hundreds of crystals carved into glittering crescent moons. There's a full bed against one wall. Beside it is another, smaller bed clearly made for a very young child. Both of these are neatly made.

A strange feeling rushes over me, and I put a hand on the doorframe to brace myself. It shifts, and I pull back in surprise.

The doorframe is broken. So is the door. Unlike in the other room, it doesn't look like the damage was done by the ravages of time. It looks like someone kicked it in long ago.

Chills roll through me, and I quickly turn and leave.

I move through the tomb-like halls once more until, finally, I reach the place I see in my dreams. A shadowed, out-of-the-way dead end with three doors.

I don't know whether it's in my memory or the dream coming through into real life, but I swear I hear the whispery, papery voice.

*There are things you must know ...*

I reach for the door on the right. When I touch it, silver light flares at its center. It's almost a letter but more complex, like a pictograph. Some kind of sigil or rune, as sharp as a wolf's teeth.

My heart slams against my ribs.

This is it.

I reach for the knob, twist, and pull. Power zings over my skin but doesn't hurt me. I pull the door open on silent hinges.

Beyond, there's only darkness and the cold scent of magic.

I feel a tug like there's a hook buried between my lungs dragging me forward. I fumble around on the wall and touch something. Lights blossom above me in volleyball-sized bubbles of orange arcane energy stuck to the ceiling. Below is a narrow, steep set of black stairs.

The magic tugs again.

I step down the stairs and close the door behind me.

The descent seems to go on forever, forward and down, twisting and turning. The hook behind my chest begins to burn, and the only thing that will stop the aching is whatever lies below.

*... things you must know ...*

She's with me. I can feel her here, and her presence makes me feel less afraid.

Finally, the stairs end at a door. An orange bubble light is beside it where a torch would be in a medieval castle.

Acting on instinct, I place my palm flat on the door.

Another sharp silver sigil flares, the same as the first. Something inside me tingles in response, like the rune is a call and my blood is the answer.

I turn the knob and push the door open.

Then I stand there, utterly bewildered.

Behind the door is a cozy subterranean library.

"Maybe I'm still dreaming," I mutter as I cross the threshold and gaze around in wonder.

Here, the bubble lights are gold-white orbs just the right brightness for reading. They hang from nothing at varying heights near the ceiling, magic swirling lazily within.

I've never seen magic like this. The magic I know is deeply tied to the land, an object, or the body of the person it originates from. It doesn't just float around. Though, admittedly, my experience with magic outside of wolves is extremely limited.

I'm standing in an alcove that looks like an office, with most of the library in a wider room beyond. Even here, though, the walls are lined with shelves that contain dozens of books. Some look moderately new, some ancient. There are even a few scrolls. There are plush red rugs underfoot and an overstuffed chair near a hollow in the wall where there's a fireplace-sized light bubble. Warmth radiates from it, and the false flames of a magical fire dance within.

Most of the alcove, however, is taken up by a heavy-looking huge mahogany desk. It's empty except for a single large open book. Possibly a journal, as handwriting is scrawled over its pages in heavy, thick pen strokes around pictures that have been glued neatly to the pages.

The hook in my chest tugs as soon as I see it. I can hear her again. Within my mind or outside of it, I genuinely don't know.

*Selenite, there are things you must know.*

*You must find them.*

I walk to the book, certain this is why I'm here. The closer I get, the more my blood feels effervescent, tingling and bubbling, light, ticklish, and energizing.

I reach the desk. On the upper right corner of the book's open page is a grainy picture of a woman. I'm reaching for it when my brain catches up with my eyes and I register what I'm seeing.

I inhale sharply and pull my hand back.

At first, just like in the dream, I think the woman in the picture is me. But when I blow away the dust of years, I see her hair is longer and leans toward gold. That she's older. That her face is sharp like mine but longer. Our noses are the same, narrow and upturned.

Beneath the photo is a name.

"Aurora Stillwater," I read.

There's another picture beneath—one of a little girl with uncanny pale, dark-ringed irises and silvery hair. The name is smudged with dust.

With my heart in my throat, I brush the dust away.

As soon as I touch the page, there's a deafening crack from above. The room plunges from bright light into dimness.

Overhead, half the golden bubbles have gone out.

Magic flares along the surface of the desk. Light flashes in concentric rings of glyphs over and over again, red and angry.

The hook in my chest releases. I nearly fall to my knees.

*Take it! Hurry! You must find them ...*

Then the voice from my nightmares. *He can never find you like this ...*

Then louder, ringing in my ears. *You must RUN!*

The whole room shakes. The glyphs on the desk flash a deeper, angrier red. Across the room, on the chair by the fire, a curl of oily smoke forms, thickens, and grows. It smells like burning tar.

"*Thiiiiieeeef.*" The voice from the smoke is creaking and ancient. It starts to coalesce into a shadowed, antlered thing.

I slam the massive tome closed, snatch it up, and run.

The earth rattles as I run, throw myself into the stairway, and shut the first door behind me. The orange stair lights dim, then brighten, then burn.

I sprint up the stairs all the way, never slowing even though my legs and lungs are burning. At the top, I slam the second rune door closed.

Everything stops. The dusty hall is cold, quiet, and utterly normal.

I look down, panting, at the book. Now that I have it, I see that the edges of its pages are yellowed with age. It's old but not too old. Maybe twenty or thirty years?

Despite how heavy it is and the fact that its edges are digging into my fingers and abdomen, I could believe that the whole episode down in the library was a dream.

On the front of the book is a title embossed in gold. *The Legacy of Alaric Bane.*

I gasp. The hook in my chest is back. Maybe I am crazy for believing that my dreams mean something, but hallucinations don't lead to real secret passages with real hidden libraries underneath.

I run my fingers over the title, feeling the rough leather, the cool smoothness of the golden words. "It's real."

All the things I've been feeling since I came to Shattered Moon are real.

The woman from my dream wants me to have this book.

Only now, free from the belief that I know who my family is, do I understand who she must be.

I pause and look around the empty, dusty hallway. "Mom?"

I don't know what I'm hoping for. Maybe that she'll appear, take me in her arms, and tell me I was always loved. At the very least, that she'll explain why she left me with the Beaumonts.

But the dusty air is still.

I touch my healed shoulder. *He won't find you.*

She stabbed me with silver, broke off the tip of the blade, and kept me from my wolf. Why? Who is *he*?

I look at the title of the book again, and with a gruesome wrench, everything falls into place.

Killian may not be the child of Alaric Bane ... but I think I am.

I open the book. It falls open right to the same page. This time, when I wipe away the dust, the ceiling doesn't shake. I look into the eyes of the child—my eyes, with frost-pale irises ringed in black—and read the name beneath.

*Selenite Bane.*

# Thirty-Four

**SELENE**

It's easy to smuggle the book into my room unseen. I'm torn between the urge to hide it and the urge to read more.

The urge to read more wins. But first, I want to see something.

I go into the bathroom, turn on the lights, and lean close to the mirror.

Once, in Finn's classroom, I studied a book cover with Alaric Bane's picture on it, searching for Killian in his face. I thought Bane looked familiar at the time but couldn't place where I'd seen him.

The answer stares back at me. It's subtle, and my features are softened by the fact that I'm a woman, but I see echoes of him in the angle of my cheekbones and the arch of my eyebrows. I see him in the shape of my lips and the pallor of my skin.

It's real. I am the daughter of Alaric Bane.

Mind buzzing, I return to my room, sit on the hard cot, and open the large tome to the beginning, balancing it on my knees. I feather my fingers over the first page. There's another woman and an entry with a child below her. There are pictures of him as a baby, then a toddler, then a boy about fourteen years old.

"Alexandrite Bane," I whisper. I see my face in his, too. There's a large *X* through the final picture. In fat black marker, the word *DECEASED* has been scrawled diagonally across the entire page.

An iron band forms around my lungs. I turn another page. Another mother and child. Another *DECEASED*. Another page, another dead child. Another. Another. Diamond, Tanzanite, Peridot, Malachite, Jet, Beryl, Garnet, Jadeite. The gemstone names just keep going.

I've heard about the terrible acts of the Alpha King but in a distant way. I have my own life, my own problems, and he's been dead for a long time.

Now I hold the evidence of how evil he was in my lap, and it hits me.

I don't realize I've started to cry until a tear plops onto the back of my hand. This book is so large. He couldn't have murdered all of his children. My siblings. A family that suddenly, sharply feels more real than the Beaumonts ever did.

*DECEASED, DECEASED, DECEASED.* I flip pages faster and faster.

The book is in order of birth date. In the first handful of years he had fewer children and many of them shared mothers. As I go on, there are children being born to more and more women.

The old paper crackles. Some of the brittle pages tear when I turn them. I'm a third of the way through the book and see my own entry. I notice that *Status: living* is hand-scrawled beneath my name. I turn more pages. Then—

"Wait!" I say it out loud, like I'm not utterly alone, and turn back to the previous page.

The child's entry has no *X*. No *DECEASED*. The mother looks out at me with eyes that burn the red-gold-orange of embers. She has light brown skin, freckles, and dark, tightly curled hair with a distinct red sheen. Her name is listed as Destiny Williams. She's an elemental fire mage.

There are only two photos beneath Destiny's entry. One of a baby, one of the same child at three or four. She has the same burning eyes and freckles as her mother, but her skin is a paler brown and her hair has a looser curl and is a much more pronounced red.

*Ruby Bane. Status: living.*

"Ruby Bane." I have a sister. I have a real sister. A *living* sister. At least she was twenty years ago, when this book was last updated. Her date of birth is listed as about eight months after mine. If she's alive, she's twenty-three.

"I need something to mark this page," I say, almost panicked, like closing the book means I'll lose her. I rise and grab a dusty box of tissues, pull one out, tear off a strip, and jam it in the crease of Ruby's page.

Ruby. Half wolf, half fire mage. A sister who might be alive.

I go back to flipping pages. More children. More death. But there are some living too.

Amethyst Bane, daughter of a divination witch. *Status: living*. She would also be twenty-three.

Emerald Bane, daughter of a nature-touched dryad healer. *Status: living*. Twenty-three again, but younger than Amethyst.

Citrine Bane, daughter of a seraph. *Status: living*. Twenty-two.

Sapphire Bane, daughter of a siren. *Status: living*. Twenty-one.

Finally, I reach the final pages of the book. A woman peers out of the last picture, looking back at the camera over her shoulder. Her features are too perfect and fine, her eyes too large, and her ears taper to fine, elegant points. The very top of her head is cut off, but she seems to be wearing some kind of circlet or crown.

My blood chills. Every aspected, from wolves to vampires to witches to nature-touched, is human.

The fae are not.

There are half-human, half-fae children, but if what I've read is true, they're so rare that there may be fewer than a dozen of them living.

Pure speculation, of course. No one really knows.

There is no name on the fae woman's page. But in the picture beneath, there are two infants with gently pointed ears. One has a thick thatch of black hair, the other has hair paler than mine. White, with a sheen like rainbows. It looks like they were hours old when the picture was snapped.

Onyx and Opal Bane. Twin girls. They'd be barely twenty now.

Did they survive?

If I thought the book would offer any kind of peace, I was wrong. Something is lodged behind my heart, deep in my chest. My whole world has been turned upside down again.

But I have found some relief; Killian isn't in this book.

To be sure, I flip back and check again, going through all of the pages. He's not here. Claudia was telling the truth when she confessed her secret to me.

*I lied to save my son's life.*

From Vandran? Why? Killian speaks of him like he's a father figure, and I don't know the warlord well enough to understand.

I flip back to my page, run my fingers over the picture of my mother, and try to piece together what I know.

Alaric Bane had dozens of children. At some point in his life, something happened, and he began to hunt and kill them.

My not-father, Frank Beaumont, used to be an under-Alpha general of Conqueror's Moon. According to his story, my mother, Aurora Stillwater, was a rogue who gave me to him and asked him to watch over me. She could have left Conqueror's Moon when the killing started, fleeing with me. While we were running, she could have stabbed me with silver to hide me from Bane, then handed me over to Frank. If they were both former members of Bane's pack, they would have known each other.

But why hide me so close by? And why on earth would Frank and Delilah ever keep me instead of sending me right back to Alaric Bane?

Aside from that, I was four. I should remember living here but I don't, except for vague impressions. Did my mother have someone else, like a witch, wipe my memories?

I trace my mother's face. She's not smiling. Rather, she's looking warily at whoever took the photo. Was it Bane? Did she choose to be with him, or did he keep her against her will?

"Selenite Bane," I whisper, tasting my true name. I wrinkle my nose. "Why did he name us all after stones?"

Seven strips of tissue mark the pages of my living sisters. All girls. None of the boys survived. I don't know whether that's because Bane thought they were more important to hunt down or it's just a coincidence.

I look at the picture of my mother again. It's said that Bane was killed by the angry mothers of his dead children. But what about the mothers of his final living children, desperate for them to survive?

Is that why she sent me away? Because she knew she'd die trying to kill him?

At last, I close the book, arch my back, and groan as my spine pops and my muscles stretch. Outside my dingy, tiny window, the light is dimming. I've been reading for hours.

"I have to tell Killian," I whisper. He's still closed off to me, and no matter how hard I try to sift through the rubble of the collapsed pack tie, I can't break through.

I have to break the spell he's under. He needs to know he doesn't have to hate himself. He doesn't deserve to be cursed. He's not Alaric Bane's son.

The thought stops me cold. He's not Bane's son, but I am Bane's daughter. Will he think I'm tainted now? Will he despise me because of who my father is, the same way he despised himself?

Inside me, my wolf stirs, restless. I've never shifted except for that first time, and it's getting uncomfortable, like not moving a limb for too long. If I'm caught shifting or trying to run in the forest, it's bound to catch Bianca's attention, and I don't want that.

Since removing the silver, my strength has slowly grown, like my blood needed time to get the poison out of my system. For weeks, I've felt magic swirling inside me, but I keep remembering how I threw Claudia into that wall and how I compelled her to tell me the truth against her will.

Instead of practicing my magic, I've hidden it, afraid of another accidental burst I can't hide. Bianca is content to let me live so she can enjoy my suffering, but if she had even an inkling that I have might power strong enough to threaten her, she wouldn't hesitate to kill me.

Now I wonder about Alaric Bane and Aurora Stillwater and what I might have inherited from them. I don't know anything about bloodline magic or the families that have it.

One thing's for certain: I didn't inherit Bane's Alpha blood. If I had, maybe I'd be strong enough to take Bianca on.

What if my mother left that bit of silver in me not just because she wanted to hide me but also because she feared what I might become?

Uneasy, I stand and tuck the book under the thin mattress of my cot. It makes an obvious bulge in the center of the mattress, so I move it beneath my barely existent pillow. The pillow is also too thin to hide something underneath, but it's the best I can do. So far, Bianca and Claudia have each visited this room once, and that's all.

Just as I reach the door, I feel something in my mind shift, stretch, almost snap. I cry out and grip the doorframe. The tearing sensation in my brain just about sends me to my knees.

"What ...?"

Howls and cries echo to me from the direction of the foyer and the great hall. Instinct grips me, and I know what it is, even as the feeling subsides.

Something is happening to our Alpha, and the bond is calling us to protect him.

Killian is in danger.

# Thirty-Five

## SELENE

I race out of my room and into the foyer. It's the middle of dinner in the great hall, and chaos is everywhere. People are milling around; some are crying. All of them are asking where Killian is. Some of them even ask me, but I have no idea.

Bianca appears at the top of the stairs. She clutches her ugly necklace to her chest.

"Lady Bianca, what's happening?"

"Where's the Alpha?"

"Is he dead? I felt something terrible!"

"Quiet!" Bianca barks, power whipping out from her. Without Killian here, she's the third most senior member of the pack, and she's never shied away from using her abilities on lower-ranking wolves. "Everyone, back to your rooms. Clear the great hall."

The throng obeys, instantly beginning to disperse. I feel the Alpha magic she wields, but I don't feel the compulsion to obey her order like the others, even with a wolf. I duck my head and move to the wall below where Bianca is standing. She didn't notice me in the crowd, and now she can't see me.

Killian is in danger. I have to know what's going on.

The great hall is generally where the pack council gathers. If she wants everyone out, I'd bet it's for a meeting.

266

I slip through the milling crowd and into the great hall, where I slice behind a floor-length tapestry in crimson, white, and moonstone blue depicting the crest of Shattered Moon. No one shouts or drags me out from behind it, so I assume no one sees me.

There's a tiny tear in the tapestry, and I position myself to look through it.

It doesn't take long for the room to empty and the pack council to appear. They take seats around the high table on the dais. Zev is supposed to stand behind the Alpha's chair, but he positions himself behind Eva's. When they think no one is looking, he leans forward and squeezes her shoulder, and she pats his hand.

Bianca arrives last. Deacon supports her, as if she can't bear to walk on her own. Her face is red and tear-streaked. There's none of the icy hardness she wore a few minutes ago when she was shouting at low-level wolves to get out of the room.

She's putting on a show. How exciting.

I watch her warily as she takes Killian's seat. The Beta sits to her right. The dozen or so council members clamor at them as soon as they sit down.

"There are still howlers pushing in on the northern border!" Sofia shouts. "For the last three nights, that's where he's been. Why has no support been sent?"

"You know why," the Beta snaps. "Between Killian and the howlers, anyone who goes out there is dead."

"He would have asked for support," Sofia snaps. "Zev and his people should be out there."

"I tried to go," Zev rumbles. "We were told to stand down."

"No support?" Bianca glares at Jones. "You said you sent soldiers!"

Jones's face is impassive. Bianca's face turns stormy. "Send them now! Beta, you have to do something!"

As Bianca speaks, Deacon leans in, and I'm surprised to see how intent his gaze is: how hungry, as if her presence alone could feed him for days.

He takes her hand. "I know this is hard for you, my lady, but it's the only choice we have. We can't go after him."

Bianca's fake tears dry as she blinks at him. His words ring hard and final in the quiet room.

"Excuse me?" Sofia's voice is as sharp as a blade.

Deacon rises and folds his hands behind his back. "The Alpha's greatest wish is to never harm someone he loves again. If we send anyone, even Zev and the Alpha's personal guard, that is exactly what will happen."

I can still feel the threads that hold the pack together through Killian. Even damaged by whatever Bianca made him do, they've always felt so strong. Now they jostle and twist, and that tearing feeling threatens in my head before subsiding again.

"We've had so little time together," Bianca sniffs, turning on the waterworks again. I know why. This is one of her favorite tactics to manipulate my father. She thinks it will work on any older man, including the Beta.

"We have to go after him." Sofia slaps her palm on the heavy, dark wood. "He's our Alpha. He built this pack. He bleeds for us every day. Now he needs us, and you want to leave him? No."

One of the council members, Ilaria Grayhorse, looks at Deacon, confused. "Gamma Perez is right. We need the Alpha. How can we afford not to go after him?"

I haven't had any one-on-one conversations with her. She's young and pretty, with russet skin, sharp features, and a way of dressing that's probably wasted this far away from the cities. Her father, Oscar, is also at this table. He's the Lore Reader and one of the pack elders who presided over my wedding to Killian.

"We can't leave him," Sofia insists. "He nearly died a few minutes ago. We all felt the call. You'd have a thousand wolves out there now if any of them knew where he was."

"And how many out of that thousand would die at his hand before sunrise? Fifty? A hundred? So he's powerful. Is he worth more than a hundred wolves?" barks Briony, the pack scoutmaster. She's Deacon's sycophant, so it's not surprising when she backs him up. She continues, "He's more than capable of dealing with howlers. When the sun rises, I'll send trackers into the forest to find him."

"I will find him," Zev growls.

"No one is asking to send out a thousand wolves," Eva says desperately. "Just his personal guard, and only those who volunteer. Maddox said there are three packs of howlers. Enough venom, and even Killian will fall."

My blood chills as I remember the attack by the rogue wolf. I imagine the same venom flowing through Killian, eating away at him. I imagine him never coming back to himself.

I won't let it happen.

"He is incredibly strong, but if he's already injured, there's a good chance he won't last the night." Even Dr. Bennett's calm voice can't hide his underlying tension. "Howler venom doesn't give us much time. We all felt the pull. If the pack magic is trying to get us to find him and protect him, we should assume venom is why. We have one hour, maybe two. If we don't get to him with treatment, our Alpha may technically be alive by morning, but it will already be too late."

Deacon stands his ground. "Sending anyone to treat him is a death sentence. Remember Grace."

Eva thrusts a finger at the Beta. "You keep my daughter's name out of your mouth."

"I am the Beta here," Deacon roars.

Zev snarls and puts himself between Eva's chair and where Deacon sits farther down the table. Eva looks pale.

"I have spoken," Jones says in a softer voice. "We wait for the sun."

He sits again and takes Bianca's hand. "Lady Beaumont, I know how difficult this must be. I swear, if the worst happens, I'll stand beside you in any way I can."

Suddenly, I understand what's happening. Deacon Jones wants to let Killian die because if that happens, he'll become Alpha. He's telling Bianca, in not so many words, that if he does become Alpha, he wants her to be his mate.

He clearly works for the Beaumonts, but I don't think he wants to. Bianca has been so caught up in her own ambition that she's missed his. She hasn't seen how much he wants her.

Bianca blinks. I watch her shocked face, see her recalculating, recalibrating, realizing what Deacon's game is, that revolting opportunist.

"What if he doesn't survive?" Ilaria Grayhorse says in a quiet voice.

Deacon's eyes are intense on Bianca's. I have to imagine what he's offering is tempting. There's no way Killian has made the last month easy for her, but he's so much more powerful than the Beta. If Bianca gives up on Killian, she'll lose her chance at running a pack at the level of strength Killian gives to it.

However, Deacon Jones will also be much easier to kill than Killian. If he becomes Alpha, they mate-bond, and Bianca murders him—which she will—it will make her the sole Alpha of Shattered Moon, able to find another, powerful Alpha mate at her leisure.

Bianca sniffs loudly and lifts her chin. "I suppose if Killian doesn't make it, the Beta and I are more than ready to lead."

"What?!" Sofia shouts.

That's it. Bianca has made her choice.

There's arguing, but I don't hear the rest. Deacon and Bianca leave shortly after, as do Briony and most of the rest of the pack council.

Only a few linger. Sofia, with Parker behind her chair. Eva, of course. Zev crouches at her side, which he has to do to be at eye level with her, and she shakes her head as she speaks to him in a low voice. Dr. Bennett. Ilaria Grayhorse. And the pack smith who made my pocketknife—a woman named Chloe DuPont.

"What are we going to do?" Josiah Bennett asks. "Their plan is so transparent, I could make a window out of it. They're going to let him die. But Deacon was right about one thing: it will break Killian to hurt someone innocent again, and no one can get close enough without that risk, not even Zev and young Maddox."

Zev looks like he's about to protest, but I slip from behind the tapestry. "I can."

They all turn to look at me. Parker grunts, like she's not surprised. Sofia presses a hand to her mouth. Eva smiles.

Sofia strides over and throws her arms around me. "Fates, Selene. You risked spying on a pack council meeting, even knowing what Bianca would do if she found you?"

I smile ruefully. "I felt the call. I had to know." I pitch my voice louder for others to hear. "Dr. Bennett, if I can reach him, I can administer whatever antivenom he needs."

The doctor rubs his bald head, then scratches his chin through his bushy beard. "Selene, I know you have a wolf now, but it isn't ... That is to say, you'd have to get close enough to touch him. If he's battling howlers, infected, his curse active, how will you manage that?"

Sofia pulls away from me and says, "If we send her with a few strong soldiers—Zev, Maddox"—she hesitates, glances at her mate, then adds—"Parker—they can deal with whatever is left or keep him occupied while Selene gets close."

My heart aches for the Gamma. I know how terrifying it would be to send someone you love into the dark to chase down the monster Killian becomes.

Parker moves behind her and wraps her arms around Sofia's waist. Sofia turns, and the two of them embrace.

"Not Zev," Parker says over Sofia's head, giving the giant man an apologetic look. "Bianca likes him to guard the Alpha's apartment. She's likely to summon him soon. If he's gone, she'll notice. Just me and the kid."

"Just Maddox and Parker?" Eva sounds strained. She turns to Zev and starts speaking rapidly. This time, he's the one who shakes his head.

Dr. Bennett frowns thoughtfully, then gives a single slow nod. "It's the plan with the least risk and highest reward."

"I agree it's a good plan—if those involved are willing to take the risk." Ilaria Grayhorse sizes me up with her head tilted to one side. "Doing nothing condemns our Alpha to death, and we all saw what Deacon is angling for, that stupid man. Killian is all that stands between us and Bianca."

I nod at her and look over the others. Eva has her fingers pressed against her lips, and tears glisten in her eyes. Zev has risen and is standing behind her again. She nods at me, and it's all I need.

"Should we call Maddox?" I ask.

"I'm here." Maddox emerges from the shadows near the door. His usual rings and earrings are missing, and he's wearing nothing but the fitted black calf-length pants Alpha shifters wear when they know they're going to change. I've never seen him without a shirt. Black tattoos crawl all over his torso, down his arms, and up his neck. Despite that, there's still something young about him. Something that reminds me of Finn.

He must see something in my look because he rolls his eyes. "Don't worry about Parker and me. Just get to Killian and give him whatever it is he needs. Try not to fuck it up by dying."

I nod, harden my resolve, and meet Maddox's violet-gold eyes. "I'll do my best."

# Thirty-Six

## KILLIAN

I stand in the forest in my hybrid form. Red eyes surround me in the darkness. One, two, three, four, five, six. Too many, or maybe finally enough. The last few nights, they haven't come at me in great enough numbers to do any harm. Tonight feels different. Maybe it's the gaping wound in my abdomen.

Just over an hour ago, I thought it was finally over. One of the monsters just about disemboweled me. It would've been a fitting way to go. It was the way Grace went. I could feel the weight of death threatening to snap my bond with the pack and the burst of magic that went out with it, warning my wolves that their Alpha's death was imminent.

In the end, its claws just didn't go deep enough. But I'm badly injured, limping, bleeding from so many places. A few more good hits, and I'm done.

*I hope you're ready to be an Alpha, Asher.*

*Selene ...*

I can't think about her.

Part of me almost expects Asher to come barreling out of the dark and help me. But since that day in the graveyard, I haven't seen or scented him.

I've used my days hunting howlers to test the limits of Bianca's control, and I think I finally found the edge of her range. For the first time in a month, the fog of the curse curls in yellow tendrils around the edges of my mind, beckoning me into the waiting oblivion. I resist, teetering between the curse and Bianca's control.

Howlers rush in, claws flashing, teeth snapping. I dodge one and grab another by the throat. I pull its struggling body close, turn my face away from its reeking breath, then grab it by a backswept horn and give one sharp twist.

Its neck snaps. One down.

Two more rush in. One leaps on my back. I wrench it from me. Its claws rake through skin and slice through muscle. The pain makes the curse rise again, and I howl.

I fight on. I fight until the world is nothing but pain and blood, torn skin and flashing teeth.

Suddenly, there's a flicker of calm in my mind. Not through the pack tie but something more intimate. I catch a flash of white from the corner of my eye and see her standing there, illuminated in moonlight.

My heart lurches. *Selene.*

No. She can't be here. She can't—

A howler lurches through her, and the vision swirls away like smoke.

The venom from the few bites I've gotten over the course of the night is taking hold. I'm losing my mind.

A howler comes out of nowhere, dodges the two I'm already fighting, and rams into my side. The thing is as big as a horse, and I go down under its weight. Others circle, no more than blurring red eyes in the dark.

I close my eyes.

It's over.

## SELENE

The forest is quiet and still. Parker whines to catch my attention and shifts directions. She's a little in front of me, a rangy gray wolf that moves silently in the night. Maddox is beyond her, leading us with his tracking spell. I forgot that his wolf is pale silver, close in color to mine.

I trot along in my own wolf form, a black pouch that's specially made for carrying things when we're going to shift back and forth fastened around my waist. Howls break the stillness. They're distant, multitoned, and haunting.

"That's them." Maddox is the only one who can speak out loud since he's the only one with a hybrid form. "We need to move."

All three of us sprint toward the sound of monsters, up and down over hills, dodging through trees. I don't know how far we go, maybe a mile or two. Suddenly, signs of battle are everywhere: broken branches, claw-gouged mud like scars in the leaf litter, and blood.

Killian's scent is here, mingled with that of the beast he becomes, and another scent like rot and bad breath.

"They're close," Maddox says.

Parker snarls. Soon we pass a mound of bloodied black fur with horns. It reeks of the bad breath smell. Its eyes are empty with death.

Howls come again, closer. The sound of snarling and crashing bodies reaches us. Suddenly, it's like I can almost feel Killian, or a ghost of him, through the incomplete mate bond. I pick up my pace, and we push over the next rise. Below, in a small hollow where several hills meet and form a bowl, we find them.

Not all eldritch are monsters, but the lurching wrongness of the howlers makes me want to turn and flee. That is, until I see one has something pinned. A wolfish large bulk that has to be Killian.

It's opening its jaws to rip out his throat.

Fear wraps its cold fingers around the primal part at the base of my brain. There's no time to save him, but I have to. I *have* to.

Without thinking, I shift, blurring up into my human form with incredible speed. "GO! Save him!"

I slam the order into Parker and Maddox without even thinking, silver light bursting like stars beneath my skin.

Maddox yelps. "What? Wait, we're not—!"

Like puppets, they surge forward and burst into the hollow. Maddox flies into the howler that has Killian a bare instant before its jaws would have ended his life.

Parker flanks him. She's not as huge as the howlers, but she's faster, smarter. They clear the beasts from Killian, and I run to him. It's extremely strange to run into battle naked except for a pouch, and it's freezing, but if I'm going to help, I need my thumbs. At least now that I have my wolf, the cold doesn't bite as hard.

I crouch at Killian's side. He's bloody and barely recognizable. A massive slash cuts across his abdomen. I think this might be the injury that almost killed him, but that was two hours ago. It should be healed more than it is, but slowed healing is one effect of howler venom.

It's been so long since I've seen him. So, so long.

"Killian, I'm here." I touch his shoulder, but his eyes are closed, and he doesn't respond. Panic threatens to overwhelm me, but I reach deep into the practical place that keeps me calm when everything around me is falling apart. There will be time to cry, throw up, or shake uncontrollably later. Right now, there's only Killian and the need to save his life.

I unzip the pouch and pull out the syringe. He has so many injuries. If we're going to get Killian out of here, we have to stop him from dying of his wounds first.

I plunge the syringe into his neck the way Dr. Bennett said to and depress the plunger. The bluish fluid inside the syringe disappears into him.

Just then, something massive and stinking slams into my body. I go flying and land hard on the ground. My head slams against a tree root. Pain bursts inside my skull. My vision blurs. It's like the burning red eyes of the howler split and multiply like a sky full of hellish stars.

It raises its head and releases its plaintive, multitoned, hair-raising song into the winter night.

Somewhere beyond my vision, Parker yelps. There are snarls. Snaps of jaws and branches and maybe bones. A piercing squeal, a whine.

All I can see is the howler looming over me. I'm still dazed and staring up at it stupidly when it raises a claw to disembowel me.

I should feel terror. Instead, the rage returns, ice-cold and unyielding.

I have not survived for so long, survived so much, to die in the woods by some random monster. As the blow falls, I plunge my will deep into that frozen well of power around my heart that I've been so afraid to touch and roar right back at those hellfire stars.

Magic answers. More than I can imagine. More than I can comprehend. More than I could ever dream of controlling. For one endless instant, it's like I've pulled the entire universe inside my body.

Then it explodes outward, blinding and silver-white, a blast of raw power that detonates like an atom bomb.

# *Thirty-Seven*

## SELENE

I'm blinded. Deafened by an impossible roar of sound. Still waiting to feel the howler slice open my stomach.

It doesn't happen. After a while, the ringing in my ears becomes silence, and all the white burned into my retinas darkens into an endless night sky with a three-quarter moon hanging low against the horizon.

The sky shouldn't be endless, but I have bigger worries than that.

"Killian!" I roll, see him, and scramble over. He's unconscious but breathing. Relief rolls through me, then disappears as soon as I take in the destruction around me.

The sky is endless because the small clearing in the hollow between the hills has become radically larger. Trees blasted flat are lying in a sunburst pattern, torn roots toward me, broken crowns outward, like a crater when a meteor hits a forest.

But there's no meteor at the epicenter. Only me.

I did that. How? I hug myself. "Parker? Maddox?"

Parker whines. Maddox groans, "The fuck was that?" in the guttural voice of his hybrid form.

Maddox rises and throws a large branch to one side to scoop up Parker, who was pinned beneath. Her fur is matted and sticky with blood. I run to them, heedless of the cold or the cutting rocks and twigs beneath the carpet of fallen leaves. When I reach them, I gently touch Parker's fur.

She has so many wounds I can't count them all. Why does she always seem to be the one who gets hurt?

Maddox's golden eyes luminesce in the dark. He turns, shielding Parker from me with his body, and repeats, "What the fuck was that?"

It occurs to me then that the howlers could be recovering from the blast and attacking any second. I turn and search among the torn remains of the trees.

Then I notice the ... parts. Limbs. Viscera. The scent of blood is everywhere.

"Don't bother," Maddox snorts when he sees what I'm searching for. "Whatever you did, it blew the one on top of you apart. The others fell like stones."

He's right. I see their fallen bodies now. Black blood trickles from their eyes, ears, and mouths in the moonlight. Their eyes are open but blank. Some of their necks are twisted back at odd angles. There's no question that they're dead.

Nausea churns in my belly. A shiver runs through me. "Wh-what have I done?"

"I don't know," Maddox growls. "You know what else I don't know? How you shoved me into that fight like a puppet."

My throat goes dry. "What do you mean?"

He leans closer. "My mother told me you don't have Alpha blood, so how did you force Parker and me into that fight before we were ready? Before we could make any kind of attempt at a stealth or strategic approach? Most of all, how did you do it when we're already bound to Killian? No other wolf should be able to command us."

My mouth opens and closes. "I-I don't know, but Killian was about to—"

"Killian can survive a hell of a lot more than you think. I've seen it. But whatever you did, you almost killed us."

Blood rushes in my ears, and I feel lightheaded. I think I'm having a panic attack. "N-no. I couldn't have done that. I wouldn't—"

I wouldn't throw my friends unthinking into battle to serve my own ends. I wouldn't take their agency away like a thoughtless, cruel Alpha.

Maddox sneers. "You did."

Leaves rustle behind us. The hair on the back of my neck rises. I turn. Slowly. Careful not to make any fast moves.

Killian has risen from the ground. He's in the exaggerated, horrific half-form of the curse. Those sickly yellow eyes are fixed on me.

"Maddox," I say very calmly, "take Parker and run. Get her to Dr. Bennett. Please."

I don't know whether it's the power he accused me of wielding or he's just that willing to abandon me, but Maddox instantly obeys.

Killian howls and lunges after him, but he has to go around me to reach them. I throw myself to the side to intercept him.

He slams into me even harder than the howler did, and my head smacks into his shoulder. Stars sparkle across my vision. He tries to throw me off, but I have my arms around his neck and my legs around his waist. I grapple with him, digging my fingers into his thick coat, but all I feel is fur.

Desperate, I let go enough to raise my hand to the sparser fur on his face.

His fangs sink into the thick part on the outside of my palm. He has his lips peeled back. Nothing touches my skin but his teeth.

The monster in his eyes looks smug.

Pressure and a feeling of wrongness slither up my nerves just before pain electrifies me. I scream and shove against his blood-smeared chest with my other hand.

"Killian, come back. Please ... Ah!"

His teeth grind down. I hear and feel the outermost bone in my palm snap. He's going to bite clean through my hand.

"Killian, *please!*" I curl the fingers of the hand he's biting so they cup his jaw and brush the skin of his lips. Desperate, I force my breathing to slow and whisper, "Remember yourself. Come back to me."

Silver light burns in my skin, flickers, then brightens again. I used so much magic in that burst, I'm surprised I have any power left at all. But in the darkness, I glow like the moon.

Killian's whole body shudders. He opens his mouth, and my hand is free. He shudders again, and suddenly, he's a whole lot less wolf and a whole lot more man.

He staggers and stumbles against a tree, propping me up with my legs still wrapped around him. Hot blood flows from my hand. It stains his lips, teeth, and chin. I can barely think around how much it hurts. But his eyes have gone from yellow to a beautiful, familiar topaz that makes my heart ache. Not cold, not unseeing. Warm and entirely focused on me.

"Selene?" His chest heaves.

I stroke his cheek and let out a sob of relief just to be held by him. Just to hear my name from his lips. It's been weeks. I thought I was okay, but the loneliness I've denied crashes onto me like a mountain dropped from the sky.

"You're here." His voice is dazed. "Why ... What happened?"

I run my fingers up and down the back of his neck, trying to calm us both. "Howlers. You almost died. Deacon and Bianca wanted to let you. I gave you an injection Dr. Bennett sent for the venom. You're all right. We're going to be all right."

Killian trembles. It can't be easy, holding me with his injuries. "Bianca is controlling me like a damned puppet. For weeks, I couldn't— I tried—I missed you."

He crushes his mouth to mine. I kiss him back with everything I have and taste my own blood. Still, it's too brief before he pulls back, touches his lips, and stares at the red staining his fingers. He grabs the wrist of my injured hand and raises it into the moonlight.

My stomach lurches at the sight of the damage. Killian's eyes go wide, and he makes an animal sound of pain.

"I'm sorry." He lowers us to the ground and presses his forehead to mine. His skin is feverish. He's still holding my wrist, elevating it. "I'm sorry. I didn't want to hurt you. Please don't leave."

Killian Darrow, the most powerful Alpha in a generation, sounds like a child caught in a nightmare, his words echoing up from a limitless well of grief.

"I'm sorry," he whispers again. He holds me against his chest, his heat and strength surrounding me. "I missed you. God, I missed you. Don't leave."

"I'm not going anywhere." Tremors set in for me now too. There's a cold inside me I can't seem to shake. All of the strength has gone out of my limbs, and I don't think I could stand if I tried. But he's a furnace, his skin blazing against mine, keeping me from turning entirely to ice. If I just rest here long enough, I might get my strength back.

If we can stay like this, alone in the nighttime forest, we might be able to keep each other.

∾

## KILLIAN

The taste of her blood scalds my tongue.

I love her.

I hurt her.

The knowledge eats into my chest, through my heart, and out again, boring thousands of bleeding tunnels. I hurt her like I hurt Grace. Her hand needs attention, but it will have to be cleaned before I can lick it to help it close.

I am a monster, and I have no right to have her leaning against me like this, so trusting.

I've always been a monster.

The smell of dead howlers is hanging in the air like rancid grease. But that hardly registers because Selene is wrapped around me. She's naked. My fingers tighten on her waist, pulling her closer. Her scent is a drug that makes me forget everything else. I want to pull her under me and taste the noises she makes while I kiss her at the same time as I slide inside her. It's been a month, and I need her like I need fucking air. So I just hold her, torn between the taste of blood and the desperate need to be so close that no one can separate us again.

"How injured are you?" Selene whispers.

I take stock of my body. I'm bruised and torn just about everywhere, and I feel weaker than usual, like my body just fought off a sickness.

Howler venom. That's why I feel weak. "You brought antivenom."

"Yes."

"You came out here to save me."

"Yes."

"And you did."

"I did something." She gives me a wan smile, but there's distance to her words, like she's going into shock.

That's when I notice we're in the middle of what appears to be a bomb blast site.

What the fuck?

"Selene. What happened here?"

She looks around and shivers. "One of the howlers tackled me. I ... did something. Reached for some kind of magic, like the light. It was there. It ... exploded. I exploded."

Another check around the moonlit clearing verifies what she said.

That and the smell of howler guts. One pile of meat in particular looks like it was blasted apart from the center.

"Killian, so much has changed. I'm ... I'm ..." She buries her head against me. Her nose and ears are like ice.

I frown. Selene is practical, not afraid to say things that will make people uncomfortable. My stomach drops. "What?"

She shakes her head, and a shiver wracks her body. "Can we go somewhere warm?"

I want to study the clearing, sniff around, but she's right. We need to deal with the cold and her injury. "Yes."

Despite the weakness in my limbs, I stand, ignoring the pain from the wound in my abdomen. I shift into hybrid form so I'm carrying her against me like I did the night we met. She's not wearing anything but the small pack with an elastic band buckled around her waist that we use to carry small things when we shift.

She winces and cradles her hand close. Guilt washes over me.

"Let's get you warm, then we'll take care of that."

# Thirty-Eight

## KILLIAN

I kick open the door to the modified cave where Selene and I spent our first nights together, give her a shirt and sweatpants, wrap her in the blanket from the bed, then start a fire in the stove. She makes sure she never stops touching me. Her uninjured hand slides across my back as I turn toward her, the pads of her work-roughened fingers catching on my skin. The last month, I barely kept enough of myself to keep Bianca out of my bed, but I did, and I am grateful.

I thought the curse was bad. Bianca's control is so much worse.

I retrieve the well-stocked medical kit from the chest at the foot of the bed and a jug of clean water and a bar of soap from a shelf. I pour some water into a bowl and wash my hands. Treating injuries in this place is routine for me; I'm just used to them being my own.

"Let me see your hand."

"My hand? Killian, your stomach, your chest, your entire body is worse than my hand."

I grunt. The wounds need attention, but after I take care of her. "It's what I do. I'm used to it."

"You're used to having your stomach sliced open?"

I shrug and ignore the dozen bright bursts of pain that accompany the motion. They're just the loudest notes in a symphony I do my best

284

to ignore. "I already carried you here. I can deal with it for a few more minutes. Your hand."

"Stubborn Alpha." Selene scowls but lifts it. I refuse to look away from the damage I've done, no matter how badly I want to. From the swelling, the outermost bone is at least fractured but doesn't seem to need to be set. Now that she's been silver-free for weeks, she's healing faster than she would have before, but the wound is still deep.

I clean the broken skin, then lift her hand to my mouth, part my lips, and drag my tongue over her torn flesh. I turn her hand over and do the same to the teeth marks on her palm. The skin begins to knit. Some of the tension goes out of her body. Her fingers curl beneath my chin.

"That feels better."

"Good." Our eyes lock. I press a gentle kiss on her palm, then her wrist, then the inside of her elbow. Her eyes close, and her head falls back.

She's here. We're together. I'm outside of Bianca's control.

I didn't think I would get to see her again, let alone be with her again.

I kiss her palm again, then splint and wrap her hand. It will heal soon, but I want to make sure it's stable while it does.

Selene tends to me next. She soaks a clean rag in a new bowl of water mixed with my own saliva, mild soap, and dried herbs from the medical kit, then gently cleans the blood and dirt from me. I stand with one arm braced against the wall even though she wants me to lie down because I want to keep the bed clean.

I have plans for the bed.

The position allows me to watch her careful hands moving over me. It's been so long, I tremble with the effort it takes not to touch her. Not to throw the bloody rag aside, tear off the too-big clothes she just put on, pin her against the wall, and do whatever it takes to remind us both that we belong to each other.

Finally, when I'm clean and bandaged, she looks up at me. "I have to tell you something. It's urgent."

The way she says it makes lead settle in my chest. I back her against the bed. "Can it wait?"

Selene sits, her hand pressed flat against my abdomen. "No."

I lean over her, bracing my hands on the blankets, forcing her to lie down and scoot back as I climb over her. I slide a hand beneath her, lift her against me, and turn down the blankets. When we're both settled, I pull them back over us, tucking her against my body and the covers tight around her shoulders.

"Are you sure?" I dreamed I'd get this moment. I am addicted to the way she feels against me. I hook a leg over her hips and bring her closer, willing her to be warm. The fire is heating the air but slowly. I can do better.

"I'm sure," she says.

I trace her cheek, then hook a silvery strand of hair behind her ear. I want to kiss her, but if I do, we're going to get way off track from whatever she wants to talk about. "Tell me."

Now that I'm listening, she hesitates. "It's going to sound insane."

"I'll believe you." Honestly, I don't give a shit what it is or how crazy she thinks it is. I'm too busy reveling in the relief her presence brings me.

"Your mother told me something. I wasn't sure if it was true, but earlier today, I was exploring, and I think I found proof."

My brows furrow. "You spoke to my mother?"

Selene's lips press together. "She came to visit me the day ... everything happened."

I growl. "She went to gloat."

For the hundredth time, I consider sending my mother back to the Free Cities.

"Yes. She came to gloat. But she accidentally told me something important. Or I might have coerced her into doing it; I'm not sure. My magic is so strange ..." Selene shakes her head and mutters, as if to herself, "One thing at a time."

Her frost-pale eyes bore into mine. "You are not Alaric Bane's son."

The world shifts on its axis. I sit up. "What?"

Selene sits up too. Her hand is on my bicep. Her voice is soothing. "Claudia admitted it to me. She said you got into trouble with Vandran and she lied to save your life. He believed her because he wanted to. I wasn't sure if *I* should believe her, but I've been having these dreams. I kept seeing halls that look like the ruined wing of the pack house and hearing a voice that tells me there are things I need to know. With the Conclave coming up and my other plans, it felt like I was running out of time to figure out what it means, so I went and explored. There was a door with a rune. I went through it, and—"

"You what?" Shock courses through me. "No one can get through the rune doors. I had a witch examine them. She said they're keyed to

Bane. It was going to take massive magic to remove them. No one but him could pass through."

Even as I speak, a cold suspicion creeps over me. When I first took the castle, one of the older wolves who was part of Conqueror's Moon told me about his secret library and hinted that the runes would let not only Bane but also anyone who shared his blood through.

I tried to go through, but I might as well have run into a wall. When I brought it up to Claudia, she shrugged it off. *Oh, Charles always acts like he knows things he doesn't. Of course, the rune doors only opened for Alaric.*

But they opened for Selene.

Her cheeks turn rosy, and her throat works. "Let me finish. At the bottom of some stairs, I found a library. There was a book on the desk called *The Legacy of Alaric Bane.* It lists all of his children and all of their mothers. It's a big book, Killian, and he murdered so many of them."

She inhales deeply. "You aren't in there, but I am. He's my father, not yours."

I can't hear past the blood rushing in my ears.

For years, Bane's legacy has defined me. I've told others that lineage doesn't matter, that the status of your wolf doesn't matter. I meant it for them but not for myself.

I'm not Bane's son. Instead, Selene is his daughter.

I said I would believe her, but I don't know whether I can. Not because I think she's lying but because this is too huge, too profound.

"How can I not be who I am?"

Selene laughs softly. "For the last month, I've asked myself the same thing."

I huff out a breath, pull her close, and tuck her head under my chin. She's quiet, giving me time to process. "If he's not my father, who is?"

Selene shrugs in my arms. "Your mother didn't say more. I haven't been alone with her since then."

"Who's your mother? Did the book say?"

"Aurora Stillwater. I don't think I've ever heard the name in my life. If what Frank said is true, she's the one who left me with Redcedar Hollow. And I think she's the one who stabbed me with that silver knife. I have this memory of pain and a voice saying if I have no wolf, he can't find me."

*Not his son. Not his son. Not his son.* The sentence plays over and over again in my mind. I try to fit the knowledge into my reality.

If I'm not his son, how am I so strong?

Though that answer also seems obvious. My mother. She squanders it, but her power is undeniable. That's why she said Bane chose her and why it was so easy to believe.

Selene's not a Beaumont; I'm not a Bane. Both of us are adrift from who we thought we were, but maybe there's reclamation in becoming someone new.

Selene watches me, brows furrowed, concern in her eyes. Tense, like she's waiting for something terrible.

"What's wrong?"

"I'm just ... waiting for your reaction."

"Reaction?" It hits me what she means. I'm not Bane's child, but she *is*.

I've spent my whole life hating myself for my blood. I still don't entirely believe I'm free of that. But Selene? Does being Bane's child make me think any differently of her whatsoever?

Hell no.

I kiss her soft silvery hair. "We're not related?"

Her nose scrunches. "Ew. No. I don't think fated mates work that way. And we wouldn't be unless you're related to the Stillwaters."

Stillwater. I think I know that name but vaguely. "I'm not a Stillwater. I think they're one of the old families. Old, old. One people thought didn't survive the Quiet."

I can't remember what magic the Stillwater line had, but if they've died off and I've still heard of them, it must have been something important. Powerful.

Maybe one of the older wolves knows.

"Does being the child of Alaric Bane make me evil?" Selene whispers, still caught in her own thoughts.

I scoff. "No."

She rolls her eyes. "If it doesn't matter when he's my father, it never mattered when he was yours."

"I'm ... not ready to tackle that yet."

"When you are, just remember I was right."

"Yes, beautiful Selene, you were right." I kiss her, and we settle back into the bed. I arrange the covers around us, making sure to tuck everything in so she'll be warm. I think of falling asleep with her, of waking up with her head on my shoulder.

Then reality crashes down around me.

288

Bianca.

I have until dawn to return to the pack house.

The Conclave begins the day after tomorrow. On the last night, during the Prism Masque, she plans to mark me. Becoming my mate and the Alpha of a pack will make her so strong, it's likely I won't be able to resist her power anymore.

I haven't given up, but I can't see past being marked. I want to hope the wolves of Shattered Moon will abandon me rather than stay under her control, but while some might, others won't. As long as there's a single wolf in my pack, I can never stop fighting.

Wildly, it occurs to me that I could try to murder Bianca tonight, but I suspect the only reason I'm in control is that I'm as far from her as I am. When I go back to the pack house, I go back to being her puppet

For Selene and me, this is our only night. Our final night.

"Killian." Selene strokes my cheek, my jaw, my neck. I savor every sensation. "What are you thinking?"

I wrap my fingers around hers. "Nothing."

Before dawn, I will have to leave this bed. Leave Selene. Go back to Bianca. If I don't, Finn will pay the price. So will the Redcedar Hollow wolfless Selene loves so much. I won't let it happen.

I pull Selene beneath me and kiss her, slow and soft and savoring. She whimpers, twines her arms around my neck, and arches her hips against mine. "I missed you."

My heart twists. "I missed you too."

One night to steal while our enemies sleep.

One night.

I kiss down her neck, drag down the loose collar of her shirt, and take one peaked, perfect nipple in my mouth. Selene cries out. The sound of her pleasure ratchets up the tension at the base of my spine and turns me as hard as steel. I swirl my tongue, and she cries out again.

Instinct draws my mouth up her chest, over her delicate collarbone to her neck. The mate bond flares, and I suddenly can't exist separately from her for another second. My teeth go sharp, and I nuzzle that spot on her neck where, if there were any fairness in life at all, I'd claim her as my own right now.

I groan and force myself to keep moving, pressing kisses up her neck to her ear.

I won't let the curse take her from me the way it took Grace.

We take our time stripping each other until there's nothing between us, kissing, touching, smiling. Slowly, that heat builds and our pace quickens, each touch and kiss more desperate than the last. I can't fill my hands with enough of her skin. I can't taste enough of her on my lips. I can't stop knowing this will be the last time.

My fingers move between her legs, which open for me. I trace her entrance, gathering her desire on my fingers and using it to circle her clit.

Her eyes go distant as her head falls back. She whimpers. I keep circling, gentle and slow, then faster. With my other hand, I roll one of her nipples between my fingers. With my mouth, I capture her sounds, swallow them down. Her hips rock against my hand, her restlessly shifting thigh rubbing against my dick in a way that sends ever-heightening spirals of pleasure through me.

Selene flips us, taking control, and I let her.

She slides her tongue along the seam of my lips. I open. She teases, then retreats. I tilt her head back and plunder her mouth. Her hand finds my cock and strokes, and fuck, it's so good. Every time she touches me, it's so good. It's the only time I feel right. At home in my own body. At peace.

I pull her forehead against mine. "I need to be inside you."

Her smile and breathy laugh as she shifts the way she's straddling me are perfect. She hovers over me. I suck in a breath as her hand wraps around my cock again, adjusting us. Then, slowly, she lowers onto me.

She's so ready that I sink deep, and for a second time, my whole body shudders with the screaming need to mark her. Above me, Selene's eyes are half-hooded, luminescent with silver. She bites her bottom lip, and her fangs are out too. She rocks her hips in short little bursts and traces the place where my shoulder meets my neck.

"Killian." She sounds heartbroken.

"We can't." I capture her hand and press it against my heart. Her fingers curl, and she whimpers.

Then she really starts to move, and the world narrows to the place where we're joined.

I fill her, thrusting as she moves over me, buried in her body and her scent, outside of time, outside of thought. My mate. Mine.

"I'm yours." The rocking becomes a pounding, urgent rhythm. "I'm always yours. I love you."

Her eyes fly open, and she comes apart, crying out as she contracts around me. I can't hold back. I groan her name as I come, pleasure wracking me in waves that don't end for long moments.

When we're spent, she doesn't let me go. She drops her head to my shoulder, and I wrap my arms around her.

"You love me?"

"Yes." Fuck how little time we've spent together. I know her. I dream of her. If the fates are real, they know what they're doing.

"I love you too." She laughs a little as she takes in my face, then lifts a hand to smooth hair away from my forehead. "You look shocked."

"I expected to say the words. I didn't expect to hear them back."

She scowls. "You are worthy of love, Killian."

She kisses me. I slide out of her, reach for the chest by the bed, and pull out a small towel. I clean her up first, then myself. Then I toss the towel aside and stoke the fire.

When I turn back toward her, she's staring at me with wide eyes.

"Killian. We aren't touching. What happened to the curse?"

# Thirty-Nine

## SELENE

He starts, then looks down at himself. He makes as if to move toward me, then stops again. He turns his hands back and forth, as if they hold the answer, then meets my gaze. "How?"

I shake my head. "I don't know."

I'm wrapped in the thick quilt that covers the bed, doing my best to keep out the sneaky drafts of frozen air that Killian doesn't seem to feel. He leans forward and tugs the blanket from my shoulders.

Barely perceptible silver light dances beneath my skin. As he watches, he takes a step back, then another. Another. When he's roughly ten feet from me, the light in my skin flickers and dies. Killian bares his teeth and puts a hand to his head. His eyes flash yellow.

He steps toward me, and the light starts again, as does the warm hum I feel in my chest when it happens.

"I haven't seen you since I got my wolf. My magic has range now. You don't have to touch me anymore." I grin.

He makes a noise that doesn't sound entirely pleased. "*You* don't have to touch *me*. I might prefer having the excuse not to let you go." He hesitates. "Or it could be that I'm affected differently here because of Bianca. Her magic holds back the curse too."

"No," I say, certain beyond words. "The curse almost took you when you got too far away just now."

He returns to me and gathers me on his lap, then wraps the blanket around us both. I curl against him, loving his warmth and the way I feel safer in his arms than I ever have anywhere else in my life. "Ever since you took that silver from my shoulder, I haven't just been getting physically more powerful, my magic is growing stronger."

It's growing frighteningly strong.

His fingers trace the scarred crescent moon mark on my shoulder. "The silver was inside you for most of your life. It makes sense that it would take time to work its way out of your system and that your power will grow until you reach whatever your limit is."

I nuzzle into him. As I think about my magic, my anxiety rises. But even as it does, it's like I'm pulling calm from all the places our bodies touch from him into me. How did I ever live without this?

"That's what I thought," I say. "But where does it end? I blew up part of the forest. I commanded Maddox and Parker to attack before they were ready, and Parker almost died. I forced your mother to reveal her greatest secret to me. No one should have power like that. And I might not even be at my limit?"

"Why do you sound afraid?"

"Because what if I do something wrong? I put your mother through a wall, Killian, and she's so strong. What if I hurt someone when I don't mean to?"

He leans his cheek on top of my head. "You'll find a way to harness it. Don't let fear immobilize you. Your enemies have power too and they certainly don't."

I'm accustomed to responsibility, but there's a different kind of heaviness to this weight. I'm not an Alpha, but I might be as strong as one. I can defend myself now. Fight for myself.

It doesn't feel fair that I can when so many can't.

"No one should have power like this," I repeat.

"Probably not." Killian scoots us back onto the bed. "But until we have the world we want, at least your strength has a use. Master it, and you can protect the people you love."

He says it casually, like someone who has been down this road, grappled with this question, and reached his conclusion a long time ago.

"You sound like you've thought a lot about this."

He strokes my back with light fingers. "Grace and I used to talk about it. It's one of the reasons I agreed when the warlord wanted me to rebuild my father's—Bane's—old pack." He pauses. "Not being the son of Alaric Bane is going to take some getting used to. You said she didn't say who my father is?"

"No, she ran before I could get her to."

"He must have been no one," Killian muses. "There's nothing she hates more than that. From what I've gathered, her parents were absolutely normal. No strength, no bloodline magic. Her Alpha abilities are a fluke." His mouth twists. "There's nothing that woman wants more than to be special."

I run my fingers over his chest. "But how does it feel, knowing you aren't the final heir single-handedly carrying the weight of one of the most ancient wolf bloodlines?"

He grins, and it's beautiful. "Free. My own name. My own path." Then his face becomes serious again. "How does it feel, knowing you do? The Stillwaters—they're older than even the Banes. That's two powerful ancient families. A lot of weight."

I pretend a casualness I don't feel. "I didn't care about names before. I don't care now."

"Other people won't let it be that easy."

"Then let's forget other people. Let's stay here forever."

"I can stay until dawn," Killian whispers. "Then I have to go back."

I jerk upright at his words. "Go back?"

"Bianca has threatened Finn." His arms tighten. In fact, his entire body draws tight, like if he can just keep hold of me, he won't have to face whatever fearful thing he sees in the future. "She said if I'm not back before sunrise, she'll kill him in front of you and make sure you know it's my fault."

Fear freezes my blood. "What?"

"I'll head back an hour before the sun rises, wash your scent off in the lake, then go in through the front door. She'll never know we were together."

"Killian—"

He cuts me off. "I swore I'd keep you and Finn safe, and I will. I thought if I ... if I died, and the pack went to Asher, it would solve things. But now the howlers are dead, and that's not an option."

The words kill any joy I might have had in tonight. "You're giving up?"

I push away from him and climb out of bed. "Is this the 'you're only safe at a distance' thing again? Or the worthiness and tainted blood thing? Be careful, Killian Darrow. Remember which one of us is actually the child of Alaric Bane."

I expect him to hang his head, to quietly give up and let my anger dig a gulf between us like he has in the past. Instead, he rises and stalks toward me. He grasps my wrists, raises them high, and pushes back until I'm pinned against the cave wall, shackled there by him. He leans the full length of his body against mine. I feel him stiffening against my belly as he captures my mouth and ravages it.

"I'm not giving up," he growls when we break for air. "I'm buying time. Run tonight. Find out what your powers are. Figure out your magic. When you do, find where the Beaumonts are hiding Finn, get him, and get away." He drops his forehead against mine. "Once the others are safe, one day, maybe you can save me too."

"You think I could save you? From Bianca?"

Facing her is something I've planned for a month, but tonight, it feels closer and more real than it ever has. I hate myself for it, but I tremble at the thought of going against her.

Killian may be cursed, but Bianca is the monster in my nightmares.

His grin is sudden and unexpected. "Of course. You just have to accept that you have the power to do it."

My knees would buckle at his faith in me if he didn't have me pinned against the wall.

"B-but I have no idea what I can do. Where my limits are. There was nothing left of those howlers but piles of guts, Killian. What if I do that to the wrong person? What if learning control takes years?"

He kisses me softly. "Then I'll wait for you."

But I don't want to wait.

What if we didn't?

My thoughts race, sparking into realization, speculation, and a wild connecting of existing plans to new ones. It all unfolds before me in an instant.

"Stay with me tonight." Killian releases me. His hands move across my skin, and all I want in the world is to melt into him and forget everything. "Let me give you the time I have."

Instead, it's my turn to capture his wrists, holding them down by his sides. "No."

He blinks. "No?"

"I ... I think you're right. I think I can do this. But I am not waiting years."

"Selene—"

"No, listen. Maddox knows where Finn is." I kiss him fiercely. "We're not waiting years, Killian. We're doing this tonight."

## Forty

### SELENE

"I still can't escape with you," Killian says.

I grit my teeth and sit on the side of the bed, my arms folded beneath my breasts. He's filled me in on everything he's learned, and he's being stubborn. "I know Alpha magic won't let you cut ties to the pack, but once we have Finn, you could still go into hiding."

I know he won't as soon as the words are out, and I know why even before he says it.

"If I leave, the pack will be at Bianca's mercy. I won't do it."

The muscles of my jaw flex, and tears burn behind my eyes as I look away. "I understand, but I hate it."

He lifts my chin with a finger. "We'll get you and Finn away. That's what matters. Vandran told me weeks ago he has a house on the beach waiting for you in Fall Line."

I laugh bitterly. "So you're sending me away, after all."

"No. I'm sending you to find us some hope, learn your magic, and come back to me. While you're gone, Sofia and the others will try to collect evidence that Bianca is using eldritch magic to control me, which is against Conclave law."

I hug my knees to my chest. "We can't just break the curse? Does Whitlock know how?"

Killian shakes his head. "The only way to know how eldritch spells work is to make deals with them, and even Whitlock isn't ambitious enough for that."

"But the Beaumonts have made a deal," I say slowly. "I tricked Bianca into waiting for the Conclave to mark you. Maybe if I stay, I can trick her into telling me how the spell works."

"No." Killian's answer is immediate and harsh. He exhales and sits next to me. "You are getting out while you can. As long as she controls me, no one can protect you, Selene. She already tried to make me hurt you once. I fought her off, but once she and I have the strength of the mate bond ..."

Silence hangs between us. Even if we save Finn, Killian won't leave the pack. That means he's going to be marked. They will be mates, and Bianca will become more powerful. Technically, so will Killian, but he's only gaining a mate. She's gaining a mate and a pack. If she's already as strong as she is, it's safe to assume her control over him will become complete.

If I stay, one day, she'll make him kill me. I can't let her do that to either of us.

I want to scream because if Killian and I could mark each other after we rescue Finn, none of this would matter.

"You're sure the curse won't take her like it did Grace?"

He grimaces. "She's certainly sure."

"If it won't affect her, maybe it won't affect me. We could try."

"No. For the last time, I'm not taking that chance."

I sigh and open the chest at the foot of the bed. Killian keeps plenty of extra clothes in here, and luckily, they aren't all sweatpants. Still, I'm surprised when I find one of the pack combat outfits in a size clearly meant for me. In fact, there are several things in my size, all folded neatly on one side of the chest.

I hold the combat outfit up and look at him. He gives me a crooked smile and shrugs. "That two weeks when things were good, I thought maybe we could use this place to get away, and I thought if I got ... overly enthusiastic with your clothes, you might like to have options."

Warmth swells in my chest, and I hug him. His arms go around me, and I want to push him backward and fall into bed. I want to show him what being thought of means to me.

Instead, we break apart with regretful looks and get dressed.

Killian precedes me out into the night. When I step out behind him, I freeze.

There's a ghost waiting for us.

She looks like my mother.

Killian throws his arm up between me and the ghost.

"You can see her?" I murmur.

"Of course I can see her. Stay behind me."

Whispers rise, pushing against my ears like I'm deep underwater, echoing strangely in my mind in a way they never have. As if being out here in these ancient hills has made her so powerful, her voice has grown too huge to be contained within something as frail as a single human mind.

*Selen-Selen-Selenite, there are things-things-things you must know-know-know.*

I try to step around Killian's arm, but he doesn't let me. I grab his shoulder and force him to look at me. "Let me speak to her."

Killian hesitates, his eyes never leaving mine, then he moves aside.

I walk toward the entity. Her hair is flowing in a breeze that doesn't exist. Her body is a blur of swirling, pulsing silver light that gives the idea of flowing robes made of mist.

As I get closer, I see that her face is shifting and blurring. One moment, she looks like Aurora Stillwater. The next, she's something else. Something ancient, with the whole of the green and misty Ozark highlands in her eyes.

I stop, a new certainty in the pit of my stomach.

This isn't my mother. It never has been.

This is something else.

*Eldritch*, my mind whispers. Not like the howlers. One of the high eldritch. The beings people mistook for angels or demons, slotting them into the mythologies of their own religions when they had no place there. When they were ancient before humans ever dreamed of heaven or hell. When they were old even when the world was formed.

"I don't want any deals," I say before I can think.

The being's expression doesn't change. It's like she's wearing a static mask of my mother's face, a cardboard cutout over something incomprehensible. In the dreams and visions before, I couldn't tell. Now I can.

She speaks again, words echoing still, her voice compressed to fit inside my skull.

*I-I-I have no desire to consume your soul-soul-soul, Selenite Bane.*

My stomach drops. Is that the cost of dealing with them? To give them your soul? "What do you want?"

*My earth tires of the taste-taste-taste of human blood. You do not know what comes-comes-comes. Your mate cannot fall-fall-fall. You must save him, or you are lost-lost-lost. Only with you both-both-both can it begin-in-in.*

Foreboding blossoms deep in my chest. "What will begin?"

The eldritch's voice falls into a singsong.

*One will guide, one will fight, one will see.*

*One will heal, one will remember, one will journey.*

*The last two, a pair. One will free, one will seal.*

She pauses, then says, *There are eight. You must gather them-them-them and the ones who would protect them.*

"Who are you talking about? And why?" Killian asks. It's the first time he's spoken, and I start because I didn't realize he could hear her voice too. He hasn't tried to move in front of me again, but he stands close, his strength at my back.

*To stop the one who brings the end.* The darkness around her seems to deepen, and I catch a whiff of burning tar, just like the scent that came from the coalescing, oily smoke in Bane's library that called me a thief.

I go cold. We have so many problems, and now it seems like we're getting caught up in some kind of war between high eldritch.

*My ability to interfere-fere-fere is limited-ed-ed. I may tell you three things. First, each magic-ic-ic my kind trades to humans has an anchor-or-or of stone. Second, if you break the stone, your mate is free-free-free. Third, Killian Darrow, what you know in your heart is true: the magic that controls you now-now-now is the same you've carried for five years-s-s; they have only learned to use-use-use it correctly. Beware—at this very moment, Bianca Beaumont moves to become stronger-er-er. Fall into the fog again, and you will lose yourself entirely.*

An anchor of stone. Bianca moving to become stronger. Killian losing himself. It's so much. I don't understand, and I can't comprehend why any of this matters to a high eldritch. "Is my sister planning something at the Conclave?"

But the entity's light dims, beats bright once, like a heart, and then disappears, leaving Killian and me alone in the night. Her absence is like having the ground pulled out from beneath me. If not for Killian's hand on the small of my back, steadying me, I'd probably collapse.

"What the hell?" I breathe. "Was that even real? What did she mean, the end? Who are we gathering? What is an anchor of stone?"

Killian's voice is grim. "The anchor is her fucking necklace. That eldritch just told us how to break the curse."

# *Forty-One*

## SELENE

Once our eyes readjust to the dark, we sneak back to the pack house. I stay close to Killian, worried about Bianca's influence and the curse, but he says he doesn't feel either. In fact, there seem to be fewer guards than usual tonight, and all of them are Shattered Moon, which is strange. But it also makes it easy to creep inside and find Eva, Sofia, and Maddox, then creep back out where we're less likely to be overheard.

We fill them in on our strange encounter with the eldritch, and Killian tells them what he suspects: that Bianca is controlling him through the stone on her gaudy necklace. To free him once and for all, all we have to do is break the stone pendant.

"She never takes it off, not even at night," he mutters as we huddle in the cold, dark forest just beyond the pack wall. "If we can get it from her and break the stone, it won't just end Bianca's mind control; it will end the entire curse. I suspected it before. I should have trusted myself."

His hand tightens on mine, and a thrill courses through me. Neither of us has said it out loud, but we both know that if we can break that stone, not only will he be free of Bianca ... he and I can also mark each other. We can mate bond.

"Once Finn is safe, I'll return to the forest just outside the castle. When Bianca realizes I'm gone, Selene believes she'll come hunting for me with guards who are loyal to her. She'll think all she has to do to take control of me is get close with that necklace. But now that Selene's magic is stronger, she may be able to protect me from the full weight of Bianca's influence. We'll ambush her, and I'll get the stone."

"We'll also have loyal pack members waiting in the woods to over-power her guards," I say. "If Killian falls back under her influence, we'll fight our way to her and take the necklace from her."

They're silent. Maddox says, "If Killian is under her control, she can turn him against us. We won't stand a chance."

Killian's expression is grim. "I have faith in Selene."

I wish I had his confidence and try to sound like I do. "If that happens, we just have to be fast. She can only control him until we break that stone."

It's the dead middle of the night. There are hours until sunrise still, but after so long under Bianca's control, so much hopelessness, it's strange to think that it could end tomorrow.

"First things first," I say. "We have to save Finn. Sofia?"

"The plan to rescue Finn is the same, but Killian will take Parker's place," Sofia replies.

"How is she?" I ask. Nerves simmer beneath my skin. Her injuries are my fault. I commanded her to attack the howlers before she was ready.

Sofia's face goes pale, but she says, "She'll recover. Maddox, can you do your part with Noelle?"

Maddox rolls his eyes. "Yes."

Aside from Noelle, there are a number of guards patrolling the surrounding streets of the abandoned town around the church—something between five and a dozen, but Maddox hasn't been able to get a confident count.

But Noelle—which apparently is her real name—is the only one who stays in the building with him.

"Why does Noelle think you're visiting her?" Killian asks.

"She thinks I want to join Redcedar Hollow and take her as a mate." His lip curls in disgust. "She has a key to the church she wears around her neck. I haven't been able to steal it. We need to get it from her."

"Can you get her to come out tonight?" I ask.

"Yeah. I've been up there a few times. We have a *system*." He looks pissed about it.

"Good," I say. "You bring her out. She tells us where the guards are and how many, then you and Killian take them out and we save Finn."

"I could find the guards myself," Maddox growls.

"If you had time, we're sure you could," Sofia says tartly. "But every time you go, you report a different number. We need to be sure, and our time is up."

"What we need to be sure of is that no one will compel me to jump into a fight I'm not ready for," Maddox retorts.

Heat flares in my cheeks. "I won't. I'm sorry. I'm just figuring this out."

Maddox glares, but when Killian growls, he backs right off.

Nerves churn my stomach. Maddox doesn't trust me, and I don't blame him.

"I contacted Vandran like you asked, Killian," Sofia adds. "He was already on his way because he wanted to get to the Conclave early. He's picked up his pace. He and his guards will be at your shelter by dawn. He's ready to back you up if it comes to a fight between Bianca's people and ours. He said Whitlock agrees that the necklace pendant, even broken, will carry enough residual power that it will prove beyond a doubt what the Beaumonts have done to you. The treaty will be broken, but the Conclave won't come after Shattered Moon; they'll go after Redcedar Hollow."

I exhale in relief. That treaty has been a sticking point. If Killian or Maddox or whoever could just murder Bianca without consequence, this would have ended weeks ago. We need to be able to prove the Beaumonts were violating the treaty, and the necklace will do it.

This can work. It's going to work. Killian and I are going to get to be together, Shattered Moon will be safe, and Finn will be safe. Then we can focus on the final problem: saving the wolfless of Redcedar Hollow.

*Gather them*, a voice whispers in my mind.

I push it away because I still don't know what it means.

"I'll meet Vandran, then we'll go to the cave and wait for you," Eva says.

Killian turns to me and takes both my hands in his, rubbing warmth back into them. "If things go wrong and we can't get the necklace, you and Finn will go with Vandran, and no one from Redcedar Hollow will threaten you again."

The muscles in my jaw tighten. "We know exactly how to break the curse now. I'm not leaving you."

He pulls me close despite the others being there. Maddox makes an irritated sound. We ignore him.

"It's a contingency," Killian pleads. "Please."

"Are you making decisions for me again?" I ask, unable to hide the thickness in my throat.

"No, Selene. I'm begging. I can hold on as long as you're out there."

I cling to him. "You're sure we can't just tell the Conclave about the necklace now?"

He sighs. "I'm afraid the Beaumonts have too many allies who will help her dodge accusations. But if we have evidence in hand, they have to listen."

Resigned, I whisper, "Okay."

We break apart. It's time to leave.

Eva huffs a sigh, then kisses both Killian and me on the cheeks. "Take care of each other. My heart will break if you can't be together."

Sofia smiles sadly and nods. Killian and I haven't told them we're fated mates, but somehow, they seem to know.

"Why are you looking at them like that?" Maddox demands.

"Never you mind," Eva says to her son. "You just do what you need to do and listen to the Alpha." Then she takes her son's face in her hands. With tears in her voice, she says, "You are my last baby. You come back to me."

Maddox doesn't seem to want to look at her, but then, as if with great effort, he does. He grasps both of her wrists and leans his forehead against hers. "I will."

## KILLIAN

Maddox leans in before we shift to make the journey and says, voice low, "She suits you better than Grace ever did. I'll try to explain it to Asher, but he won't like it. Watch yourself."

Selene is less than ten feet away—she's being careful to stay within a range that prevents the curse—but she doesn't seem to hear. I grab Maddox's shoulder as he goes to walk away. "Wait. Asher is still here?"

Maddox shrugs one shoulder. "He comes and goes. I don't know where he is now, but he'll be back again. He ... might know that you're supposed to mark Bianca at the Conclave. He doesn't like that."

I let out a humorless laugh. "Of course he doesn't."

I look out into the dark forest, half expecting to see Asher, relieved when I don't. I have a hell of a lot more to live for now than I did last time he tried to kill me.

The three of us undress, pack our clothing into small bags we can wear as wolves, shift, and run through the woods. Tonight has been brutal. When Selene found me with the howlers, it wasn't late. Maybe nine o'clock. Now it's sometime after one in the morning. We have miles of hilly forest to cover, with half-frozen rivers, icy streams, and an untold number of bluffs and ravines between. I've barely recovered from the howler attack. Selene doesn't know her magic, and with that forest-leveling blast, she's already unleashed more raw power than I've ever seen a wolf use in one night. Magic isn't endless. It's like a well—draw too much, and it goes dry.

I just hope she has enough for what's to come.

A normal wolf can travel over a hundred miles a day when it's necessary. We are larger, faster, and have greater stamina, which gives us the ability to cover twice that distance if we go without rest. Finn is about fifty miles from us. We'll reach the town where he's being held in two and a half hours.

Selene and I run side by side through ravines and along the ridges of hills, through thick forest and out into fallow old farmland. Spring isn't far, but winter hasn't released its hold yet. The world is shades of shadow and silver and white. Snow glitters in patches like scattered diamonds.

We break into an open spot at the top of a cliff. Selene skids to a stop for just a moment. The moon hangs heavy and low, and she's framed against its sharp crescent. Its light limns her wolf form, turning her pure silver.

She's beautiful. For an instant, I lose all sense of purpose. All I want to do is run through the forest with her. Play. Chase. Catch. Fuck.

Our oldest legends say that before the Quiet, there were priestess-queens who ruled all the wolf packs. Selene Beaumont—Selenite Bane—could be one of those ancient queens. Clever, compassionate, wise.

She could be mine. My mate. My queen.

If we succeed tonight, she will be.

Selene bounds on. I push forward to keep close to her, Maddox darting ahead, then appearing from behind.

I can't get that image of her before the moon out of my mind, or the idea of her as one of the old queens, and I wonder.

～

# SELENE

Killian and I crouch in the dark a mile outside of the abandoned town. We're in our human forms again. My hand aches from the cold where Killian bit me, but thanks to his ministrations, it was healed in time for me to make the run. He seems mostly healed as well, only wincing every once in a while.

"Do you hear them yet?" I whisper.

Killian shakes his head.

"It's been twenty minutes. What if something went wrong?"

Killian leans over and brushes his lips across mine. "He'll be here."

Like his words are a prophecy, I hear the faint sounds of people moving through the woods. A second later, Maddox and Noelle enter the clearing. She's giggling and has her head tilted toward him. I expect Maddox to be his usual taciturn self. To trudge, ignoring her, head down and hands stuffed in his pockets. But that's not what's happening.

He leads her forward by the hand, laughing with her. As they enter the middle of the moonlit clearing, the key shines on its chain around her neck. Maddox stops and tugs her close, their intertwined hands between them. His grin flashes in the night. He is everything charming.

Even so, I can't believe she doesn't see how full of broken glass edges he is. How dangerous.

He extends the arm holding her hand like he's going to pull her into a dance. Noelle's breath catches; her eyes are wide, her expression blissful. I recognize that look. The man she's wanted for years has finally— *finally*—noticed her.

I would feel sad for her if not for the part she played with Finn.

Maddox's golden-violet eyes flash as he catches sight of me in the shadows. He tugs her in close to his chest, turning them so Noelle's back is to me as I step out of the trees and into the clearing. I open and close my fists, hoping I'll be ready.

I've never used my power on purpose, but I feel it flow through me now. Magic gathers around me. Silver light flickers, then swirls beneath my skin. The warm hum starts in my chest. I extend it toward her.

So far, I've only compelled obedience by accident. Can I do it on purpose?

Maddox leans down so that his lips brush Noelle's ear and says, "I hope you suffer when they kill you. I hope you feel exactly as afraid as you made that little boy feel."

As if they're dancing, he steps back and sharply spins her away from him. She stumbles to a stop and sees me. She gasps, but it's too late.

Power pounds in my blood with every beat of my heart and spills from my mouth as I command, "Cut yourself off from your pack tie."

Noelle lets out a strangled sound, but so does someone else. Maddox? Killian?

She turns and tries to run. Killian emerges from the darkness and grabs her by the back of the neck, spinning her to face me again, quick to return to my ten-foot range.

"Maddox?" she cries.

Only the silence of the snow-muffled night answers. Maddox has retreated into the shadows, but I still know he's near. I can feel him somehow when the power flows through me like this. I can feel all three of them.

I'm beginning to get a sense of this magic. It pounds in time with my heart, like a rhythm I've danced to my entire life but can hear only now. I reach out my mind for Noelle, for her life force. I sense the wolf in her, and my wolf stirs.

*Mine*, that part of me says. It's not the same rabid possession that I feel for Killian, but there's possessiveness in it all the same.

All wolves are mine. Mine to protect. Mine to punish.

The thought shocks me, which breaks the magic for an instant. In that moment, Noelle tries to run again. She lets out half a scream before Killian slams her face-down into the snow, then drags her upright and back to me.

I step toward her, but my eyes are on Killian. This moment together, our purposes darkly intertwined. Hunting our enemies as a pair. It is right.

My confidence swells, and I pull power around me like a cloak of mist and moonlight. "Tell me the location of every guard Redcedar Hollow has in this area."

The night ripples with the power. *My* power. It hits Noelle, and she whimpers and throws her head back, her body seizing until only Killian's fist twisted in the back of her shirt keeps her upright.

"Killian—"

"Keep going," he snarls.

I wince but push harder. "Tell me!"

Blood dribbles from Noelle's nose. "All around, in the alleys."

"We need better answers than that," Killian says.

"Be specific," I insist. And then I *push* with the magic.

It works. She lists every single guard and location. By the end, her words are a jagged moan, as if I've reached into her head and torn them out of her mind in chunks.

When we're done, she gags. Her limbs twitch uncontrollably. Blood leaks from her mouth, her nose, her eyes.

Killian lets her go, and she doubles over as she coughs up bile. Killian shudders too. His nose is bleeding.

All the magic falls from me, horror flooding in to replace it. "What did I do?"

His face is grim as he wipes away blood from beneath his nose. "You were right. Your power is strong. *Very* strong."

I made his nose bleed. I used too much, but it didn't feel like I was pushing at even half my strength. I clutch my hands together in front of me. Noelle is still convulsing on the ground. "What have I done?"

The lines around Killian's mouth deepen. "Her Alphas must have commanded her to keep everything about this location a secret. She was bound by their command but compelled to obey yours. I think it … tore her."

"What do we do?" I hate this. I hate that I caused so much suffering, even for someone like her. "I stopped, but she's not getting better."

Killian lifts Noelle as she writhes and makes terrible mewling noises. Then, with a quick, precise motion, he snaps her neck.

Noelle's body jerks, then falls. Her face is a rictus of pain. Death was so clearly a mercy.

*It tore her.* I press my hands to my mouth as bile rises in my throat.

"What about you?" I demand. "Your nose was bleeding. How strong was the magic?"

"You hit both of us," Maddox growls as he comes out of the dark. Blood is smeared beneath his nose as well. "You've got to learn to aim that shit or narrow it down or something. I'll get the key. You need it to open the church."

Shit, shit, shit. I knew it.

I walk on unsteady legs over to one side as Maddox jerks the chain from Noelle's neck. I don't vomit, but I wish I could. Instead, I spit a couple of times to get rid of the flood of saliva in my mouth.

I reach a hand behind me. Killian is there.

"I'm sorry," he murmurs, pulling me against his chest.

"No! I'm sorry." I wipe my streaming eyes.

"I'm fine. Maddox is fine."

"Because you two are impossibly strong Alpha bloods. Noelle is just a normal wolf. Look what I did to her!"

"I'm the one who killed her."

"I'm not sick because you killed her. I'm sick because of me. I'm a bull in a china shop, but the porcelain is lives. Killian, what the hell am I?"

He strokes my back. He hesitates for a moment, then says, "When this is over, we'll figure it out."

"But what if Finn had been here? What if I hit him, he's just little—"

"Shh. Selene. It's over."

I lean my head against him and try to breathe, steadied by the sound of his heartbeat against my ear. "I understand you now. Why you wanted distance. Why you were afraid to let anyone get close."

He just squeezes tighter. "You're not like me. It's power, not a curse. You'll be able to control it."

I'm not so sure.

"If it makes you feel better, I was going to kill her anyway. She betrayed Shattered Moon."

It doesn't make me feel better. Execution by Killian would have at least meant a clean death. But I am grimly satisfied, and that worries me. Only now, in this moment, do I truly realize how easy it is to believe that everything I do is justified when I have the power to do whatever I want.

I swallow and pull away from Killian as Maddox makes an impatient noise.

"Are you done? We have a kid to save." The air around the younger wolf already radiates with violence.

Killian nods. "With Noelle gone, will anyone be inside with him?"

Maddox snorts and stalks over to press the cold metal key into my hand. "No. She didn't tell them when she left. She just waited until he was asleep and snuck out."

I thought I could use my magic to help save Finn. Now I don't know whether I can. "Okay," I say, pretending a confidence I no longer feel. "Let's get my brother."

# Forty-Two

## KILLIAN

I have to stay close to her. That's the most important thing. As long as I stay within ten feet or so of Selene, I'm shielded.

But that means she has to come into the thick of the action with me. Which means, in turn, I need to try to keep the fights to one or two guards at a time.

Stealth has never been my method. I prefer to attack head-on. Asher is the stealthy one. And Maddox, I realize as I watch him fade away into the dark. Selene's and Maddox's silver coats, almost identical in color, aren't as obvious as usual because of the snow. It's a small advantage, but I'm grateful for it.

"Shift," I murmur to Selene. "Try to stay down and out of the way. If you have to run ..."

I wish we had time to wait for sunrise, when I'm not in danger of losing control. Despite the plan, separation feels inevitable. But I don't fear becoming the beast as much as I used to knowing I can't even get near her without returning to my right mind.

Selene undresses, and despite where we are, my eyes linger on her body while she stashes her clothes and my shirt in her cross body bag and tucks it away in the hollow of a tree. Since we're going into a fight, it's better not to wear something the enemy can grab.

I have to tear my eyes away. All I want is to tumble this woman into bed. To lie with her, the room dark, fire crackling. I want to study her face and trail my fingers up and down her skin while we talk about inconsequential things—or serious things—or don't speak at all. And then I want to roll her beneath me, hear the way her breath catches, and feel her nails dig into my back as I move inside her, knowing everyone we love is safe.

Warm breath mists against my hand as Selene, now a wolf, nudges my palm with her nose, and I have the sudden urge to grab her and run.

Going into a fight was never difficult until I had this much to lose.

"Do you have the key?"

She opens her mouth. The key shines just behind her front teeth.

"Remember to stay close, stay low."

She huffs.

I shift into my hybrid form. For an instant, the curse bubbles in the dark, a faint whisper from the depths. *Breakthemkillthembleedthemeatthem.* Then it subsides.

We move into the night, leave the forest, and cross into the town. The woods are encroaching on this once-human place. The streets are cracked and sprouted with tall yellow grass, the brick buildings of the small downtown half-fallen. I can't tell whether any of the damage came from the Wars of Power or whether it's just age.

We move silently beneath the eyes of the broken-out old windows, and I'm curious to see whether the information Selene got from Noelle is accurate or whether the other woman was able to lie despite Selene's magic.

Two blocks from the church, we duck down an alley and toward the first guard, exactly where Noelle said he would be. The gray wolf doesn't see me coming until I slash his throat with my claws. Neither does the second guard or the third. I wonder how many Maddox has taken out.

The fourth guard is smarter than the others. She isn't tucked away somewhere easy to sneak up on—she's standing on a balcony overhead. The door of the building is collapsed, so she must have jumped on the awning of the building next to it to get there. The railing around it is mostly missing, leaving a bare platform where she's perching. Against the old brick, her stillness and patchy, black-tipped tawny fur hide her until it's too late.

She spots us, tilts her head back, and howls. The sound rolls away, echoing across the empty town.

Shit.

I leap up, wrap a hand around her ankle, and jerk her down from the balcony. She crashes down on me already slashing with clawed hands and feet, opening a few minor cuts along my arm and chest.

Close—far too close—a chorus of howls lifts into the night.

The guard is strong, but it's short work after that. In less than a minute, she's dead in a bank of snow clinging to the sidewalk, her throat open and spilling a widening patch of crimson on white.

My vision blurs. It's not the Redcedar Hollow guard in the snow; it's Grace.

*Killian, what's happening to me?*

Screaming.

The snow is stained red.

*Breakthemkillthembleedthemeatthem.*

I fall to one knee, bracing against the ground to stop myself from going all the way down. Selene, who is crouched behind an ancient dumpster, whimpers, and I know I need to move. I need to move. The howls are closing in. They're only a street or so away.

Selene nudges me with her nose, and I force myself to rise, even though the world is spinning and I keep seeing Grace and Jackson. More howls. The other guards are coming all at once. The church is only two blocks away. "We need to run."

I take off. Selene bounds at my side.

We don't get far before they're on us.

Half a dozen Redcedar Hollow wolves stream from multiple dark alleys. One is a hybrid, five are normal wolves.

If they were all non-Alpha blood wolves, I could take them without a problem and protect Selene.

But the hybrid is massive, and as he bounds toward me, his eyes burn red.

He's got some kind of bloodline magic, probably a berserker. I barely have a chance to turn toward him and brace myself.

He hits me like a freight train and takes me to the ground. I rip and claw at him, but he's so fucking strong. As strong as Zev. Maybe as strong as Maddox.

The other wolves tear at my legs and feet. One claws at Selene. She dodges, still trying to keep close. The berserker turns his head toward her.

*Breakthemkillthembleedthemeatthem.*

Selene yelps as the wolf tears into her.

Yellow fog rises in my mind. For the first time in my life, I reach out to embrace the monster.

"Selene," I growl. "Run."

# SELENE

I don't want to leave him. I don't want him to lose himself to the darkness. But he's right.

We need the monster now.

I dodge another swipe from a wolf with a white belly and gray head and back. My side burns where his claws have already split my skin, even through my thick layer of fur.

I never trained with the pack soldiers, mostly because the Beta was in charge of them, and Deacon Jones has made me uncomfortable from the beginning.

Now I wish I had.

I try to use my momentum from the dodge to get farther from Killian. My shoulder slams painfully into the side of a building, and I trip over a pile of rubble before I can get my feet under me and really move. The gray-and-white wolf opens up another set of slashes in my rump before I can scramble far enough that Killian isn't shielded by my magic.

The change takes seconds. I can't see exactly what happens to him because I'm running away, but I feel the cold ancient magic of the curse ripple through the air.

Killian roars. It's not a sound wolves make, and it turns my blood to ice.

The roar shocks my pursuer into stillness long enough for me to dart away and scramble between slats in a boarded-up doorway. The building has partially collapsed, and I have to crouch low. I don't stop, dragging my belly to get deeper, away from the sounds of carnage.

There's sudden, shrieking pain in my back foot. I turn to see the gray-and-white wolf has his teeth clamped around my paw. I fight and kick, but he only digs in deeper.

Then, with a yelp, he disappears. Blood splatters across the ground where he was.

Fear pounds in my chest as I wait for the monster to finish with that wolf and find me.

It doesn't. The sound of fighting grows more distant.

Is it Killian, still fighting for control, pushing himself away from me?

In the distance, more wolves howl. They're probably calling to each other through the pack tie. They've probably already alerted Frank and Delilah that we're here.

Maddox said there would be no other wolves with Finn. I have to pray he's right. I also pray they don't have more soldiers stationed nearby or between us and home. This place is miles from the Redcedar Hollow pack house—a fact I'm sure Frank thought meant that Finn would stay hidden. But we're also so deep in Redcedar Hollow land that they'll have a long time to chase us, a long time to catch us.

I feel sick, remembering what it is to be hunted. And now I don't have Killian's protection.

Just like that first night, it will be Finn and me running alone.

But I'm not who I was then. I know I can do this. I have to be fast while Killian is hunting the guards, distracting them.

I squirm out from the collapsed building and onto a street that's empty except for three wolf bodies. None are Killian or the red-eyed hybrid. To the east, the white steeple of the old church rises, so close.

I dart the last two blocks and crouch in the shadows across the street. The dingy white building is smaller and more dilapidated than I thought it would be—more like an old clapboard house than anything else. It's maybe twenty feet wide and forty feet long. There's a slight glow in one of the windows, and I catch a whiff of woodsmoke in the winter air. Embers from a fire. At least they aren't letting my brother freeze.

I stand and pace into the road in front of the building. It's thirty feet from my position to the door.

No one attacks me. Nothing moves.

I take a few more steps.

Nothing.

I run all the way to the door. Still nothing.

All the guards have gone to chase Killian. They think Noelle is here. They don't know they've left Finn alone.

I shiver, then spit the key into the snow and shift out of my wolf form. Can't unlock a door without thumbs.

The whole time I crouch there, freezing and naked, I wait for claws or teeth to tear into my back.

They don't. The key turns. The door swings open. I move inside.

The scent of old furniture and dust assaults my nose, and I sneeze. I let the door close behind me without shutting it all the way and move deeper into the room.

This main part of the church is filled with two columns of old pews. There's a raised area with a podium where the preacher would speak at the front. Off to the side and back are a couple of empty doorways.

I walk until I'm almost to the front of the pews. This place smells of Finn. I know he was here, but the dust is so thick, I can't tell what's recent and what isn't. It's pitch black, and I've heard nothing move.

"Finn?" I whisper.

"You get away from me!"

Something gleams, and a tiny body comes flying out of the dark. I throw my forearm up to block, and a blade bites into my skin. I cry out in pain, and the attack immediately ceases.

"Selene?" my brother whispers in a tiny, frightened voice.

"Rocket! It's me."

The knife clatters to the ground. He throws himself at me and wraps his arms around my neck. I hug him back but have to put space between us. He must have hit a vein in my arm because even with my fast healing, I can hear blood dripping on the ground and the limb is rapidly growing cold.

"You got me pretty good. Is there something in here I can use as a bandage?"

"I'm sorry! I'm sorry!"

"It's okay, buddy. Think. Do you have a blanket or something? Where have you been sleeping?" Nudity is not a big deal in wolf packs. It can't be with people shifting all the time. But I'd still rather have something to wrap up in right now.

"Yeah! They make me sleep on a pallet in the old kitchen. I'll get you the blanket!"

He scurries off. I wrap my hand around the wound, squeeze, and grit my teeth against the pain. In a moment, he's back. He hands me a thin sheet.

"Does it hurt?"

"It's okay, but I think I need to bind it to keep pressure on it. I'm going to rip this up, okay?"

Finn sniffs. Then a sob breaks from him. He tries to speak, but the words are incoherent. "Oh, Finn." I wrap the sheet around me, then pull him in for a quick hug despite the bleeding. "It's okay. You're going to be okay."

"How can it be okay?" He fists his hands in the sheet and buries his face in my shoulder. "They're so strong. You and me keep trying to get away, but they keep taking me. How will it ever be okay?"

I squeeze him again. "It will be. I have a wolf now, and do you want to know a secret?"

The sobbing slows, and he sniffs. "What?"

I drop my voice to the lowest of whispers. "Killian and I are fated mates. Once we have you safe and we break the curse, we're going to mark each other. We'll get stronger, and so will the whole pack. Not even Frank and Delilah will bother Shattered Moon after that."

He gasps and pulls away from me. A sliver of moonlight slants across his face. "Promise?"

I grin. "I promise. But we have to get away from here first, okay?"

He wipes a sleeve across his nose. "Okay."

"Peek out the door and make sure no one is coming. I'm going to wrap this wound, and we'll get out of here."

And hopefully find Killian and Maddox.

I tear a strip from the sheet and wrap my arm as he scurries between the rows of broken pews. Even as I wrap it, I realize the bleeding has basically stopped.

I don't know whether I'll ever get used to healing like this.

There's a creak, and I shiver as a draft of cold air whispers against my skin. "Do you see anyone?"

"Um. S-Selene?"

I turn, and my heart drops. Finn is most of the way across the church, probably thirty feet from me, only ten feet from the door.

He's not the one who opened it.

Yellow eyes flash high over his head, and a soft snarl rumbles out of the dark.

The door is blocked by Killian, completely in the grip of the monster.

He lunges.

In that instant, I know that there's nothing—*nothing*—I can do to reach them in time. Not my brother to save him, and not Killian to force him back into his right mind, even with my extended range.

I have nothing but my magic and no choice but to use it.

"Stop!" I scream as I wrench energy up from my body. Magic bursts from me. Desperately, I picture the power parting, going around Finn, sparing him.

There's a blinding flash of light, but it's weaker than what I did to the howlers. Between them and Noelle, I've used so much magic. Forcing out this burst leaves me hollow and shaking. Even so, my ears ring, and the afterimage burns away my night vision.

Finn screams. Killian howls. I stumble forward blindly on unsteady legs. I've never felt this way before, like my insides have been carved out with a spoon. Like I am a desert, dry as dust.

I can't see, but if the blast doesn't keep Killian down, I have to get close.

God, what if I used all my magic and I can't shield him? What if this is the moment Finn and I both die?

The afterimage fades just as my foot touches something warm and soft. I drop to my knees and blink rapidly.

There's dim moonlight filtering in from outside through the place where the door used to be.

The door ... is gone. There's nothing left but a hole in the wall twice its size.

Finn is lying on the ground before me. He's not moving. His face is turned away from me, and his eyes are closed. Blood is running from his nose.

I have never felt terror like I do in that moment. "Finn?"

Footsteps pound on the street outside. I gather my brother in my arms and try to pull another burst of power, but nothing responds.

I found my limit.

I almost sob with relief when Maddox appears in the hole blasted through the wall. The fur of his silver hybrid form is streaked with blood. His gold-violet eyes are wild, and his chest is heaving. As he stands there, I wonder whether he's still under the influence of his berserker bloodlust. But then he shakes his head and looks back over his shoulder to where I assume Killian is lying in front of the church.

"Holy shit, Selene," Maddox says in a near whisper.

A whimper escapes my throat. Did I kill him? Did I kill them both?

Just then, Finn moves in my arms and starts to cough.

I pull him against me, my breath coming in sobbing huge gasps. "Finn, I'm sorry, I'm so sorry!"

He hugs me weakly. "I'm okay."

Outside, there's an ominous growl.

"You'd better get over here," Maddox says dryly. "Killian is already waking up. All the guards are dead, but there's no way they didn't alert the Redcedar Hollow Alphas. My guess is, if they're not almost here, they're blocking the way home."

~

THANKFULLY, Maddox is wrong. No one from Redcedar Hollow shows up. No one pursues us.

I'm grateful but uneasy. They should be chasing us.

I stick close to Killian's side as we make our way back to Shattered Moon land. Maddox is carrying Finn. The lack of pursuit feels more and more ominous as we go. But once we cross into our own territory, I'm too relieved to care.

Miraculously, both Killian and Finn are okay. My attempt to force my power to pass around Finn seems to have at least partially worked, but I didn't do enough and it clipped him in passing.

Killian took the full brunt of the blast, but it was so much weaker than what I did to the howlers that he was just blown back. It cracked a few ribs, but the injuries were relatively minor.

Dawn breaks at the same time as we reach Killian's shelter; I'm exhausted but so happy. Every time I look at Finn, I realize how close I came to losing everything and how close we are to being free now. There's only one more phase in our plan: lure Bianca out, get the necklace, and break it.

A couple more hours, and we are going to be free.

"Where's Eva?" Killian asks.

Maddox's eyes go distant. Killian is cut off from speaking to his pack, but whatever Bianca forced him to do to himself, he managed to preserve the pack's ability to speak to each other. I'm cut off only because I was isolated when Killian's ability to use the pack tie was damaged.

Maddox grunts. "Sofia says Vandran was running late, couldn't find the place. Mom had to go meet them. They'll be here soon."

"Get back to the pack house and help Fia gather the people we need for the next phase," Killian says.

Maddox nods, transfers Finn to Killian's arms, then disappears.

I go into the shelter, shift to human, and quickly dress. Killian does the same.

Finn is so tired, we lay him on the bed. I sit on the side next to him and smooth back his hair. They had him for a month, but he looks okay. "Are you all right, Rocket?"

He gives me a sleepy smile and turns toward me. "Yeah. I knew you and Alpha Killian would come for me, even when it took you a long time."

That smile holds such perfect trust, such heartbreaking innocence, I want to cry. Finn sighs, turns back over, and falls asleep. I press a kiss to his cheek, then go join Killian outside, where he's waiting, quiet.

"He knew we'd come for him." My voice wobbles.

Killian opens his arms. "Of course he did. We're his family."

The tears I've been holding back flood from my eyes. I go into his arms, he wraps me tight, and we stand in silence. The sun is shining down into the clearing where the cave is tucked at the base of the bluff, turning the last patches of the year's melting snow pale gold. Bare branches are turning our view of the blue sky to lace.

Neither of us speaks—it's enough to exist in that single moment with his warmth around me and his heartbeat in my ear.

I never thought I'd find someone who understands the weight of my life, my past. But he does. He listens, he's intelligent, he has so much compassion, and he would die to protect the people he loves. He would also live for them despite his own suffering, which is so much harder to do than go out in some sacrificial blaze of glory. Every time I look at him, I melt, and every time he touches me, he sets me on fire.

. "I love you," I whisper, tightening my arms around him.

"I love you too."

"I hope this works. I want to mate bond with you."

Killian sighs. "I want that too, but if it doesn't—"

I growl softly. "It will."

Twigs snap, and Killian and I both tense. We expect to see Eva. Instead, a silver wolf in hybrid form comes hurtling out of the trees. It's Maddox.

"Killian!" Maddox skids to a halt in front of us. His chest is heaving.

"What happened?" Killian snaps. He's moved between me and the younger wolf.

"Bianca knows. She's coming. When she didn't come out of her room at dawn this morning as usual, Zev checked on her. She wasn't inside. As far as he can tell, she was never actually inside. Scouts at the Redcedar Hollow border reported to Zev a little while ago. She must have snuck through last night, but she's coming back now, and she has fifty Redcedar Hollow wolves with her. Zev thought they were marching on the pack house, but I just saw them in the woods. She's coming here."

Killian is already moving. "Selene, get Finn. You have to go. Maddox, find your mother and Vandran. Tell them to turn around."

"Wait!" Maddox's voice is harsh. He takes another step toward Killian, his voice pleading. "It's too late. She has Mom."

Dead silence.

"What?" Killian snarls.

"No!" I whisper.

Killian grabs me. I look up into his heartbreakingly handsome face, fall into the topaz depths of his eyes. "Selene, if they take me—"

A stick snaps in the forest. As one, the three of us turn our heads toward it.

Vandran steps out of the trees about sixty feet away. A dozen guards flank him. Whitlock is at his side, pulling his long, high-collared coat free of the grasping undergrowth.

"Killian." Vandran grins. "Looks like we arrived just in time."

# Forty-Three

## KILLIAN

I move between Vandran and Selene.

I don't know why; we were expecting him. But there's something in the way he's watching me, a small smile playing around the corners of his mouth.

I know that smile. It's the one he wears when he's maneuvered an enemy into a corner.

Beside me, Maddox growls. Selene has gone still.

"Eva said you couldn't find us," I call out across the clearing. "She went to find you and ran into Bianca. They're on their way. I want to get Finn and Selene out before the fighting starts."

I wait for him to come closer. I want him to prove this eerie feeling wrong. Cold wind whispers through the trees, and he doesn't move.

Vandran heaves a sigh and runs a hand through his thick, gray-streaked hair. "Ah, Killian. I didn't want it to come to this."

A growl starts in my chest. A sweet, dark rage pulses deep in my brain. "Come to what, Marcus?"

The warlord's soldiers shift subtly.

I let my claws grow. Maddox said Bianca is coming, but I don't feel her. When I glance down, the silver light in Selene's skin is brighter than it's ever been and brightening by the second. I move to hide her more completely. "Sofia filled you in, didn't she? The Beaumonts are responsible for the curse. Bianca has recently harnessed it in a more targeted way. We think the pendant on the necklace she wears is some kind of anchor stone. Redcedar Hollow is inches away from destroying everything we've built, but we can stop them. We just need that stone as proof to show to the Conclave."

The Conclave is only two days away. Most of it will be held at the pack house, but some events—like the Prism Masque traditionally held on the third and final night—will be held in the old canyon park that serves as a no-man's-land between Redcedar Hollow and Shattered Moon.

"Everything *you* built, Killian," Vandran gives me a wry smile. "My vision has always encompassed greater things. You assumed Shattered Moon is the only project I have, and it is a bit of a pet of mine—after all, you are the son of Alaric Bane. An Alpha of hundred-thousands. Imagine the fear it would strike in people, having you at the head of my army—but my investment in you didn't pan out the way I had hoped. I've had to shift my focus and my resources to other, more promising ventures."

Blood rushes in my ears. He still thinks I'm Bane's son. They all do.

But then his words hit me. An army of wolves?

I hear the words of the eldritch like a distant song caught on the breeze. *Stop the one who brings the end …*

A rising sense of danger dumps adrenaline into my blood, heightening my senses, tensing my muscles. Beside me, Selene starts to speak. "He's not—"

I put my hand up, cutting Selene off sharply.

Vandran and Whitlock have always been obsessed with legacy and old family names. I will die before I let them find out she's the person they think I am. "Army?"

Vandran waves a hand dismissively. "Ah, no need to worry about that now." He looks me over, his expression wistful. "You were a good kid, Killian. Cunning, patient, willing to do violence as long as you thought it was necessary. The problem is, your standards for 'necessary' are too high, and you're stubborn, especially when it comes to"—he waves a hand vaguely at Selene—"relationships. You should have listened to me when I told you to get rid of her. I gave you the perfect way to just let it happen when I infected that rogue with howler venom and set it loose in your pack house."

*What?*

"Hell, honestly?" Vandran continues. "You should've listened way back when I told you to ditch the Quinn girl. Look how that turned out. Your mind is strong, but hers broke, and she started all this war."

I stiffen, my brain following his words too slowly. He can't mean what I think he does. The betrayal can't run that deep.

"What the fuck does that mean?" Maddox snarls. Power rises around him, crackling like a bonfire.

Vandran's easy grin falters, and his eyes cut to Whitlock's. The arcanist lifts his hands, opens and closes his fingers, rings glittering.

But they're too bare. One of his rings is missing—a big one.

An image jumps into my mind. An overlarge ovular black stone that flashes yellow.

Finally, my mind catches up. Realization makes the world tilt.

It's the same stone as the one on Bianca's necklace.

But Whitlock has had that ring—had the anchor stone—for years.

Vandran isn't working for the Beaumonts; they're working for him. He had Whitlock curse me. I've been his puppet all along.

It makes sense. As soon as he learned I was the son of Alaric Bane, Vandran helped elevate me to power. He convinced me that power as rare as mine destined me to be an Alpha. He convinced me I shouldn't just create my own pack—I should retake Conqueror's Moon. He made my rise possible because he wanted me to become Alaric Bane ... but this time, Vandran would be the king, and I would be the head of his werewolf horde.

Except his plan didn't work. I respected Vandran, but I never let him control me. Grace must have been the final straw. He cursed me. It didn't work how he intended, but it still got rid of Grace. Got rid of Asher. Started a war. Hell, Vandran even introduced me to Deacon Jones and recommended he replace Asher as my Beta.

My mind reels.

"Maddox! Killian!"

I turn at the sound of Eva's voice in time to see Bianca appear from the trees at the head of a pack of wolves. She's human. Beside her, two hybrid form soldiers are frog-marching Eva toward us.

Maddox tenses, and I can tell he's about to lunge for his mother. I throw out a hand, grab a handful of fur, and haul him back.

"Stand down," I command, throwing Alpha aura into the words. My life, Selene's, and the lives of Eva, Maddox, and Finn all balance on a razor's edge. "They'll kill her before you get close."

Maddox snarls. For an instant, our wills grapple for dominance. But I'm older, I have more control, and I have a pack. He shoves away from me, chest heaving, eyes on his mother, but he doesn't charge.

"Vandran," Bianca says conversationally. "You made it."

Selene's hand finds mine. She's shaking. Fuck me. We thought we were close to freedom, but we never had a chance.

Vandran has been behind everything all along.

Maddox snarls again. Bianca does a fake little pout at him. "Aw, be careful, puppy." She pulls a dagger out of a sheath on her hip and holds the tip of the blade against the base of Eva's throat. The metal catches the light. Not steel—silver.

"The silver might not harm a wolfless, but her throat will slice all the same," Bianca says sweetly. Her eyes cut to me, and she grins. "Oh, and Killian, *be still.*"

Feverish heat slides down my neck. Pain prickles at the back of my mind. Both are met by a cool sweetness that washes them away. The command doesn't take hold.

As drained as Selene is, her presence does what we hoped it would— it shields me.

Still, I want Bianca to believe she's in control, so I don't move.

"No one has to get hurt," I say to both Bianca and Vandran. "We can come to an agreement. Me for the rest of them."

"No," Selene hisses beside me.

Still smiling, Bianca presses the dagger against Eva's skin. A line of red appears. "You aren't in a position to negotiate."

Selene growls. I squeeze her hand.

Eva lets out a muffled sound of pain as blood drips down her chest and into the neckline of her shirt, but she keeps her eyes on mine. They're defiant and full of rage. She doesn't have to speak; I know what she'd say. *Don't you dare trade yourself for me, Killian Darrow.*

But I've lost too many Quinns, and the choice isn't hers to make.

My eyes go to the pendant Bianca is wearing around her neck. In the sun, it's shining that disgusting yellow. I just need to get to it—the source of all the death I've dealt, all the suffering I've gone through, everything I've inflicted on others. So close but out of reach.

"That stone," I say, unable to take my eyes from it. "It was yours, Whitlock."

Yellow mists around the edges of my mind as I stare at it. Whispers swirl like smoke.

*Breakthemkillthembleedthemeatthem.*

Warden Whitlock holds up his hand and wiggles his fingers. "You always were quick, boy. Like Vandran said, it's too bad you're so stubborn."

"But the stone has a limited range," I say, still trying to understand. "Fall Line is outside of it."

"Well, I didn't get it quite right at first," Whitlock says, drawing a long breath like he tends to before launching into overly long, technical descriptions of magic. "The deal with the eldritch was supposed to grant us control over you. But the thing tricked me, didn't tell me the details of how it worked. I put too much power into it over too much distance with too much interference, and the effects were ... Well, I believe you're familiar with the effects by now."

He tuts, like that part was unfortunate but mostly inconsequential. "I've had time to refine my understanding, however, and after offering the eldritch in question a second trade, it showed me how to do the ritual correctly. The anchor needs to be wielded by an Alpha wolf to control an Alpha wolf."

It takes everything in me to keep my feet rooted to the ground. "It wasn't the Beaumonts. It was *you*. You wanted to build an army, but you couldn't even get me to choose the right mate."

There's a beat of quiet. Selene whispers, "Oh, no," in a trembling voice.

"You killed Grace?!" Maddox snarls and surges against me again. His power is like a wildfire caught by the wind. It takes everything I have to hold him back.

A cry of pain and grief tears from Eva's throat. "That's why my daughter is dead?"

Bianca tilts her head at me, giving me the most incredulous look, like I've just said something so stupid, so obvious, it made everyone else dumber for hearing it.

She scoffs. "I'm sorry, did you think my parents had the guts to pull something like that off? Fuck no. Frank would've shit himself at the very idea of making a deal with an eldritch. And Momma? Too complacent." She tosses a grin at Vandran, and even though she's human, I can see the wolf in her smile. "Not a problem anymore. As promised."

"What do you mean, not a problem?" Selene demands.

"Oh, sweetie. They're dead." Bianca snaps her teeth in Selene's direction, then smiles at me and strokes the necklace. "Whitlock figured

I could use the power boost to keep you under control, baby. You're looking at the new Alpha of Redcedar Hollow. We're going to end the pack war for real, and I am going to be *so* strong with you as my mate."

She lets loose. Her Alpha aura rises and rises and rises, billowing from her like a storm. She was always strong, but this ...

Behind her, the wolves of Redcedar Hollow lift their muzzles to the sky and howl.

A new voice pipes up from behind me, and my stomach drops when I realize it's Finn. He pokes his head between me and Selene and shouts with all his might, "You can't have Killian as a mate! He has to be with Selene! The moon fate said so! And they love each other!"

The howls cease. Silence falls across the clearing. All eyes are on the little boy.

I close my eyes. Leaves rustle as Selene kneels next to Finn.

She pulls him into her arms, and her voice is so calm, so kind. "Hey, Rocket. Thank you so much for standing up for me, but right now, I need you to stay by Maddox and keep quiet, okay?"

He looks at her with huge eyes and nods. I want to howl. I want to rip something apart.

Not Finn. All he meant to do was stand up for Selene against the biggest bully either of them has ever had.

He has no idea what he's done.

Selene rises and takes my hand again. I have to be careful not to crush hers, I'm holding on so tight. I have to be careful not to move so Bianca believes I'm under her power.

Bianca lets out a short, sharp, incredulous laugh. "Oh, my god. It's true? All this time, you two have been keeping secrets from me." She laughs again, then wipes tears from her eyes before her gaze sharpens on Selene. "Oh, Sister. I'm so glad I haven't killed you yet. This is the best moment of my life."

Selene's eyes dart. Under her breath, she says, "Eva is next to her. Finn is right here. If it goes wrong ... I only have one chance."

"Take it," I say.

"I love you," she whispers. It sounds like goodbye.

"I love you too."

~

# SELENE

Bianca's words almost break my will, but I fight against them. I have to hold on to hope.

I let power build inside me, careful to keep the look of defeat on my face. Warmth tingles in my chest, but it's stuttering and weak. I'm scraping the bottom of the well of power inside me and coming up with only dust. I think the only reason I'm shielding Killian from Bianca's influence is because it's something that happens automatically. It's not the same as me consciously trying to use compulsion or blast someone back.

*Please*, I beg the magic.

My mind can't wrap around what's happening. Vandran's betrayal. The fact that he's behind the curse. Behind Jackson's death.

And the Beaumonts ... They can't be dead. It's impossible. Even Bianca isn't enough of a monster to murder her own parents.

But I remember how angry she was when they didn't want to beat me the night I tried to escape with Finn. Harper Lloyd, the Redcedar Hollow Beta, warned me.

*Bianca is the one pushing us forward. It's over for Shattered Moon and for you.*

We wanted to stop Bianca from marking Killian because of how powerful it would make her. It didn't occur to me that she'd find another way. *This* way. If she takes Killian as a mate now, his power—and the additional thousand wolves of Shattered Moon—will make her unstoppable.

Vandran wanted Killian to lead his army. But Killian turned out to be too good. Vandran broke him, discarded him, and left him to struggle against Redcedar Hollow.

Now the warlord has found a use for him again. But instead of leading the army, Killian will serve as no more than an accessory for Bianca. An amplifier for her magic, an Alpha powerful enough to serve as a nexus for a hundred thousand wolves, completely under her control.

I wonder whether Vandran realizes Bianca is already plotting against him. Waiting until she can depose him the way she did our—her parents. Not that I know it for a fact; I just know her.

All this passes through my mind in seconds as Bianca's words ring in the air. "This is the best moment of my life."

I curl my lip. God, she's a heinous bitch.

Whispering so quietly I can barely hear him, Killian says, "Don't tell anyone you're the daughter of Alaric Bane or the Stillwaters. They'll never let you go."

The Stillwaters? Why does my mother's supposedly extinct side of the family matter?

But I can't ask. I've gathered every scrap of power I can, and I have to act before they do.

I lift a hand and push, unleashing my magic on Bianca, putting everything I have into the compulsion. "Let go of Eva and command your wolves to attack the Warlord's guards!"

The words ripple and swell as they crash against her. She shudders and blinks and then ...

My power whiffs out.

A beat passes. Bianca looks around, then breaks the silence with an incredulous laugh. "I'm sorry, what?"

She laughs again, harder, until she's cackling. Howling. She braces her hands on her knees, the knife still clutched in one of them. The wolves behind her yip and bark and howl with her.

Bianca gestures sharply, and her soldiers drag Eva along as Bianca stalks closer to me. "Say it again." She points the dagger at me. Her voice takes on a high-pitched, mocking lilt. "Let go of Eva and command your wolves to attack!"

She doesn't stop laughing. The guards from the Fall Line Protectorate join in. Vandran and Whitlock exchange pitying glances.

Humiliation sets fire to my cheeks.

Bianca gasps and holds her stomach. "Did you think that was going to do something to me? Do you think you have some kind of Alpha power now? If you had magic, Selene, why have you been cleaning my toilet for a month? God, you are stupid."

She wipes tears from her eyes and waves the silver knife at Finn before she presses it to Eva's throat again. "Take him."

"No!" I cry.

Her soldiers reach for my brother. With a roar, Killian bursts into his hybrid form. He leaps for Bianca and Eva. Bianca's eyes go wide with shock.

Her surprise is the only thing that saves Eva as Killian knocks the new Alpha of Redcedar Hollow on her ass.

But the movement takes him too far from me. The light beneath my skin winks out. The warm hum in my chest stutters and dies.

"Stop!" Bianca screams, one hand clasping the black stone at her throat.

Killian freezes like he's been turned to stone. Maddox lunges and grabs Eva. I run toward Killian, trying to get close enough that my magic will protect him.

Before I can take two steps, Bianca leaps to her feet and presses her silver blade to his throat.

"Don't you even fucking think about it, Selene," she purrs. "Weak wolves like you aren't meant to have nice things."

I go as still as Killian, like she's frozen me with magic too. "Bianca—" I plead.

"Not a step closer. I don't give a shit if you're fated. Do you think I would *ever* let you have something I want for myself?" She bares her teeth in a terrible smile and leans the full length of her body against his "And I intend to have him."

"Killian ..." I reach for him, trying to feel him through the partially formed mate bond. There's nothing. His eyes are as blank as empty stones.

Bianca goes on tiptoe and stage whispers in his ear, "Killian, honey, reject your mate bond with Selene."

"*No!*" I shout.

I try to pull my magic again. To do something, anything.

Killian's face contorts. He's fighting her command. He's still in there. Maybe he can break her control. Maybe he can deny her this part of himself. Her power over him was never complete before.

But then he speaks, the words a horrible snarl that come from behind clenched teeth, filled with power. Intention. Wolf magic. "I reject you, Selene."

There's a shocking ripping sensation in my chest. I let out a strangled scream and go to my knees.

Behind me, Maddox shouts. Vandran's guards have moved in. They have Finn. Maddox is fighting them, but there are so many. The campfire scent of wolf magic mingles with the spice of witch spells. More cries, snarls, whimpers. For a second, I think Maddox will get free.

Then Bianca's wolves converge. Eva cries, "Maddox!"

A moment later, they have him too.

It all feels so distant. My heart is tearing in half. I press a hand to my chest and am surprised when it doesn't come away covered in blood.

Bianca's smile is pure, venomous evil as she presses the silver blade against Killian's throat. "Now, Selene, you reject the bond too."

"Bianca, please."

"Do it!"

"No," I sob.

"You want to play games?" Bianca's eyes dart to where the Protectorate soldiers have Finn. "That's my heir," she says. "He belongs to me. Give him here."

No!" I beg Vandran. "Don't give him to her."

"You heard the Alpha." Vandran dips his head to Bianca. "She wants her brother."

I can only watch, slumped on my knees, pain beating against thought and sense as they drag Finn over and hand him to the Redcedar Hollow wolves.

"Selene!" Finn reaches for me.

"Reject your mate bond, Selene," Bianca says with false patience, "or I'll have them break his neck."

One of the soldiers grips Finn by the top of the head and chin, ready for her command.

Tears run down my brother's face. He strains against the wolf who holds him, reaching for me. "Selene!"

"It's going to be okay, Rocket." I force a smile as tears spill from my eyes too.

I look up at Killian. He's in his hybrid form. His lupine face is blank, his eyes forward. Is there wetness in the corner of his eye too? I don't know whether hybrid form wolves can cry.

It's easy to break a mate bond. All you have to do is speak.

Still, if not for Finn, I wouldn't be able to because nothing but saving my brother's life could make me mean it.

"I reject you, Killian," I whisper.

*I love you.*

Magic tightens around my throat, my lungs, my heart. I throw my head back and scream. It feels like invisible claws are delving into my chest. They eviscerate my heart and pull it out, piece by bloody piece. I collapse on my side in the mud and leaves.

"Are you satisfied, Alpha?" Vandran asks Bianca, coming to stand next to her.

I hear the words as if from a distance. The pain won't end. Finn sobs and calls my name.

I roll onto my back, writhing in agony.

I've been beaten so many times, but nothing—*nothing*—compares to this.

"Almost," Bianca says. She steps away from Killian and kneels beside me, smirking as she looms.

"I'd say I don't know what I'm going to do without you, Sister," she whispers. Then she shrugs. "But, then again, I have Finn. I'm sure he'll be just as fun to play with as you were."

No, no, no!

She raises the silver knife high. It gleams in the morning light for a moment.

I look to Killian, reach for him.

Bianca drives the blade into my chest with both hands.

I scream. My body spasms. The silver hits my system, burning through my blood, sending a terrible, familiar weakness through my body.

Bianca rises. Finn is screaming now. The silver knife is still buried just beneath my collarbone. Pain slices every time I try to breathe.

I can't. I can't breathe.

It burns.

I blink, and Bianca is gone from my side. She's next to Killian. I swear I see him trembling. Is he in there? Does he know what just happened?

If he could just break free, he could kill her, take this knife from my chest. We could live.

Finn is screaming. People move around me. Time warps and stretches.

I blink. The sun has risen high in the sky. I'm on my back. The hilt of the knife protrudes from my chest. I lift a shaking hand. There's silver light beneath my skin. It flickers, weak.

I blink. The sun is setting. The world is agony. I just want it to be over. Why isn't it over?

The next time I close my eyes, it all stays blessedly dark.

# Forty-Four

## KILLIAN

Selene is dead.

My mate is dead.

My love is dead.

I'm trapped by the sickly yellow fog that invades my mind. A puppet with no one at the strings. Finn screaming, Eva crying, Maddox roaring angrily as he fights like a demon.

But they have his mother, and when Bianca threatens to break her neck too, Maddox finally submits.

Bianca is exponentially stronger than she was before. Last time, I could fight. I still had a sense of movement inside my own mind.

This time, I am completely paralyzed.

I fade in and out of awareness as we leave the forest and return to the Shattered Moon pack house. Consciousness is agony. My heart is a ragged hole where Selene used to be. The scene plays over and over in my mind: The shock on her face. The knife in her chest. How still she'd gone by the time Bianca forced me to walk away.

The oblivion of this new version of the curse is my only relief. Hours pass. Or maybe it's centuries. I don't know. I don't care.

In the vaguest way, I'm aware that the pack is in a flurry of activity. Hundreds of Redcedar Hollow's wolves have joined us in the pack house, filling it for the first time since Alaric Bane's day.

The members of the Conclave have just begun to arrive.

It hasn't been years, then. It's been only a day.

I retreat to the yellow again.

"What did you find?"

Bianca's voice tugs me up from the depths. I fight against it. If I can sink deep enough into the oblivion, maybe I can stay there. Any time I'm conscious, her name beats in my mind in rhythm with my pulse. *Selene. Selene. Selene.*

"A book." It's Deacon's voice.

The sound of my traitor Beta speaking sparks a rage that immediately yanks me to the present. I blink and come to. I'm standing in my bedroom wearing a suit. Bianca is in a deep green dress. She's leaning over, glaring at Deacon in the mirror, applying a shade of lipstick that looks like old blood.

"I can see it's a book." Bianca's voice is dry.

I stand off to one side out of the way, left like a forgotten toy. Before, I could move a little unless I was commanded not to. Now her control is so complete, I have to be commanded to do anything at all.

Jones places a huge leather-bound tome on the vanity. He points to the cover excitedly. "Selene had it hidden in her room in the servants' hall. Look at the title."

"The Legacy of Alaric Bane," Bianca reads in a whisper. She puts down her lipstick and excitedly opens the book, then turns a few pages. "These are his children." She glances at me and grins a feral grin. "This will prove Killian's legitimacy. Vandran will be pleased."

"What will please me?" Vandran appears at the bedroom door. He steps inside, eyes skating over me like I'm furniture. Then he sees the book. "What's that?"

If Selene were alive, I'd be going out of my mind at the possibility of them finding out she's Bane's true heir. But she's dead, and I don't give a shit whether they find out I'm not a Bane at all. They're the ones who chose this. Who killed her.

Bianca jabs the book with one green-painted, sharp-nailed finger. "A book of Bane's children. I made Selene stay in the old wing of the castle, and she had it stashed in her rooms. She must have found it while she was skittering around down there like a rat."

"Let's see it," Vandran says excitedly.

He leans over Bianca as she begins to turn the pages. They're slightly yellowed around the edges and filled with dark handwriting and pasted-in pictures.

"It's in chronological order," Vandran says after a minute. He reaches over Bianca and flips ahead, then back a few pages, then ahead a few more. "Killian should be in this spot. Where is he?"

Confusion wrinkles Bianca's nose and brow. "I don't know."

They go back and start paging through from the beginning. They look through the entire book, then go quiet. Vandran goes back to the beginning, but Bianca approaches me.

"Look at me, Killian."

My body obeys.

"Is this a joke? Did you set this up with Selene? Be honest."

It's like having a gag pulled out of my mouth. "No. Selene found it in the abandoned wing, like you said."

"Where?" Bianca demands.

"Through a door sealed with Bane's blood-rune."

The sound of flipping pages stops. Vandran lumbers over, holding the book open, the spine braced against one of his meaty forearms.

He's quiet, which means he's on the verge of being very, very dangerous.

"Why aren't you in there?" Bianca demands.

They didn't notice Selene's entry. It would be funny if I could think of her without spiraling into agony.

I shrug. It feels like I'm lifting boulders on each shoulder. "Maybe I'm not Bane's son."

Vandran grabs me by the throat. I surge against the mental walls of fog that prevent me from reaching my own body, but they're as impenetrable as ever. I can't defend myself.

"What do you mean, you're not Bane's son? All these years, you were lying to me? Command him to answer!" Vandran barks the last at Bianca.

She does, but Vandran's giant hand is still around my throat. I cough. "I never lied. I thought I was a Bane."

The warlord bares his teeth. They're flat and utterly human, but the expression is still menacing. "Claudia," he growls.

Vandran releases me, tosses the book onto a table, and stalks to one end of the room, then back. Then he stops, like something just occurred to him, and goes back to the table. He begins furiously flipping through the book, muttering to himself. One word over and over.

Then, a little past the midpoint of the book, he presses his finger to a page.

"Tell Warden Whitlock to get his decrepit ass in here," Vandran snarls at a guard.

"What is it?" Bianca strides over, looks at the page, frowns, and then gasps as all the blood drains from her cheeks. "No. *NO!* This is a lie! She planted this!"

If I could, I'd smile.

"Oh, was the woman doing arts and crafts in all that extra time you gave her?" Vandran retorts. He pulls the book toward him, and his eyes dart over whatever is written inside.

Abruptly, he slams a fist on the table and roars. I've seen him angry, but Vandran is good at his cultivated appearance of nonchalance. I've never seen him lose control like this.

"Stillwater? That girl was a Bane *and* a Stillwater, and you *killed her*? Do you know what you've done?"

He lunges toward Bianca. Vandran is a massive man who has spent almost all of his five and a half decades as a soldier, but the Alpha Lady of Redcedar Hollow is a warrior too. Almost six feet tall, ripped as hell, in her prime, and the Alpha of a pack of one thousand wolves.

She grabs him by the collar, uses his own momentum against him, and throws him to the floor. She swings her leg over and crouches above him, her evening gown rucking up to her knees.

Vandran's guards jump toward them, but Bianca holds out a finger. The claws on her other hand are extended, poised right at the hollow of Vandran's throat. "I wouldn't."

They stop. She smiles.

"Good boys. Now, back up, or I'll have to puncture your warlord's windpipe and then unleash my pet on you." Her eyes dart to me, and my body tenses, readying to move without my say-so.

The guards back away.

Bianca's voice remains a seductive purr as she returns her attention to Vandran and drags one clawed finger down his cheek. "Did you forget that you're in *my* house, you dusty old fuck? This isn't Fall Line. Don't you dare disrespect me."

Whitlock enters the room. One of his rings flares, and there's a blinding flash I can do nothing to protect my eyes from.

There's a thud. Bianca yelps. By the time the afterimage clears from my eyes, she's climbing up from the floor, snarling. Whitlock apparently blasted her back. The arcanist has a ball of black lightning pulsing above his hand, a different ring glowing. Downstairs, I hear my apartment door fly open and crash into the wall. A few seconds later, the hallway outside my room is flooded with Redcedar Hollow wolves.

The tension in the air becomes a solid thing. Then an irritated voice sounds from beyond the clump of wolves. "Move!"

Sofia wiggles her way through them.

"You are supposed to be making sure the Conclave guests are settled," Bianca snaps.

My Gamma raises a brow, unimpressed. "Yes. I am. And *you* are supposed to be hosting." She glares around. When her eyes fall on me, sadness crosses her face. "But don't end things on my account. By all means, go ahead and tear each other apart while the rest of the Conclave and their guests settle in for dinner."

Vandran is the first to hold up his hands in a gesture of surrender, his signature easy grin back on his face. "My apologies, Alpha. I was out of line."

Bianca doesn't respond for a long moment. Then she snorts and relaxes. She jerks her head at the gathered wolves and Sofia. "Get out."

"Wait!" Vandran calls. He glances at Bianca. "Tell them to bring Claudia Darrow here. I want to get to the bottom of this"—he gestures at the book—"right now."

My blood chills. Sofia gives me a longing look, and I know she wants to speak to me. But when Bianca shoos her again, she leaves.

It doesn't take them long to find my mother and haul her upstairs.

The Redcedar Hollow guards attempt to throw Claudia down in front of Bianca. My mother is in heels, glittering with jewelry, dressed all in black with her chin-length hair in perfect order and her favorite bloodred lipstick on her lips. She stumbles a little when the guards toss her, but she doesn't fall. She sticks her nose right in the air and says, "I am the mother of the Alpha. What is the meaning of this?"

When she looks at me, is there sadness in her eyes too?

I've been so angry with her for neglecting me as a kid and a teenager, I haven't bothered looking in years.

Vandran looms over my mother. Disgust for the way he's looking at her worms its slimy way down my spine. "Claudia. Who is Killian's father?"

To her credit, my mother doesn't blanch or flinch; she just looks at him like he's an idiot. "Alaric Bane."

Bianca stalks to the table, grabs the book, and shoves it in my mother's face. "Then why isn't he in this book?"

My mother's eyes drop to the cover. Her eyes widen, and her throat works as she swallows. But, being my mother, she doesn't give up. "I tore out his page."

"There are no torn pages in that book except the final one that talks about some half-fae twins," Vandran snaps.

He stalks closer to her, menace in every movement. I claw and ram and tear at the walls in my mind. Claudia is the way she is, but she's still my mother.

"He's just not listed, then," she says with an unconvincing sniff.

Vandran puts a heavy hand on her shoulder. "Bane knew *all* of his children. He created them carefully, purposefully. The truth, Claudia. Now."

She bares her teeth at him. They go back and forth a few more times. But when Vandran casually wraps a huge hand around the back of her neck and squeezes, my mother breaks.

"Fine! He's not Bane's son." Her eyes find mine, and I realize I wasn't mistaken. There is sadness there. "Your father's name was Jack Owens, Killian." Her lower lip trembles. "He was a good man."

"Jack Owens?" Bianca screeches. "Who the fuck is that?!"

Vandran shoves, and my mother stumbles to the floor on hands and knees. "He was a Conqueror's Moon Gamma," Vandran snarls. "He was no one. Barely an Alpha blood, no bloodline magic, no name. Nothing."

"No one?!" Bianca shrieks. "Do you understand how ancient my bloodlines are? And you think I want some nobody as a mate?!"

Jack Owens. I stare at my vicious, drunken, irritating mother crumpled on the floor.

*He was a good man.*

Jack Owens.

Claudia rises while Vandran and Bianca shout at each other and toddles over to me on those impossible heels. As she gets close, I realize I can see lines around her mouth and eyes I never noticed before. She looks ... lonely.

Claudia examines me. And all I can do is stand there, impassive. Useless.

She sniffs like she's holding back tears and speaks in a low voice. "No one expected Bane to raise a former rogue to be his primary pack's

Gamma, but your father—Jack—he was just that good. He cared, and people could tell, so they followed him." Her throat works. "He got us out. He was supposed to follow, but he never came. I thought he abandoned us. Later, I found out Bane murdered him because he helped some of the mothers of his children escape."

She folds her arms over her chest and looks away. "He chose them over us, Killian. Nothing useful comes from being a good man. But it didn't stop him, and it's never stopped you."

I wish I could do something other than stare at her. I wish she would have told me this a lifetime ago.

My mother's eyes are distant for a second, then she shakes herself and curls her lip at Bianca, as if just now hearing what the other woman said an entire minute ago. "Excuse me? *Your* bloodlines are ancient?"

Bianca and Vandran stop arguing and look at my mother.

Claudia scoffs, and it's the single most dismissive sound I've ever heard. "Selenite was a Stillwater *and* a Bane, and even she wasn't good enough for my son. Mostly because her mother was a sniveling little bitch." She sniffs again. "And I thought the silverlight priestesses were supposed to be wolf kind's fearless leaders."

For who knows how many times in recent days, my world rocks on its axis again.

I had my suspicions about who the Stillwaters might be. My mother just confirmed I was right.

No wonder Vandran is so angry. No wonder Selene's power bloomed so quickly, so wildly out of control.

They aren't just an old family; they are *the* old family. The first werewolves. The priestess-queens from the ancient days before the Quiet who led all of wolfkind. Queens who could command Alphas and were immune to being commanded. Who could shape raw magic in defense of their packs and the people they loved.

"Impossible," Whitlock says. "Their line was never recovered after the Waking. They died off."

He stares at Vandran, but the warlord only says, "Her entry is in the book."

"Oh, no, they didn't die off." My mother strides over to the small cabinet where I keep a few bottles of alcohol, yanks out a bottle of wine, and pours herself a jewel-dark glass. "They found them right in this area, actually. Just Aurora and her ancient grandma, living like peasants in the woods. Then that old bat died, and it was just her. His *precious* Aurora. That pasty little trollop."

She throws back the wine.

Vandran runs his tongue over his teeth and turns to Bianca. At first, I think he's going to order my mother's execution. But I forgot, he's known her for a long time and he can be incredibly cruel.

"Alpha Beaumont," he says, "I suggest commanding Killian to exile Claudia from Shattered Moon."

My mother drops the glass of wine. Red liquid sprays all over the floor. "No!"

Bianca bares her teeth, and I want to close my eyes. The instant my mother showed her how much being part of a pack meant, it was over for her.

"No! You can't do this! I'm his mother!"

Bianca bares her teeth. "He is no one, and so are you. Killian, exile your mother from Shattered Moon, and hurry up about it. We have a feast to host and the final touches to put on your *real* mating ceremony."

"No!" my mother cries again.

Bianca flashes her teeth. "Claudia, if you aren't off these lands by the time we close the first session of the Conclave tonight, I will send your son to hunt you down and kill you."

# *Forty-Five*

## SELENE

I wake to an angel's face, a devil's smile, and a pair of eyes as blue as a freshwater spring.

"Well," the man says as he sits back on his haunches. "Looks like you'll survive."

I'm lying on the hard ground in a cave. Not like the one Killian turned into a cozy little home—just raw, natural stone and the scent and sound of water. I sit partway up and scramble backward until my shoulder smacks the stone wall. "Who are you?"

"Whoa. All right." The man holds up both hands and pulls back. I know he's a werewolf, but I don't recognize him. "It's fine. I am no longer planning to kill you."

"*Excuse* me?"

He grins as if it never occurred to him that he's anything other than charming, which isn't surprising given his looks. Tousled brown hair, deeply bronzed skin, bone structure like artwork, and those goddamn blue eyes.

Then, despite the smug expression on his face, I suddenly know where I've heard his voice. Seen those eyes. As soon as I realize it, I also recognize his long, straight nose, the shape of his brow, and those eyes.

He looks like Eva. Those irises are the same blue as hers and the same as the brown wolf with metallic claws I saw in the forest in what feels like another life. The same as the eyes in the darkness that told me Killian murdered my brother in a jealous rage.

"You're Asher Quinn."

The cave isn't deep—no longer or wider than a medium-sized room, barely an indent in the side of some bluff. We're in a dip between some hills, and there's half a fallen tree blocking the opening, but from the red light spilling inside, I can tell the forested hills outside are rapidly growing dark.

I have no idea where I am.

"I am." Asher sits back and draws up his knees, bracing his forearms against them and clasping his hands. The smile flashes from wicked to cruel. "And you're Grace's ... replacement. Or you were. I suppose that dubious honor belongs to your sister now."

I press a hand to my forehead, my stomach. I feel like my thoughts are slogging through mud. "You know a lot of things for a man who's been lurking in the woods for the last six weeks."

"I hear things, *Selene*." He says my name like he's tasting it.

"So, what? I'm no longer on your hit list?"

"No. I think you've suffered enough." He nods at my shirt.

There's a gaping, bloody hole in my sweater. I gasp and press my hand there, and everything comes rushing back. I try to stand but fall before I can even push myself to my knees, so dizzy the cave tilts and spins.

Killian would've moved to help. Even before he knew me, he would've grabbed me to stop me from falling on my ass or smacking my head.

Asher just watches, unmoved, as I hit the ground. "That was stupid."

I press the heel of my hand hard into my forehead, willing the world to be still. "Have you changed much in the last five years, or does Killian have terrible taste in friends?"

Asher's grin settles back into something less cruel. "Terrible taste."

There's a massive bruised spot right below my collarbone. Images flash across my mind in a nightmare slide show.

Vandran's betrayal.

Bianca showing up with the Redcedar Hollow wolves.

The utterly blank look on Killian's face when he rejected me.

Finn screaming.

Bianca and her silver knife.

The blade driving, biting, penetrating into my chest.

I make an involuntary little sound at the memory and move my shirt to look beneath. I have a new scar—an angry red line just to the right of the crescent moon mark.

Asher clicks his tongue at whatever he sees on my face and says, "I go away for a while for my own personal reasons, then come back to discover I missed the fun and all that's left at the scene of the chaos is you with this in your chest."

He draws Bianca's silver knife from a sheath on his belt, flips it, catches it by the tip of the blade, and waves it at me, holding the bare silver in his hand without a flinch. "You had a mountain lion circling your not-quite corpse. Naturally, I was curious about how you passed. I drove the cat away and got right up close to you, and you weren't fucking dead. That surprises the shit out of both of us, I assume."

I touch the healed wound. "It does. How am I alive?"

He shrugs. "Fuck if I know. You're extra special? Whoever stabbed you missed?"

He flips the blade, catches it by the hilt, then whips it forward.

I cringe, pulling up my knees and throwing my arms in front of me, waiting for the bite of the blade, terror bursting through me.

The knife never hits. When I peek between my arms, Asher smiles a cold little smile, flips the knife one more time, then slides it back into its sheath in a single smooth motion.

"If it'd been me," he says quietly, "I wouldn't have missed."

Cold rage wraps around me like armor. I brace myself on the wall and rise to my feet. "That was an asshole thing to do."

He shrugs, and suddenly, I hate him. I am so sick to death of callous cruelty. Of bullies. I have been sick of bullies for such a long damn time.

I don't know whether my magic is back. Even if it is, Asher's reputation says he can kill me before I can blink.

I don't care anymore. Fuck Asher Quinn. Fuck everyone who's strong but who uses that strength to frighten instead of protect. I don't care how much he's suffered or what made him turn off his empathy. The apathy of the weak toward each other is the greatest tool of the powerful.

Devils never have to lift a finger when the damned are dead set on dragging each other into hell.

Calm and cold, I say, "Your mother would be ashamed of the man you've become."

The grin falls from Asher's face. Something terribly sad flashes in his eyes but only for an instant before that emotion is replaced by a smirking mask. He rises too, looming over me.

The rogue has a lean build—broad shoulders, if not as broad as Killian's, and Asher could be an inch or two taller. But the biggest difference is how they move. Where Killian has a predator's grace, Asher flows like liquid.

"You don't know a fucking thing about my mother." His voice is quiet. Deadly.

I lift my chin. "I know she'd be ashamed of a son who gets off on frightening people."

He grimaces, then turns on his heel and stalks toward the cave opening. He's wearing weathered brown pants, a gray T-shirt, a red leather jacket, and fingerless motorcycle gloves. A belt in the same brown leather as the gloves holds two daggers and a sword sheathed at his hips.

Usually, pack wolves wear dark, fitted combat clothing with accents in pack colors. Asher's outfit screams "fuck your uniforms; I'm an edgy badass rogue," and I could not roll my eyes any harder.

"Where are you going?"

He glances at me over one shoulder like I'm an idiot. "I have a promise to keep."

To murder Killian. That's what he means. I push off the cave wall and wobble after him. "He made his life hell to keep his promise not to take a mate! All he ever wanted to do was protect the people he loves!"

Asher turns on me with a snarl. "Like your brother? Like my sister?"

I grit my teeth. "Killian didn't murder my brother. The curse seeped through his mate bond to Grace. She turned. She killed Jackson. Killian ended her life before she could get to the rest of the pack. Neither of them is responsible for what happened that night."

Asher stares at me, eyes wide. The muscles in his jaw work. I expect him to deny it. Instead, he turns away from me. "Listen. Right now, we're in Steel Alliance territory. Half a mile from here, the forest ends. Walk north until you find a road or a house. You won't be a servant. You won't be an Alpha's mate. You can just ... live a life. Forget about Shattered Moon."

I stare after him, wide-eyed, as he walks out of the cave.

For a heartbeat, I just stand there.

I'm in Steel Alliance territory?

Dozens of packs united under an Alpha Prime they all voted for.

Wolves, other aspected, and mundane humans mingle freely. The peace the Alliance maintains, plus mile upon mile of fertile land, makes it one of the most populated places left on the continent since the Waking.

I can head for the heart of the territory, maybe go to a city. I've never seen a real city, but I've read about them, seen them in pre-Waking movies. I can lose myself in a place with so many people. Forget my powers ever existed. That I ever held responsibility for anyone or anything. I can also forget that I've ever been no one—wolfless and hated.

All it will cost me is Killian and Finn. All it will cost is Shattered Moon.

"No!" I stagger to the cave mouth and fall against one side, ready to launch myself after Asher despite my unsteady legs.

But Asher has stopped dead in his tracks. He's got his back to me, his arms folded across his chest.

"Shit," he mutters.

A woman stands beyond him. Her sleek, dark bob is wild and tangled with twigs and leaves, her black designer evening dress ripped, the hem ragged. Crimson lipstick is smeared across her face. Her eyes are red as if she's been weeping.

When she sees us, Claudia lifts her chin and pops her hands on her hips and sniffs. "Well. Asher Quinn. Is the little Stillwater whore fucking you too?"

Oh, my god.

Asher scoffs. "She's too frigid for me. I like my women with a little more heat. Now, if you're interested, Ms. Claudia—"

"Claudia," I grate out. "What the *hell* are you doing here?"

If possible, the older woman sticks her chin further in the air. She's as shrill as ever, but her voice trembles. "They found your little book, Selenite. They know about Killian not being a Bane and that you are. Or were, as far as they're concerned. That bitch Bianca made Killian exile me."

Oh, wow. "Exiled?"

"Yes!" Claudia shrieks.

It's the hardest thing I've ever done in my life to swallow the hysterical laugh that bubbles up inside me. This is vengeance, and it should feel good.

But looking at her now, how bedraggled she is, how close to breaking, it only feels hollow. "How are you *here*, Claudia? How did you find us?"

"Were you followed?" Asher asks.

She sniffles. "They threw me out of the pack house. I went to my son's little shelter and found your body wasn't there, Selenite. I thought a witch came and stole your bones, but then I recognized this hooligan's scent. I suppose even if I wasn't followed, they'll come looking for whatever the scavengers left soon enough."

I lock eyes with Asher. "How deep in Alliance territory are we?"

"Not so deep that anyone will know if your sister's people track you down and drag you back until it's too late." He shrugs. "If I were you, I'd get moving."

I return my attention to Claudia, bemused. "Why did you come to find me?"

She huffs and wipes beneath both eyes with delicate fingers. "Well. Since you're alive, I thought I would see if you want to help me kill Bianca and free my son. Quinn, I suppose you can help too."

Asher makes a face. "Bianca? If you want her dead, I suppose I can add her to the list."

"You are not going to murder Killian!" I snap.

Asher stalks right up to me. I expect another outburst, but he's completely cold when he says, "I knelt in a puddle of Grace's blood and a pile of her gore and swore that I would kill the man who murdered her."

"So keep your oath," I retort, "and kill Eli Whitlock and Marcus Vandran."

Asher frowns. "Explain."

"So you know Bianca took my place but you don't know this?"

"*Explain*," Asher snarls.

"Hooligan," Claudia mutters.

I lift a brow and wait one heartbeat, then another, until his eyes flick away from mine with a hint of shame. Then I gesture to the silver knife sheathed on his belt. "Killian didn't murder Grace any more than that knife stabbed me. Any more than she was responsible for killing Jackson. You know so much about what has happened. You *know* he's cursed."

The muscles in Asher's jaw flex. "I have recently been made aware of what my mother and brother believe. The excuses Killian has made to try and convince everyone he isn't like his father."

I gesture to Claudia. "Who is Killian's father, Claudia?"

Asher looks at me like I'm insane. "Everyone knows—"

Claudia sighs loudly. "Jack Owens."

Asher frowns. "No."

"Yes," Claudia snaps. "Bane is *her* father. The child of him and his favorite little"—she looks at me and seems to remember she wants my help to get rid of Bianca—"*friend*, Aurora Stillwater."

I jump in. "Killian is cursed. Eldritch magic was laid on him at Vandran's command by his arcanist, Eli Whitlock, the Warden of Rowan Ridge. They doubled down, and now Killian's being mind-controlled with some stone Bianca wears on a necklace."

Asher moves so fast, I don't see it. He grabs my arms and squeezes. "You're lying."

I grit my teeth. Warmth tingles in my chest. Light swirls beneath my skin. "Let. Me. Go."

Asher lets out a startled curse and pulls his hands from me like he's been burned. He takes several steps back, then blinks and barks a laugh. "Stillwater?"

Claudia hisses, "Stillwater."

Asher turns to her. "The silverlights are dead. They went extinct in the Quiet."

"Not dead enough," Claudia mutters. She waves a hand at me.

I give her a withering look.

"What?" she demands.

Asher says, "I thought your name was Selene Beaumont."

In the spirit of this three-way hostile conversation, I tilt my head, smile, and delicately hold a hand out to him as if he might shake it or kneel and kiss it. "Oh, no. My name is Selenite Bane. I am the last Stillwater, the eldest surviving child of Alaric Bane, and if you help me get my fated mate back, I will help you kill the men actually responsible for your sister's death. Will you come with us?"

Asher's grin is pure wolf as he takes my hand, brings it to his mouth, and brushes his lips across my knuckles. "My long-lost queen. For you? Anything."

# Forty-Six

## KILLIAN

For maybe the first time since the Conclave began in the years after the Wars of Power, it passes mostly without incident. The days are taken up with meetings, the nights with feasts and balls. I'm surrounded by allies. Friends. But Bianca's control over me is complete. A single command to act like nothing is wrong, to tell no one, not to speak to Zev, Eva, or Sofia has imprisoned me more than any cage ever could.

Tonight, the last night, during the Prism Masque, Bianca will force me to mark her, and she'll mark me. She controls the magic of the curse, so it can't hurt her the way it did Grace. Between my power and the combined packs, who knows what she'll become.

For two days, I've saved my energy. I was able to resist in small ways before. I need to resist one more time.

The final meetings of the Conclave end. Attendees retreat to their rooms. There are only hours until they begin making their way, by car, carriage, or horseback, to the waterfall-lined canyon where the Prism Masque will take place. I wait until Bianca is distracted as she begins to get ready for the Masque, then fight off her influence just enough to walk and talk on my own.

Bianca has allowed Zev to stay close during the Conclave because she has her own pack stretched so thin. The instant she leaves me alone, I open the door to the hall, where Zev stands guard on the apartment with a wolf from Redcedar Hollow. "Zev, the Alpha Lady would like to speak with you."

He gives me a pitying look and then comes inside. I push against the fog walls in my mind with all my might. I'm shaking, nauseated with the effort this single small rebellion is taking. As soon as the door closes, I stagger and have to grab the massive man for support.

"Alpha?" he asks.

Sweat beads on my brow. "Asher," I whisper. "He's still here. Find him, Zev. Tonight, if he comes to the Masque—if he comes for me—let him the fuck in."

Zev growls. "Not a chance."

"Do it," I snarl. I drop my voice to a low whisper. "If I die, the pack goes to him. Bianca and Vandran can't control him. He's the only one who can kill me, and it's the only way to save Shattered Moon. If he can't—or if he left ... the next best choice is you or Maddox. Together, you could ... but if it comes to that, don't let Maddox strike the killing blow."

Zev jerks back, his face contorted, conflicted.

"It's my final order, Zev." I can already feel the curse tightening, closing me off from my own body. "He's out there. Find his trail and follow it. Go now, before Bianca finishes her bath."

The older man's upset expression fades into one of sadness. "Maddox says Asher wants to kill you."

"Selene is gone," I whisper. "Let me follow her. Let me set all of you free."

He blinks rapidly, then nods. "Yes, Alpha."

I squeeze his shoulder, and my bodyguard leaves. I hear him through the door, telling the other guards that Bianca has dismissed him from my personal guard. It's a good lie. Believable.

Then he's gone, and I'm alone with nothing but my thoughts.

If I could, I'd exhale in relief.

It will all be over soon.

# SELENE

The first thing we do is abandon the cave. If Claudia could track us there, anyone could.

I wasn't sure where to go, but Asher spent two years as the Beta of Shattered Moon, and he still knows the land well. After we cross several streams and do everything we can to cover our trail, we shift. Asher leads us back into Shattered Moon territory, down to a cove where yet another cave is carved into a bluff right at the lake's muddy shore.

There isn't much there beyond a beat-up sleeping bag and some food, but we have to wade through the lake to get there, which hides our scent and makes it the perfect hiding place.

At first, we try to think of a way to sneak into the pack house. Once again, Finn needs to be rescued, and I'm afraid Eva does too. I'm sick thinking about them both, but Asher bluntly tells me to fuck off. It's too heavily guarded. We can't even figure out a way to contact anyone inside, especially with security heightened while the Conclave is taking place.

There's only one chance to stop Bianca, and I hate it.

"The Prism Masque tonight," I say. "It's at the amphitheater, which is more open and harder to guard than the castle. Plus, it's a masquerade. If we find clothes, we could get in."

As soon as I say it, I realize how terrible of a plan it is. "*If* we can find clothes. And if we fail, there won't be a second chance."

"Cute of you to think there would be a second chance no matter how we do this," Asher says.

I rub my temples. "This is so stupid. There's no way we'll get past the guards there either."

Asher shrugs noncommittally. "Once you're in, then what?"

I roll my eyes because I don't have the energy to go back and forth with him. "We need the necklace if we're going to prove that Vandran and Whitlock are involved too. If I let someone loyal to Bianca spot me and I say just the right things, they'll relay it to her through the pack tie, and I think she'll come after me herself. I was able to trick her into delaying marking Killian. I can do this too. We lure her into the dark, and you grab her, Asher. Then we take the necklace."

"And kill her," Claudia snarls. "If you don't want to do it, Selene, I will."

My mind flashes back to Noelle dying in the forest. My gorge rises, and I swallow it down. "No. She's evidence. We have to turn her, Vandran, and Whitlock over to the justice of the Conclave."

Not long after, Asher leaves to scout the area, which means I spend a few silent hours worrying while Claudia ignores me. When Asher returns, he's not alone. A massive pale gray wolf trots through the water alongside him. He's so huge, even the stuffed-full giant bag strapped to his back looks comically small.

When the wolf reaches the cave, he shifts into a hulking blond man with a buzz cut.

"Zev!"

He tosses down the bag and quickly pulls on pants, then opens his arms. I throw myself into them.

"Lady Selene! I can't believe you're alive! This changes everything."

I grab his shoulders and lean back to look into his face. "How is Killian?"

Zev's face falls. "Not well. The Alpha heard Asher was nearby. He was able to fight the curse back just long enough to speak to me. He wanted ..."

Zev and Asher exchange a glance I can't read, and Asher gives a small shake of his head.

"He wanted what?" I demand.

"He wanted me to find Beta Quinn to help save the pack," Zev says

"I'm not your Beta, Zev," Asher mutters.

Zev ignores him and gestures at the bag. "Supplies from Sofia. I was here to get the Beta into the Masque. Now I can do that for all of you. One more trip, and you'll have everything you need."

My heart races. "You can get us in?"

Zev grins. "Of course, I can. Sofia already had your dress and your mask. They're ready to go."

"Oh," I breathe. "Zev, that is perfect. Will you tell Killian I'm alive?"

His face falls. "Bianca doesn't let any of us near him."

Heaviness settles on my chest. I can't imagine what Killian is going through.

Claudia snaps her fingers at us. "Bring my dress when you return, too, Zev. And some wine. Mommy needs a beverage to calm her nerves."

# *Forty-Seven*

## SELENE

After Zev gets us the rest of the supplies, Asher breaks into an old house in the woods. It looks like it's been abandoned since the Wars of Power, but it's our best option to get ready for the Masque, despite the rotted bits of floor and the spiders.

We get dressed. Sofia's supplies include everything—toiletries, clothes, makeup, and more.

I expect to have to make do by myself with no water or power, but Asher wordlessly hauls a bucket of water from a nearby stream into the house, and to my shock, Claudia offers to help with my hair and makeup.

We go into a dusty old bedroom on the top floor that has decent light and a full-length mirror. She does my makeup with practiced care, steps back, and sniffs. "I was wasted on a son. Not that your face matters. We'll be wearing those awful masks."

I look in the mirror and am astonished. She didn't paint me like a clown like I half expected. My brows have been darkened slightly, my lips deepened to rose. There's color on my cheeks and life in my eyes. Honestly, she's done a better job than even Sofia's team would have.

I'm surprised, also, by her steady hand and the lack of wine on her breath, even though there was wine in the second round of supplies.

"Thank you," I say.

Claudia harrumphs. "It won't happen again. Just be grateful I hate your sister more than you."

"Can we leave?" Asher snaps from the bottom of the stairs.

We go out of the bedroom and to the top of the stairs. I raise a brow at the sight of Asher. He's wearing a suit with no tie, the dark blue shirt beneath not quite buttoned all the way to the top. His chestnut hair is tousled but more intentionally than usual. When he sees me staring, he flashes that wicked grin, and I roll my eyes.

Even I have to admit the rogue cleans up very, very well. I frown at the sword buckled on his hip. "Won't they find that suspicious?"

He winks and rests a hand on the hilt. "I have my ways."

I pull on the heavy velvet cloak Sofia provided and pull the draping hood over my hair. Claudia wears a cloak too, and Asher a coat long enough to mostly hide the sword.

From the house, we trek a mile and a half through the woods down old roads. The air is crisp, and the clouds that dripped steady rain down on us earlier today have cleared, leaving only the crystal night. We go three-quarters of the way before we stop to put on the blank ovular white masks everyone will be wearing.

Asher meets my eyes, his mask perched high on his head, paused halfway through putting it on. "Are you sure he's worth it? If this goes wrong, we die."

"Yes." My voice is calm. Inside, I am screaming, shaking, terrified.

Asher gives me a look I can't read. "If we live, I'll tell him he's lucky to have you."

"How benevolent." I pull his mask over his face and adjust my own. Despite his flippant delivery, I hear what he doesn't say—he won't try to assassinate Killian. "Thank you."

We don't speak again.

We reach the main road that runs through both Redcedar Hollow and Shattered Moon and join the throng of people making their way to the masque. The members of the Conclave have vehicles or horses, but plenty of people are walking. When we're within view of the canyon and the outermost guards, Asher ducks into the forest for a moment. When he comes back, the sword is missing.

"What—?"

"Shh." He winks again.

I roll my eyes, and we carry on. Soon enough, we're there.

The neutral zone between Shattered Moon and Redcedar Hollow is actually a wide, shallow canyon where streams have carved deep into the limestone and turned the land into latticework. Bridges cross steep ravines over fast-flowing torrents, and waterfalls flow into pools and down naturally tiered steps at intervals.

We enter the canyon, moving down as we go deeper, and pass through several layers of security. According to Asher, Zev has smoothed the way for us. At each layer, Asher silently leads us to one specific checkpoint or another, each one manned only by Shattered Moon wolves. They aren't wearing masks, and I recognize Wes Bennett and several other of Killian's personal guards.

Without Zev setting up a way for us, we would never have gotten through.

The canyon ends in a wide, shallow U-shaped wall split by the yawning mouth of a cave. Waterfalls frame the entrance, which leads to a massive cavern three times as large as the great hall in the pack house. From the depths of that cavern, a dark river emerges, cutting close to one wall before it splashes down into the labyrinth of waterways on the canyon floor.

During the Quiet, this was a park. The bridges were built back then, as was the path along the canyon wall we used to get here. There also used to be a sprawling stone lodge at the crest of the southern hills. The building lies in ruins now, a fallen remnant of the disappeared, non-magical age.

The cavern we move toward now used to be a restaurant. Its natural floor was leveled and extended into a cement patio that's just as large as the space within. The level area, both inside and out, is bordered with metal railings along where the river flows and then along the sheer edge outside where the falls drop. The result is a huge indoor-outdoor event space that still has its original, refurbished old sound system.

It's not something I've experienced before—music with no visible source. But somewhere, hidden, staticky speakers are amplifying a woman's mournful voice as she sings about lost love over the sighing of a fiddle and twanging of a banjo.

Strings of hanging electric lights make golden lines along the edge of the patio, arc along the cavern mouth, and disappear inside, casting just enough of a glow to illuminate the shadowy crowd.

I fidget as we wait in line to cross the final bridge, where Zev and Maddox are standing guard at the far end. I've served at many events like

358

this but never the Conclave and nothing approaching the decadence of the Prism Masque.

I was afraid Sofia went overboard with my dress, but from the gemstone-rich flashes of fabric I can see in the swirling, spinning mass inside the cavern—ruby silk, sapphire satin, glittering golden brocade— I'll blend right in.

As guards instead of attendees, Maddox and Zev aren't wearing the blank ovular white masks that are covering the faces of everyone else in attendance yet. Theirs hang at their sides, waiting for the toast that will release a wave of magic and truly begin the night.

My arm is through Asher's, and he stiffens beside me as he catches sight of his brother.

"He's grown up," he whispers. "He's got a spell we can speak through, but I haven't seen him."

"I imagine he has grown. More than you know." I touch my oval mask with my fingertips to ensure it's in place. My heartbeat quickens. The couple in front of us lift their masks to show their faces. Zev and Maddox wave them on, looking bored.

Then it's our turn. Heart hammering, I face Zev and pull my mask up just enough, careful not to knock the draping hood of my velvet cloak aside. Even in this crowd, my pale hair is a dead giveaway.

Beside me, Asher does the same, revealing his face to his brother. I hear Maddox's sharp intake of breath and feel the air ripple with a rise in his power, but it's quickly tamped down. Zev would have warned him that we were coming. Maddox and Asher exchange brief, intense words I can't hear and then clasp each other's wrists so tight, their knuckles turn white.

"Hurry up," Claudia hisses. "I want to get this over with."

I settle my mask in place and go to move past Zev, but his hand darts out and he leans close to my ear. "There's been a development. The wolfless of Redcedar Hollow are here. So is Finn ... so is Eva."

He meets my gaze, eyes pleading for me to be careful. My stomach feels like it's fallen to somewhere in the vicinity of my toes. Surprises are popping up and we haven't even gotten inside yet.

I have to keep moving, but I nod to Zev. "If this plan goes how it should, they'll be okay."

I wish I were as confident as I sounded.

"Good luck, Lady," he murmurs. "Move fast. The marking will take place immediately after the Prism toast."

I nod again. Asher takes my arm. After a brief pause for Claudia, we finally enter the Conclave's infamous Prism Masque.

Out on the patio, the crowd is thin. Music from the live performers inside pipes through hidden pre-Waking speakers. We circle slowly, making subtle contact with our few allies. Parker is standing guard on one side of the cavern entrance. Inside, where bodies are pressing together, heating the space, Sofia is overseeing the staff. Even with her mask, her quick, efficient movements give her away.

"On the table," she whispers to a woman older than Eva with white hair and papery skin. "Please bring a lighter load next time."

My heart catches as I recognize Greta carrying the heavy tray of food. The wolfless Redcedar Hollow woman dips her head, and I can hardly hear her thin voice over the ambient noise. "Yes, Gamma."

Asher tightens his grip on me before I can rush over. I see them everywhere now. In the crowd, weaving their way through the richly dressed pack and Conclave members, wolfless in simple black tunics and pants. Jenny, Sam, Natalia, Gabriel, and a dozen more. The wolfless are the only ones in the cavern without masks.

"If she thinks I'm dead, why are they here?" I whisper.

Asher snorts in derision. "Because even if Killian thinks you're dead, he's the kind of idiot who will martyr himself to protect anyone you ever loved."

My heart aches. I search the cavern for Killian but don't see him anywhere.

Sofia's eyes catch on us. At first, they narrow, then widen. She makes her way over as if she's still inspecting things, unhurried.

I turn to the long table along the back of the cavern as she approaches and pretend to peruse a tray of hors d'oeuvres. She leans close, as if examining the number of deviled eggs on a tray. Her hand darts out to catch mine, our mutual grip on each other hidden by my full skirt.

"I'm so glad to see you," she whispers. "You look beautiful."

"Thanks to you."

"Killian and Bianca are seated over there by the rest of the senior members of the Conclave." She nods to a roped-off area where important-looking people are sitting in groups at round tables, but I still can't find him.

"I tried to get Bianca to schedule the marking for later in the night," Sofia continues, "but she wouldn't. They're about to—"

The music ends. Redcedar Hollow wolfless stream from the kitchen carrying full trays of jeweled golden goblets. Goblets also line the tables set up along the back of the cavern. Claudia already has one in her hand, and she frowns down into the wine inside.

"Shit," Sofia whispers She grabs goblets and hands one to me, then to Asher.

My heart pounds. If this is for the toast, the mating ceremony will be right after. We're already low on time.

"Beta," she says low. "What kind of trouble are you here to cause?"

I can't see Asher's expression, but I can hear the wicked grin in his voice. "As much as I possibly can."

Behind her mask, Sofia rolls her eyes.

Asher turns serious then. His gaze darts over the wolfless servants handing out wine. "If the toast is happening, our plans have changed. Where's my mother?"

"Asher," I whisper urgently, "we need to—"

I'm cut off by a ringing chime. Dancers clear the center of the room. In the roped-off area, several people rise and make their way toward the now-clear dance floor.

I study them in awe, knowing that behind the masks are some of the most powerful people in the world. Every major aspect is represented: human warlords, Alpha werewolves, vampire lords, seraph archivists, coven high witches, archmages of the elements, nature-touched chieftains, even—if the rumors from over a month ago are true—a siren clan leader.

In the middle of them all, holding their own jeweled goblets, are Killian and Bianca.

I recognize both, even with the masks. Bianca's strapless deep blue-green dress is clinging to her curves and accentuating her golden skin, draping into a trailing skirt that's alive with shimmering beadwork.

She grins and waves at several people, but it's Killian who draws my eyes. Killian who steals my breath. Killian whose presence, even though we have both rejected the mate bond between us, tugs on my soul like a lodestone.

He's wearing a black suit, the jacket open over an embroidered black vest, the breadth of his shoulders straining the fabric. Beneath, his black button-up shirt is undone at the collar. His dark hair is tumbling back from the white mask. For an instant, I catch a flash of topaz from the depths of the mask's eyeholes. Even from here, even in that short time, I can tell they're blank.

I rein in the desire to run to him. All I want is to burrow into his arms, lean my head against his chest, and hear the steady beat of his heart. Just one more time, if that's all I can have. One more embrace.

Smoothly, he lifts the goblet in his hand. His voice sounds stiff and practiced. "My friends, tonight we celebrate another successful Conclave. Raise your glass to the Waking, and each aspect of humanity it restored like light shining through a prism. To peace, prosperity, and a unified Conclave."

Around us, as if these words are rote, everyone lifts their goblets and repeats, "To the Waking."

Killian drinks, then so does everyone else. I hesitate, but a hiss from Claudia has me following suit.

The wine flows smooth and slightly sweet over my tongue. As I watch, Killian's white mask shimmers, distorts, and then transforms into an impossibly intricate metal mask of a snarling wolf's head. Bianca's does the same, though her wolf is white.

A wave of minor magic washes over the room in a slow ripple. The rest of the central group's masks shimmer and change, and then the crowd's.

Wolves' masks become a copy of Killian's and Bianca's in a variety of metallic shades. Vampires' curl back to become half masks that look carved from a solid piece of bloodred ruby. Witch masks turn into trailing clouds of shimmering amethyst mist that swirl around their eyes and trail into their hair. The masks of the nature-touched reveal the bottom halves of their faces, the tops as varied as they are. Sylph masks become spread moth, dragonfly, bird, or bat wings. Oread masks take the shape of jagged mountains. Naiad masks shine with round river stones. Elemental mages suddenly seem to be wearing living flame, flowing water, glittering gems and gold, or roiling white cloud. Seraph masks take on the radiance of small suns, glow of the moon, or the mysterious shifting lights of the aurora borealis.

One figure in the center, slender and feminine with brunette hair that streams to her lower back. At her throat, she wears a starburst sapphire on a choker of silver ribbon. A mask of coral, pearl, and bone covers her face.

The siren.

My breath catches. They're so rare after decades of conflict among themselves, I never expected to see one in my life.

But there's no opening in the mask for her mouth. The space is blank, closed.

The effect is unsettling.

The masks of the mundane humans catch my eye then. I assumed they would remain blank or just disappear. Instead, they become eye masks carved of crystal, glittering in prismatic rainbows.

The symbolism is apt, considering the metaphorical theme of the ball.

Bianca raises her goblet. Beneath the face of the wolf, her smile is sharp. "To the leaders of the Conclave, those with power earned, granted, or inherited. To those who guide the way into the future."

She turns toward Killian. Her voice is smug. "To Killian and me, who, with this marking, join our packs and become Alpha Lord and Alpha Lady of Redcedar Hollow and Shattered Moon."

Shock turns my veins into ice.

"She's doing it now," I whisper frantically to Asher. "I thought they'd set up for a completely different ceremony. She's doing it *now*."

"To the leaders of the Conclave," the crowd intones.

Everyone drinks. Bianca smiles up at Killian and tilts her head to one side, exposing her neck.

The masks of those in the center shift again, their edges limning with a glowing rainbow of colors. Not just their masks but also their entire bodies, the prismatic light filling the room. I have eyes only for Killian, who begins to burn gold. He is so beautiful.

I've heard of this. The luminescence is a party trick, like fireworks. Part of the entertainment and a way to make faction leaders look even more mysterious and powerful. It's a witch spell, just like the masks are a witch spell. I have no idea how it works.

Killian bends toward Bianca, lips curled back. Beneath the mask, his canines are long.

No. No. No.

There's no time to think. I wrench my arm from Asher's and shove through the crowd.

I'm too far. There are so many people here.

I could blast them out of my way or compel them to move, but if I use my power wrong and hurt someone, I will start a war. Several wars. And I don't know where Finn or Eva is.

"Oh, *fuck*," Asher hisses behind me. "Selene, you're—"

Killian's lips hover above Bianca's shoulder.

"NO!" I scream, reaching out to them, the hood of my cloak falling back with the violence of the movement.

No magic. No power. Just my voice. But it startles Bianca and leaves the cavern in ringing silence.

Everyone's eyes turn to me.

That's when I notice that, unlike the other leaders, Bianca isn't glowing at all. She's a spot of dull mundanity among them.

My outstretched hand, however, is shining as brightly silver as the moon.

# Forty-Eight

## KILLIAN

"**N**O!"

That voice.

Silver light streams through the yellow fog where I'm confined. The mist hardens, fractures. I can't see, can hardly think. But my nose is filled with the wrong scent. The warm skin beneath my hand isn't hers. The body pressed against mine isn't *hers*.

With everything I have, I wrench free from the mist. For an instant, feeling rushes back into my brain like prickles from a sleeping limb.

Bianca is standing in front of me, her neck craned to see who shouted. I can't see either, my vision hemmed in by something on my face.

The Masque. It's the last day of the Conclave. I'm about to mark Bianca.

I shove her away and take several steps back, then rip off my mask.

Bianca flails but keeps on her feet. She snarls and yanks up her wolf mask. Angry apple-green eyes glare at me. "What are you doing?"

Beyond her, a light is shining through the mass of people. A light that's moving toward me like a beacon.

The crowd parts for a woman in a silver wolf mask. Her chin-length pale hair is half-pulled back, braided and glittering with jewels. She's wearing a heavy pewter-gray velvet cloak, which opens to show a Vshaped bodice that hugs her lovingly, the neckline dipping low between her breasts, the area covered by sheer fabric that hints at more than it hides. The shape emphasizes the curve of her waist where it meets the full, layered skirts that ripple around her. She's wearing a simple necklace of moonstone with a single white gold crescent moon.

My lungs seize. "Selene?"

She's alive. My mate is alive.

Bianca grasps the large black jewel at her throat and hisses, "No. You are *mine*."

An inexorable wave, the yellow fog rises and takes me again.

I bare my teeth. "No!"

This time, I fight.

≈

## SELENE

"Guards!" Bianca cries. "Take her!"

"Why? Who is this?" demands a man as large as Zev in a wolf mask of silvery steel. He pushes it up, revealing deep brown skin, a neat gray beard, and bright copper eyes. He's wearing a high-collared black and blue-gray jacket with gold buttons. More gold touches his shoulders and throat. He looks curiously from Bianca to me. "Why has the light spell chosen her?"

"I'm not sure," says a woman beside him—a witch who's glowing in shades of lavender and violet.

I don't stop moving forward. I just have to reach Bianca. I don't know whether I'm strong enough to break the stone, but if I can snatch the necklace, maybe it will be enough.

The woman next to the steel-masked wolf pushes up her own mask, which is white with golden swirls along the nose and ears. "Alpha Beaumont, who is this woman?"

She also has dark skin and a powerful build. Her onyx eyes are lined with metallic gold, her short hair done in twists decorated with jewels and gold and steel bands. Like her mask, her dress is gold and white. She speaks as if she expects to be answered.

With a start, I realize who these wolves are. Locke and Morgana Winters. The Alphas Prime of the Steel Alliance.

They peruse me curiously, examining the silver glow around my body. I glance down, twisting my hands and arms. It's not like the swirling stars of my magic. I'm limned, like the rest of the Conclave leaders.

The crowd whispers.

I'm caught completely off guard, but I have been given this moment, and I will use it to my advantage.

"I am Killian's mate." I remove my mask, then undo my cloak and let it fall to the ground, exposing more skin, letting the silver glow shine bright. "Killian and I were bonded in a mating ceremony weeks ago. The Beaumonts claimed they sent me as a proxy, but that was a lie. They meant to send the wrong daughter. They meant for him to kill me so that Redcedar Hollow would have an excuse to attack Shattered Moon within the terms of the treaty."

Erebos, the male witch who came with the Beaumonts that day, steps out from the crowd of leaders and speaks up. "She is not a Beaumont. I tested her blood. So did the esteemed First Arcanist."

"They told me I was theirs," I argue. "It's not Killian's fault or mine that they lied."

As I speak, I scan the room for Finn and Eva. I finally find them pressed together against a far wall surrounded by a cluster of guards. Eva is clutching Finn's shoulders. He looks like he's trying to break free and run to me. His eyes meet mine, and I mouth, *Stay.*

He stops struggling.

"No farther," shouts Bianca.

My path is blocked by Deacon Jones. Suddenly, Asher appears at my side, blue eyes flashing in the depths of his bronze wolf mask. "I think the Conclave should hear what the lady has to say."

I bare my teeth at Jones. "Move, traitor."

"Traitor?" Jones chuckles. "I've only ever wanted to strengthen my pack, Selene. It's a Beta's job."

Asher tilts his head and looks Jones up and down with new eyes. Too softly for most of those gathered to hear, he says, "Ah. So *you're* the new Beta." He sucks air through his teeth. "A little old."

"Young enough to kick your ass, pup," growls Jones.

With the mask on, I don't think he realizes who Asher is.

"Oh, yeah?" The words are dark, an invitation. Asher's chuckle makes ice slide down my spine. He holds out a hand to one side. There's a knotting, twisting sensation in reality, and then his sword pops out of nowhere, right into his hand.

In the crowd, people gasp. I hear whispers of "Asher Quinn" and "steelborn" and "last one left."

"Quinn," Vandran asks in a low, dangerous voice. "What are you doing here?"

Asher pushes up his mask. His eyes go to Whitlock. "Just needed a quick vacation after the last war crime."

"That woman is a liar and a traitor," Bianca shouts pulling my attention from whatever is passing between Asher and the warden, likely sensing she's losing the crowd. "My parents adopted her, raised her, and she tried to undermine their attempts at peace. She demanded to be sent to the Alpha of Shattered Moon so she could assassinate him! We found out about her plot and put a stop to it. I exiled her, but she won't give up!"

The lie is so outrageous, I laugh.

"Didn't you just murder your parents?" Claudia asks idly, walking up on my other side, still swirling wine around the goblet in her hand like she's bored. Even so, her words carry.

Bianca bares her teeth. "What is done by right of challenge within my own pack is of no concern to the Conclave. Wolves may challenge their Alphas. It is the law. And you were exiled, you sodden old bitch! Your life is forfeit for being here!"

"You aren't *my* Alpha, you little Redcedar despot!" Claudia snips back. Like an afterthought—or maybe because she realizes she's not likely to get to Bianca with it to throw it on her—Claudia tosses the wine aside, goblet and all. It clatters to the ground and rolls, spilling over the cave floor.

"Double parricide does seem more concerning," mutters the siren woman. Even speaking casually, her voice is the most beautiful I've ever heard.

All around us, the general crowd has drawn back. It seems larger than it's supposed to be. I suppose because we've been joined by the Masque attendees who were outside. Zev and Maddox appear and make their way toward us, confirming my suspicions. They stop a little ways away from where Asher, Claudia, and I are facing down the Conclave.

"Alpha Beaumont is right," Vandran booms, still shooting narrow-eyed glances at Asher. He stands on one side of the cluster of leaders, his prismatic mask shining. "The Conclave doesn't interfere with internal pack politics. But this woman tried to keep the bloodshed going between Redcedar Hollow and Shattered Moon."

"No, you—"

"Yes!" the warlord shouts, drowning me out. "Who will you listen to? Some unknown girl, or the ruler of the second-largest nation on this side of the continent?"

I grit my teeth. "Does the size of your nation exempt you from the law that says you can't use eldritch magic to control the sovereign leader of another nation or of a Conclave-allied werewolf pack? I notice your arcanist is missing one of his rings, and that stone now seems to be around my sister's throat. That stone is the anchor for a curse—"

I'm cut off when Deacon Jones wraps a meaty hand around my throat. Asher raises his sword, but Bianca shouts, "Back off, Quinn, or I'll kill your mother."

Finn shouts and Eva cries out as the guards drag both of them forward to stand at Bianca's side. Asher stills, his eyes going to Eva, hers locking on him. He takes a half step toward her.

"Asher, don't let them hurt Selene!" Eva shouts. Then she cries out in pain as one of the guards grabs her and pulls her back against his chest. His claws extend, and he presses one to her neck.

"Eva!" Zev bellows, and I hear Maddox snarl.

"Drop the sword," Bianca commands.

"Yes, Quinn," Vandran says, voice dangerous. "Drop the sword."

Asher's eyes dart between them. Like Claudia's wine goblet, his sword clatters to the ground.

"No!" Eva shouts.

Deacon's hand is still around my throat. He drags me forward until I'm right in front of Bianca. Just beyond arm's reach, another guard is holding onto Finn. Finn's lip is trembling, but he's standing straight. I want to tell him it's okay, but I can't breathe.

In the days since Killian was captured, my magic has recharged. I feel it there, the power in my chest. I practiced some with Asher but had to stop when his ears and nose started bleeding.

Now Jones has me too close to Finn and Eva. The wolfless I've loved as family my whole life are peppered in with the crowd, pressing too close. Jenny has come right to the front of it, not fifteen feet away. Her freckled round face is pinched with confusion and terror.

Bianca is so strong. If I lash out with enough power to affect her, I could kill them all.

"Stop this immediately, Alpha Beaumont," Alpha Lady Morgana Winters commands. "You've been accused of using eldritch magic against Killian Darrow. From the way the man is standing here like a puppet while you're threatening his family, I'm going to guess there's something to that." She looks at her husband. "I move that Alpha Bianca Beaumont, Warlord Marcus Vandran, and Warden Eli Whitlock be detained immediately."

"Let it be done," Locke Winters booms.

Immediately, wolves I don't know wearing combat uniforms in black and gray-blue—Steel Alliance colors—press forward from the main crowd.

Bianca sneers. "Well. I was going to wait until I was marked to do this, but I suppose my pack is strong enough as it is. Redcedar Hollow! Take the Conclave!"

A few moments ago, I thought the room looked too full. Now I see why. It's not just Masque attendees from outside.

Slowly, steadily, hundreds of Redcedar Hollow wolves have trickled into the room.

At Bianca's command, all hell breaks loose.

# Forty-Nine

## KILLIAN

Selene is alive. She's *alive*, and she's right in front of me. But I can't move.

I throw myself against the prison of my mind over and over. I beat myself bloody against the inside of my own head. My own battle mirrors the one that's raging all round us in the cavern, the Redcedar Hollow wolves versus the Steel Alliance and the forces the rest of the Conclave brought. But this was a diplomatic event, not a fight. Soon enough, Redcedar Hollow will overpower them all.

Two or three dozen Redcedar Hollow wolves have pushed into the center and surrounded us, cutting us off from help. Deacon has Selene. He drags her forward, and my whole world narrows to her.

As if from a distance, I hear Bianca. Her voice starts far away but gets closer as she demands my attention. She leans against me, her lips close to my ear, her breasts pressing into my arm. One hand is resting on my chest.

"I want you to watch this, Killian. Look into her eyes. I want you to be present for this. I want you to know that no matter what happens, you have no option but me."

I suck in a breath. It's unsteady. A tremor runs through my body. My fingers twitch at the sight of the Beta who betrayed me—no, who was never loyal to me—with his hands around Selene's slender neck.

Then Bianca straightens and says, "Bring her close, Deacon. Let's let them say goodbye."

The Beta smirks and thrusts Selene closer to me. Her face is red from how tightly he's squeezing her throat.

"You heard the Alpha," Deacon growls at Selene. "Say goodbye."

"Killian," Selene whispers, voice strangled.

And then, for the first time in days, I feel something.

The lightest touch of Selene's fingertips as she grazes the back of my hand.

The silver light of Selene's magic pushes at the fog, but Bianca is so strong, just a touch isn't enough anymore.

Selene's brow furrows. Then her eyes flutter closed, and her face tenses with focus.

"Deacon," Bianca drawls. "Break her neck."

No. No, please.

"As you command, Alpha," Jones says. He moves one hand to her chin, the other to the back of her head.

"Killian," Selene murmurs, "be free."

Silver light blazes like the sun, burning away the yellow mist.

I lunge.

~

## SELENE

Killian knocks me out of the way as he leaps on Deacon. There's only one guttural half shout from the Beta, which cuts off abruptly among all the other sounds of fighting.

Killian crouches over Jones. He's in his massive silvery-black hybrid form.

Beneath him, Deacon Jones's head is lying at an impossible angle. The Beta seems to be missing his face.

My stomach lurches.

"Selene—" Killian's voice is agonized. His topaz eyes find mine. His clawed hands are drenched in blood. I try to stand, to reach for him.

"No!" Bianca shrieks. It's hard to hear among all the other chaos, the shouting and screaming. There are the scents of spice and smoke, petrichor and ozone on the air, and magic bursts from the wolves and the other members of the Conclave.

Here, though, Bianca's guards form a circle around us in our little tableau at the center of the room, allowing it to play out while a battle rages all around.

I'm on my feet, reaching for Killian, when Bianca speaks again, her voice ringing with cold, dark power. "Killian, end her."

He shakes his head. He looks dazed. I can see him fighting her power. "Selene ..."

Bianca's eyes blaze. "If you won't do it, then the beast will. Let the curse take you."

Killian shudders, stumbles, chokes. Then he throws back his head and howls. His body stretches, warps, becomes the thing I first saw in the woods.

When he opens his eyes again, they're a pale sickly yellow.

Before I can react, the monster leaps for me.

He lands already swiping for my head with his claws, impossibly fast. I duck but feel a tug and see silver strands fall. He's sliced through some of my hair.

Almost at the same time, his clawed foot connects with my stomach, tearing into my dress, knocking the wind out of me, and sending me flying back. I land hard on the cavern floor.

The monstrous version of the man I love stalks over until he looms above me. He kicked me so hard, I can't catch my breath. I keep hoping that as he gets closer, the yellow will fade from his eyes. That my power will work like it did before and bring him back into his right mind.

But Bianca is in control, and she's too strong.

Outside the circle, the Winters and their wolves are tearing through Redcedar Hollow. There's a burst of fire, then one of wind as the mages go to work. Witch magic crackles in the air. These are the most powerful supernatural beings in the world, and I want to believe they have a chance, but the number of Redcedar Hollow wolves feels endless.

I think it might have been Bianca's plan, or Vandran's, to murder the Conclave all along.

Killian bends and wraps his fingers around my throat. He lifts me off the ground, squeezing so hard. It's already bruised from Beta Jones and I'm afraid Killian going to break me. I cough and kick and bury my fingers in the fur on his arm. His rough palm is against my neck. He's touching my skin.

*Come back to me. Come back!*

367

This should be working, but it isn't, and I can't speak to compel him. I squeak out, "Killian, please."

Silver light leaps into my skin. The yellow in his eyes flickers.

"Kill her!" Bianca screams. Then, "No! Stop them!"

I roll my eyes to the side and see Zev, Maddox, Parker, and other wolves loyal to Killian. They've fought through the ring of guards. Zev bellows Eva's name and tackles the wolf holding her while Maddox takes on the one who has Finn.

Bianca is distracted. Killian's grip loosens, but he can't seem to let me go. His eyes flicker to topaz. "Selene?"

His voice is all gravel and stone, but it's him. Tears rush to my eyes. "Let me go."

I put power into it. It flickers and sparks. His monstrous form starts to fade, but his hand is still wrapped around my throat.

"Killian." Asher emerges from the chaos. His sword is back in his hand.

Zev howls. I hear Eva shout, "Come, Finn, run!"

They're free. Everything is happening so fast, but Killian's clawed hand is still around my throat, and I'm struggling to breathe.

Killian sags in relief at the sight of his friend. "I can't ... I n-need ... I didn't ..."

Asher looks sad. "I know."

Killian is shaking. He looks at me. "You have to let—let him—"

Then yellow flickers back into his eyes, and his grip tightens again.

"I said *end her*!" Bianca screams. She's no longer distracted but stalking this way.

"No, Ki—"

"Do it," Killian snarls.

Asher's form ripples. The scent of campfire smoke hits the air as he takes his chocolate-furred hybrid form. The sword shimmers and disappears.

When Asher puts a hand on Killian's shoulder, his claws are pure silver. I don't know whether he's speaking to me, Killian, or himself when he says, "I wish things had gone another way."

Then Asher pulls back and slams his entire weight into Killian. Killian's claws slice into my skin as I'm ripped from his grasp and go flying.

I land and roll onto my side, coughing and drawing air in deep, wheezing gasps. Someone almost steps on me in the chaos. I roll out of the way, and my hand splats into the cooling pool of Deacon Jones's blood.

"Killian, you useless nobody!" Bianca shrieks over the din. "Kill him! Kill them all!"

The tingling in my chest has turned to roaring heat. Killian and Asher grapple, snarling. They get too close, and I have to scramble away. Bianca's circle of guards is holding, but Jones's isn't the only body on the floor.

"Where are you, Selene?" Bianca snarls. She's lost me in the chaos, and I don't see her either.

Killian's and Asher's snarls are deafening. They move almost too fast to see, slashing at each other, jumping back, tackling, rolling around, kicking, biting. Blood streaks and spatters on the floor all around them.

When I locate Bianca, she's no longer shouting for me. Her attention has been caught by the two Alphas. She's standing just far enough back from their fight not to get caught in it, raw hunger in her eyes. Killian is in his cursed form, and he howls and strikes. A deep gash appears on Asher's side.

Beyond the circle of guards, the battle is going badly for the Conclave. There are just too many of Bianca's wolves. They're too strong. These may be the most powerful leaders in the world, but they're still losing.

From my place on the floor, I can't see Finn or Eva, but I do see Zev nearby. He's lying on the ground, head turned to one side, eyes closed. He's bleeding from deep lacerations covering him from chest to abdomen, and I can't tell whether he's alive.

But the wolf Bianca commanded to kill Eva is lying on the ground beside him, and that wolf is definitely dead.

"Parker!"

It's Sofia's voice. My eyes find her in the crowd. Her mate is in wolf form, surrounded by at least five enemies. She's bleeding. As I watch, Sofia tears her dress and shifts into her Alpha form. She leaps into the battle, even though she has no idea how to fight.

"You leave him alone! He's just a kid!" A knot of wolfless have formed at the back of the room, led by Jenny. I don't have to see who they're protecting to know. It's Finn. The wolfless are his family too. He would've run right for them. Which means that's also where Eva is. They're standing between the older woman and the child, facing down their tormentors with whatever they can grab—trays, ladles, the broken leg of a chair.

I take all of this in in seconds that feel like eternities. As I watch, Jenny screams and goes down under a wolf's claws. Parker howls. I hear the booming voice of the Alpha Lord of the Steel Alliance. "Fall back! Open a way to the cavern entrance!"

I can end this.

I must end this.

*"STOP!"*

Power explodes from me in a wave, rushing out and over the crowd. I try to control it. There are so many of them, I *have* to control it. *Wolves,* I think, *Redcedar Hollow wolves.*

There are yelps and screams as fighters are thrown to the ground. Some slam against walls. Others freeze like they've been turned to stone. Several others cry out. I fight to contain the power until my head pounds. Until I'm biting my lip so hard, blood flows.

"Stop," I whisper.

And then it's like a thousand threads snap into place. I can feel every single wolf in the room as if they're bound to me by invisible cords. Some are easy to tug and manipulate. Some I couldn't move if I tried. But I can feel them, and the longer I do, the more I realize I can tell who they are. Which are my pack and which are *other*. I can distinguish between them.

I choose the wolves of Redcedar Hollow and *hold*.

Bianca screams. "Attack! What are you doing?"

I rise on shaking legs. I can feel Bianca too. I know, now, exactly how terrifyingly strong she is, how strong she'd be if she joined with Killian, because I can feel it. Alphas of one hundred thousands, just like Alaric Bane.

Bianca tears at my power, but her back is to me. She has no idea what's going on. Doesn't know I'm the one whose magic is thrumming like thunder in the air.

I can't hold the Redcedar wolves for long. If I do, they'll all end up like Noelle. But I hold them anyway as the Conclave members regroup, retreat, pick up the wounded, and run.

"Shattered Moon!" I call. "Get the Conclave somewhere safe!"

Parker jumps into action, Sofia with her. "This way!" shouts the Gamma.

I haven't tried to halt Killian and Asher, and they're still tearing at each other at the center of the room. Killian roars as Asher opens up a slash in his chest.

"No!" I shout.

Asher redoubles his attack, and it's clear the tide has turned.

I know what Killian wants. I know what he was begging Asher to do. I remember him telling me, what feels like a lifetime ago, that if anyone can kill him, it's Asher.

Someone slams into me from the side. "You stupid *bitch*, Selene! You stupid, stupid bitch!"

We fall to the floor, Bianca's solid weight pinning me down. She threads her fingers into my hair and slams my skull against the stone floor once, twice, three times. I cry out as pain explodes on the side of my head. My hold on the magic connection to every wolf in the room snaps, and the backlash whips against my mind, something I've never experienced before. It's like a thousand molten needles digging into my brain. My vision blurs and swims.

Bianca lifts my head to smash it down again. I buck hard.

She is stronger than me by far but always did underestimate me, and not once in the last month has she taken into account my new strength now that I have a wolf.

I don't send her flying, but I do dislodge her and dump her onto the ground.

Since I was thirteen years old, I've never dared to fight back against Bianca physically. I was so afraid of what would happen, afraid of what my parents would do.

I'm not afraid anymore.

I snarl and dive onto her, rolling her over onto her back. When she tries to push me off with the same move I used on her, I wrap my legs around her and hold on.

I grab the necklace and yank it off her neck. The chain snaps. I hold it up in the air, triumphant.

Killian and Asher fight on.

I yelp as Bianca's claws rake my ribs, splitting my dress and leaving deep bleeding gashes that make a tic-tac-toe board with the ones Killian's foot left when he kicked me. They immediately start to heal, but they still burn.

Bianca throws me off, and I roll across the floor, my skirts dragging. When my command snapped back on me, it released the Redcedar Hollow wolves. All around, the chaos has started again.

The necklace is in my hand, but Killian is fighting Asher as fiercely as ever.

I struggle to my feet and have to dodge out of the way of the two huge hybrid wolves. Asher lets out a pained yowl as Killian opens a gash nearly the length of his torso.

Maddox has been fighting back Bianca's soldiers, but at his brother's cry, he drops the wolf he's just killed and leaps to Asher's aid.

Now Killian is fighting both of them.

I can't tell who will win. I think they may overcome him but not before he takes one or both of them out.

I can't let Eva lose both of her sons. I can't let Killian hurt the men he thinks of as brothers.

There's a quiet laugh beside me, and I realize I'm just standing, frozen, watching them. Bianca has come to stand at my side. Her eyes are on them too. She doesn't even look at me, even though I have the necklace in my hand.

She still doesn't believe I'm a threat.

"Give me the necklace, Selene."

"No."

She scoffs. "All right, then. Hold it for me until this ends."

And that's the thing ... she'll never believe I could hurt her. Maybe I'm not a threat to her, for all of my power. What is it worth without control? Without knowledge of how to use it?

What is power worth to me at all when ruthless people like Bianca will always wield it to greater effect than I could ever stomach?

"Look at him," she breathes. "God, he's perfect like this."

"That isn't Killian," I say, so tired. "That's your monstrousness that you've forced into his head—you and Vandran. It's your reflection, not his."

She rolls her eyes. "Fates, shut up. Enjoy watching your man in the last few minutes you have before I make him kill you. Look, you're the one with the stone, and he's still obeying me. Whitlock said the focus had to be wielded by an Alpha blood, and you aren't one. You can't do anything with it. You can't help him or the wolfless or Finn or yourself. Even with a wolf, you're as weak as you ever were. Did you know our parents had a witch modify both of our memories so we'd believe we were siblings? I never felt so much relief as I did the day I learned we don't share blood."

I tighten my grip on the necklace, the edges of the pendant digging into my palm. "We were sisters, Bianca."

"No. We weren't."

I take a breath, letting go at last. Of the Beaumonts, of my fear. "You're going to lose."

That gets her attention. She fully turns toward me, her expression incredulous. "Do you think just because you have a wolf and Alaric Bane was your father I'm going to let you back talk me? You aren't better than me, *Selenite Bane*. When I force Killian to murder you, I'm going to make him do it slowly, and I'm going to make sure he looks into your eyes as you die."

I pull power to me, winding it like a skein of yarn. I let it gather in my veins, building and thickening, until my blood sizzles and boils.

"I never said I was better than you, Bianca."

"You always thought it. I could tell. You never accepted your place in the hierarchy."

"The hierarchy is bullshit."

She snaps her teeth. "Of course the weak think that. The strong know better. You were meant to be a servant. You could never be the Alpha of Redcedar Hollow, and you're jealous that I am. You've always been jealous."

Absolutely not. But I shrug. "I'd certainly be a better Alpha than you."

Bianca laughs out loud. "Is that a challenge, little sister?"

This time, I don't turn that tingling, boiling, burning outward. I let it sink down inside me until I can't tell the difference between the burn and the freeze. Until it melts into my bones like ice. Like the rage I have held deep inside since I was thirteen years old.

Or maybe the ice entered my blood when the silver did. When my own mother stabbed me and broke off the tip of her knife inside my body so that I would never get a wolf and never be found by Alaric Bane.

"Yes, Bianca," I say, rubbing my thumb in circles over the curse-anchoring pendant. "I challenge you."

The scent of smoke is in the air, and wolf magic tightens around us like a noose. Bianca laughs again. She laughs and laughs.

While she does, I channel magic through my muscles, my organs, my blood and brain. My senses sharpen. My instincts balance on a fine wire. My teeth lengthen, and my claws grow. Strength suffuses my body.

It's not an Alpha form—I am not an Alpha blood wolf. But some kind of transformation rushes along my nerves and prickles beneath my skin, and in it, I feel the presence of my mother and her mother and mothers going back to the beginning of wolfkind.

I grip the necklace and imagine magic spearing through the pendant. Crushing it. Releasing my mate from his torment.

It doesn't work. My magic can't penetrate the stone. Not as long as it's connected to its source of power: Bianca.

The sister I used to love finally straightens. "Well. I didn't expect tonight to include comedy. Maybe I won't kill you, Selene. Maybe I'll keep you around as my jester. You can watch while I fuck Killian if you're very, very good."

"I never thought I was better than you," I say quietly. "If you couldn't love me, I only wanted you to leave me alone."

There are no games now.

I used to fear that when it came to this moment—when using power responsibly meant something extreme—that I would be too afraid to do it. That I would hesitate.

But in the end, I'm what I always have been: very practical.

So while Bianca stands there looking at me like I'm an idiot, like there could be no lesser threat in the world than me, like she's just beginning to anticipate the pleasure she'll find in my suffering, I dart my partially transformed hand forward, sink my long claws deep into her flesh, and tear out her throat.

Only as she falls, blood spurting hot over my arm and my dress, spraying over the stone floor, does Bianca finally look afraid.

Rushing fills my ears. The feeling of being the *center* as a thousand strands of gossamer wrap my body and climb right up into my head. Connections, connections, connections forming like spokes of a wheel, plugging into my brain.

*Is that a challenge, little sister?*

*Yes, Bianca. I challenge you.*

I have been using power in ripples. In rivulets. In shore-licking tiny waves. But now, as the lives of three thousand Redcedar Hollow wolves connect to mine, I drown in a tsunami that drives me to my knees, soaking my skirt through with more of Bianca's blood as I hit the ground.

There's a tentative touch on my mind. "*Alpha?*" the first one whispers, followed by more.

*"Alpha?"*
*"Bianca is dead!"*
*"Who are you?"*

There is so much noise, but I can already see how this works.

*"Stop."* I send the command down every one of the gossamer threads. *"No more violence."*

Around me, the chaos slowly goes still. More voices in my mind clamor for attention. I gently block them out.

When I am battered beyond bearing, all I can do is the next task in front of me.

Bianca is dead, and I am filled with the strength of thousands.

There's a *pop* in the stone in my hand. When I open my clawed fist —the one not covered in blood—the yellow sheen in the stone flares, nearly blinding.

Killian is still fighting Asher and Maddox. I feel him, not in my mind like my new pack but through this stone. I feel his mind trapped, his body like a puppet on strings.

I close my eyes and pour my power, amplified by the pack, into the stone. More. More. More. Until the yellow is flushed out with pure silver-white.

I command the stone to shatter.

There's another *pop* in my palm. I squeeze the anchor with all of my strength.

It cracks. Then it crumbles to dust.

I feel Killian shudder, and then ... his presence is gone.

He is free.

But Bianca and Vandran were both right about one thing.

I don't have Alpha blood.

I am powerful. But I'm not made for this kind of magic. I'm not built to be a nexus at all, let alone one that connects this many wolves.

All of the gossamer threads binding me to the Redcedar Hollow pack become wires pulling tight, cutting, rending. Pain screams through my mind and echoes in my body. Liquid wells from my eyes. I touch it. When my fingers come away, they're crimson with blood.

Darkness presses in on me.

At least I set them free. Killian. Finn. The wolfless.

I set myself free.

I am at peace.

## KILLIAN

There is an impossible silence.

For five years, the whispers have never been far from me. Even when the sun is up or the moon is new, I sense them in the depths of my mind.

Now they're gone. With the pack tie still disabled, I am truly alone in my own head.

I groan. I feel like I've been put through a meat grinder. The floor beneath me is hard and cold. Above me, instead of sky, there's stone.

And then there's a pair of bright blue eyes and a shit-eating grin.

"She did it," Asher whispers. "She fucking did it!"

He hauls me up into a sitting position. The world spins. Someone else supports me from the side.

"Easy, Alpha," says Maddox. He steadies me, then looks at something over my shoulder. Quickly, he gets up and walks in that direction.

The last few minutes come back to me in flashes. Fighting Asher, then Asher and Maddox. And before that—

"Selene!" I look around wildly and finally see the carnage. Wolves and members of the Conclave are tending to the wounded. Some are clustering, whispering. The bodies of the dead litter the ground.

For some reason, there are hundreds of wolves on their knees.

371

Redcedar Hollow wolves. One of Bianca's favorite soldiers groans and hugs his stomach not six feet away.

"Shit!" he groans. "Bianca died, and now that idiot Selene is dying. I'm going to be fucking sick."

Bianca is dead? Selene is dying?

My brain slips like tires in mud, spinning and finding no traction.

I need to catch up. I have to find her.

"Oh, Zev." Eva's voice. She leans over my bodyguard. He's still a wolf, prone on the floor. There's so much blood around him. She strokes his face softly. I rise and start to move toward them.

"Killian!"

My head snaps around. I've never heard Maddox shout like that before, desperate and afraid. He kneels over what looks like a pile of crumpled silver fabric with a pale arm extending from it.

Next to the pile is Bianca's corpse. Her throat is red ribbons, her blood a dark puddle beneath her.

"Killian, get over here!" Maddox shouts again. "Selene took Redcedar Hollow. They're tearing her apart!"

Everything inside me turns to stone as I understand what happened. What is happening. Who Maddox is pulling into his arms.

I run.

I reach Selene in a dozen strides, dropping to slide the last of the distance on my knees. Maddox has her propped up against his shoulder. Selene's gaze is unfocused. Her breathing shallow. Her pale face has gone as white as death except for the crimson tears that are dripping from the inner corners of her eyes. Blood is also darkening the inside and corners of her lips.

"Selene!" Sofia appears, Parker clearing their way through the crowd so they can reach us.

Asher wanders over as I take my wife gently from Maddox and pull her onto my lap.

When she's settled into my arms, Selene turns her face toward me and inhales deeply. Then she smiles. Her voice is barely a breath. "You're free. No more treaties. No more Beaumonts. No more war. No more monster ... but that was never really you."

There's the sound of retching as some of the Redcedar Hollow wolves start to get sick. A dying Alpha can do that to a pack.

I cup her face. "If I'm free, so are you."

"I know."

"Stay with me."

"I'm trying, but I don't think I can."

"Did you challenge Bianca and then kill her?"

"Yes."

"Why?" The question tears from me. An Alpha can't reject their pack. She can't undo this.

Selene's laugh is a weak chuckle that ends in a cough. There's more blood around her mouth. "All that power … told you it would … go to my head. I had to stop them from killing."

"Killian," Sofia's voice, as always, is matter-of-fact, though it's more gentle than usual. "There's an obvious solution to this."

"Is there?" I snap. "I can't mate bond with her. It will do to her what it did to Grace. She'll die."

"What are you talking about?" Maddox snarls. "Killian, do it."

Asher crouches beside me. The serious expression on his face is unfamiliar. He puts a hand on my shoulder, then holds up a broken chain. A ragged bit of black stone clings to it. "She broke the stone. She broke the curse. You won't hurt her."

"You're fated, for gods' sake!" Parker barks.

I can't stop staring at the necklace in Asher's hand.

The silence in my head rings loud.

I don't know whether I can believe I'm not cursed. Either way there's still terrible violence in me. What if something about me infects her anyway? What if it wasn't the curse that destroyed Grace—what if it was me?

But if I am shadow, she is light.

I move Selene so she's sitting up. The shift into my hybrid form and the fight with Asher shredded my clothes, so it's easy to pull her against my bare chest and position her so her lips rest at the place where my shoulder meets my neck.

"What are you doing?" Selene's words wheeze. I am running out of time.

"We are going to mark each other," I say. "Just say the words, then grow your fangs. You just need to break the skin."

She shivers. "I don't know if I can."

"You can." I'm not wasting any more time arguing.

"Killian, what if we do this and I die? It will hurt you."

I turn my head so my lips brush her ear and whisper, "I love you.

Selenite Bane, I take back my rejection of our bond, and I accept you as my fated mate."

A prickle of connection in my heart jolts back to life. It's so easy. So ridiculously easy.

I lean forward, nuzzling her neck until I find the right place. I kiss the spot and shake her gently.

"Say it."

She shudders again. Her words are barely audible. "Killian Darrow, I ... take back ..."

I jostle her again. "Selene!"

She whimpers. "I take back my rejection of our bond ... and I accept you as my fated mate."

A feeling of raw emptiness in my chest closes like a healing wound. Her lips touch my skin, part, and I feel her teeth. At the same time, I open my mouth and sink mine deep into her shoulder.

"Ah!" The pain must revive her because suddenly, her fangs are sharp. They press into my shoulder. I put my hand on top of her head and push down to help her break through and draw blood.

I have never felt sweeter pain than I do the moment when her teeth bury themselves in my skin.

Abruptly, she goes limp, her head lolling to the side, all the breath going out of her at once.

"Selene!" My heart pounds, shattering with each beat.

Then magic slams into me like a goddamned freight train. My mind opens to hers. The first thing I see is the way she's being sliced to pieces by the pull of her pack.

"Excuse me," someone says, "I need to speak with—"

Asher turns to face whoever it is, and Maddox jumps to his feet, standing shoulder to shoulder with his brother. "Absolutely not fucking now!"

I unleash my aura and let magic flow into Selene, through her. I peel those killing threads away and take them into me. They snap into place among the threads I already hold that tie me to the wolves of Shattered Moon.

Selene gasps and stirs. I feel the lightness in her mind. I can feel all of her now, her pain, her sorrow, her will to live.

I take away the thing that was killing her, but so much damage has been done.

Those threads settle, twining around me, pulling tight. My head throbs with the sudden addition of a pack more than twice the size of the one I already have. The tethers that hold me together threaten to snap.

Before, when I thought I was the son of Alaric Bane, I would have been confident that becoming the nexus of this many wolves wouldn't kill me. Now I have no idea what I'm actually capable of, if I have the power others have claimed.

On the floor of that cavern, with Bianca's dead body beside us, our friends around us, and the Conclave clamoring to speak to me, I wrap myself around Selene and wait for both of us to live.

# Fifty-One

## *SELENE*

I'm surrounded by warm strength, the scent of cedar and rain, and the feeling of being so loved, so treasured, it makes my chest ache.

Killian's heart beats against my ear, his mind intertwines with mine, and I realize we have survived.

"Selene?"

Gods and fates, his voice. I could listen to it every day for the rest of my life. And unless I'm mistaken or already dead, I think I get to.

I open my eyes and find myself drowning in pools of topaz. "Killian."

He buries his face in my hair. "It worked."

His emotions are there, close enough to touch. Relief, exhaustion, love. Power flows between us and from us to the pack and back again.

My magic doesn't do what an Alpha's does. Mine is ... broader. I can tell I'm in his head now that I can sense exactly what wielding his magic feels like for him. But we seem to be functioning the way Alpha Pairs are supposed to, and the strength generated by our bond is staggering.

What did Asher call me? Silverlight?

This bloodline magic I carry isn't something new—it's something ancient. Something forgotten. It will take time to explore, to see where our limits are. Where *my* limits are.

I wonder whether there are answers in the library of Alaric Bane.

"Alphas." Sofia approaches, which breaks my attention from Killian and my own thoughts.

We're still in the cavern. All around us, people are cleaning up from the battle. About three hundred Redcedar Hollow pack warriors are kneeling in a group at the back of the chamber, their hands on their heads, guarded by a variety of Aspected guards—several of whom are still wearing their enchanted masks.

That toast feels like a million years ago, but I'm not sure whether it's even been an hour. Though I'm no longer tied to those wolves by Alpha threads, I can feel them. I know them. Several people who made my entire life a living hell are among them, and the light inside me whispers that they are mine. Not to control but to guide. Protect. From the strongest of them all the way down to the wolfless.

"Yes, Sofia?" Killian asks.

The Gamma's face is drawn. Her ripped dress has been somehow rigged to stay up with ribbons that look like they came from someone else. The curls at the ends of her sleek brown hair have come loose, and there are purple circles under her eyes. "The Conclave wants to speak with you."

Killian rises with me in his arms. My dress is stiff and disgusting with blood. My silver wolf mask is long gone. At some point while I was unconscious, Killian apparently swapped the tattered remains of his suit for a pair of black sweatpants. I want to shower, put on soft pajamas, hug Finn, check on the people I love, and then sleep buried halfway beneath Killian's weight for a year.

"Not now," he says to Sofia. A growl vibrates beneath the words. "We need to clean up, to rest. She's tired. She almost died."

I splay my hand across his chest and notice it's also crusted with flaking dried blood.

Blood.

Bianca's blood. It's on my hands, under my nails.

The memory is a slap. I startle and look at the floor. Her body is gone, but there's still a congealing puddle where she fell. I remember the feeling of my claws punching through her skin, the way her throat felt as I crushed it in my hand and tore ...

I shudder, and then I push the darkness down. "We'll see them now."

Killian's eyes meet mine, and the most miraculous thing happens.

He speaks into my mind. Not through the pack tie but through our mate bond.

We are mate bonded.

*"Are you sure?"* he asks.

*"I'm sure. Where's Vandran?"*

*"Maddox said he ran early on in the fight. So did Whitlock, but several of his cronies on the Conclave, like Erebos, are still here."*

A wave of exhaustion almost overwhelms me at hearing Vandran is gone. *"We have to tell them the truth, or lies are all they'll have."*

Killian sets me on my feet, and I lean on him. Asher stands not far away, arms folded. He and Maddox seem to be having a low, intense discussion with a female witch. Killian whistles, and Asher looks up. He says something to the other two, then jogs over.

"You summoned?" Asher's tone is cutting, but Killian doesn't flinch.

"Deacon is dead. Act as my Beta."

"Fuck off."

"You fuck off."

Asher bares his teeth. "Five years you let me believe the worst of you. Five years I stayed away because I thought, if it wasn't his fault, he would find a way to tell me. He wouldn't rely on my mother and little brother to fight his battles for him."

"It's not my fault you're a skeptical bastard who believes the worst of people," Killian retorts.

"It's not *my* fault you spent your life like a fucking martyr trying to push everyone into believing the worst of you and I finally did," Asher snaps. "And don't give me some bullshit about me being better off away from you or you trying to protect everyone you could from your 'nature,' because we both know which of us is actually the problem. You can fuck off again."

A muscle in Killian's jaw works. "I need you."

Asher folds his arms. "Fine. For today. That's it."

"I'm sorry for not telling you."

"Fuck off." Asher runs a hand through his hair, and for an instant, I see how upset he is and how deeply the last five years away from the people he loves must have impacted him. His eyes skip over all the carnage in the cavern and fix on something in the corner. When I look, there's nothing there.

I shiver. I can sense him now, and there is some kind of shadow over Asher Quinn.

But in this moment, all he does is shrug and say, "I guess I'm sorry I made you swear never to take a mate and your idiotic martyr complex took it so far it almost led to your death and Selene's and the downfall of the entire pack."

"Okay," Killian says, pinching the bridge of his nose. "That's not what happened."

"Do we hug?" Asher opens his arms.

Killian lets out the heaviest sigh I've ever heard.

I watch the end of the exchange like a tennis match, amused despite my misgivings about Asher. I take Killian's hand and pull it farther around me. "He's hugging me right now."

Asher scoffs. "He was my friend first."

"She's prettier than you," Killian interjects.

Asher gasps. "Bastard!"

Killian shakes his head and pushes his friend out of the way. We walk toward the front of the cavern, where the leaders of the Conclave have gathered. Asher and Sofia flank us. Parker and Maddox walk behind.

"Wait! Where's Zev?" I remember seeing him go down.

Killian jerks his head to one side. Zev is propped up against the far wall. Eva is with him. Their hands are clasped.

Asher follows our gaze, then narrows his eyes. "What the hell?"

Maddox sees them next and half pivots that way. "I'm going to fucking—"

Parker catches him with a hand to the chest.

"Leave them alone," Sofia barks. "You, both of you, are going to leave your mother alone. She's not dead, and Zev has been in love with her for years."

The brothers exchange glances, seeming to communicate silently. Asher shrugs. Maddox makes an irritated sound. Then they follow us forward.

We approach the circle of guards surrounding the Conclave leaders where they sit in the cordoned-off area. The chairs are gathered in a semicircle, the tables pushed to the sides.

The guards part for us, and we walk into their midst. The Steel Alliance Alphas sit at the apex, flanked by coven heads, chieftains, lords, and the few humans who remained when Vandran fled. Claudia is already there, seated in a chair a little off to one side.

Killian drops his gaze as a sign of respect before the Steel Alliance Alphas, and so do I.

"Alphas Prime, Conclave members," he says.

"Alpha Darrow." Morgana Winters's gaze lingers on Killian, then me.

"My question from before all this chaos still hasn't been answered," she says, voice calm. "Are you a Beaumont or not?"

"I'm not a Beaumont," I say. I have, at last, come to terms with that.

Morgana leans forward, eyes keen. "If you're not a Beaumont, who are you?" She squints. "You look so familiar."

Claudia heaves a sigh. There's a wine goblet in her hand again. Like the last one, it seems to still be full. She swirls the liquid, and I wonder whether she just finds some comfort in holding it. "That's because she's Selenite Bane, the daughter of Aurora Stillwater and Alaric Bane. You probably saw Aurora a few times, though once Bane decided she was his favorite, he did like to keep her hidden from view."

Morgana Winters looks at Claudia like she's lost her mind. Before she can speak, Claudia heaves another sigh, rolls her eyes, and says in a monotone, "I lied. Killian's father was Jack Owens, Bane's Gamma. They don't share any blood, so stop looking at me like that. Alpha Lady Winters."

She tags on the title belatedly when the Alpha Lord of the Steel Alliance narrows his eyes.

"She's a Stillwater?" Morgana says, brows rising. "A silverlight?"

"She's a Bane?" That comes from Erebos, the High Priest who helped Vandran.

Killian has gone tense. He takes a long, slow breath.

*"What's wrong?"* I ask.

*"I didn't want them knowing you're a Stillwater or a Bane. It's going to cause problems."*

"Oh, yes. There's proof, back at the pack house," Claudia says. "There's a book with all of his children listed."

I sigh. *"Well, I suppose it's too late to keep it secret now. We have got to stop her from finding out so many things. Maybe if we pay attention to her, she'll stop acting out like a child. Or you could just let her stay exiled."*

Killian chuckles under his breath.

"So," Morgana Winters says, eyeing me with an unreadable expression in her eyes. "You two have mate bonded. You're now Alpha Lady ... Beaumont? Bane? Darrow?"

I blink. My lips part, but I don't know what to say. Am I an Alpha Lady with no Alpha blood? "I think I'll be Selene Stillwater for now, Alpha Prime. I'm still coming to terms with both the events and the revelations of the last several days."

"Mm." Morgana Winters taps sharp gold nails against her lips, then gestures to Claudia. "We've heard a fascinating tale from your mother, Alpha Darrow. Five years under an eldritch curse. That's quite the burden. Others who've dealt with similar things have gone on killing rampages and had to be taken down at great cost. But you kept it in check. Impressive."

"I did as much as I could," Killian says tightly.

I know he's thinking of Grace and Jackson. I squeeze his hand.

"This is ridiculous," says Erebos. "This is a coup the Bane girl planned from the beginning. You can't let this bald-faced power grab stand. Do you want another tyrant?"

"Strange," Locke Winters says. "You always told us we didn't have to worry about Killian when *he* was the son of Bane and Warlord Vandran was supporting him. Speaking of which, where is Vandran? Because there are very serious accusations being leveled against him and his arcanist, and I'd like to hear what he has to say."

"Beaumont had the anchor stone," one of the vampires says lazily. "There's no evidence Vandran had anything to do with it."

"The question is, what are we going to do about Shattered Moon? They violated the treaty," Erebos insists.

I step aggressively toward the coven head. "That treaty was a sham in the first place, designed by my parents—and who knows who else—with the sole intent of entrapping Killian in a way that would bring you all down on his head."

I scan the Conclave, taking stock of their expressions, their postures.

One of the vampires lifts a brow. "So bold. I like her."

I frown but continue. "I am Killian's rightful mate. I do not concede that Vandran had nothing to do with Killian's curse, but it is irrefutable that Bianca did. I acted within my rights to protect my mate from a person manipulating him with magic."

A murmur goes through them. It sounds mostly like agreement, but I see who Vandran's allies are. I memorize their faces. Later, I'll find out their names.

"One of the reasons you came here tonight was to see the pack war between Shattered Moon and Redcedar Hollow officially ended," Killian says. "You did. It's over. There's only one pack now. You got what you wanted, even if it nearly killed us. Your trade routes will no longer be disrupted by unrest in this area."

"What about the former Redcedar Hollow wolves?" the siren woman asks. Her voice is soft. Even so, it draws the gaze of everyone who hears it.

Sofia speaks up. "Under Conclave law, any wolves who acted under an antagonistic Alpha's control but who remain in the newly formed pack are for their new Alphas to deal with. If any choose to leave Shattered Moon and become rogues, they'll fall under the jurisdiction of the Conclave. I'll make sure a record is kept."

Her tone is final, and the meaning behind her words is clear. This is pack business now, which means the Conclave need to keep their noses out. I make a mental note to have Sofia teach me Conclave law. I have a feeling I'm going to need to know it.

"We'll provide medical care and compensation for damages." Killian's arm tightens around me, and I feel how unsteady he is on his feet. "Consider this our formal apology and our formal thanks."

"I thought it was exciting," a naiad chieftainess whispers.

Killian wavers. Asher puts a hand on his shoulder. "Okay, enough politics. We have to get our Alphas to our pack healer before they try to drop dead again."

I want to say more. To reassure the Conclave that with Killian and me in charge, there will be peace. It would come wildly out of nowhere, but I also want to bring up the law about the wolfless. The next Conclave won't happen for three years. If I don't speak now, I'll miss my chance.

*But the Redcedar Hollow wolfless are mine now. No matter what, they're safe.*

Except now that I am who I am, it isn't enough to only save the ones I know and love.

But before I can do or say anything, Asher, Sofia, and the others usher Killian and me out.

Killian, apparently sensing my distress, takes my hand. *"We won't wait for the next Conclave. We'll figure it out."*

I look up at him, amazed to be so known. *"Thank you."*

*"Always."*

# Fifty-Two

## KILLIAN

My mate is a goddess in the moonlight.

Selene lies back on the blanket, silver and shadow pooling on her skin. We've run a long way from the pack house to a place where a grassy clearing runs right up against the edge of the lake. It's been a month since the Conclave. A busy, exhausting month.

The new version of our pack isn't settled. The threat of the Conclave's justice kept a lot of former Redcedar Hollow wolves who I'd rather not have as part of Shattered Moon from leaving. Despite that, there has been only one instance of insubordination against Selene: a low-level pack guard thought he could bully her the way he used to.

He thought that right up to the moment when I opened his throat

Selene was shocked and horrified, but no one else was surprised. My justice tends toward mercy, but I have no mercy for anyone who made her scars.

I kiss my way up her stomach, and her eyes luminesce silver with the presence of her wolf. She slides her fingers into my hair and pulls me up so that I cover her, then parts her legs so that we're pressed together in just the right way. I open the seam of her lips with my tongue and explore her, her taste and scent, my whole world narrowed to just her as I rock against her.

"Killian, I need—"

I move my lips to her neck, hook my hands behind her knees, guide her legs around my body, and bury myself inside her.

Selene cries out and bucks, shifting her hips to take me as deep as she can. She wraps her arms around me, cradling my head as I close my teeth over the place I marked her. I bite down, and she cries out in ecstasy, her legs shaking as she comes hard, her walls pulsing around me and sending me over the edge.

I think I'm spent even though she's still going. Then she pulls me down, finds where she marked me, and bites. I make a guttural sound and spend myself inside her all over again.

We hold each other for a long time, our hearts slowing, our skin cooling in the chill spring night.

I roll onto my back and pull her close so that her head is pillowed against my chest, and we watch the stars.

Finally, she lifts her head and smiles down at me. She presses a kiss to my forehead, then each of my cheeks before she finds my mouth and lingers there. When she pulls back, she sighs.

I cup her cheek and run my thumb along her lips. "It's our night off. You're not supposed to worry."

She gives me a wry, sideways smile. "I'm not."

I pull her down and kiss her again. "Tell me what it is."

"It's our night off," she protests.

"If you aren't taking one, neither am I."

She settles back against my side. Finally, she says, "It's the book."

My head falls back. "Yeah. The book is a problem."

After everything, when the smoke cleared and the danger passed and the members of the Conclave went home, Selene wanted to show me the book she found that lists all the surviving daughters of Alaric Bane. I saw it when Bianca showed it to Vandran but never got a close look.

But when we searched for it, it was gone.

I'm almost positive I know who has it.

"I have sisters out there," Selene says quietly. "You said Vandran is obsessed with Bane's legacy. What if he tries to find them?"

"We'll find them first."

"I can't remember the names of the survivors. It's just a bunch of gemstone names jumbled in my head. I know there was Ruby. Maybe Beryl? Or maybe she was one who was dead. Shit. I should've written their names down, but I didn't have a chance."

"Like I said, love, we'll find them," I reply.

Selene's brows pinch with worry. "Soon, Killian. I'm safe, but they don't have you or silverlight magic or the power of the Conclave protecting them. Or what's left of it now that Vandran and his sycophants have broken off."

I stroke her hair. "We'll figure it out."

She gets a determined look on her face. "Ruby. Quartz. Citrine? Emerald, I think. Obsidian? No, a different black stone. I am going to remember, and we're going to find them."

I kiss her forehead. "We are. And we'll bring them here and keep them safe until Vandran and Whitlock can be brought to justice."

Selene nods decisively. "We will."

She settles back on my shoulder. The air smells of spring and growing things and her scent of waterlilies in a clear pond. For five years, I was determined to be alone. For the last month, nothing has separated me from her. I've stopped fearing the curse will come back. I've stopped subconsciously doing things to push people away.

For the first time since Grace died, I've rediscovered hope.

I can see a future.

Selene turns toward me, her breasts grazing my skin. "What are you thinking about?"

I grin and roll her beneath me again. "You. Always."

## SELENE

"Selene!" Finn sprints over to me, giggling maniacally as he's chased by two little girls from his class.

"Don't hide behind me!" I laugh as he tries to do exactly that.

Night has barely fallen. Bonfires are lighting the pack grounds at intervals. Tables full of food are everywhere.

In an effort to bring the formerly enemy packs together, Killian and I have started holding these feast nights once a month. It's amazing how uniting food and music can be. It's especially deserved this month, as the pack has been working hard to build more housing in the nearby woods and restore the ruined old wing that used to belong to Alaric Bane.

Finn pushes away from me, cackles, and darts into the night, the girls running behind him.

"He's grown so much since coming here," Eva says.

"He really has," Sofia replies. "I think he's the tallest kid in his age group now."

We're standing near one of the tables, chatting as the festivities of the night wind down. Of course, Parker is never far from me, but she and Sofia keep exchanging smoldering looks, and I don't know how much longer they'll last.

"He might be," I agree. He's taller, stronger, and healthier. Every day, I am so grateful for the night we were brave enough to run. That Finn was brave enough to go into the darkness alone.

Warmth brushes my mind as Killian approaches and wraps his arms around me from behind. Asher and Maddox trail after him. Maddox wrinkles his nose. Asher whistles and wiggles his eyebrows.

Eva's eyes light the way they always do when she sees her sons. She goes on her toes and kisses them both on the cheek. Then she smacks Asher lightly on the shoulder. "Don't be tasteless."

"Mother, I have never had taste."

Eva rolls her eyes. Asher grins down at her, but then his smile fades, and he grabs his mom and pulls her into a tight hug.

I've had a month to observe Asher now, and I wonder about him. He's always smiling, flirting, and joking. But there's something disconnected beneath, like he's pretending to feel instead of really feeling. And there is that shadow I feel over him, and the times I catch him looking at things that aren't there.

He also hasn't opened himself to rejoin the pack bond. Killian is waiting, trying to give him space, and maybe space is for the best.

In the last few weeks, we've made some discreet inquiries as to where Asher has been. There are rumors. Whispers that he has something to do with Whitlock's secret military experiments. Or that he took his and Killian's old trainer, Hagan's, place, and became the warlord's personal killer.

Killian thinks Asher will tell us eventually. I'm not sure I want to know. But still, he's pack.

*"Are you sure you can't convince him to stay?"* I ask. *"Eva is going to miss him, and I think it would be good for him to keep spending time with her."*

Killian is quiet for a minute, than says, *"He said he made a promise to Grace. He intends to keep it."*

I lean back into Killian's arms. *"Eva wants him to let it go."*

*"He can't. She's never understood that about him."* Killian squeezes

me closer. I close my eyes. I love the way it feels to be surrounded by him. I love this moment, encompassed by him and the people who've become family.

"Selenite!"

My eyes fly open at the sound of Claudia's shrill voice. Killian sighs, and we both turn toward her.

"Yes, Claudia?"

"The canapés are gone. The children are animals. You *must* contain them."

"Claudia," I say, "you lived in a shack in the Free Cities for a decade. You are not helpless. If you want canapés, go into the kitchen, find a tray, and bring them out yourself."

The wolfless certainly won't be bringing them. I look to where they are, seated by one of the fires. Guilt prickles me when I see Jenny. My injuries from the battle are faint scars while hers have barely healed. It's a reminder that I am not who I spent my entire life thinking I was. That I have the power I have not because I'm more deserving, but because of luck and birth. A reminder that it's up to me to make sure I use that power for good, even though I never asked for it.

Claudia sticks her imperious nose in the air. "Get my own? Well, I never."

"Mother," Killian says ominously.

Claudia sniffs, turns on her heel, and walks away.

"She's hopeless," Killian mutters, pressing a kiss to the side of my neck.

I tilt my head to give him easier access. "She did head in the direction of the kitchens. Maybe she'll surprise us."

"Mm." The hum is disbelieving and distracted.

"Things are winding down." I turn in his arms. "Sofia and Parker are sneaking away as I speak. Maybe it's time we take Finn upstairs and put him to bed. Then ... we can put us to bed."

Killian's warm honey-brown eyes darken. "Yes."

I call for my brother, who runs over. Killian hauls Finn up onto his shoulders, and we climb the stairs to the pack house. Before we go in, I glance over my shoulder and look out over the pack, the fires, the spring night.

I don't know why I was chosen for this—to be with Killian, to have the power I have—but I no longer fear it.

Last night, I dreamed of the eldritch who took the form of my mother.

We stood near the edge of the cliff overlooking the lake. In the east, dawn lightened the sky.

This time, her words didn't echo.

*You have saved him, silverlight. That is the first step. Only together can you begin. Each must have their other. Gather them.*

I didn't ask who. I think I know.

Her words came in memory instead of the dream.

*One will guide, one will fight, one will see.*

*One will heal, one will remember, one will journey.*

*The last two, a pair. One will free, one will seal.*

Eight roles. Eight living daughters of Alaric Bane, if what was true when the book was written is true now.

"I am the guide," I said.

The being in my dream dimmed as dawn brightened. *Seven remain.*

Killian and I reach our suite of rooms. We put Finn to bed, then find ours.

"You've been quiet," he says, his fingers stroking up and down the bare skin of my back.

"Mm. I'm thinking about my sisters. And Vandran. And Asher leaving. At first, when we defeated Bianca, I thought it was some kind of conclusion, but it wasn't. It was the beginning. We might face that kind of danger again."

He kisses the top of my head and floods the mate bond with love. "If we do, we'll face it together."

# Epilogue

## ASHER

I thought by leaving the pack house in the middle of the night, I could avoid my mother.

Yeah. I fucking forgot who I was dealing with.

My fingers are just closing around the doorknob that will let me out of her apartment when the lamp flips on.

"Shit," I hiss, shoulders hunching.

"Yeah," my mother agrees from her chair in the corner. "Shit."

"I thought you were with your burly man friend."

She raises a brow. "I'm sure you did."

Age has only deepened Eva Quinn's beauty, as far as I'm concerned, even as it's grayed her hair and etched smile lines around her mouth and eyes. She used to worry so much when Killian and I were young. Now, as Preceptor and a pack Elder, she's come into her own.

Do I feel guilty that Killian, not I, is responsible for giving her that?

I'm not going to think about it.

She's got her chin propped on one hand, pretending nonchalance. I fold my arms and lean back against the door.

"Asher Quinn."

"Eva Quinn," I retort.

Her eyes narrow. "Where the hell do you think you're going?"

"Killian lets you teach the kids here with that mouth?"

394

Her lips press together in a thin line, and I see how close to the edge she is. I sigh and push away from the door, shifting the pack on my back to a more comfortable position as I go to a knee in front of her chair. I take her hand in mine. "Mom, I have to do this."

She touches my face. Her fingers are gentle. "No, you don't. She's gone, Asher. She's not holding you to any promises she never asked you to make."

"I promised her when she was alive. I told her I'd be there. I wasn't."

A cold chill slides down the back of my neck like ghostly fingers.

*"Asher..."* a disembodied voice whispers. A voice only I can hear.

I ignore it for now and pull my mom into an embrace. It's a long time before she releases me.

"It's not forever." I never used to be able to lie to her. Now, it's so easy.

Her lips tremble. "Yes, it is. If you think you can go after the damn warlord of the Fall Line Protectorate and his most powerful warden and arcanist alone, *yes, it is*. Give Killian and Selene time. Give the Conclave time."

"The Conclave can't do a damn thing," I say bitterly. "They're broken, and Vandran still has too many allies among them."

"Grace never wanted you throwing your life away. She's gone. Let her rest! Stay here and let me rest."

The words almost reach me. Almost touch something inside me that died when my sister did.

Almost.

I rise. "I know she's gone, Mom."

The cold comes again. A ghostly, rasping laugh echoes in my mind. *"Gone..."*

"So why can't you leave it and live your life?" my mother asks, pleading.

"Why can they breathe when she can't?" I snap. "Why can Vandran and Whitlock walk around and enjoy the sun or be with the people they love or have their miserable fucking lives when Grace and so many other people can't?"

People I killed, or kidnapped, or maimed for them. Entire lives, destroyed.

My mind flashes to a woman with red curls and rage in her ember-glow eyes. I put a hand on my bicep, over the scar of bullet wound. Just a graze, but a good one, and hear her voice again.

*You don't have to do this. You don't have to be a monster who works for monsters.*

But I am. I see it in the way my mother stares at me now with wide, terrified eyes. For an instant, it's like she finally sees the blood on my hands.

I rein in the violence that's shivering through my limbs. The silver-edged sword on my hip hums, and I feel a hunger to be away from here. To spill blood that deserves to be spilled.

I don't feel much of anything anymore except the anger that burns in my chest day and night, an unquenchable fire. I'm so tired of keeping it lit, but it won't burn out.

When I kill the people responsible for Grace's death, maybe the fire will die. Maybe I can rest, too.

Or maybe I'll die. That counts as resting, too.

Unless you're Grace, whose wraith, pale and bloody, stands just at the corner of my vision. A white dress and her chestnut hair swirl around her in a wind that doesn't exist. *"Asher,"* she hisses through that torn-out throat, spraying fine droplets of blood, *"It's time. You must return."*

I bend and kiss my mother's cheek. "I love you."

She catches my hand. "Stay."

I disentangle myself and move to the door. "Tell Maddox I said goodbye."

I never rejoined the pack tie, so I won't be able to tell him myself.

Mom presses a hand to her mouth and looks away. When I'm sure she's not going to say anything more, I leave.

My sister's wraith follows after me.

I walk along the old road through the woods for a long time. Sometimes Grace's wraith is there, sometimes she's not. Finally, I find the motorcycle I hid in a half-fallen barn a few months ago. I've checked on it regularly, and when I turn the key, the ancient thing roars to life.

I guide the bike onto the shit excuse for a road and turn east toward the Fall Line Protectorate.

Toward my past and the sins I should've known I'd never be able to leave behind.

Grace will have her vengeance, even if I have to burn Fall Line and everyone in it to the ground.

# Acknowledgments

Writing this book was a rollercoaster and I won't lie, I almost gave up in the middle of all the rewrites and attempted to become a florist. Thank you to my husband Will and my three kids for giving me a reason to keep pushing forward.

Thank you to the Ozark woods and hills in which this story is set. You have always inspired me. In a lifetime filled with cross-country moves, you have always been home.

Thank you to my small writing circle: Charlie N. Holmberg, Tricia Levenseller, and Mikki Helmer for major, gigantic, enormous help brainstorming, overhauling, and brainstorming again. Even when I didn't want to listen, you guys were right.

Thank you to my D&D group—Joon, Nathan, Raylene, Cole, Natasha, Mikki again, and Will again—for giving me a social outlet that keeps me sane. Thanks especially to Raylene, Natasha, and Nathan for reading early drafts of this story.

Thank you to Alison R., Carly S., and Natalie G., who also answered my call for readers.

Thank you to Tanya and the amazing people at Oliver Heber Books for the time, care, edits, etc. I can't tell you how much I appreciate you taking a chance on me.

Thank you to my old job for laying me off and finally giving me the push I need to try writing for myself, to Will a third time for working so hard and giving me the breathing room to do this, and to my parents for being amazing, as always.

Most of all, thank you to my local flower shops, who were not hiring.

# Also by Caitlyn McFarland

**Dragonsworn Trilogy**

Soul of Smoke

Shadow of Flame

Truth of Embers

**Daughters of the Shattered Moon**

Echoes of Night

Crimson Dusk

*About the Author*

After spending most of her adult life in UT, Caitlyn McFarland has returned to the Midwest and currently lives by a lake in Missouri with her husband and three daughters. She has a Bachelor's degree in linguistics from Brigham Young University. When she's not writing romantic fantasy, Caitlyn can be found wandering the woods, crafting, or playing TTRPGs.

A small press bound by the belief that every voice matters.

Sign up for our newsletter to learn about new releases and more.

*Buy directly from us to save on ebooks, book bundles, and special editions.*

Follow us on social media:

facebook.com/oliverheberbooks

instagram.com/oliverheberbooks

tiktok.com/@oliverheberbooks

bsky.app/profile/oliverheberbooks.bsky.social

youtube.com/@OliverHeberBooksPublisher

oliverheberbooks.substack.com

amazon.com/oliverheberbooks